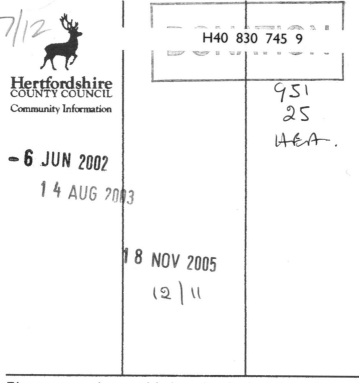

7/12

Hertfordshire
COUNTY COUNCIL
Community Information

H40 830 745 9

951
25
HEA.

– 6 JUN 2002

1 4 AUG 2003

1 8 NOV 2005

12 | 11

Please renew/return this item by the last date shown.

So that your telephone call is charged at local rate, please call the numbers as set out below:

	From Area codes 01923 or 020:	From the rest of Herts:
Renewals:	01923 471373	01438 737373
Enquiries:	01923 471333	01438 737333
Minicom:	01923 471599	01438 737599

L32   www.hertsdirect.org

D1320913

Beating Retreat

TIM HEALD

BEATING RETREAT

Hong Kong Under the Last Governor

SINCLAIR–STEVENSON

First published in Great Britain in 1997
by Sinclair-Stevenson
an imprint of Reed International Books Ltd
Michelin House, 81 Fulham Road, London SW3 6RB
and Auckland, Melbourne, Singapore and Toronto

Copyright © 1997 by Tim Heald

The right of Tim Heald to be identified as author of
this work has been asserted by him in accordance with
the Copyright, Designs and Patents Act 1988.

A CIP catalogue record for this book
is available at the British Library
ISBN 1 85619 357 8

Typeset in 12 on 15 point Sabon
by Deltatype Ltd, Birkenhead, Merseyside
Printed and bound in Great Britain
by Clays Ltd, St Ives plc

For Richard Cobb

As he gazed through the rear window of the car, it seemed to him that the very world that he was moving through had been abandoned also. The street markets were deserted, the pavements, even the doorways. Above them, the Peak loomed fitfully, its crocodile spine daubed by a ragged moon. It's the Colony's last day, he decided. Peking has made its proverbial telephone call, 'Get out, party over'. The last hotel was closing, he saw the empty Rolls-Royces lying like scrap around the harbour, and the last blue-rinse roundeye matron, laden with her tax-free furs and jewellery, tottering up the gang-way of the last cruise-ship, the last China-watcher frantically feeding his last mis-calculations into the shredder, the looted ships, the empty city waiting like a carcass for the hordes.

John le Carré, *The Honourable Schoolboy*

Contents

List of Illustrations

Acknowledgements

The general assumption among authors seems to be that one should acknowledge as many sources as possible. It adds to the book's credibility and it is only fair to those who have taken the trouble to be of help. While the former may be true, my experience is that the latter is often not . . . On at least one occasion in the past I have paid tribute to a particularly helpful source only to be rewarded by a yelp of protest because the source said he wished to be unattributed. Saying thank you can be a thankless occupation.

Of course I am grateful to all those who helped me. Most of them are clearly identified in the text. One or two, however, pleaded for anonymity, not for any sinister reason but simply because they didn't like the idea of publicity. I have tried to respect privacy while demonstrating authenticity. Unfortunately, this can sometimes be a bit of a tight-rope. Under these circumstances I hope I will be forgiven for not including the conventional acknowledgements to those who have helped my researches.

I would, however, like to say thank you to the publisher Christopher Sinclair-Stevenson, who first commissioned the book and was a constant source of enthusiasm and inspiration; to Roger Cazalet, a zealous and knowledgeable editor who did his job with a rigour and correctness that is popularly supposed to be long dead; and to my agent, Vivien Green, whose loyalty and terrier-like persistence shine out like good deeds in a naughty world.

The extract from *The Honourable Schoolboy* by John le Carré is printed by kind permission of Hodder & Stoughton and John le Carré.

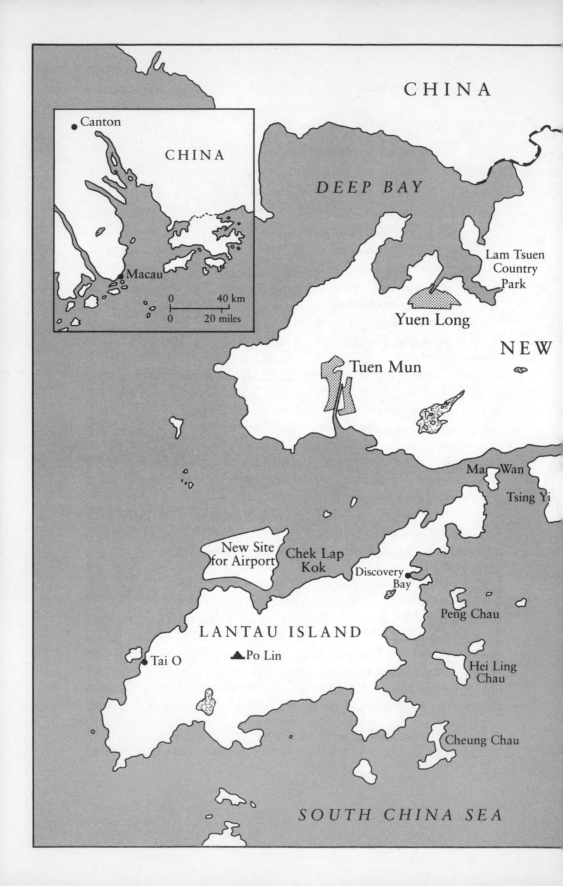

CHINA

Canton

CHINA

Macau

0   40 km

0   20 miles

DEEP BAY

Lam Tsuen
Country
Park

Yuen Long

NEW

Tuen Mun

Ma Wan

Tsing Yi

New Site
for Airport

Chek Lap
Kok

Discovery
Bay

Peng Chau

LANTAU ISLAND

Tai O

Po Lin

Hei Ling
Chau

Cheung Chau

SOUTH CHINA SEA

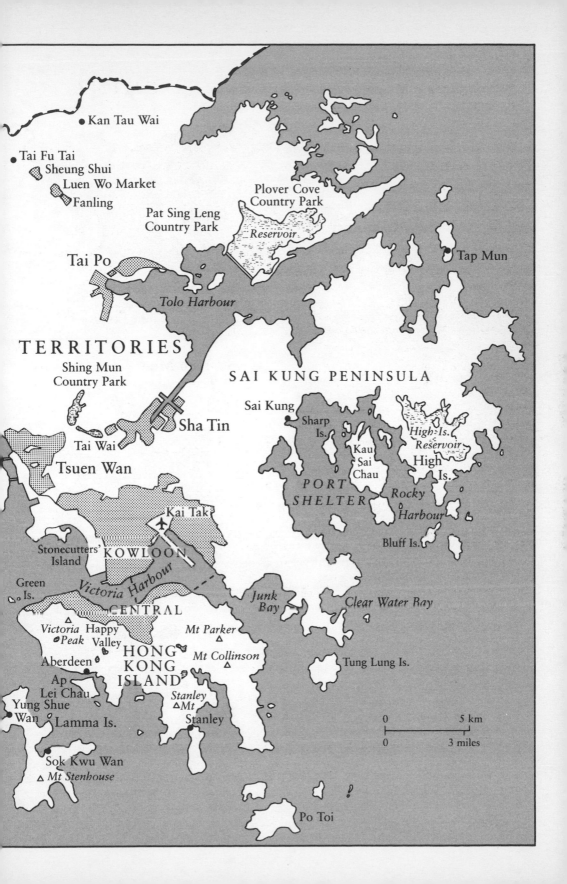

Kan Tau Wai

Tai Fu Tai
Sheung Shui
Luen Wo Market
Fanling

Pat Sing Leng
Country Park

Plover Cove
Country Park

Reservoir

Tai Po

Tap Mun

Tolo Harbour

TERRITORIES

Shing Mun
Country Park

SAI KUNG PENINSULA

Sai Kung

Sha Tin

Sharp
Is.

*High Is.
Reservoir*

Tai Wai

Kau
Sai
Chau

High
Is.

Tsuen Wan

PORT
SHELTER

*Rocky
Harbour*

Kai Tak

Bluff Is.

Stonecutters'
Island

KOWLOON

Green
Is.

Victoria Harbour

CENTRAL

*Junk
Bay*

Clear Water Bay

Victoria Happy
Peak Valley

Mt Parker
△

Aberdeen

HONG
KONG
ISLAND

Mt Collinson
△

Tung Lung Is.

Ap
Lei Chau

Stanley
△*Mt*
Stanley

Yung Shue
Wan

Lamma Is.

Sok Kwu Wan
△ *Mt Stenhouse*

0   5 km

0   3 miles

Po Toi

ONE

For forty years I nurtured a forlorn obsession with Hong Kong.

One of my earliest memories is of a September day in 1952. I was eight years old and I was saying good-bye to my mother. She was almost more tearful than me. Indeed after our parting she was apparently incapable of coherent speech for several hours, to the embarrassment of my great-aunt, who was chaperoning her and had to explain her distress to everyone they met with the words, 'My niece has just left her son at boarding school because she is going to Hong Kong.'

My father was already in the Colony with the 1st Battalion of the Dorset Regiment and my mother and younger brother James were shortly to set sail from Liverpool in order to join him. I was not to see any of them until after the Queen's Coronation the following year. So while they experienced imperial echoes in the Orient I struggled with Kennedy's *Latin Primer* and rudimentary cricket at Connaught House School, Bishop's Lydeard in the lee of the Quantock Hills.

They returned that August, driving down from Liverpool to my aunt's house in Aberdovey, where I had spent all my school holidays. In the interim our only source of contact had been letters written once a week – mine on pale-blue flimsy airmail letter forms, my parents' on khaki ditto. One

1

could only write so much on these, which meant that our news to each other was circumscribed. I don't remember any telephone calls. In those days I suppose that would have seemed too exotic and expensive. A few years later I flew by BOAC stratocruiser for holidays in Canada when my father was posted there, but the idea of flying to Hong Kong for Christmas was never seriously mooted.

In those days when so much of the map was still tinted pink, 'Army brats' like me were commonplace. Boarding schools were stuffed with children whose fathers were serving with the armed forces all over the disintegrating Empire and there appeared to be as many offspring of men working abroad for international companies such as Shell, which sometimes seemed to be almost as much a part of the imperial bureaucracy as the Army or Navy. Hong Kong had a sizeable garrison and dockyard, a judiciary and civil service, as well as a commercial infrastructure which was effectively British. In those days it was far from being unique. It is only in the intervening years that it has become such an oddity.

I wish I had kept those khaki airmail letters, but they are lost for ever and my vicarious memories of Hong Kong during the first year of the Queen's reign are blurred. My father, determinedly individualistic, never lived in conventional officers' quarters and on this occasion he and a fellow Dorset officer, John Archer, rented a house out in the New Territories near Fanling, where the Governor has his country retreat.*

---

* The area generally known as 'Hong Kong' is about 90 miles southeast of Canton and consists of Hong Kong Island and the Kowloon peninsula, both of which have traditionally been regarded as British possessions, and 'the New Territories' which were leased from mainland China. Technically 'the New Territories' were the only part of the colony which had to be returned to Chinese rule in 1997. They comprised some 359 square miles of a total area of just over 390 square miles and include mountains and islands as well as some spectacular new towns. The

Their landlord was called Major Macomber Churn and his house Lena Lodge. It sounded remote and mildly dangerous. My brother James, then three or four years old, had very red hair which the local villagers found fascinating. On one occasion my mother left him in the care of his amah and returned to find that he had wandered off and was surrounded by a crowd of fascinated Chinese fondling his alien locks. They seemed to intend him no harm but my mother was horrified, not least on grounds of hygiene. I seem to remember talk too of a village idiot who wandered about with an axe stuck in his head. And there was a houseboy, Kam, whom I did later meet when he came to London to work as a waiter in a Soho restaurant called Maxim's. Kam had many gold teeth and was long remembered for one particular morning catchphrase with which he regularly summoned my brother to toast and cornflakes. 'Yame, Yame! Bleffust, bleffust!' He also taught the rest of my family the only Cantonese they ever learnt: 'Kung Hei Fat Choy.' This was his phonetic rendering of 'Happy New Year!'

I can't pretend that Hong Kong became a burning issue for me, but in a mild way it rankled. It was an early experience from which I had been excluded, an element in the family life and argot from which I had been left out. Hong Kong was, for me, a gap.

My father left the Army a few years later and was never posted there again. His colleague John Archer, however, rose to the rank of general and returned to the Colony as commander of the British forces there. So did Roy Redgrave, who was a pupil at the Canadian Army Staff College in Kingston, Ontario when my father was a member of the

---

capital on the south of the famous harbour is actually named Victoria although I never heard anyone call it that. Kowloon is about half a mile across the water although as more and more land is reclaimed the distance diminishes almost daily.

3

Directing Staff. General Sir John so impressed that, after leaving the Army, he was signed up by the Royal Hong Kong Jockey Club as their chief executive and was the presiding genius when the club decided that their downtown Happy Valley course was not enough and in the 1980s built a huge new course and stadium at Sha Tin in the New Territories.

Coincidences such as these were an incentive, particularly because, from the mid-1960s onwards, I was a journalist and occasional travel-writer. Opportunities for a visit did occur but somehow it never happened. *Vogue* once sent me to Malaysia and Singapore but I never made the final leap east. Then in the 1980s it was agreed that the Colony, the last substantial jewel in what had once been an imperial crown, would return to Chinese rule in 1997. I had a brief frisson of frustration and desire but it quickly subsided into inertia and I resigned myself to the knowledge that Hong Kong was, for me, an opportunity missed in perpetuity.

Then, in 1992, a very odd thing happened. The Conservative Party won a general election. This was widely unexpected. Indeed, a triumphal rally by Neil Kinnock and his Labour Party shortly before polling day may have been all that tipped the balance. The British hate other people counting eggs before they are hatched and in this case, to compound the cliché, pride went before a fall and Labour lost.

The Chairman of the Conservative Party during this campaign, and therefore, though controversially, the indubitable architect of this victory, was Chris Patten, who since 1979 had been the Member for Bath. His had never been a safe seat and was under permanent threat from the Liberal Democrats. Largely because of his high-profile and violently partisan position as party chairman and also because the national job meant that he was frequently away from the constituency, Chris lost out. I watched the declaration of the poll and saw, along with the rest of the country, what a devastating shock it was to Chris, his wife Lavender and their friends. Somehow it was more than just a political calamity. This was something personal – a sense of real betrayal hung in the air. There were tears.

I had known the Pattens for only a decade less than I had – at a remove – known Hong Kong. Chris and I had been undergraduates together at Balliol College, Oxford. We had shared tutorials, played occasional agricultural tennis together, debated in the Arnold and Brackenbury Society and contributed to *Mesopotamia*, the allegedly humorous magazine which was the precursor of *Private Eye*. Lavender was a St Hilda's girl of the same vintage. A little later Chris became godfather to my son Alexander and I took on Kate Patten, their first-born, as my goddaughter. Our subsequent lives had been very different, but we remained friends, even though we saw each other less than I, at least, would have liked.

A few weeks later they came to a kitchen supper. It was the night before the opening of Parliament. Traditionally the Prime Minister hosts a dinner for his MPs at Number Ten. The Pattens couldn't face it. The idea of all their friends going back to Parliament without them was more than they could bear. They preferred to lick their wounds in private.

Until that unexpected defeat, the idea of Hong Kong was for them remote, if not ridiculous. Chris had for a time been Minister for Overseas Development and coveted the foreign secretaryship. Lavender had once visited Hong Kong on a twenty-four-hour stop over. Hong Kong was, in effect, a far-away place of which they knew nothing. Besides, the governorship had long been, in effect, a diplomatic posting, occupied by a Sinologist from the Foreign Office well versed in Mandarin and diplomacy. There was no precedent for giving the job to a career politician. Before the general election that year the idea of Governor Patten had never been voiced.

Nevertheless, in the 1990s a view was emerging that in the run-down to 1997 the Governor of the colony should not be a shadowy 'expert' but a more substantial figure with a significant public image. The names of Prince Charles and Lord (David) Owen were invoked. And after the election Chris Patten's name came into the frame as well.

I did not know at the time – and I doubt if by the end of this book I will know any more – precisely what deliberations took place. John Major clearly felt a sense of responsibility if not exactly guilt. There was an obligation to find a proper job for someone who had, in effect, laid down his constituency for the party and the Premier. Hong Kong was an obvious plum.

Many of his friends and acquaintances offered advice. I, presumptuously, was among them and said he should take it. Others, more sophisticated in the wiles of political intrigue, suggested otherwise. After due deliberation Chris decided to take the job, to eschew the traditional plumed feathers and knighthood, and, in the summer of 1992, arrived to a fireboat welcome aboard the Governor's yacht, the *Lady Maureen*, to become almost certainly the last governor of the last significant relic of Britain's once proud Empire. A long step from Balliol, and I for one found it difficult to reconcile the idea with my recollection of the mop-haired teenager in denims and CND badge who had bowled fizzy medium pace for the College XI and whose ambition had been to become a copy-writer with the J. Walter Thompson advertising agency.

Nevertheless life is a dance to the music of time and there was no escaping the verdict of history.

For me it was the final chance. Given that lingering sense of disappointment, the Patten governorship represented a last opportunity which I simply had to take.

The pretext was a book. The publisher was gratifyingly easy to find. Christopher Sinclair-Stevenson's father-in-law was Lavender Patten's guardian, and his own father had spent much of his life in Hong Kong. I don't believe that these were the only reasons for Christopher taking on the project but network connections such as these always help. At least I have spent a lifetime believing with some justification that this is so.

I was hardly the first person to have the idea, though I do think my reasons and qualifications are peculiar if not unique. Lavender herself is keeping a journal with a view to publication; Jonathan Dimbleby is making a TV documentary followed by a book, rather in the manner of his Prince of Wales TV and print biography – he, too, is a friend of the Pattens, and can therefore expect some sort of privileged access. Jan Morris has already written a book which she is supposed to be updating from time to time whenever it goes out of print; Robert Cottrell, an old journalistic Hong Kong hand, got in early with *The End of Hong Kong*; Timothy Mo wrote a much praised novel called *An Insular Possession*. And so on.

In the early 1960s when I first worked for a national newspaper, my mentors, in particular an awe-inspiring news editor at the *Daily Mirror*, spent hours teaching me to erase the first-person singular, to eliminate 'I' and 'me' from my writing. At the time and in that context they were absolutely correct, but all these years later I have come to the conclusion that, for better or for worse, it is the first-person singular and the 'I' and 'me' that makes writing distinctive and different. Dickens is Dickens and Tolstoy is Tolstoy not because of the material with which they deal but the individual way in which they deal with it. My book about this moment in the history of Hong Kong is, at the end of the day, different and distinctive because it is *my* book: my connections, my prejudices, my memories, my perceptions, my insights, my style. This is going to be a truthful book but not, contrary to what was said in an article in Hong Kong's

Eastern Express, an 'objective' book. It's *my* book. It is the way I saw things through my little eye.

Because my parents and my brother had arrived in Hong Kong by sea I had always wanted to do the same. Opportunities for doing so diminished year by year. So I was profoundly fortunate to be offered, in 1992, a voyage down the Chinese coast aboard the good ship *Ocean Pearl*, a French liner with Filipino crew. It was an odd and sybaritic experience, light years away from the Insect-class gunship my uncle Basil commanded in these waters some sixty years earlier, and not, I imagine, much like the troopship on which my parents sailed from Blighty. One Sunday I sat on deck with Kenneth Rose, the distinguished biographer of Curzon and George V. Lunch was stuffed quail and chilled Sancerre, and all around us on the Yangtse Kiang China was on the move in laden barges with woks steaming in the stern.

The sense of cultural disparity was quite shocking.

Despite the luxury of the ship and the insulated sense you inevitably get when on a cruise, my first sight of Hong Kong was as dramatic, almost numbing, as I had hoped. We arrived in the late afternoon having come from Shanghai. Shanghai was obviously a city in transition. It seemed immense and pulsating, but, although modern buildings and bridges were rising, the old Bund appeared essentially as it must have done when the Europeans built it. It looked like Liverpool.

Hong Kong at first glance was not remotely like Liverpool. We had been steaming through fog in the South China Sea, but this lifted. The first sign that we were nearing civilisation was an empty plastic bottle bobbing in the waves. Real Western-style litter. Then a smart motor yacht came in sight with a red ensign fluttering in the breeze. The little square of the Union flag seemed so incongruous in this far-away sea. Britannia, I thought, no longer rules the waves, and yet . . .

Then tower blocks started to appear. I was unprepared for

the sheer size and quantity. Every time we rounded another point there would be another space-age panorama. It was like climbing a mountain and finding that there is always another summit beyond the one you have just scaled. In the end, just as the first lights began to flicker from the offices, we hove to at the entrance to the harbour and I settled down on deck with a cigar to contemplate Hong Kong by night. It would have been a magnificent urban seascape anywhere in the world, but here on these rocks on the tip of China it seemed almost grotesque.

The Governor and Mrs Patten were out of town. They were visiting Mr Clinton in the White House. I put up at the Peninsula Hotel, which another of my uncles had, sort of, liberated after the war in an aircraft carrier called HMS *Chaser*. He said that he and his brother officers had introduced the first Western-style lavatory paper seen in the hotel since the Japanese took over at the beginning of the war.

The Peninsula had printed personalised stationery and visiting cards, gold-embossed in English and Cantonese, and I was welcomed with a pot of jasmine tea as well as a scroll explaining its significance. Some months earlier I had watched Michael Palin on a televised round-the-world journey playing with the remote-control blinds and curtains and was pleased to find that they were functioning just as he had demonstrated. Behind the gentle opulence of the surroundings, however, there was a massive building site. One of the hazards of the Hong Kong waterfront is that there is a continuing process of land reclamation. The Peninsula used to enjoy an unrivalled view of the water looking across to Hong Kong Island itself, but this had been blocked out by a new cultural centre on a site which had once been water. Until recently there had been height restrictions on new building on the Kowloon side because of the danger from planes taking off and landing at Kai Tak airport near by.

The newest generation of jets, however, could perform at steeper, less threatening gradients and the height restrictions had therefore been eased. Hence the hotel was building a new thirty-storey tower in order to get its view back.

It was a rush of a stay dictated largely by a variety of enjoyable but possibly misleading public-relations functions. One day, however, I managed to slip across on the slick subway system, for which my brother-in-law, since relocated to Singapore, was one of the architects, and took tea with 'Charlie' Churn, the youngest of the sons of Major Macomber.

I found a soft-spoken, silver-haired man who, like his father, enjoyed the title 'Major', having served with the Hong Kong Regiment as a territorial. He seemed prosperous and confident. His company sold and serviced Hondas in southern China. 'Motorcycles are rampant there,' he said. What struck me most about his business dealing was that, whereas the hand-over of power in 1997 was being presented back in the UK as a watershed with all sorts of concomitant uncertainties, this was not the case here. It seemed to me, on the basis admittedly of a very brief conversation, that this Major Churn had passed through his own personal 1997. His systems were all in place. He was already dealing with mainland China in what was effectively a post-imperial manner.

'It was paradise when I was young,' he said, referring to Lena Lodge. It had been surrounded by paddy fields then, much as my mother remembered. Now there was a four-lane highway. In even earlier days, before the 1920s, people had travelled out to Lena Lodge by train and horse-drawn carriage. 'They went under the pretext of shooting,' said the Major, 'but actually it was floosies!' In those days it was called the Cheerio and it was run as an informal club with seven members. Gradually Major Churn senior had bought out his fellow members until the house was his alone. The downstairs drawing room had once been the stables or mews.

He produced some very old photographs. There was one of his father in a three-piece suit looking stiff and another of his stepmother Ruby – 'who your mother would remember'. There were two Yorkshire terriers.

'My father loved sweetpeas,' he said reflectively. And then: 'It's twenty years since we owned it. We sold it after the Mud Slide.'

I promised myself that when I returned I would make a little pilgrimage to Lena Lodge.

It was over a year before I returned to Hong Kong.

The Times asked me to go and see how the Peninsula was getting on with its new tower at the end of October 1994.

In the meantime the Governor had been having a rocky ride. There was an inevitable honeymoon period lent a faintly ridiculous extra dimension when the second Patten daughter arrived wearing a very short skirt and achieved instant star status. Patten himself, smiling and pressing flesh in the style of the modern Western politician, was immediately perceived as a genuine, friendly man of the people in direct contrast to the frock and feathered froideur of his predecessors. His walkabouts and photo-opportunities were innovative and apparently popular. His new dogs, Norfolk terriers called Whisky and Soda, also acquired cult status.

The old guard in Peking[*] looked on him with rather more disfavour and soon began regular melodramatic castigations. 'Fat Pang', as he was affectionately known in the Colony, was granted all sorts of new names and descriptions, though Peking seemed most keen on describing him as a 'prostitute'.

[*] Some people say 'Peking' and some 'Beijing'. In the end I came to believe it was a matter of taste or affectation rather than right or wrong. I tend to prefer 'Peking', but when others use 'Beijing' I haven't changed it.

11

More hurtful was the opposition of a Hong Kong old guard most obviously personified by Sir Percy Cradock, formerly British Ambassador to Peking and foreign policy adviser to Mrs Thatcher. Cradock had been instrumental in drafting and negotiating much of the 1984 Joint Declaration between the British and Chinese governments. Cradock, along with many others, especially those with commercial interests in Hong Kong, was strongly critical of the new Governor's robust attitude to Peking and his plans to widen the scope of democracy in the colony before the flag came down at midnight on 30 June 1997.

The details of this disagreement can appear abstruse, and much of the vehemence seemed unduly personal. Later when I spent more time in Hong Kong I supposed that I would have to master some of the intricacies, but at this stage I was, and am, more concerned to deal with the essentials. I may have changed my view by the end of the book but here, almost at the beginning, it seemed that the Governor's difficulties had as much to do with style as with substance. To those – Chinese, British and Hong Kong – who had spent a lifetime steeped in Sino-British relations, Patten was seen as a Johnny-come-lately. And, in most people's view, it was much too late. By the time he arrived at Government House the deal was long done and the seconds were ticking away.

My concern in writing about some of these last moments is not so much to argue the rights and wrongs, let alone the meanings of individual clauses in the Joint Declaration, as to see how people reacted to the situation – what effect it had on their mood, and their behaviour.

The most obvious effect was that, between my two visits, the Governor suffered a heart attack. It seemed not to be tremendously serious. No by-pass surgery was involved. He was treated in Hong Kong by having a tube inserted in the groin and a series of what felt to him like miniature heart attacks to expand and clear the arteries. Lavender and senior hospital staff watched the entire performance from a viewing gallery. Afterwards he was put on a strict diet, and told to take more exercise and avoid quite so much stress. Nevertheless it was a nasty warning. I remembered that his father had died after suffering a heart attack when we were up at Balliol. He must have been much the same age as his son, the Governor, when he suffered his.

Sod's law seemed to be at work over my second visit, for when I faxed Government House with my plan I had a reply asking, 'Do you really have to come on 25th October?' The Pattens were due in London that week and the nearest we would get to meeting would be when our planes passed each other somewhere over Baghdad. As the Governor wrote, 'It really would be too tiresome if your only four days in Hong Kong coincided with our five or six days out of the country.'

Quite so. Too tiresome. I therefore extended my trip to take in two days as the Governor's guest.

On the first day of my visit the front page of the *South China Morning Post* had a picture of the Pattens *en route* to the airport in the gubernatorial limousine with a rather carping little piece drawing attention to the number of air miles Chris had travelled in the year so far. This seemed harsh but I later discovered that the *Post*'s line, unlike that of its newest rival, the *Eastern Express*, was generally inclined to be hostile.

It was strange to see old friends in this sort of limelight. The Patten profile had been high in the British media but suddenly, *in situ*, one realised that his was the hottest running story in town. Whether or not he had made more trips to London than his predecessor, Lord Wilson, was front-page news. It did seem a little preposterous.

I was kept busy throughout the week discovering what a village of networks and universal acquaintance Hong Kong was. Before long I became used to people saying, 'I hear you were at the so-and-so's last night.' One old friend from Fleet

Street days even did an interview about my latest project which covered a whole page in the *Eastern Express* with an alarming banner headline which said, 'Bringing the Guv to Book!' I hoped this wouldn't be misconstrued.

On the Monday afternoon I made the journey from the Peninsula in Kowloon to Government House on Upper Albert Road, the other side of the harbour. Hitherto I had been making this journey on the upper deck of the Star Ferry, which cost a princely HK$1.50 (between 5p and 10p in English money). This time, with my suitcase, I was ferried in one of the Peninsula's Rolls-Royces. These have become a hotel trademark to such an extent that their particular shade of green which used to be called 'Brewster' green has now been officially redesignated 'Peninsula' green. The latest fleet had been specially fitted out to meet the hotel's requirements with special handgrips for passengers and a freezer for refrigerated towels.

Luxury indeed, but the Star Ferry takes no cars and we had to use the tunnel. Traffic was heavy and it seemed to take an age.

Later I remarked to Lavender on the inconvenience; she frowned lightly and said that she supposed I was right but that of course they were entitled to use the bus-lane or, if in a real hurry, to have an escort of Royal Hong Kong Police. I mused on this for days afterwards. As a young reporter on the *Daily Express* I had once been asked to take Members of Parliament from the three main parties on public transport. My editor believed that they were becoming pampered and cut off from reality. I accompanied Eric Lubbock, as he then was, on the train from Orpington and Norman St John Stevas, as he also then was, on a bus down Victoria Street. Lubbock was quite happy on the train but Stevas made a terrible palaver on the bus. Of course, I agreed privately, it was not proper that a busy and important person such as the Governor of Hong Kong should get stuck in the tunnel between the island and Kowloon. And yet privileged transport, it seems to me, insulates like almost nothing else. Life seen from the back of a Rolls-Royce or through the windows of a royal train is not life in the usual sense.

The Pattens had not yet returned when I finally swept through the front gate manned by Hong Kong Police in their paramilitary khaki with black cap and Sam Browne belt. Louise the social secretary and Elspeth the housekeeper met me in the light but cavernous hall, made me welcome, gave me a brief run-down on the basic drill, and asked if I'd like tea. I was then taken to the Tennis Court Suite, which does indeed overlook the tennis courts where, since his heart problems, the Governor had taken prodigious amounts of exercise, playing some three times a week and having a couple of lessons as well. He was even working out with the Hong Kong Davis Cup team. It seemed a far cry from the sort of tennis I remembered him playing at Oxford.

The suite was enormous, with a drawing room, a double bedroom, another single bedroom leading off it, two spacious bathrooms and a closet for hanging clothes which could accommodate a medium-sized Chinese family in less privileged parts of town. I had two separate telephone lines and my own uniformed steward, a charming, beaming man called Ah Cheuk, who really did seem to want to make me happy. 'You like press shirt? You like scrambled egg for breakfast?' He looked quite crestfallen when I said no to both. (So did Chris when I said I wasn't having cooked breakfast. He said all his staff always had cooked breakfast, which was more, now, than he was allowed.)

I was amused by the reading matter set out by my bedside, though I forgot to ask if it was personally selected or standard choice for inhabitants of the Tennis Court Suite. It consisted of *The Collision of Two Civilisations* by Alain Peyrefitte; *The Wisden Book of Obituaries* compiled by Benny Green; *The Lion and the Dragon* by Aubrey Singer –

15

the story of the first British Embassy in Peking; *Berry and Co.* by Dornford Yates; *Famous Trials* by John Mortimer; and a *Colour Guide to Hong Kong Animals*. In my diary I recorded, 'Somehow I feel this says something though I'm not entirely sure what.'

After Ah Cheuk had brought in afternoon tea I spent a little time reading through my instruction kit, presented in a stiff folder with my name stencilled on the cover. It was military in its precision. Dinner the following night was quite an informal affair but a full seating plan was included together with the guests' *Who's Who* entries or whatever other information seemed appropriate. One sheet of paper was given over to me as 'Government House House Guest'. It gave my 'phone numbers and my arrival and departure times, and was distributed to no fewer than twenty-six different people beginning with the Governor and ending with the gardener. I was impressed, though also slightly appalled.

I spent the rest of that afternoon in the garden, scribbling. It is an extraordinary garden with lush lawns and shrubs and even a *Prunus persica* planted by Lavender on 30 October to mark the thirtieth anniversary of the Hong Kong Society for Handicapped Children. What makes it bizarre is not the expansive greenery but the towers of Mammon which surround it. The housekeeper, Elspeth, said that when she first arrived four years earlier there was still one little chink in the concrete curtain through which you could see the harbour. Now that had gone, and as I sat by the fountain I felt the future all around and above me looking down from thousands of soaring office windows almost as if waiting to pounce.

After touching down at Kai Tak that evening Chris had to go immediately to present the Governor's Awards for Industry – widely reported the following day, but uncontroversial. Lavender, however, came straight home. The social secretary, the housekeeper, the fifteen-year-old Alice (decked out for a Hallowe'en party) and I formed the main reception party in the hall, attended by sundry uniformed staff and an eager Whisky and Soda.

Again I was struck by the curious imbalance between Lavender, who is quintessentially unstarchy, and this level of formality. Formality is not quite the right word, though, because when Lavender did struggle in, burdened by bags, there were kisses all round, presents for the girls, leaps and bounds from the dogs and a general sense of easy euphoria. Even so it wasn't the sort of homecoming given to the average housewife. Or even to the average successful barrister, which is what, in another incarnation, Lavender was.

A little later I wandered over to their private quarters for a pre-dinner drink. These are in and around the building's tower and include a good-sized drawing room and bedrooms for the whole family. Talking to Alice the next day, we were discussing the problems of living in such a public residence. Could it ever feel like a proper home? Alice, who was loving the Oriental experience – school field trips to Shanghai and Vietnam, for instance – agreed that much of the house was a sort of hybrid. However, her room in the tower was 'definitely home'.

Presently the Governor appeared, looking fresh and ebullient despite the flight and his awards ceremony. He showered and changed, and the three of us went down for supper in the small informal dining area off the main dining room. It was a quiet domestic evening devoted mainly to catching up on mutual family news, though I was struck by the fact that drinks upstairs were brought in by the staff, who also served us at supper. Informal, but not quite the same as a family evening at the country house just outside his Bath constituency.

I was wearing one of the shirts made for me in a few hours

by 'Sam the Tailor'. 'Sam', whose real name is Manoo, had a tiny shop in 'The Burlington Arcade' just off Nathan Road in Kowloon. I had been sent to him by Kent Hayden Sadler, marketing director of the Hong Kong Tourist Association. Kent's father had known Manoo's father, and Kent wrote a little note of introduction asking Manoo to take care of me. 'It'll be a three-shirt job at least,' warned Kent, 'but he's worth it.' He was right. He was also right in thinking that I would be given a cold beer and, within a minute, shown Manoo's picture of himself posing with Mrs Thatcher. He had not warned me that underneath the glass on the counter I would see facsimiles of several quite large cheques signed by Chris. Little did I think, thirty years earlier, that I would find C. F. Patten's cheques displayed as trophies in a Hong Kong tailor's shop.

The Pattens had a chuckle at this and said that Manoo's intelligence system was the best in Hong Kong. 'He knows who's staying at Government House before we do.' They were also amused to hear that my MCC membership card had failed to gain me admission to the Kowloon Cricket Club. 'But I'm the president,' said Chris.

After supper they gave me a quick guided tour. The house had been extensively, though inexpensively, redecorated and furnished. Their friend, the Anglophile entrepreneur David Tang, had lent them a number of contemporary Chinese works of art; the bathrooms had reassumed an authentic colonial grandeur; plastic chairs on the verandahs had been replaced by elegant wooden ones from Suffolk. No question, I thought, the place had style.

Next morning I 'phoned through to Lavender's room at 9.30 after toast and melon on my verandah served by the trusty Ah Cheuk. She was running late but had at least managed to have a planning session with the housekeeper. We agreed that after Sonny Wong had taken my photograph for the *Eastern Express* we would meet in the hall, have lunch on the Peak* and walk the dogs, hopefully with Alice.

My copy of the day's programme revealed that both the Pattens were busy. The Governor had a 9 a.m. conference in his office and a morning with ExCo, the Executive Council, which he described as his 'cabinet'. There was a lunch-time tennis game and then a 'first call' from the newly arrived Consul General of Guinea-Bissau, a meeting with Hong Kong's Commissioner in London, Sir David Ford, and a reception at the Hong Kong Country Club to celebrate the seventieth anniversary of the founding of the Republic of Turkey. Lavender was fairly free until 5 p.m. when she had a meeting with a Mr Chen and a Mr Wu followed by a board meeting of the Community Chest. Her predecessor, Lady Wilson, was titular head of forty-seven different charities. Lavender had already accumulated sixty. No shortage of work for either of them, but Lavender made the point that although it involved time and effort not nearly enough was intellectually taxing. I had forgotten – or not realised – how much of their work was ceremonial and vice-regal and how frustrating that could be for anyone of intelligence.

At lunch-time Lavender and I drove up winding roads with imperial names such as Magazine Gap for a light meal at the Peak Café. This is authentic nouveau-Pacific Rim, all seafood, satay and Chardonnay. We were joined by Alice, full of the night before, and the Range Rover went back downhill to pick up the dogs, who were not allowed in the restaurant. There were numerous 'round-eye' Hong Kong jokes about pets like Whisky and Soda ending up in a wok

---

* 'The Peak' is described by one writer as 'Surbiton or Wimbledon, in an atmosphere as truly British as roast beef or muffins'. Jan Morris has called it 'snootier' than any Indian hill station. On the hilltop overlooking the harbour, connected to sea level by a dramatic funicular tramway, it is as much a symbol of (European) affluence and achievement as a geographical region.

19

with noodles and soy sauce. This was not that sort of restaurant. All the same . . .

The views both from the restaurant and from the footpath afterwards were spectacular. From high up one had a panoramic vision not only of the city state laid out beneath but also of the incessant bang and clang of construction. On their brief trip to Europe the Pattens had exchanged contracts on a remote farmhouse near Albi in south-western France. It was the silence which Lavender found most therapeutic after the constant cacophony of the Colony even in the relative fastness of Government House. High on the Peak you could hear the yack of the drills and the pounding of earth-breakers as building after building soared improbably skywards in a flimsy casing of bamboo scaffolding.

Halfway round the walk a family glanced in our direction and the father spoke a single sentence in clacking Cantonese. Lavender looked slightly cross. 'That means "Governor's wife",' she said. Later as we loaded the dogs into the back of our vehicle there was more pointing and Chinese chat in the middle of which the words 'Whisky' and 'Soda' could be distinctly discerned. 'The dogs,' said Lavender, 'are much more famous than the Governor's wife.'

Another sheet of official paper was given over entirely to my departure arrangements. My luggage, passport and $HK50 departure tax left Government House at 8.00 p.m., fifteen minutes before we sat down to dinner. There were the Pattens including Alice and a friend of hers called Trilby Glover, who sounded as if she were the star of a touring theatre group but was actually a former schoolfriend; the Fords; Jung Chang, author of *Wild Swans*, and her husband Jon Halliday; Lord Skidelsky, Professor of Political Economy at Warwick, who was in town on a fact-finding mission; and me. Conversation was mainly one to one and mainly apolitical. At one point the Governor made it general in an informal fashion and sought Jung Chang's views on the

20

present situation in China, whence she and Jon had recently returned from a month or so researching their biography of Chairman Mao.

At around ten a member of staff tiptoed in to tell me, in a whisper, that my car was at the door. I said my farewells and climbed into the back of the Governor's stately Daimler, flag furled at the far end of the bonnet. Smoothly we drove through Hong Kong to the airport. I sat back in leather luxury and gazed alternately at the impassive back of the chauffeur with his red-banded peaked cap and at the tumultuous world outside. We passed through heavy gates barred to the rest of the world, paused briefly at a very VIP lounge and then, behind a car with a flashing light on top, smoothed across the tarmac to the waiting British Airways jumbo. Up the steps and into the cabin, where everyone else was already buckled up. The doors closed, we taxied away, accelerated and climbed up over the Peninsula and Government House and Sam the Tailor's and Lena Lodge, and headed back to the grey damp of a Heathrow dawn.

My initiation into the transient wonderland of Hong Kong was complete. Soon, I decided, I would return to try to capture in more detail a little slice of history on the wing. Already I was captivated, perplexed and half fulfilled.

I had been afforded a privileged glimpse of a strange place in a strange time. Now I had to plan a longer, harder look, assimilate as much as possible and communicate the experience. The received wisdom was that here an old lion was finally whimpering into extinction while a new dragon was rearing its head. My experience, however, was that received wisdom is never as simple as it sounds that this was an extraordinarily complex situation and that, for a variety of reasons, I had a chance to immerse myself in it.

I wanted to swim for a while in these choppy waters and, having, I hoped, made dry land, tell it as it was.

TWO

Six months later I went back through the looking glass.

Between the autumn of 1994 and the spring of 1995 I had rather lost touch with events in Hong Kong. Coverage in the British press seemed fitful and inconclusive. Obviously the clock was still ticking away towards the 1997 hand-over but there didn't seem to have been any great drama, no further verbal fisticuffs between the Governor and Peking. I had seen enough to know that the apparent indifference of the British press did not mean that there had been no activity in the Territory. It was simply that Fleet Street was more interested in 'sleaze' among Conservative Members of Parliament than in the intricacies of the Basic Law* and its interpretation. Royal trivia sold more copies of newspapers than abstruse debates in the Hong Kong Legislative Council.

Even so I sensed a faint hiatus. Shortly before I was due for a second stay in Upper Albert Road the former Prime

---

* Adopted at the Third Session of the Seventh National People's Congress of the People's Republic of China on 4 April 1990 and to be put into effect as of 1 July 1997. The decree promulgating it was signed by Yang Shangkun, President of the People's Republic of China. If I were a cynical Hong Konger I would be inclined to think that what the People's Congress adopts one day, the People's Congress could unadopt the next. If you took that view then all the political debate within Hong Kong during the Patten governorship would be meaningless. My impression was that there were many who did indeed take this view.

Minister, Edward Heath, was the Pattens' guest. The Princess of Wales was also in town and had been expected at Government House. They seemed an ill-assorted pair and it was perhaps the realisation of this that caused HRH to decamp instead to the Mandarin Hotel. Nevertheless it was she who made the papers in the UK, pictured with the Governor, and the ubiquitous, beaming David Tang. Mr Heath's visit passed largely unremarked.

I flew out on Virgin Atlantic thanks to the good offices of the Hong Kong Tourist Association and, in particular, Kent Hayden Sadler. For years Kent had been the HKTA's London-based European boss but he had recently been offered a job back in the Territory, which meant, in effect, that he would be the organisation's top gweilo, or 'foreign devil'. Many of his friends thought he was ill-advised but he was third-generation Hong Kong and committed to its future. He wanted to be in the Territory when it was handed over to the Chinese, and he wanted to be a part of it thereafter. He was an optimist. More to the point, although he seemed to me a conventional enough English person – he was educated in an English boarding school and had held the Queen's commission, albeit in the not wholly conventional Brigade of Gurkhas – he evidently thought of himself as a Hong Konger. That was not the same as being British. Nor, though in the years to come this might prove the greater problem and paradox, was it the same as being Chinese. Quite what this Hong Kong identity consisted of was not clear to me. It obviously took many forms and it did not necessarily have anything to do with racial origins or passports or even domicile.

The business of the airline ticket, a complimentary one for which I was duly grateful, was a small pointer to the difference between London and the Colony.* I tried for

* I later realised that the word 'Colony' had become redundant and had been replaced by 'Territory', which had fewer awkward imperial echoes.

weeks to negotiate some sort of deal in London with no success and a great deal of prevarication and obfuscation. Even saying no seemed to take for ever. Once the request was transferred to Hong Kong, however, things seemed to change, though there was precious little liaison between the two places. My ticket was issued in Hong Kong and sent to England by courier. I even had to pay Hong Kong airport tax on it, and the Virgin office in London never even knew it had been issued until I told them. I sensed that it might be easier to cut corners and pull strings out there than in the larger world of London.

I travelled on a crutch, because some two months before my departure I had ruptured my Achilles tendon playing real tennis. This meant surgery and eight weeks in plaster. The doctors warned me that I wouldn't be playing games for a year, which was a bore because I had hoped to challenge the Governor at lawn tennis. I knew how much he had improved, but even so . . .* Instead I was going to have to undergo some prolonged physiotherapy. This would, I hoped, give me another slant on Hong Kong.

Lavender had written encouragingly, 'You poor old thing . . . it sounds agony . . . we do have a good physio here but not on the NHS so they cost quite a bit. We can provide all other comforts while you're here and taxis are cheap.' My GP and Queen Mary's, Roehampton, assured me that Hong Kong would be able to provide free physiotherapy, but I wasn't entirely convinced. On a previous visit I had been obliged to go to the dentist and had been disconcerted by the American Express sign prominently displayed in his recep-

---

* A further irritation was that Jonathan Dimbleby was an avid tennis player. Dimbleby was making a TV programme with a tie-in book which would, presumably, be in competition with mine. Apparently sound in wind and limb he was able to enjoy regular early-morning sessions on court at Government House.

tion area. The subsequent bill had confirmed my fears.

I had also had my lap-top computer stolen. It was uninsured, thanks to the obduracy of my insurance company. Luckily the most vital material was stored on floppy disk, but I would need a replacement. It seemed to me that Hong Kong would, on balance, be a better place to make such a purchase than the UK. I had been told that electronics were cheap and plentiful. Purchase of a new machine could be another small litmus test.

The Hong Kong Tourist Association had done its stuff, for when I arrived at Virgin check-in, bleating about the need for extra space for my afflicted leg, I was told that they had 'authority for an upgrade'. This meant that I was almost immediately in a VIP lounge being invited to take part in a complimentary game of blackjack before being ushered into 'Virgin Upper Class', a classification which struck me as fraught with politically incorrect ambiguity. The airline had won prizes for the sophistication of its in-flight entertainment system, though I felt as technologically challenged by it as a latter-day Monsieur Hulot. I was so fazed by the various knobs and buttons that I even had some difficulty getting into the lavatory. More importantly there were only twenty-eight Upper Class Virgins for thirty-eight seats, so I had even more space than would normally have been afforded by their almost completely reclining seats. It was all a far cry from a slow boat to China.

As I dozed between sumptuous dinner and elegant breakfast I dreamed of my brother and parents steaming from Liverpool by troopship for six long claustrophobic sultry weeks. Our scheduled flight time was sixteen hours and in the event we lopped off a full ninety minutes. In their day, if you did fly, you went by flying-boat – a contrivance now memorialised by the decor in the area between the Philippe Starck restaurant and the twin helipads at the summit of the Peninsula Hotel's now completed tower. Odd how the ever increasing pace of progress has shortened our sense of history, so that aeroplanes in which living people have flown already possess the cobwebs of nostalgia. Nothing, least of all in Hong Kong, has a shelf life any more.

It was, I think, Simon Winchester, for some years a sort of Hong Kong writer-in-residence, who chided Jan Morris for suggesting that the best way to arrive in Hong Kong is by boat. Winchester favoured the airborne approach and, although, for reasons I've already given, I think he's wrong, I have to concede that the descent into Kai Tak is a dramatic, nay hair-raising introduction to southern China. Pilots love it. The thrill comes with a sudden sharp right-hand turn low on the approach over Kowloon. On a hillside there is an orange-and-white-painted square known as the Chequer Board. This is the point at which the planes have to bank steeply in order to line up the runway, which itself is a narrow finger of reclaimed land stretching out into the harbour. It's not, as far as I can tell, a dangerous manoeuvre, but it demands skill and, for a pilot, it sets the adrenalin flowing. Most airport approaches are routine, but not Hong Kong. Every pilot worth his salt wants to be at the controls coming in here. There is a special programme devoted to Kai Tak on training simulators throughout the world.

The other part of the fun is that this is one of the most urban airports in the world. As you come in you fly through the blocks of flats, and every traveller has a tale of what he or she saw through the windows: a housewife stir-frying in her wok, men playing mah-jong, a couple copulating. I'm inclined to disbelieve such stories but there's no question that the sensation of flying through rather than over a housing estate is peculiar, alarming and, as far as I know, unique. The airport should have vanished by the time the Chinese take over, replaced by a vast new one at Chek Lap Kok far away on the fringe of Lantau Island. But that's another long-running story, a bone of contention chewed remorselessly by

26

governments in London, Peking and Hong Kong itself. It promises to be a wonder of the world and yet it will be sad to see the end of Kai Tak.

My friend Fred Metcalf, who makes a living writing jokes for famous people's speeches, had given me a graphic account of his arrival to stay with the Pattens. Fred's plane evidently came to a halt halfway across the tarmac, landing steps were wheeled up and Fred alighted in solitary splendour to be wafted away in the Governor's limousine. I was over-neurotic about my disability and did not fancy the idea of long walks and queues through the teeming airport.

Lavender had assured me that there would be a car to meet me, but as we taxied down the runway I could see no sign of the personal reception which had greeted Fred Metcalf. Perhaps news of our early arrival had not reached Government House. When the airbus came to a halt I limped down the steps feeling disappointed and apprehensive. Then, halfway down, I saw a diminutive Chinese girl in a blue suit. She had shiny black hair and she was holding a notice with my name on it. Already I could sense the envious irritation of the serried ranks of businessmen as they were herded towards the waiting airport bus.

I introduced myself to the girl and she flashed a gleaming smile and did a little bob of welcome which was well short of a curtsey but nevertheless conveyed much more than a simple handshake.

'Our Governor has sent his car for you,' she said and asked for my passport and baggage check. There with the familiar red crown on its bumper and the familiar driver in white tunic and red-banded peaked cap was Chris's big black Daimler.

I especially liked the way she said 'our' Governor. It suggested a sense of proprietorial pride, which I like to think the Governor would have found gratifying.

I experienced a curious feeling of *déjà vu* over the next few

27

minutes. It felt, as I gazed from the depths of the back seat at the back of the driver's neck, as if I was replaying a video of my departure in reverse. At the entrance of Government House, one of the khaki-clad, black-Sam Browned Royal Hong Kong Policemen on the gate strode into the middle of Upper Albert Road, stopped the traffic to allow us in and offered a smart military salute. I smiled back at him, not having the gall to wave.

Elspeth and Louise were in the hall to greet me and shortly afterwards Lavender came tumbling out of the private apartments complaining, good-naturedly, that I was an hour and a half early. The Governor was elsewhere, governing.

This time I was in the Harbour Suite, so called because, once upon a time, it overlooked the harbour. Now, of course, like the house itself, it was not so much overlooking as overlooked. There were paintings of old Hong Kong on the walls and two bathrooms with gold taps. In one there was a shower with a huge rose like a gigantic watering can. Lavender, eyeing my limp, explained nervously that guests had been known to slip on the marble floor.

Luckily it was to be a quiet night: a private wine-tasting followed by a family supper. I had a bath and changed into a curious grey tracksuit which Virgin had given out to their Upper Class passengers. Presently my luggage arrived and my charming, smiling steward Ah Hon began to unpack. I was immediately devoted to Ah Hon. He seemed to me exactly the sort of 'scout' or college servant that Chris and I would have hoped for at Balliol but never quite achieved. Naturally I was appalled at the idea of him delving into my suitcase. I had packed in my usual fashion, throwing everything in haphazardly and closing the case by sitting on it. Half the stuff was dirty and it was all unironed. From time to time Ah Hon would shimmer in, like an Oriental Jeeves. Would I like so-and-so dry-cleaned? Would I like a button sewn on such-and-such? In one of their more inspired

28

innovations Chris and Lavender had commissioned portraits of the staff. They are on the walls downstairs. I wonder where they will be after 1997. I wonder too where their subjects will be. Ah Hon, like most of his colleagues, served in the Royal Navy. He was proud of this. Lavender told me he liked to talk about being on Her Majesty's Service, not least because he had fought in the Falklands War. When I broached the subject he did indeed seem pleased. He rolled up his sleeve to reveal the scarring on his arm, a souvenir of his service on the *Galahad*, the assault craft in which so many Welsh Guards were killed by the Argentine Air Force.

Ah Hon had a family up in the New Territories whom he visited whenever possible. Most of the time, however, he lived in staff quarters on the Upper Albert Road, where he listened to music on an extremely sophisticated sound system. One felt, however, that he was as happy on duty in Government House as he was anywhere else. One night I met him on the stairs after I had been dining out. He wanted to know if I'd like a cup of coffee. No? Well, how about a pot of tea? No? I told him I'd had a long day and just wanted to go to bed.

He looked at me knowingly. 'You like whisky soda?' For a moment I wondered uneasily if he was referring to the dogs. But no, he was being more literal.

Oh, very well, yes, I said, I'd love a whisky soda. A large well-iced drink duly arrived with Ah Hon looking triumph-ant and conspiratorial.

A day or so later, after I had moved out of Government House, I returned for an engagement with the Pattens shortly after lunch, at about 2.15. Ah Hon met me in the hall and greeted me like a long-lost friend.

'You like coffee?'

'Thank you very much, Ah Hon, but no.'

'You like tea?'

Again I said no.

29

And then he looked at me with the expression of a golfer who has just achieved a hole in one. 'You like whisky soda!'

Lavender, arriving minutes later, seemed only half amused.

That first afternoon as I slid around the bathroom floor in my Virgin grey two-piece I heard a throat-clearing from the door of the drawing room and found the Governor hovering. He was looking very fit. The hair was whiter than I remembered and though he seemed chunky I certainly wouldn't have described him as overweight. He was wearing a suit and looked clean, scrubbed and presentable without seeming exactly well dressed, imposing or even gubernatorial. It was a recurring problem for me. I found it difficult to think of him as Governor of Hong Kong, just as I had found it difficult to think of him as Chairman of the Conservative Party, Secretary of State for the Environment or even a Member of Parliament. To me he seemed no more and no less than Chris in a suit.

I showed him my scar and he appeared duly impressed. A serious wince. He too had been experiencing problems with legs. His physiotherapist, a partner, it later transpired, of the one recommended to me, came to the house quite regularly. Our chat was mildly desultory. The most serious exchange concerned our former tutor Richard Cobb,[*] now in his late seventies. Richard was in hospital and when I had spoken to his wife Margaret she had sounded grim. I told Chris that I was afraid we should prepare for the worst. We both, being very fond of the old boy, were silent and thoughtful for a time. Then the Governor said he'd see me at the wine-tasting

[*] Richard Cobb's resilience appeared boundless. When I returned to England some months later he was back home and working hard to finish two books. The last time I had spoken to him he told me he thought his writing days were over. Sadly he did die in the spring of 1996, but not before completing a final volume of autobiography to be published posthumously.

if I liked or, failing that, in the private drawing room for a drink before supper. Hong Kong, which in a curious way seemed miles away, was not discussed.

The wine-tasting was a domestic affair with a local, French wine merchant presenting her wares. There were a dozen or so of us quaffing and not spitting much – the ADC, Mike Ellis of the Royal Hong Kong Police, various members of the private office, Louise and Elspeth. I didn't remember the Governor having any particular interest in wines during his student days, but in the intervening years he has become a serious francophile and something of an oenologist to boot. His predecessor, Lord Wilson, was reputed to have exhibited an indifference to fine wine verging on the disdainful. Indeed I was told that the Wilsons were alleged to have bought their wine two bottles at a time and, like Her Majesty the Queen, really only liked German whites. The Pattens, in particular Chris, were not only keen on good wine, they also regarded serving it to their guests as an important part of the act. An invitation to the Governor's table during the Patten regime was a guarantee of what another of our tutors, the medievalist Maurice Keen, habitually described as 'good scoff'. 'Scoff' included drink as well as food.

The staff, while happy to sup, seemed, I thought, fairly reluctant to venture an opinion. The most obvious exception was Elspeth, who as housekeeper was, Governor apart, the person most responsible. But it was the Guv who dominated. He approved the Fleurie, a typically honeyed Monbazillac and the Pouilly Fumé. A case or so of these would find its way into the cellars and would, I surmised, be consumed before the Chinese commandeered the house on 1 July 1997. On the other hand I got the impression that Chris rather relished the thought of bequeathing his successors a few fine bottles they would be too untutored to appreciate.

Supper that night was quiet and domestic. Such family

31

meals are taken in the small area off the main dining room, the same place as we had used for the wine-tasting. The only time when 'shop' intruded was when discussing the arrangements for a formal function on Friday night. Chris had been hoping to slip away early. Lavender said they'd be lucky to escape before midnight. Chris was tetchy about this. Had Lavender's secretary talked to *his* aide-de-camp. Surely everyone knew that he wanted an early night? I mischievously thought to myself that they sounded almost as I imagined the Queen and the Duke of Edinburgh might sound arguing about a snafu between their respective households. After an uncharacteristically scratchy exchange Chris glanced at me with a grin. 'Don't think we always argue like this,' he said.

I spent only a few days at Government House. The Hong Kong perception was that I was writing a biography of the Governor, but that was not the case. He was the single most important figure in the story and he was the crucial introduction to the place, but I knew, as did he and Lavender, that the view from Government House was a partial and selective one. It was wonderful and seductive to be pampered in my Harbour Suite, spoiled rotten by the attentive Ah Hon, saluted by the police and eased around on the strength of being the 'Governor's friend', but before too long I had to break out of this privileged bunker and experience, relatively at least, a more normal Hong Kong existence.

Those few days were enormous fun. On Thursday, for instance, the Governor was scheduled to field questions at the Legislative Council. At Ah Hon's beaming insistence I breakfasted that morning on scrambled eggs and bacon, made 'phone calls all morning, lunched, as the Governor often does, on soup and sandwiches and then joined him and the diminutive Edward Llewellyn, one of his private secretaries, in the back of the Daimler. The tone of conversation on the journey was light and bantering. 'How would you like me to play this?' the Governor wanted to know. 'Should I be statesmanlike ... humorous ... witty but weighty?'

I was reminded, inevitably, of the TV series *Yes, Minister*. Llewellyn, in the role of Nigel Hawthorne's Sir Humphrey, managed to seem enormously shrewd without actually saying very much at all. If I knew the Governor he would make up his own mind in his own way. Llewellyn's role on the short drive to the Council was, I thought, to act as a sounding board.

As we approached the building we were confronted by a crowd with placards. They appeared to be wholly Chinese and mainly elderly. The burden of their complaint was to do with old-age pensions.

'Ah,' said the Governor, smiling a smile which was part sardonic, part self-deprecating and wholly characteristic. 'Democracy in action.' It was a friendly demo with no hint of real hostility, danger, or even real confrontation.

Inside the building, formerly the law courts, we were met by the chairman, Sir John Swaine, a smooth-looking local lawyer, and I was ushered upstairs to the public gallery and given a headset for simultaneous translation. The galleries, one at each end of the chamber, were full. There were journalists taking notes, photographers, and twenty or thirty local Hong Kong people of what looked like pensionable age and reduced circumstances. Enter right the Governor. All stand. Governor sits. All sit. After a few moments, when he is in mid-sentence, the elderly folk in the galleries stand up, unfurl a banner, throw pieces of paper about the place, point fingers and fists at the Governor and chant in Cantonese. Uniformed attendants start to remove them, using minimal force, while the Governor remains silent, pursed lips indicating a palpable but only mild irritation. This too is democracy in action, his body language suggests. The demonstration is tiresome and ill-conceived, but in a free society one must

33

expect this sort of thing. Under British rule order will be maintained but dissent tolerated. No arrests were made but 'details were taken' (a mildly sinister phrase) of the two men who held the banner, a Mr Wilson Li Man-yeung and a Mr Wong Kim-ho. The maximum penalty for disrupting LegCo proceedings was apparently HK$10,000.

Taking my cue from the Governor I too maintained a stiff upper lip, observing the scene, writing notes and, I hoped, displaying a sang-froid appropriate when batting abroad for Balliol and Britain. There was a curious sequel to this. Sitting in the Harbour Suite later on I heard my 'phone ring and, on picking it up, was told that I was listening to someone called Andrew Lynch of the *South China Morning Post*. Lynch, it transpired, had once worked for a paper in Bristol and had accompanied the Lord Mayor of the city on a trip to Venice on the Orient Express. I had reported it for the *Daily Telegraph*. Now Lynch was in the *Post*'s office looking at a photograph of me in the middle of the LegCo demo. Would I care to explain myself? This I did for a few minutes, as judiciously as I was able, though not enjoying the experience. No one feels more awkward at the receiving end of a hack's interrogation than a hack himself. When the piece appeared that Sunday there was the photograph of me looking rather quaintly stoic amid the fracas, and a short diary item which said, alas not for the last time, that I was writing a biography of the Governor. Throughout my time in Hong Kong I tried to convince various interrogators that I was trying to find out about the place and not the person. I was seldom successful.

'With the characteristic British stiff upper lip,' wrote the *Post*, 'he appeared to ignore the whole thing.' But of course. The words that rankled were those describing me as 'a ruddy-faced expatriate'. It made me sound like some freakish and endangered species. A few days later as I sat in the botanical gardens I watched a female 'red-cheeked crested gibbon' swinging about her cage with a baby red-cheeked gibbon in her pouch. The sight reminded me disturbingly of the words in the *Post*. I suddenly realised that, to the natives of Hong Kong, I was just a red-faced foreign monkey lurching about their cage on a quest they probably found presumptuous and irritating. This reaction was not to prove universal, but it was certainly widespread. I could understand it. It is irritating if you are a native to find some truculent interloper swanning in for a few days and then writing the definitive verdict on your home as if he were an expert. I resolved to attempt a decent humility.

Several visitors called during my few days as a house guest of the Governor. The most flattering was the millionaire entrepreneur and socialite David Tang. I had met Mr Tang on a previous visit through the good offices of Kenneth Rose. Kenneth knows everybody who is anybody. So does Mr Tang. Last time I had been to a sumptuous luncheon party on the lawn of his exquisite house in the New Territories. Champagne flowed like water, Havana cigars were handed around as if they were everyday joss-sticks, and I sat next to India Birley, the daughter of Mark, the founder of Annabel's. He was also there, as was Jacob Rothschild, the banker; Lady Dunn, the politician; Belinda Harley, Prince Charles's former factotum; and many others in similar vein. Mr Tang had shown me his collection of first editions (ninety-eight out of Cyril Connolly's top hundred) and sent me home in his yacht.

I had been told beforehand that, if I knew Chris Patten and David Tang, all Hong Kong doors were open to me. As it turned out this was less than the whole truth, but it was not without substance. This time David Tang was practically the first person I called, and his secretary rang back to say that he would be round for tea the following day. There was some confusion here because I wasn't entirely clear whether he was coming to see the Governor, Lavender or me, but in the event there was a knock on the door of my suite and in he came.

When I had previously encountered him he had struck me as a profoundly Westernised figure, speaking the sort of English I associate with P. G. Wodehouse or Old Harrovian maharajahs, enjoying such European pleasures as vintage wines and fat cigars, and favouring Savile Row suiting. On this occasion, however, there had been a transformation and the Tang who entered the Harbour Suite for tea was wearing mandarin gear – a fetching khaki tunic and baggy trousers. He looked like a walking advertisement for his upmarket shop, Shanghai Tang. It was the first time that he had been in the suite since visiting David Linley, son of Princess Margaret and the Earl of Snowdon. Linley, a modish and talented furniture-maker, had been involved in manufacturing special cigar boxes for Tang's divan at the Mandarin Hotel.

I already knew he was a phenomenon, but not only was I unsure of the nature of the phenomenon, I was also unclear whether he was in any way typical of Hong Kong. Since the Pattens' arrival he had become one of their closest friends, yet he was also a regular visitor to Peking and had friends in high places there too. The stylish and fashionable China Club, which he had opened at the top of the old Bank of China building, was shortly to be matched by a Peking counterpart.

Tang is a common name in this part of the world, and the local Tang clan have been around for hundreds of years. David Tang's fortune, he told me, derives from his grandfather, who imported ten double-decker buses from England and thus began the Kowloon Motor Bus Company. David, young middle-aged with a shock of jet-black hair, was one of the first Hong Kong Chinese to go abroad for his education. His father and grandfather fell out, though later David became the apple of grandfather's eye. At first he went to

36

state school in England, which sounds disastrous. Then he found a place at the Perse School in Cambridge. He must have been an oddity, for he spoke virtually no English. Indeed he says he failed his English 'O' level five times while, typically somehow, passing French and Russian at the first attempt. I can't believe many other Perse old boys speak English as he does, but he obviously benefited from the education. He told me, a touch whimsically, that he was first woken to the concept of European culture when he walked past an open study door at school and heard the sounds of Brahms's Fourth Symphony emanating from within.

At King's College London he began by studying nuclear physics before switching to philosophy and finally attending law school (it was this last which endeared him to his hard-headed grandfather). Then, after a spell in Hong Kong, he travelled to Peking, to the university, where he wished to sit at the feet of a brilliant German professor who was the world's leading authority on Wittgenstein. Tang, surprisingly, had no German and the professor no English. This was a problem never wholly resolved and Tang spent most of his time teaching English and English literature to PhD students (the first such since the Communists assumed power in 1949). When not engaged in this he was translating Roald Dahl's book *Charlie and the Chocolate Factory* into Mandarin. I was going to say that this was an improbable activity, but on reflection I'm not sure that would be correct. Nothing about David Tang is entirely improbable.

He talked at some length about the Patten predicament, about the attitudes of the Chinese,[*] and the likely prognosis

---

[*] David Tang used the word 'Chinese' when he was talking about people from the mainland or more specifically about the Peking regime. At first I found this mildly disconcerting but after a while I realised that the usage was effectively ubiquitous. Hong Kong people, whether of European or Chinese descent, always appeared to use the word in a similar way.

for 1997. He did this in part because he assumed, with some justice, that this was what I was interested in, but also because these questions were paramount. Obviously I was in a very particular position but nevertheless it seemed to me that it was virtually impossible to have a conversation with an intelligent, educated Hong Kong person without these subjects being mooted. Chris once said to me that he wished local people didn't all think that life began and ended in Hong Kong. Yet their predicament was so profound, the denouement at once so inevitable yet so uncertain, that it was hardly surprising if they talked of little else – especially to me.

Tang was a great supporter of the Governor, though I was already known as an old friend of the Guv's, which meant that even enemies were apt to preface their criticisms with disclaimers. Thus, 'personally I find him the most stimulating company but . . .' or 'I have absolutely nothing against him but . . .' Tang, on the other hand, seemed to have no problem with approving the deeds as much as the man himself.

He said that his Chinese friends had real difficulties in understanding that Chris enjoyed a unique position vis-à-vis the British government. Whereas previous governors had been career colonial civil servants or diplomats, Chris was a heavyweight politician. The Chinese, more careful of status and protocol than contemporary Britain – especially Chris and John Major – felt that the Governor was a relatively lowly figure who was subservient to Foreign Office bigwigs in Whitehall, who were in turn at the beck and call of the Foreign Secretary, who in turn did as he was told by the Prime Minister. The reality, thought Tang, was that Chris, as a former Cabinet minister and Conservative Party Chairman, was in an altogether different league. Not only did he enjoy the confidence of the Prime Minister, he also had an autonomy granted to no previous Governor in living memory. He more than anyone else on the British side was the architect of Britain's Hong Kong policy. He called the shots.

China felt that Chris was lucky to be engaged in a dialogue with *any* of their officials, no matter how junior. The British – in other words, Chris – reckoned that this particular governor should be allowed to negotiate face to face with Deng himself. (Always assuming that Deng was still alive.)* The two sides seemed to have completely irreconcilable opinions about the Governor's status and importance. The British thought him a big cheese; the Chinese didn't (or at least they pretended not to).

David Tang also said that his Chinese friends were quite as suspicious of us as we, the British, were of them. We regarded them as 'wily Orientals', but they regarded us as equally 'wily Occidentals'. They were convinced that the British were engaged in a sinister plot designed to ensure on the one hand that what the Chinese inherited was worth far less than it should have been and on the other that British power and influence would, despite a superficial transfer of sovereignty, actually continue undiminished after 1997.

In personal terms Tang's position was complicated. His Peking friends thought him naive, duped by the cunning Patten and his Foreign Office friends. Some of his British connections thought he was altogether too pally with Peking and their chums in Hong Kong.

My own view, at this absurdly early stage in my time in Hong Kong, was that he was an engaging, charming, generous fellow riding two volatile horses with enviable skill. I liked him a lot and was grateful for his kindness and

---

* Chris Patten said, on my first evening, that it looked as if I had arrived in the proverbially 'interesting times' because Chairman Deng's death was likely to be announced at any moment. The announcement had still to be made when I left Hong Kong some four months later!

confidence. But I wouldn't be surprised to see him fall off, possibly in a spectacular fashion.

Another visitor was Lord Hunt, who came to luncheon.* When I saw his name on my daily programme I rang Lavender in some excitement, because I assumed it was the Lord Hunt who had led the 1953 Everest expedition and who had been an old friend and colleague of my father. However, I had got the wrong Lord Hunt. This one was the Lord Hunt who had been Cabinet Secretary in the 1970s. His wife, as Chris told me after lunch, is 'Basil Hume's sister'. I don't really believe in the Catholic mafia, but there are some interesting connections even in Hong Kong. I knew, at Oxford, that Chris came from a Roman Catholic school, St Benedict's Ealing, but I didn't remember him being any more religious than the rest of us. I would have thought of us as being cheerfully agnostic. In middle age, however, his Roman Catholicism seemed to loom large.

The other guests were both interesting examples of the British in Hong Kong. Anthony Lawrence came to Hong Kong as the BBC correspondent in 1960 and, though retired since 1975, has stayed on with his German wife Irmgard, who taught Mandarin classes to beginners at the YWCA. I remembered Lawrence's dispatches as classic old-fashioned BBC broadcasts, clipped, cool, dispassionate, authoritative and very professional. He was now eighty-two but seemed sharp and knowledgeable. I said I'd like a chance to talk to him on his own later. Francis Cornish, the Senior British Trade Commissioner, and his wife Jane had been at a dinner party on the Peak during one of my previous visits. Cornish, Charterhouse and 14th/20th King's Hussars, struck me as a very different kettle of fish from Chris Patten, and his job

* I would have expected the more casual usage, 'lunch', but Government House style was unrepentantly, and slightly unexpectedly, formal. Thus the background notes for this occasion were headed 'Luncheon at Government House on Friday 28th April 1995.

significantly at odds. After all, in 1997 he seemed likely to stay on as the first British Consul General, operating from the imposing new Terry Farrel-designed Consulate. In a sense he represented the British future in Hong Kong, while the Governor stood for its past. Cornish was very dry and agreeably indiscreet on occasion, but also patrician; I would have guessed he was ex-Army and probably ex-cavalry even if I hadn't known. He and the Governor gave the impression of civilised accord, but I couldn't help wondering. Chris is the least military of men . . .

Government House was stylish and comfortable but, like Buckingham Palace, very much an office block. The private office was on the right-hand side as you entered, and very visible. You could not fail to be aware of minions at desks from the moment you arrived. It was quite usual to see some Foreign Office *éminence* from London such as Christopher Hum,* first posted to Hong Kong in 1968, gliding through the hall looking *grise*. Not many homes have a grand ballroom with a royal coat of arms.

As a weekend retreat the Pattens had the use of Fanling Lodge in the New Territories next to the Royal Hong Kong Golf Club. In my parents' day the Governor had eschewed it and handed it over to the GOC (General Officer Commanding). (My mother remembered taking my little brother to a party there at which he inadvertently bit through the glass he was drinking from. My mother panicked, thinking that he might have swallowed a lethal sliver, so all the senior officers present were made to get down on all fours to comb the carpet for the missing fragment. I assume it was found safely. At any rate my brother survived.)

---

* I had already met Hum at dinner in Hampstead. A career sinologist, he was, shortly after I spotted him at Government House, given a knighthood and posted to Warsaw as British Ambassador to Poland. Whatever its critics might say, the Foreign Office is singularly adept at keeping the rest of us guessing.

It seemed extraordinary that any Governor should voluntarily have given up Fanling. It was a lifesaver, a perfect country retreat. Early on the Saturday morning the 'pantry wagon' departed with bags and essential supplies. A little later the Pattens and I Daimlered to the helipad and flew across Kowloon and the hills of the New Territories, skirted some bird sanctuaries which had greatly impressed Michael Heseltine, and touched down on the lawn outside the lodge.* It was a wonderful escape. Sherry before lunch . . . the meal taken on the terrace . . . a long ramble through a nearby country park . . . favourite custard tarts for tea . . . a swim in the large private pool with Chinese urns full of flowers . . . Ayala champagne before dinner . . . a volume of *Times* Fourth Leaders by my bed . . . Sunday morning Gregorian chant on the hi-fi to compensate for not going to church . . . by Range Rover to the quayside to join the gubernatorial yacht, the *Lady Maureen*, named after the wife of Governor Grantham ('Rather a good governor,' said the present Governor) . . . large crew . . . Alice and boyfriend . . . passing marine police station Governor emerges from working on papers in cabin dishevelled in US Navy cap to acknowledge salute . . . swim round yacht . . . lunch on deck moored in Double Haven . . . ashore with Lavender for walk along pebbly beach littered with big black sea slugs . . . tea on the return voyage with crustless cucumber sandwiches . . . met by Daimler . . . and so to Upper Albert Road.

The usual Patten custom is to try to have an informal Chinese supper on Sunday nights. One of the other guests on

* A new acquaintance had already told me that by helicopter was the only way to see Hong Kong. 'I didn't expect you to take me so seriously,' he said, a day or so later. 'I was driving near Fanling on Saturday and took a wrong turning. The next minute I was just outside the Governor's front gate and I saw you and him getting out of a helicopter and going into the house.' They say Hong Kong is a village but I hadn't expected quite that level of coincidence.

this my last night staying in such splendour was an old Oxford friend, now a professor at Royal Holloway College. Professor Penny Corfield* was the niece of Christopher Hill, the great Marxist historian and our senior tutor at Balliol. The Professor's politics, while not perhaps quite as austere as her uncle's, were nevertheless far from Conservative. It was amusing and reassuring to see how, especially after dinner, the atmosphere relaxed and the years receded until we might have been sitting once again in Christopher Hill's rooms at one of his beery parties, discussing life. It was all as friendly and playfully adversarial as it had been thirty years before, and I had to pinch myself to remember that she was a London University professor and he the Governor of Hong Kong.

Next morning, Lavender bade me farewell as I climbed into one of the Governor's smaller cars.

'I'm sorry you can't stay longer,' she said. 'But it's probably time you saw more of the *real* Hong Kong.'

---

* Discussing my project, Professor Corfield had only one piece of adamant and unbending advice. I absolutely had to include footnotes. The idea had not occurred to me before, so their inclusion is entirely due to her.

THREE

I had a problem with the *real* Hong Kong.

The city state seemed more fragmented and illusory than any place I have ever visited. In many respects, and certainly from inside the walls of Government House, it resembled a bustling European city with its crowded but efficient underground railway system, its modern 'phone boxes (and ubiquitous mobiles), its gleaming tower blocks and mall upon mall of chic boutiques. The Governor was still, dammit, a British governor; the military commander was the very model of a British major-general; another British general ran the Jockey Club; the upper echelons of many, if not all, the great merchant houses were still dominated by people with names like Swire and Keswick.

Yet I already knew, because it is one of the most often repeated of all Hong Kong statistics, that my own people, pinko-greys of European origin, represented only 2 per cent of the population. It was a disproportionately dominant 2 per cent, but it was nonetheless a statistically insignificant fiftieth part of Hong Kong's population. Occasionally, in the pages of the Territory's English-language press, I caught a sudden brief aroma of the other Hong Kong. On one of my earlier visits, for example, I read a horribly thought-provoking and evocative piece of court reporting in the *South China Morning Post*. A witness was quoted as saying, 'I always thought my husband was in the restaurant business until he told me he was in charge of a fishball stall and had control over a number of under-age girls.'

It haunted me, that image of deceit and poverty and exploitation. It spoke of a world which I, a transient gweilo, could never hope to penetrate. Not only was I only in Hong Kong for a few months, I was also excluded by my appearance, my lack of knowledge and my ignorance of Chinese languages from acquiring any but the most superficial understanding of the world of the 98 per cent. Other Europeans, of course, knew far, far more than I could ever know. I met such people over the summer – priests, politicians, businessmen, journalists. Many of them were fluent in Cantonese and Mandarin; some had Chinese wives or husbands. In a few cases they had lived in Hong Kong all their lives. Some could trace their local ancestry back to the nineteenth century; some were humble, others positively truculent. I could only guess at the extent to which they had been accepted into the local Chinese world, but I sensed and still sense that in every case there was ultimately a barrier beyond which even the most erudite or sympathetic or privileged could never hope to penetrate. For my part I hoped I could enter a reality beyond the big white house on Upper Albert Road, but I knew it would never be a Cantonese reality. 'You're just sticking needles in an orange,' said one sceptic. 'Sometimes you may get the needle to go in quite a long way. Sometimes you won't get through the skin. But, whatever you do, you'll never cover the whole orange.' The image was a recurring echo.

My immediate post-Albert Road excursion was a temporary residence about a mile away in an apartment building in Bonham Road. George Bonham was governor between 1848 and 1854, a period of unusual tranquillity in Hong Kong's history. He was remarkable chiefly for his suspicion of the native Chinese and regularly blocked the promotion of

Chinese-speakers on the ground that they would be too sympathetic to the local community. Most governors and many other British bigwigs of the past have streets named after them. Whether these names will last long after 1997 is anybody's guess. As a participant on a notably inbred Hong Kong *Any Questions* on BBC radio, Governor Patten told his audience that he expected his public memorial to be a sewage-treatment plant. Many a true word . . .

The road named after Bonham is a busy thoroughfare which threads through the Mid-Levels on its way towards the smart suburb of Pok Fu Lam.[*] As the name suggests, Mid-Levels[†] are situated socially as well as geographically somewhere between the slums and the Peak. The road is lined with tall, thin residential blocks. Small supermarkets and stores like Park'n'Shop or 7–11 are interspersed with modest restaurants, some local Chinese but also Korean, Thai and even an elderly Russian relic called the Czarina. Every so often a steep ladder street of steps lined with market stalls drops downhill towards the harbour far below.

The immediate contrast was striking. My uniformed chauffeur helped me in with my luggage and together we staggered past a surprised-looking concierge sitting under an alarming Cantonese-captioned poster of a giant rat. The hall was gloomy, the stairway dark. The double front door of my basement flat seemed seriously fortified.

Inside, the apartment was unexpectedly light and airy. The windows of the drawing room gave out on to the playground of the school next door, where immaculately uniformed

[*] Sometimes it's Pokfulam and sometimes Pok Fu Lam. In Cantonese the name has three separate characters but sometimes the Anglicisation has elided the syllables. Both usages are commonplace, and I hesitate to say whether one is more correct than the other.
[†] Some people talk of 'the Mid-Levels' and others simply of 'Mid-Levels'. I was quite unable to determine which was the correct usage and which the solecism.

Chinese children played well-mannered games between lessons. Steps alongside were titivated with shrubs in pots, and inside there was a variety of rather alarmingly priceless-looking Oriental objets. The stylishness of the decor was an unexpected repudiation of the rat on the poster in the hall.

This was not altogether surprising because the flat belonged to a successful interior designer, Liz Dewar. Liz was away on a prolonged European holiday and I was sharing her place along with two dogs, three cats and an amah. I had never met Liz until the second night of my visit, when I had dinner with her and two friends at the Royal Hong Kong Yacht Club. Of all the expatriate mafias the Yacht Club seemed one of the most potent. Its networking potential appeared virtually limitless.

I was caught in its entrails almost entirely by accident. A friend in England who had once publicised a book of mine said months earlier that she had a Hong Kong acquaintance by the name of Mike Sinfield who would almost certainly be able to lend me a hand with accommodation. I knew I could intrude on the Pattens for a few days but I didn't want to push my luck, nor did I want to become so closely identified with the Governor that I was regarded simply as his Boswell. Hotels were a prohibitive price and commercial rents for apartments almost as bad. Luckily, however, Sinfield said that during the clammy humid summer months many Europeans still took extended leave and might be prevailed upon to allow someone to house- or flat-sit for them.

I confess to being surprised by this. I imagined that long leaves went out with the East India Company or at least the flying boat. I was wrong, however. Many expatriates still seemed to absent themselves for two or three months around the typhoon season, and Sinfield's friends were remarkably generous. More than that, of course, it gave me a glimpse of how Hong Kong people other than the Pattens actually lived. Whether you would describe their lifestyle as *real* is another matter. One night I was on the receiving end of a good-natured lecture from the veteran journalist Kevin Sinclair. Sinclair lives in the New Territories and writes reams about all manner of subjects, including *real* people. Not unreasonably he said that I was spending all my time with the *unreal* elite of the tycoon tendency like the Governor and David Tang. He was keen to take me on an extended bicycle ride to the Chinese frontier so that I might meet some *real* peasants, flower vendors and the like. I'm afraid I used the ruptured Achilles tendon as an excuse, but even so I found myself wondering what I would have learned from the flower sellers and whether a meaningful dialogue would have taken place. I'm not sure I would have got a tremendous amount from interviewing their counterparts in England, let alone on the Hong Kong–Chinese border. The Governor himself frequently went on such excursions, though not on bicycle. I had several chances of joining these and pondering their worth.

Nevertheless and notwithstanding, the experience of borrowing apartments and houses was instructive. I feel the three cats were probably atypical. One of the dogs was a mildly portly boxer, the other a village animal of uncertain pedigree and erratic behaviour called Hong Hong. The latter chewed everything he could sink his teeth into, including my pocket 'phone book and the flex of his mistress's fax machine. He never actually bit the cats but would occasionally cuff them around the ears. On one occasion he managed to lock himself into the bathroom, and from time to time he and the boxer would hurl themselves around the flat, never quite destroying Liz's valuable works of art but causing the amah and myself severe palpitations. At weekends various friends would come to take them off to the country park near Sai Kung, where Liz had a cottage. Every morning a special trainer arrived to remove the delinquent dog for half an hour of instruction. After he had returned, the amah and I would despairingly order the dog to 'sit', using our most authoritative voices. It sometimes worked for an instant and then he would start leaping about, grabbing me by the wrist and attempting to get the humans to join in his game.

I suspect the whole menagerie was atypical. It certainly seemed un*real*.

The amah was different. Her name was Ah Non, not to be confused with Ah Hon at Government House, though I, naturally, did become horribly confused by this similarity in nomenclature. Ah Non was short, chunky, shy at first, wonderfully smiley and disarmingly dedicated. She was also a brilliant cook. 'Master like drink? Master like breakfast? Master like lunch?'

Master, not used to such service, would mutter that for breakfast coffee and fruit would be more than enough. Next morning Ah Non, almost literally on bended knee, produced a multi-coloured sculpture of mango, grapefruit, melon and mangosteen. Around lunchtime Master would say that he'd be happy with a sandwich. Sometimes she took me at face value, though the sandwich was always sumptuous. After a while she stopped asking but would just arrive bearing a tray with delicate curries involving coconut and lemon grass, fresh prawns from the market or delicious, exotic but unidentifiable vegetables. She ironed my pyjamas daily and washed and ironed my shirts almost before they were off my back. She was so conscientious that one day I found her crouching inside the bath, scrubbing. She lived in a room just inside the front door, little bigger than an airing cupboard, seldom stirring out of the flat except to go to market. But on Sundays, her day off, she would dress up and go off to spend the day with her friends, other amahs from her native Thailand.

There are said to be 130,000 foreign maids in Hong Kong, mainly from the Philippines. On Sunday almost all of them seemed to congregate underneath Terry Farrel's functional grey monolith, housing the Hongkong and Shanghai Banking Corporation, or outside the Mandarin Hotel or the Anglican cathedral. There they enjoyed picnics, exchanged jewellery and clothing and filled the air with starling-like chatter in Tagalog, the principal language of the Philippines. The roads are closed to traffic and the affair has become a semi-formalised ritual. What would happen to it and to them after 1997 was just another aspect of the universal guessing game.

Statistically speaking, 130,000 is not a hugely significant figure in a total population of around six million,[*] but if you were to assume that on average one amah looked after a family of two adults and two children the numbers become more impressive. That means that half a million Hong Kong people were being released from everyday chores thanks to cheap foreign labour. In my case Ah Non washed and ironed, cooked and cleaned and catered. All I had to do was work at my job. I don't know what the figures are for domestic servants in the UK, but whereas at least half those I met in Hong Kong employed at least one amah (not necessarily living in but working on a regular basis), I know hardly anyone in the UK who now employs full-time staff.

The amahs' contribution to Hong Kong's vibrant and booming economy must be colossal, yet it sounds so trivial that I never heard it acknowledged in public. There must be literally thousands of married women in Hong Kong able to hold down serious full-time jobs simply because they employ cheap domestic labour. When the Governor or the Chief Secretary or one of the famous local millionaires trumpeted Hong Kong's success to the world they talked about democracy and the rule of law, the thrift and industry of the Cantonese, the intelligent laissez-faire apparatus of British

[*] The estimated population in the middle of 1994 was 6,061,400.

50

rule and all sorts of rather pompous peculiarities of the Colony. But I never heard them talk about the foreign maids.

On a personal basis I kept wondering what employing these sort of servants did to one psychologically. Very few of the expatriates would ever have employed domestic servants before coming to Hong Kong. It would be too strong to describe the situation as slave labour, yet the subservience of the servant class seemed to me quite unlike anything that would be tolerated in the West. How quickly, I wondered, would the novelty wear off? And in how many employers would the unequal relationship bring out a latent streak of bullying. Naturally all my friends and acquaintances were exemplary employers, but one kept hearing horror stories. Interestingly too I kept hearing, and not just from fellow gweilos, that the Chinese were often much more brutal employers than the Europeans.

In any event Ah Non spoiled me as indulgently as Ah Hon at Government House. And I'm bound to say that though I hope I always treated her with respect I very quickly came to take her attentions for granted. I even stopped privately wincing whenever she addressed me as 'Master'.

Not having a conventional nine-to-five job I had no externally imposed routine to observe. Actually I soon realised that most of Hong Kong operates a far longer working day than nine-to-five, and nearly everyone works on Saturday mornings. Waking at seven I tuned into the BBC World Service. I should really have listened to one of the local RTHK* channels or to the British Forces Broadcasting Service, but for some reason I found them difficult to pick up on my little radio. Besides, I've always used the World Service as a solace when far from home. I find comfort in the

---

* Radio Television Hongkong. Whether Hongkong was one or two words seemed to me both arbitrary and confusing. It seemed to be one word when banking and broadcasting were concerned but two when it involved the Governor.

little snatch of *Lillibullero* on the hour, the chimes of Big Ben and such odd domesticities as the Football League Third Division.

Having bathed, shaved and dressed, I would then nip up to the 7–11 convenience store with its disconcerting array of exotic Oriental contraceptives prominently displayed by the cash register. There I would buy a morning newspaper. For some reason they seemed not to stock the *South China Morning Post*, much the largest-selling English newspaper.* I wasn't too unhappy about this. The *Post* was required reading because it was the nearest English-speaking Hong Kong had to a newspaper of record. If the Governor wished to voice an opinion he would voice it in the *Post*. On the whole, however, I found the paper dull and flaccid. Perhaps the Chinese proprietor, who had purchased the paper from Rupert Murdoch, thought the same, for he had recently hired a new editor from England, Jonathan Fenby, formerly deputy editor of the *Guardian* and editor of the *Observer*.†

I much preferred the *Eastern Express*, whose founding editor, another former *Observer* journalist, Steve Vines, had recently been fired in acrimonious circumstances. Writs had been issued. The *Express* was much racier-looking, and written, I thought, in a far sprightlier fashion. It also carried more items lifted verbatim from the English press, though the *Post* too relied heavily on Fleet Street and the agency for its international coverage. The *Express*, however, was massively outsold by the *Post* and was generally regarded as unviable. So too was the *Hongkong Standard*, which, though largely unread and ill-considered, consistently

---

* When I mentioned this to the Governor he looked pleasantly surprised. 'I wish there were more 7–11s like that,' he said.
† At this point Fenby was so little known in Hong Kong that I was told more than once that he was Chinese. Not Jonathan Fenby with the stress on the first syllable of his surname but 'Jonathan Fen-Bee' with the emphasis on the 'Bee'.

boasted scoops and stories which eluded its two main rivals. Both these last two were allegedly kept going for that most Chinese of all reasons, 'face'.

After a breakfast spent reading the paper and fending off the attentions of Hong Hong, I would make a 'phone call or two. I had arrived with the telephone numbers, not just of the Governor and David Tang, but of innumerable friends of friends and acquaintances of acquaintances. This list, plus the public-relations apparatus associated with various arms of government and the main commercial organisations, was my principal key to unlocking the secrets of Hong Kong.

After the calls, I would shuffle my ever expanding pile of papers and look through my collection of business cards. I had been warned about the business card before leaving England. Indeed while staying for the first time at the Peninsula Hotel I had been presented with a small set of my own, embossed in gold, giving the hotel as my address and with a Cantonese translation on the reverse side. Kent Hayden Sadler, at the HKTA, had offered to have some cards printed, but as I had no fixed abode or 'phone number it seemed slightly pointless. I soon realised, however, that I must have been the only person in Hong Kong who did not possess such identification. This omission, I fear, caused me loss of face. Receptionists in grand offices would always ask me for my card and would look dumbfounded and mildly scandalised when I said I didn't have one. When I first met someone on either a business or social occasion I found that I was invariably presented with a card held in both hands and accompanied by a modest bow. It was a formal greeting, as much a part of local life as a tea ceremony. My failure to reply in kind was plainly regarded as bad form, and for a time it made me feel gauche and inferior. I was obviously losing face by not being able to follow suit when someone else dealt a high trump. After a while, however, I took a perverse satisfaction in not carrying my own pack. I felt it made me seem not so much inadequate as eccentric. How far I was able to get this message across I could never, of course, discover.

Eventually I would venture out and catch a bus to Central. The buses were a source of excitement and mystery and remained so throughout my stay. They came in a variety of shapes, sizes and colours. Betty Wei, in her informative and amusing guide, writes that 'bus stops are places to test the Darwinian theory of the survival of the fittest'. This seemed pretty accurate to me, but I found the actual journey just as much of a struggle. There were 4,500 buses in Hong Kong, of which over a thousand were double-deckers. These ranged from noisy, fume-belching old Leylands to sleek air-conditioned numbers, often of German or Japanese origin. There were also almost 7,000 minibuses seating sixteen or eighteen: the 'public' ones green and beige, the 'private' ones red and beige.

At this stage in my Hong Kong career I had no idea where the buses were going. My geography was so uncertain that when a bus had the words 'Admiralty' or 'Wan Chai Ferry' I had no idea what they meant or where they were. My usual first port of call was the Hong Kong Club, in the middle of Central, but the bus indicators did not, reasonably enough, say whether a particular route passed by the club or not. Worse, I had no means of finding out. I spoke no Cantonese and the drivers seldom seemed to have any English. Even if they did they found great difficulty in understanding my accent and inflection.

Thus I might say, enunciating carefully, 'Central?'

The driver would look completely blank.

I would repeat the words several times. Sometimes the incomprehension would persist. Sometimes, however, after three or four attempts the man would give a sudden exasperated grin of recognition and repeat 'Central' and shake his head in wonder as if to say, 'Central. Of course, you stupid gweilo, why on earth didn't you say so in the first place?'

But getting on the bus was nothing like as much of a problem as getting off. The old double-deckers of the China Motor Bus Company[*] were much the easiest because they appeared to use regular, clearly identified bus stops. Some were compulsory stops and others voluntary. Most of these buses didn't have bell-pushes like the ones I was used to in London. Instead they had a rubber strip running the length of the vehicle. Pressure applied anywhere along the rubber rang the bell and caused the bus to halt at the next stop. The minibuses were altogether more problematic. At least the green ones operated with fixed fares, timetables and schedules. The red ones did not have fixed routes, timetables or fares, yet there were over 2,500 of them carrying almost a million passengers every day. The concept of a million people a day getting on buses without knowing where they were going, when they were going or how much they were expected to pay, strikes me as fairly mind-boggling. I knew it was the state in which I undertook most of my bus journeys, but I had no idea there were a million others in a similar condition of uncertainty.

It was the bells and the compulsory stops which made the double-deckers my preferred transport. The minibus stops seemed more or less arbitrary and to get the driver to stop you had first to shout at him. Later on I acquired the

[*] The China Motor Bus Company is the biggest operator on Hong Kong Island with ninety-three routes and 930 double-deckers, apart from the thirty-eight cross-harbour routes operated jointly with the Kowloon Motor Bus Company (founded by David Tang's grandfather). The KMB is much the largest operator in Hong Kong with 3,369 vehicles, 2,619 of them double-deckers. But it operates almost exclusively in Kowloon and the New Territories. A new company, City Bus, started on Hong Kong Island in September 1993. By the end of the year it was already running 144 double-deckers, 141 of them air-conditioned.

confidence, sometimes, to call out 'Stop!' in firm, authoritative English. This usually produced the required result, but in the main, and certainly to begin with, I was far too embarrassed to shout in English in a bus full of Cantonese-speakers. According to Betty Wei, I should have shouted something which sounded like 'look chair' without the 'k' or the 'r' being sounded. Other authorities said the correct noise was 'Yau Lok'. My impression was that any old noise would have done.

I never really warmed to the Hong Kong Club, even though it was convenient. As a member of the Travellers Club in London I was allowed the privilege of visiting membership in Hong Kong. I had written from London to confirm this and to ask if I could use the Club as a poste restante for incoming mail. This was agreed, though I sensed a marginal reluctance as if, in some loosely defined manner, I was taking an unfair advantage. I was reasonably certain that as many members of the Hong Kong used the Travellers in London as vice versa, and in several respects the Travellers was much to be preferred. It had bedrooms, members for the use of, and it was still housed in the same historic, cavernous and appropriate Pall Mall building it has occupied for over 150 years. There were travellers at the Travellers before the British even occupied Hong Kong. The Hong Kong Club was non-residential and although it used to be housed in a wonderful building overlooking the cricket ground (also long gone) it was now in what looked to my untutored eye like a multi-storey car park in a Hertfordshire new town. It was the work of the Austro-Australian architect Harry Seidler. There were considerable commercial advantages in the demolition and development. Much bitterness was aroused at the time and there was even a petition to the Queen. I saw one bitter cartoon on the wall of a member's house. The drawing showed the new club with the Cenotaph in front of it. On the side of the war memorial the words 'Glorious Dead' had been changed to read 'Glorious Deal'.

It was difficult to put a finger on my misgivings. The membership secretary was perfectly correct and civil when I called to present my credit card so that I could sign for food and drink, but she also managed to make it plain that I was very lucky to be able to use the facilities and that there were a great many people in the Colony who had been on the waiting list for years and who would give their eye teeth to be in my position. After a while the hall porters unbent, recognised me when I came to check the pigeonholes and even sometimes smiled. At first, however, they had seemed distinctly flinty-faced. To be fair, I should admit that Grafton, who manned the front desk in Pall Mall, was cast in a similar mould.

Apart from the poste restante pigeonholes there was a very comprehensive little library with a number of useful books, comfortable armchairs and agreeable views of the harbour. Next door was a silent reading room with more armchairs so deep and enticing that, as if in a parody of Pall Mall, members would curl up in them and snore the afternoon away, their faces covered in old copies of the London *Times* or *Daily Telegraph*. On the top two floors there was a light, airy, spacious Garden Lounge; there were several formal, and expensive, restaurants, and on the third floor a large, sepulchral, dark-panelled bar where I used occasionally to have a glass of wine and a club sandwich. I thought the staff there were notably jollier than on the desk, but it still struck me as stuffy. There were some Chinese members but they seemed very few. I know also that it is unfair to judge by appearances but too many of the other members reminded me of the prefects who used to beat me in the dormitory at school – now, almost forty years on, prosperous but gone to seed.

'Central' is *very* central and, for the visitor, particularly

57

the visiting businessman, there was no need to stray outside its confines. Indeed many businessmen never did so, with the result that there is a popular image of Hong Kong which derives entirely from that small area around which one can easily walk on foot, though in the stifling humidity of the Hong Kong summer that would be unwise. I never did get used to the atmosphere, which wrung the last drop of moisture out of me after only a few moments of hobbling along the city's teeming pavements.

Exile, however temporary, inevitably breeds a degree of homesickness. I wanted to immerse myself in this strange place and yet still I craved news from England and wanted to send my news to England too. Thus, as often as not, my second port of call was the General Post Office, a few hundred yards from the Club and hard by the Star Ferry Terminal. Every schoolboy knows about the Star Ferry. The evening Professor Corfield came to dinner at Government House, Chris, looking sage, said that, hackneyed though they were, the three absolute tourist 'musts' were the Star Ferry, the tram from Kennedy Town to Shau Kei Wan and the Peak tramway.

With limited time you would hardly include the General Post Office in that list, yet it was a place of which I became absurdly fond, partly because of the way it represented a conduit to the world I had left behind, partly because it was, with its orderly queues (only disorderly on the days of first issues when the clerks were too few to cope with demand), so like a British post office of the 1950s, and partly because of the plaque to mark its opening. I never failed to be moved by the quotation: 'As cold waters to a thirsty soul – so is good news from a far country.' Underneath was the legend, 'This building was opened by His Excellency Sir Murray Maclehose, GBE, KCMG, KCVO, Governor of Hong Kong.' I always wondered, as I waited to post my home thoughts from abroad in their flimsy red, white and blue envelopes, how long that imperial souvenir would survive the transfer of sovereignty. Maclehose's name seemed to crop up all over the place, though those who remembered him, and there were many, talked of him not just as the most physically imposing of recent governors, but also, fondly yet irreverently, as Jock the Sock.* He was Governor from 1971 to 1982, then took a peerage and retired to the United Kingdom.

Retiring to the old country is not inevitable among expatriate Britons, though the path followed by Jock the Sock is more usual than not. I even came across one woman whose parents had never lived in the UK but nevertheless retired 'home' to a Jardine Matheson enclave in south-west Scotland where they were apparently blissfully happy. I wondered how many of us British pinko-greys thought wistfully of home, waited anxiously for 'good news from a far country', and sent out cold waters for thirsty souls ourselves. Exile is an uneasy condition and I was not the only exile in Hong Kong. On the bus one day I overheard two Indian girls conversing. One said to the other that she couldn't bear to make any new friends because just as a new relationship was established the other person left. There was so little permanence in the place. Chris's complaint about those who thought life began and ended in Hong Kong kept coming back to me. If the Governor saw his tenure through he would have spent five years of his life in the Territory. I was here for only a few months. We were gypsies, vagrants, and so too were most, if not all, of the 2 per cent. The majority of the 98 per cent, however, were stuck, for better or for worse.

Our own brief stays were microcosms of the imperial

---

* The nickname was allegedly coined by Donald Wise, sometime foreign correspondent of the *Daily Mirror* in its halcyon Cudlipp days. Wise was one of those journalists to whom famous anecdotes, nay sometimes lunchtime legends, inevitably attach.

presence itself. 'A thousand ages in thy sight are but an evening gone.' A hundred and fifty years of British rule, five years of Patten governorship, four months of a writer's visit . . . these were as nothing in the context of thousands of years of Chinese civilisation.

No wonder I had problems with seeking out the *real* Hong Kong.

FOUR

If ever a place was cut out for clubland heroics it was Hong
Kong. The very fact of expatriate existence made the
unclubbable clubbable. All but the most misanthropic
appeared eager to seek out kindred spirits when they
suddenly found themselves thousands of miles from home
with few of the support systems upon which they usually
relied. The Pattens were blessed with spacious accommodation and obviously entertained at home; so did a small
number of other exalted figures. In the main, however, the
inhabitants of Hong Kong suffered from the fact that space
was at a premium. This meant that housing, even for the
relatively well off, tended to be pokey. Quite affluent homes
were too small for serious regular entertaining. Some expats
managed bigger accommodation by moving to the outlying
islands or up into the New Territories, but, as a very general
rule, a high proportion of middle-class people lived within
walking distance of downtown. Besides, taxis were supposed
to be among the cheapest in the world. The combination of
modest dwellings and easy accessibility meant that the Hong
Kong clubs tended to seem like homes from home in a sense
which the St James's clubs of London hardly ever seemed to
emulate.

My first club was the Hong Kong itself but, useful though
it proved, the conviviality quotient continued low. It simply

wasn't the sort of place where you could go and bump into someone for a drink and a chat. Nor, I suppose, was the Royal Hong Kong Yacht Club. The Yacht Club was not particularly convenient, being on the harbour's edge and cut off from the rest of civilisation by a multi-lane urban motorway. Unless I was with someone in a private car or a taxi I approached it by taking the underground to Causeway Bay and then negotiating the lugubrious low-ceilinged tunnel that ran under the road from the car park by the Excelsior Hotel.

At the harbour's edge was Jardine Matheson's famous Noël Coward-celebrated noonday gun[*] (disappointingly small), and below and beyond was an extraordinary assemblage of boats. I was always being stunned by the contrasts of wealth and poverty in Hong Kong and there are few better examples. Some of the boats appeared to be Chinese homes, modest wooden sampans wallowing in fetid water, their owners in singlets and lampshade hats, squatting over fishing nets or the family wok. At the other extreme were the yachts from the club, gleaming veterans of Admiral's Cups, Sydney–Hobart and China Sea Races, sleek with spit and polish and fluttering pennants. Ball-park figure half a million Hong Kong dollars.[†]

The footpath took you past the premises of the Royal Hong Kong Police Officers' Club, which looked almost as impressive as the Yacht Club, through a chandlery and boat

[*] 'In Hong Kong/They strike a gong/And fire off a noonday gun . . .' ('Mad Dogs and Englishmen'). I was unable to see a gong, though there is a bell. The present three-pounder gun seems to date from 1905 and was given to Jardines by the Marine Police after local residents complained that its predecessor, a six-pounder, was too noisy. The original was taken by the Japanese in the Second World War. The precise origins of the custom and the weapon are confused.
[†] During my visit the Hong Kong dollar was worth approximately a twelfth of a pound sterling.

yard and into the clubhouse itself. It was a serious building: two bars, a smart restaurant with wraparound panoramic harbour views and a bistro in the former cellars with an outdoor terrace which also enjoyed amazing harbour views. Outside there was a replica of the sculpture of the Copenhagen mermaid.

The club had reciprocal arrangements with other sailing clubs from the Royal Thames and Royal Cornwall to Bermuda, Bombay, Belgium and Brunei. In other words it was major league. The Governor – not alas, a sailing man – was, unsurprisingly, the patron. The status of the club after 1997 was a touch uncertain and a matter of debate and controversy. There were those who thought the 'Royal' prefix should be dropped voluntarily before it was forced on them by the new regime. Others, more sanguine, pointed out that sister clubs in other republics had happily retained the 'Royal'. There is the Royal Bombay in India, the Royal Cape in South Africa and the Royal Cork in Eire. On the other hand, and perhaps more pertinently, the Singapore Club is now the Republic of Singapore Yacht Club. The buzz in the bar suggested to me that in the end the Royal Hong Kong was more likely to follow the Singaporean than the Irish example.

The first time I went was to see my new friend and benefactor, Mike Sinfield. We met in the main bar, a serious drinking establishment, which was fun enough if you were with friends, but I found it inhibitingly 'yachtie' and closed-shop if I went in on my own. Had I been a sailor myself I might have felt less of an interloper, but I wasn't sure.

Sinfield generously arranged a visiting membership, though I felt rather fraudulent entering 'Marylebone Cricket Club' under the heading for 'visitor's home club'. This meant I could use the club's facilities for a couple of weeks with an option to take a longer temporary membership if I wanted. I had been told by the doctors at Queen Mary's, Roehampton, that swimming was the best possible therapy, and the Yacht Club had a good-sized pool where I could swim lengths, buy a sandwich lunch and eavesdrop on bored expat wives discussing the prices of property in Surrey.

Swimming was good for the ruptured Achilles tendon and so, up to a point, was hobbling around on my stick or crutch. Early on at Government House I was proud of being able to stagger in some pain and at some risk to the Hong Kong Club and to the Hongkong and Shanghai Bank, where I opened an account. I say 'risk' because the streets of Hong Kong were more crowded than any I have ever known and the disregard for oncoming pedestrian traffic quite ruthless. I was not actually knocked over and did not actually use my stick in self-defence, but I was glad to have it.

Despite these two therapeutic recreations I had been told I needed professional help and arrived in Hong Kong armed with a letter of explanation from the Queen Mary's consultant in the UK. This, I was assured, would smooth my path. It seemed to me in the safety of the UK to be rather a good test and a chance to assimilate local colour. The waiting room at the orthopaedic clinic at the National Health Queen Mary's was a very good slice of life and an excellent opportunity to observe human behaviour. However, when I suggested going public to my early Hong Kong contacts the idea was met with disbelief. Nobody in the monied or well-insured expatriate community would, it seemed, even consider public medical treatment. That was for the man on the Kowloon omnibus.

There seemed to be two contenders for physiotherapy. One was the Governor's physio, who came with a powerful endorsement from Upper Albert Road. The other was the Sinfield–Yacht Club candidate. As the two were partners, it didn't really make much difference who I plumped for. Grateful to Sinfield and anxious not to appear too obviously in the Governor's pocket, I opted for the Yacht Club candidate, Lesley Hickman, Grad Dip Phys, MCSP (UK), MCPA (Canada). She operated from cramped premises in an office building in Ice House Street, though because the landlords were proposing a massive and apparently arbitrary rent increase she was contemplating a move.

The atmosphere was very similar to that in the dentist's I had visited on my last trip and at the doctor's I was to consult a few weeks later. The poster in the reception area illustrating the spinal column and adjacent joints was much as I would have expected back home. It was the credit-card signs which pulled me up short. Despite first-hand experience of the capitalist approach to medicine in North America I am essentially a child of the Welfare State. I associate American Express and Diners' Club with restaurants and airlines, not aches and pains, let alone life and death.

Lesley and her young Canadian assistant seemed first-class physiotherapists, but nevertheless an hour of whirlpool, massage, ultrasound and clever tricks with electricity came to HK$350. On top of that there were various extras like a heavy-duty red elastic band with which I was supposed to do knees-bending in any spare moments. She even said that my trusty stick from the petfood shop in Shaftesbury was an inch or two too long and should have a rubber tip rather than the metal one which I'd insisted on, admittedly for reasons of style rather than safety. Worst of all she wanted me to have the treatment two or three times a week. That way I could see a brilliant new bionic leg but also financial disaster, and I'm afraid that after a few sessions and a definite improvement in the afflicted limb I cancelled an appointment and never went back. I felt slightly guilty but a few weeks later I bumped into the young Canadian on an island ferry and she greeted me like a long-lost friend. She was just off to Bosnia on a physiotherapy assignment with the United Nations. By then I was unsurprised. People in

Hong Kong always seemed to be charging off on sudden exotic enterprises.

Lesley herself had been in Hong Kong for twenty-four years. She viewed the 1997 change-over with cautious equanimity. Some valued possessions were stored in a bolt-hole house in Glastonbury. She had her British passport, but on the other hand she expected business to continue in much the same vein, not least because, as she put it, 'the PLA* get bad backs'. Her Hong Kong home was a 47-foot ketch moored near the Yacht Club in Causeway Bay. As she put it laconically, the boat had sailed to the Philippines several times already and she didn't see why, if it proved necessary, she shouldn't make the voyage again. As I talked my way round the community I found a lot of this sort of bet-hedging, especially among those expats who did not enjoy the umbrella protection of a multi-national organisation or – to a much lesser extent – an arm of government.

Further up Ice House Street, a ten-minute walk from Lesley's clinic, it turned into the Lower Albert Road, which skirted the northern perimeter of the Governor's garden. Here, at No. 2, was one of Hong Kong's few surviving ancient monuments. The term is necessarily relative. Given Lord Palmerston's famous early-Victorian judgement that Hong Kong was a barren rock with barely a house on it, there is very little indeed of genuine antiquity. Obviously there is nothing British which predates the 1840s, and the few really old Chinese buildings are miles away from the soaring modern heights of the city centre.

The curious timbered building in Ice House Street used to be the Dairy Farm Depot. Built by the Dairy Farm Company in 1913 and extended in 1917, it was the downtown storage place for the fresh milk and dairy produce of the herds of cattle then grazing in Pokfulam. In the 1990s one part of the

* People's Liberation Army.

building had been taken up by the Fringe Club, described a little prissily in one of the HKTA's guides as 'a performance venue catering to those with progressive tastes in art'.*

The rest of the building was the home of the Foreign Correspondents' Club. The FCC has enjoyed a peripatetic existence, lurching from palatial buildings of its own to modest suites in office blocks. For a time it was housed in the Hilton, and it had occupied the Dairy Farm Depot for a decade or so. By some curious, almost magical, sleight of hand, however, it felt as if it had been there for ever. More than any other club I have ever known, its premises seemed exactly right for its purpose. The main rooms were a first-floor dining room with a long conservatory at one side and a downstairs bar area serving drinks and fairly basic food. FCC members were always apologising for the food, though it struck me as perfectly adequate, with one or two of their specials like the rockfish soup, the rack of lamb and the crêpes being, as Michelin would put it, 'worth a detour'.

But the FCC was not a Hong Kong institution for gastronomic reasons. For any journalist who remembered Fleet Street in the 1960s and 1970s it was an essay in instant nostalgia. Indeed several of the faces belonged to hacks who were El Vino habitués during those last excessive days of the old journalism. There was one night at the FCC when Tony Clifton, now with Hong Kong's *Newsweek* bureau, was there along with Ken and Pat Pearson, in town pitching for the job of setting up a new permanent museum for the Royal Hong Kong Jockey Club. All of us had worked together for

---

* The only Fringe show I attended was a two-man exhibition of new portraits of every single Hong Kong Governor from Napier to Patten. They didn't strike me as the least bit progressive, being for the most part little more than attempts to copy contemporary portraits or photographs. The one of Governor Patten was conspicuously unflattering and, I thought, inaccurate. The artists were both Chinese, which, to me, was unexpected, though it might go some way to explaining the porcine portrayal of the last Governor.

the pre-Harold Evans *Sunday Times*, when Denis Hamilton was editor and Lord Thomson the proprietor. The doyen and doyenne of the FFC were Anthony Lawrence, the former BBC correspondent whom I met at that early lunch with the 'wrong' Lord Hunt at Government House, and Clare Hollingworth, still active on behalf of the *Telegraph*'s Conrad Black. She had begun a legendary journalistic career by being the first person to report Hitler's invasion of Poland. Both were in their eighties, but both spry, garrulous and worthy successors to the late Richard Hughes, who used to hold court in former FCC premises and was immortalised by John le Carré as Old Craw in *The Honourable School-boy*. A bust of Hughes stands between the pigeonholes and noticeboards and the bar. Years ago when Fleet Street was Fleet Street, no journalist could come to work from the eastern end of the Street without passing a plaque in memory of one of the patron saints of journalism and popular writing. Edgar Wallace had been given a bust on a wall in Ludgate Circus. Every day for years I would pass that memorial and perform a silent, momentary act of homage. The same is true of Richard Hughes. You could not go for a drink at the FCC without passing the father of all Hong Kong hacks.

Like El Vino, the Stab in the Back and Poppins, the three most famous old Fleet Street hostelries, the FCC had a louche air of not always suppressed debauchery, especially on Friday, which was categorised as 'zoo night'. This was when the animals emerged. One unkind aphorism had it that the FCC was where 'women with a past meet men with no future'.

The main bar, claimed to be the biggest in all Asia, occupied most of the downstairs room and was an elliptical island sitting on a sea of terracotta Canton quarry tiles punctuated with irregular inlets. The effect of this arrangement was a little like the notion propounded, I think, by

68

Jonathan Miller, of a theatre with no stage but two auditoriums. When the curtain goes up the audience is confronted simply by a mirror image of itself. I often felt at the FCC as if I was watching a stage play but was being watched at the same time. This surreal effect was compounded by the fact that around the walls were framed magazine covers, many of them – a *Spectator* cartoon, a *Far Eastern Economic Review* photograph with the independent legislator Emily Lau – portrayals of my friend the Governor looking, for the most part, sage, statesmanlike and fantastically important. Other photographs on the walls included the infamous shot of the Saigon police chief killing a young Vietnamese with his pistol at point-blank range and the helicopter in the same city as it evacuates the last of the Americans escaping from the victorious forces of Ho Chi-minh and General Giap. Hubert van Es, the Dutch photographer who took the picture, was still often to be found at the bar, a tall, disconcerting presence with unblinking eyes. The shadow of the Vietnam war still hung heavy in this room.

Its enemies and there were many, especially among the politically correct, regarded the FCC with suspicion and contempt. Like all such places it was rife with gossip, often wild, and opinion, nearly always vigorously expressed, but frequently just as unsubstantiated as the gossip. Inevitably it had its share of bores and misfits, but it was nearly always generous to me and I found that, whenever I came in, sat down and produced my visitor's membership card and dog-eared book of coupons, I would be engaged in conversation by a member. Early on in my visit the Rugby World Cup took place in South Africa and the FCC showed it on a big screen. It was an unusual, and not always easy, experience to watch the England XV surrounded by patriotic New Zealanders and Australians, not to mention even more xenophobic Welshmen and Scots, but nevertheless those matches encapsulated the atmosphere perfectly. The foreign correspondent in Hong Kong still seemed to me to have something of the footloose swagger of the last frontiersmen and this, his watering hole, much of the quality of the Last Chance Saloon. I doubt whether it or its inhabitants will find much favour with the new regime. It would be a shame if it became as mournful a shadow of its former self as Fleet Street's El Vino, yet it was not too difficult to imagine it as one of the most lugubriously haunted houses in post-imperial Hong Kong.

Neither the FCC nor the Royal Hong Kong Yacht Club nor Lesley's physiotherapy represented reality in a truly local sense. They were essentially gweilo enclaves, mere pimples on the body politic. Yet for all their expatriate character, they exerted a fascination – not least, I felt, because it was they who were likely to change most dramatically when Hong Kong became reabsorbed into Mother China. *Che sera, sera*, whatever will be will be. All three might survive with minimal changes of style or nomenclature, but it was not entirely fanciful to imagine them vanishing altogether.

The Governor had his legs manipulated by Lesley's partner (though she went to the Governor rather than the Governor going to the clinic); he addressed the FCC at one of their regular speakers' lunches; and he went to the Yacht Club for dinner with the Commodore. I sensed, however, that he was less than patient with these manifestations of gweilo culture and, after his fashion, he remained assiduous in his own quest for the *real* Hong Kong. He pursued this in a number of ways, one of which was to make regular visits to parts of his bailiwick, sometimes quite formally and at other times virtually unannounced and certainly unknown to the press.

I went with him on several of these trips, the first of which was to the Northern New Territories, including the town of

Fanling near his country house. Indeed we made a quick pit-stop at the lodge to inspect the fine wooden screen he had just bought.

We travelled by helicopter and car and went first to the North-East New Territories Landfill. This was, in effect, a very big rubbish dump, and part of the Strategic Waste Disposal Plan endorsed by the Governor-in-Council in 1989. In other words it was an initiative of his predecessor, Governor Wilson. As befitted a previous UK environment minister, Governor Patten was tremendously keen on environmental issues and these, of course, included such apparently prosaic matters as sewage and waste disposal.

I felt I had been here on previous occasions, notably while researching a biography of the Duke of Edinburgh. I said as much to the Governor and, though he gave one of his short barkish laughs, I was not entirely sure he enjoyed being lumped in with Prince Philip. It was eerily familiar though. We all put on yellow hard hats, stared at the hole in the ground with expressions of what we hoped were intelligence and understanding, and nodded attentively as the site engineer ran through his detailed exposition.

The Governor had mastered his brief. He knew that the Landfill was due to start receiving waste in July, that it had a maximum depth of 140 metres and a void space of 37 million cubic metres, which made it about 120 times as big as Jardine House.[*] He remembered that it was filled with two layers of low-permeability membrane to prevent leaching of gas. And so on.

The engineer and the Governor swapped statistics about extra vehicles on the road, and the engineer mentioned that a major problem had been the existence of a family grave on the site. This had taken a year to negotiate. Family graves in

[*] The flagship headquarters of Jardine Matheson near the harbour in Central.

tiresome places often, it seemed, placed a brake on 'development' of various kinds, a notion I found rather appealing.

Lavender, *sotto voce*, remarked, 'What a shame to fill a lovely place like this with rubbish.'

I think several of the party probably agreed, but such is the price of progress. Or something like that.

The next stop was Kan Tau Wai village. This was a small farming community near the Chinese border. The population was 180 from four different clans, most of whom seemed to have come out to meet the Governor. They had suffered from severe floods in both the previous years and had been given emergency relief grants. A month or so earlier they had held a village election and a Mr Wong Wai-yim was elected unopposed. Mr Wong was obviously a significant local figure, for he was also on the Sha Ta District Board and was vice-chairman of the Ta Kwu Ling Rural Committee.

The scene in the village reminded me of a harvest festival in Wiltshire. There was a banner which said 'Welcome Governor Mr Chris Patten, Regards from Kan Tau Wai village'. I liked the courteous restraint of the 'Regards'. All the vegetables on display looked succulent, but it was the cucumbers that caught the eye. We were clearly at the height of the cucumber season.

The Governor alighted from the Daimler and worked the crowd just as he might have worked a crowd on the stump in Bath during a Westminster election. He smiled broadly and warmly, he pumped flesh, he enthused about infants and cucumbers, and he told them all how pleased he was to see them and how happy he was to be there. He spoke to them in English. I asked one of his aides whether he was learning Cantonese or Mandarin and he replied, half joking, that the Governor was far too busy learning French. His predecessor had prided himself on the fluency of his Chinese and it would have been impossible for Chris, who is not in any case a natural linguist, to have matched Wilson's expertise. Had I been Governor I'm not sure I wouldn't have invested in a funny little booklet called *Instant Cantonese!*[*] and learned one or two phrases from 'The Polite Section', subtitled 'How to win friends and influence six million people'. A few 'Hung woo-ee's would have been appropriate. 'Hung woo-ee' is apparently a phonetic rendering of 'Nice to meet you'. 'Ngor hor-mm-hor yee bong lay' would have been another useful one. That's Canto-speak for 'I'm sorry, my Cantonese is not very good.'

However, the Governor conducted himself in English and no one seemed to mind in the least. The villagers all beamed back. They seemed curious but genuinely friendly. The background brief suggested that people here were well-disposed to government. The introduction of elected instead of appointed representatives, greeted at first with hostility, was now not only accepted but enthusiastically endorsed. Or so the background brief suggested. Certainly nothing happened in Kan Tau Wai that afternoon to indicate anything else.

From there we moved on to the Tang Chung Ling Ancestral Hall. This was my first experience of such a place, though not my last. The Tangs, I was told, first arrived in this part of the world in the tenth century and came to Fanling 300 years later. I assumed that these Tangs were related to David Tang and the founder of the Motor Bus Company, but I felt this might be the wrong question to ask at this precise moment.

The building we were now inspecting was built in 1525 to honour the first Tang and had recently been renovated, thanks to a HK$2.35 million grant from the Jockey Club. The jumble of intricately carved exotic creatures, the pervasive scent of joss-sticks, the religious and cultural

[*] This was, fortuitously, published a week or so after my arrival, but I was as feeble as the Governor and never put it to the test, relying, like him, on a broad smile and English spoken slowly and firmly.

73

significance of the place, all impressed yet confused me. I stayed some paces from the Pattens and watched them walking slowly around the hall, nodding at their guide's explanations and assuming the same sort of deferential reverence one would have deployed for a guided tour of Chartres Cathedral or the Blue Mosque. I wondered if we really understood what we were looking at, any more than the camera-happy Japanese tourists whom we used to find so amusing as they snapped away at our academic gowns and mortarboards in Oxford.

And so to market. The Governor's gourmet propensities were widely remarked. One journalist had already told me that he was plotting two articles, one on the 'Governor's luvvies', meaning the Pattens' core of close friends, and another on the Governor's restaurants. Sometimes one felt that every restaurant in Hong Kong had the equivalent of a blue plaque saying 'Chris Patten ate here'. Actually the market was not just a market; it was a five-storey 'regional complex' which also housed the North District Public Library and the North District Office of the Regional Services Department. But the market was the focus of our visit. This was my first market. Over the next months I visited a number of them, just as I visited a number of ancestral halls. On the whole I felt more at ease with the markets. I suspect the Governor felt the same.

This one was air-conditioned and had been opened, at a cost of HK$206 million, in June 1994. Previously, licensed hawkers had been scattered all over the Sheung Shui District. Now they were all safely gathered in this one building. It comprised 16,500 square metres and 365 stalls. Apart from the sheer variety of produce on display, what struck me most was that all the food was illuminated by overhead lights with red plastic shades. I was told that this was designed to make the food more luminous, shiny and enticing. I was disappointed and mildly sceptical about this. I felt the red lights should have had a more symbolic significance to do with religion or superstition.

The final act of the day was a meeting with local officials. Again I was reminded of my tours with Prince Philip: the suits, the fixed smiles, the handshakes, the mild embarrassment. The locals stood around the walls of the room while Chris and Lavender circulated, starting at opposite ends and passing in the middle. Over the years many have criticised the stilted quality of royal greetings and yet how, passing down a line of strangers, such as this, is it possible not to be repetitive and slightly stilted? There is a limit to the number of ways in which one can say 'Hello' or ask what someone does for a living. The secret, of course, is to look genuinely interested, warm and enthusiastic, even while secretly one is bored, possibly nervous and, frequently, as stumped for something to say as the person you are meeting so very fleetingly. It is also axiomatic that 'office', however modest, carries an aura with it. I have frequently seen mature, sophisticated, intelligent grown-ups reduced to shambling incoherence in the presence of royalty, however minor. Something of that mystery attached to the Governor and his wife. No matter that I knew they were just Chris and Lavender, or that part of me, inevitably, felt that the Governor had no clothes, I could not deny that their very presence induced not precisely awe or reverence but at least a feeling of nervousness and apprehension.

Finally the Governor made a speech. He spoke in English with a simultaneous translation, though it was evident from the occasional titter that several in his audience were perfectly capable of understanding his slow, carefully articulated words.

Apart from the expected sentiments designed, on the whole, to make the company feel pleased with life and proud of their achievements and their position in society, there were two tiny moments that seemed characteristic, at once

75

both very Chris and very English. Being locals themselves, in a sense, spending as many weekends as possible at Fanling, he and Lavender had become involved with the community. Every year, for example, Lavender attends the 'Flower, insects, bird and fish show' and does the judging. When Chris mentioned this, Lavender smiled a conspiratorial smile, and so did I. The idea of her awarding rosettes for prize-winning insects obviously struck her as funny. Equally obviously there was no reason for any of the locals to find it even remotely amusing.

Then, at the very end, the Governor got to his final thank-you, looked around the crowded room and said, 'I leave once again with very pleasant memories,' a pause, a faintly sheepish smile, 'and two bags of tomatoes.'

It was a typically stylish minor irony: precisely the self-deprecating little flourish one learned in the college debating society. Yet looking round the smiling suits I felt that it would have passed straight over their heads. I also felt, unprovably, that such tiny, very English touches were quite important in keeping the Governor sane.

I had little idea whether I had learned much about the New Territories that day, though I did feel I had learned a little about the Governor's *modus operandi*.

One of my main sources of research was, of course, the local press. Shortly after this afternoon out I read a story about the New Territories. I learned that customs officers had seized a million dollars worth of fake birds' nests in the New Territories. They had in fact been constructed from deep-fried pig skins.

Reading this strange story I knew, though I hardly needed telling, that I had a lot to learn and, moreover, always would.

FIVE

I was glad that my mother was not coming to see Hong Kong, for there were so few traces of the Colony she knew. As I had promised myself, one of the first people I tried to contact was her old landlord's surviving son, 'Charlie' Churn. The second-generation Major was frantically busy with his Japanese cars and motorbikes but agreed that he would indeed try to arrange an excursion to view Lena Lodge. However, long-term planning was impossible. I would have to rely on him to telephone early one morning at short notice when he had a sudden unexpected 'window of opportunity'. But I sensed that his heart was not in it. Did he really want to visit an old family retreat with happy memories only to find it a run-down drug rehabilitation centre with a four-lane highway screaming past the front door? It didn't sound to me as if he did. And suddenly I was no longer sure that I did. Lena Lodge belonged in the past, to another country.

The pace of change is frantic. Even in my brief absence the harbour seemed to have changed shape and shrunk still further. Around the ferry terminals on the Hong Kong side great pile-drivers banged incessantly and a navy of dredgers performed a daily miracle of turning water into land. Everywhere I went there were logic-defying cats'-cradles of bamboo scaffolding stretching skywards as yet another new office building took shape.

The weekend after I arrived the Hilton Hotel closed after just over thirty years to make way for new offices and further enrich the already fabulously wealthy Mr Li Ka Shing. At first this seemed a matter of little consequence. On my previous visits I had been lucky enough to stay at the Peninsula. In my parents' day that had been the Colony's grand hotel. Felix Bieger, for years the hotel's manager, and now memorialised in the eponymous restaurant in the new extension, reminisced with me once about the various regiments stationed in Hong Kong which had conducted their rest and recreation under his roof. His favourite had been one of the cavalry regiments, not least because shortly after their arrival their commanding officer told him that if any of his men failed to pay his bills the CO was to be informed and the account would be settled, if necessary out of the colonel's own pocket. At the end of that regiment's tour of duty the Pen hosted a special farewell party in its honour.

Magnificent hotel though it unquestionably was, I came to entertain slight doubts about the Peninsula's pre-eminence. This had nothing to do with the hotel itself. It was simply because of its situation. The longer I stayed in Hong Kong, the more I got the sense that the hub of activity was in the Central District on Hong Kong Island. The Kowloon side, accessible only by Star Ferry or an arduous detour through the harbour tunnel, was where I had been based on my first two visits, but after a while it seemed ever more peripheral.

If this were indeed the case then the palm seemed to go to the Mandarin Hotel, which, though a characterless 1960s box compared to the Peninsula or some of the more recently constructed futuristic hostelries, had, internally, style and buzz. The Mandarin was where the Princess of Wales elected to stay rather than share Government House with Edward

Heath. It was where David Tang had his cigar divan. If the city's makers and shakers were having a power lunch, the Mandarin Grill occupied the same sort of position in the local firmament as the Savoy Grill in London. The shadowy Captain's Bar, crowded though it could be, had the same sense of being at the centre.

Of the Hilton, however, I knew nothing. To my mind, with a few exceptions, a Hilton is a Hilton is a Hilton. The last Hilton I had visited was the Hilton in Watford, where I attended a 'literary luncheon' with Denis Compton and Lynda La Plante. There was nothing wrong, or at least not quite right, with it but it was hardly one of the world's great hotels and I tended to put the Hong Kong Hilton in the same category.

Wrong. Like the Mandarin it had opened only in 1963. At the time it had seemed ultra-modern and, before the skyline began its recent transformation, it was one of the relatively few buildings of any height. Twenty-six storeys no less. It dominated, whereas by the time I first saw the hotel it had shrunk to insignificance beside its peers.

In the 1966 riots which accompanied the Cultural Revolution the Hilton was a focus of resistance.* It was the soup kitchen for the international press and for the police themselves. In defiance of the Red Guard loudspeakers blaring propaganda, the Hilton management set up its own loudspeaker arrangement to provide a British counterblast. When finally it was judged that public opinion in the Colony would countenance such an action, it was outside the Hilton that the Hong Kong Police were first given the command to meet the rioters' force with a force of their own. It was after their bravery in these troubled times that the police were

---

* In Hong Kong local rioters sought to emulate their Red Guard counterparts on the mainland. Their efforts seemed to be orchestrated from the Xinhua or New China News Agency building where loud-speakers broadcast revolutionary, anti-colonial sentiments to the people.

granted the honour of being called the 'Royal' Hong Kong Police.

For a time the FCC was housed there, which sounds understandable. Less expected was that the coffee shop was a regular rendezvous for the cathedral clergy and lay staff. 'If I wanted a quiet word with the Dean,' I was told by his secretary, Mary Whitticase, 'we would always go and take a mid-morning break at the Hilton.' For more than twenty years the actor/impresario Derek Nimmo brought his touring troupe of actors to the hotel, where he always occupied the same room.

Plainly, therefore, the Hongkong Hilton was not just any old hotel.

In 1994 Li Ka Shing's Hutchison Whampoa company bought out the recently renewed twenty-year management contract on the hotel for a reputed HK$125 million. Mr Li, who is said to have begun his business career in the manufacture of plastic flowers, is best known as a property developer, and it came as no great shock in Hong Kong when he announced that the hotel was coming down to make way for an office development. James Smith,* the Hilton's much admired general manager, was reported as saying gloomily that 'as a hotel it's worth $500 million; as an office block it's worth $1 billion'. The loss of 750 beds is something Hong Kong could ill afford, but the economics are apparently unassailable. The manager of the rival Furama-Kempinski suggested that running an office block was anything between five and eight times as profitable as running a hotel. And the mega-rich tycoons of Hong Kong did not get where they are by being sentimental about the past – even a past as recent as the Hilton's.

Interested to see what the fuss was about, I visited the

* After the closure Mr Smith went to work for Mr Li at Hutchison Whampoa. This being Hong Kong, no one seemed particularly shocked.

Hilton one evening just before its final closure on Sunday, 30 April. It happened to be the night of the annual dinner-dance of the Hong Kong Rugby Football Club, and the stairs and foyer were a scrum of black tie and ballgown. The old girl was going out in style, though the hotel boutiques, many already deserted and most of the remainder offering closing-down sales, were a gloomier prospect.

The following final night saw a wake at which the singer Frances Yip, who had performed at Hilton Christmas and New Year parties for fifteen years, sang a requiem to the tune of 'Those Were the Days', which included the words:

> But we have to bow to market forces
> They think: 'More rent in commercial property'
> The Hilton Hotel soon will be demolished
> For that great decision, we must thank Mr Li.

According to my Orient Express colleague, Andrew Lynch, writing in the *Post* that morning, Li Ka Shing was unamused by this.

You could see the Hilton from the windows of Government House. On the night of its closure I was dining with the Pattens and looked up at the old building. Already, only hours after the departure of the final guest, the 'Hilton' sign had been obscured by a mask of blue material. The wheels of progress seemed to be grinding exceeding fast and I was full of foreboding. To me the symbolism was glum.

One of the Governor's staff recommended a small computer shop in the Prince's Building as a sensible place to buy a replacement for the machine I had had stolen before leaving the UK. As it was within easy hobbling distance I tried this place first and found more or less what I wanted at what seemed a reasonable price. However, when I said I wanted to pay by credit card the assistant immediately said that there

81

would be a significant surcharge for plastic. He wasn't aggressive or unpleasant or particularly offhand, although some people complain that your average Hong Kong shop assistant is all these things. Also, playing silly buggers with credit cards is a worldwide malaise. Nevertheless, I decided to take my custom elsewhere.

My computer whiz at Government House had said that the widest selection was at Windsor House in the Causeway Bay area. I found it with difficulty, stumbling past Elizabeth House, Vancouver House and Paterson Street in the pouring rain. The names sounded so reassuringly Anglo-Saxon and yet the context was wholly Chinese. It was probably the way I was pronouncing it, but no one seemed to have the faintest idea what I was talking about when I said 'Windsor House'. However, in the end I found what I wanted on the eleventh floor of the building at a tiny shop called CompuStation, where they gave me a better price than anywhere else and were prepared to accept plastic as well. The assistant was willing and knowledgeable and prepared to install any number of programmes. I settled for a small Compaq and a Canon Bubblejet printer. The programme which I would, in effect, have to teach myself was called Microsoft Works for Windows. Although Compaq is a British firm with its main factory in Scotland, I later realised that my machine had an American keyboard, not only with a dollar rather than a pound sign but also with a marginally different configuration. It didn't bother me unduly but it was slightly disturbing that this should happen in what, after all, was still a British colony.

I felt moderately at home in the computer shop. Any incomprehension was due as much to computer illiteracy as to a lack of Cantonese. And clearly I had no problem in the clubs and grand hotels, let alone at Government House. All these were, in their different ways, gweilo ghettos where English was the lingua franca. Near Windsor House I ventured into a cheap ethnic-looking restaurant, where I shared a table with a shrivelled elderly Chinese woman. We smiled at each other but said nothing. At the next table a group of schoolgirls in fantastically clean, neat, white starched uniforms were giggling noisily over bowls of noodles. I soon found that school lunches were habitually taken in restaurants, some of which seemed to become virtual school canteens for an hour or so every day. On this occasion I had a glass of tea and a bowl of shrimps and rice recommended by *le patron*, who did have a modicum of English.

I tried to be reasonably adventurous about eating out, but it wasn't always easy, especially if I was on my own. The shrimp and rice suggestion was perfectly welcome, but I had a feeling that part of the reason he wanted me to have it was that it was safe. On more than one occasion I was actually refused dishes because the waiter felt it was too exotic, fiery or plain disgusting for a gweilo to handle. In my first week at the Bonham Road flat, for instance, I tried a meal at the Korean restaurant almost next door – another eating place which became transformed into a school canteen every lunchtime – and asked for squid with a chili sauce, but it was forbidden. I had to make do with a perfectly agreeable but comparatively bland barbecued beef dish instead.

I had wondered, before arriving, whether there would be any traces of what I thought of as the Malta–Gibraltar effect. In both those places I have always a strong sense of the vestigial legacy of British military eating and drinking habits. They seem to be the only places on earth where Fray Bentos Corned Beef, semolina and condensed milk are among the most popular items in shops and even restaurants. This seemed not to be as pervasive in Hong Kong, presumably because the Cantonese and several other ethnic though less numerous groups have such strong culinary traditions. Very early on, however, I took shelter in a rainstorm at a tea shop in Central where the menu included 'Chocolate, Horlicks, Ovaltine', all priced at HK$16 hot and HK$19 cold. I've no idea why cold drinks should have been three dollars more expensive than hot. Also on offer were boiled milk with egg and ginger, instant noodles with luncheon meat and egg; and toast with condensed milk. I felt that here my mother might have caught an echo of the past.

That Saturday, almost a week after my voyage with the Pattens on the *Lady Maureen*, I was invited to sea again. My hosts on this occasion were some international bankers. In the aftermath of the Nick Leeson affair in Singapore, an invitation to sail on a corporate junk induced a collage of contrary frissons. I was quite surprised to find that banks still had junks. Indeed it seemed that this particular merchant bank had two, as well as a more recognisable motor launch on Western gin-palace lines. These junks were shared on a sort of rota system between their 300 employees in Hong Kong. In the interests of fair play, a new rule had recently been instituted so that not even senior personnel could have the use of the gin-palace more than once every six weeks.

The reason for the invitation was that a local merchant-bank honcho, shortly to be promoted to an even more exalted pan-Asian post, was married to my friend Angela. She was now living an *echt*-memsahib existence with three children and two amahs in a large house on the Peak, and seemed to have taken to her new life with gusto, though she had experienced one or two mishaps. She had suffered a bad case of food-poisoning after lunch with Jonathon Mirsky, the local *Times* correspondent, and had also been hospitalised for several months during a recent, difficult pregnancy. Unfortunately Angela had not been told of the new six-week rule about the junk and had inadvertently put her foot in it by attempting to book the boat for more than her share of outings. 'There has been talk,' I was told, darkly but not too seriously. Such are the pitfalls of life as an expatriate wife.

I was bidden to present myself at the Aberdeen Marina Club (yet another of those gweilo clubs)* at 10 a.m. The best way was to take a taxi, said Angela. Absolutely no problem, dear boy. Every taxi driver in Hong Kong knows the Aberdeen Marina Club. Well, I'm sorry to have to report that Hong Kong taxi driver number ED 3211, Mr Kam Wai Yea, was the exception to this rule.

He scratched his head. He got out his map, at which we both stared uncomprehendingly. He spoke no English. I'm afraid my temporary loss of humour is reflected in what I wrote at the time. 'Absolutely *no* English whatever. On the one hand, of course, the place is Chinese, but on the other it's been a bloody British colony for over a hundred years. I can't think of a single such place anywhere in the world where the English language has made so little impression.' I had only been in Hong Kong a few days (it seemed highly probable that Kam Wai Yea was in a similar situation) and I had no right to such sweeping and intemperate generalisations. On the other hand it was what I felt at the time, and I have a feeling I was not alone.†

What I was really irritated about was the driver's obvious belief that I hadn't the first idea what I was talking about. The exasperation was entirely mutual. We were approaching the situation from completely different directions. As far as he was concerned I was an idiotic foreigner, truculent to

---

* In fact I was told that the Aberdeen Marina was well known as a haunt of very rich local Chinese yacht owners. I can only say that they were not in evidence when I was there.
† It was more than just a feeling. According to the Hong Kong Examinations Authority, there has been a progressive deterioration in the results of the school Form 7 Use of English Tests; and, under the headline 'Territory fails the English Test', the *Hongkong Standard* echoed my thoughts with the words: 'It must surely amaze English speakers visiting Hong Kong from all over the world to discover that such a high-profile British colony should express itself in the official language so poorly.'

boot, who couldn't speak the language and didn't know where he wanted to go. Oh well, he'd have to take charge and show me. I was relieved, a few minutes later, to find that we were entering something called the Aberdeen Tunnel. Perhaps he had understood after all. Shortly after leaving the tunnel we executed a left and pulled up at the impressive gates of an institution called the Hong Kong Country Club. Mr Kam turned to me with an expression of contemptuous triumph. I'm sure he said 'Told you so' in Cantonese.

Further argument ensued, this time involving the men on the gate. Eventually the message seemed to get through. Mr Kam got back into his cab and we drove on. In a matter of moments we were at the Aberdeen Marina and here indeed was the front door to the Club. And here I forgave, for, instead of muttering sullenly and complaining about the size of the tip, Mr Kam looked positively abject. 'I am sorry. I am sorry,' he said, betraying an unexpected knowledge of what I feared might have to be a phrase crucial to his career at least until 1997. And he really did look sorry, in a way I suspected few Western taxi drivers would. I wondered, idly, if the Governor had ever travelled in a Hong Kong taxi and felt perhaps he should.*

We were a small party: Angela and her husband with children; Sheila Macnamara, formerly of the *Edinburgh Evening News*, *Observer Magazine* and *Elle* and now writing leaders and a column for the *Eastern Express*; and a visitor from the UK who was something in textiles. We took, of course, a picnic with cold boxes for liberal quantities of

---

* The idea is not *quite* as fanciful as it sounds. Once, in London, a cab driver told me that when Harold Macmillan was Prime Minister he would, from time to time, 'escape' from 10 Downing Street, using a side or back entrance and hail a taxi to take him to lunch at his club. On one such occasion my taxi driver picked up Macmillan, who regaled him with mild and uninterrupted indiscretions all the way to St James's. As he paid him off the Prime Minister smiled benignly at the driver and said, 'Thank you so much. I *have* enjoyed our conversation.'

beer and wine. The junk itself was a custom-built craft modelled on the traditional Chinese fishing vessel but designed for pleasure. As such she was no different from hundreds, possibly thousands, of similar craft all through Hong Kong. You could make a very strong case for the *Lady Maureen* with her traditional old-fashioned European lines, but as a seagoing picnic area with ample space for sun-bathing the junk was arguably preferable. Stripped of the usual paraphernalia of masts, sails and fishing gear, the recreational junk had a large covered deck area with seating all round a good-sized table, a small deck up front with a larger one above the cabin. Engine-driven with a local Chinese boatman at the helm, the junks were made of gleaming wooden planks which looked like teak. This one gave a strong impression, as did all the other ones I encountered, of having been built by hand.

Heading out of the harbour, past the vast, ornately garish floating restaurants owned by the tycoon Stanley Ho, we were part of an armada of such vessels. It was as if the whole of the Hong Kong Stock Exchange was going to sea in a junk. A freak storm could have sent the Hang Seng Index into a terminal decline. About ten minutes out an apparently identical junk came cruising past us at speed. Her name was *Fortunes of Asia*. My host regarded it beadily. 'Ah,' he said, 'Crédit Lyonnais.' Most junks have inventive names, the punnier the better. BZW (Barclays de Zoete Wedd) is called *The Bee's Knees*. Duty Free Shoppers is *Off Duty*. And so on.

It was a very pleasant day out. We moored off a sandy beach, went ashore in the dinghy, paddled. The more energetic or able-bodied went for a walk round what appeared to be a deserted island. Some of us swam and were disconcerted by the sudden appearance of large and menac-ing jellyfish. As it happened, this was the last time I swam in the open sea around Hong Kong, and in retrospect I was not altogether sure I should have swum in the first place. On his very first day out in the *Lady Maureen*, the Governor had given his bodyguard palpitations by almost being run over by a smuggler's boat as he breast-stroked some distance from the yacht. But this and jellyfish were not the only hazards for swimmers in the South China Sea, as I was later to discover.

Such is the claustrophobic pace of business and indeed social life in Hong Kong that for many people some form of weekend escape is essential if sanity is to be preserved. Stuart Wolfendale, then the *Post*'s regular Sunday columnist and a habitué of the FCC, wrote a sad article about the tedium of the Hong Kong weekend in which he denigrated junk-trips. The main burden of his complaint seemed to be that they were cocktail parties from which there was no escape. Once on board there was no getting off until you returned to port. His experience was that one always got stuck with the boat bore. However, I was grateful for my handful of junk voyages, for the fresh sea air, for the glimpses of a rural and maritime Hong Kong I would never otherwise have seen, for good food, drink and company. Perhaps repetition numbed the fun, but my view was that a man who was bored with junks was bored with life.

From the very first I sensed that the British community in Hong Kong was full of people I had been to school with. Originally I meant that metaphorically. My preparatory school, now sadly defunct, was originally well known as a feeder for the Royal Naval Colleges at Osborne and Dartmouth. It even had special Royal Naval Honours Boards. After moving from the south coast at Weymouth to inland Somerset, the seagoing tradition lapsed somewhat, but there was still an institutional belief that boys were being trained to go out and lead men, preferably in a far-flung corner of what had once been the Empire. Sherborne, where I next went to school, now boasted more Army generals among its Old Boys than any other school in England, a statistic with which I had been chided after I had suggested in print that the highest to which a military Old Shirburnian could aspire was the rank of brigadier. I dimly recollected that Jardine's, Swire's or the Hongkong and Shanghai Bank was considered a socially acceptable career destination, particularly for those who didn't make Oxford, Cambridge, Trinity College, Dublin, or Sandhurst.

One night Mike Sinfield invited me to an art exhibition in a hotel suite. Already I recognised several of the Yacht Club crew, particularly the members of the Echell class. The Echell is, I'm told, a sporty racing dinghy of relatively recent invention, sometimes patronisingly known as the 'rich man's Dragon'.* It was an eclectic little exhibition with three John Pipers, some safe Italian landscapes and a handful of nudes which reminded me of the paintings on the walls of the London Sketch Club in Chelsea. It would be pushing things too far to say that guests were only here for the wine but it was a convivial party. The second person Mike Sinfield introduced me to was a fiftysomething government employee called David Browning. He was the District Officer in Sha Tin, a new town in the New Territories, known to me principally because it was the home of the new race track associated in my mind with the stewardship of my father's old comrade-in-arms General Sir John Archer.

On hearing my name, Browning looked at me quizzically. 'That's funny,' he said, 'I was at school in Somerset with a boy called Heald. I understand he went on to be some sort of writer.'

I perused Browning with a less perfunctory appraisal than one usually gives a new introduction at a cocktail party.

* Another Western-style sailing boat and not to be confused with the Chinese 'dragon boat', now enjoying a Hong Kong-led craze around the world. Of which more later.

Suddenly the grey-haired middle-aged head became transformed to its essential components of downturned, almost hooded, eyes, an impish smile and prominent chin. Of course. Connaught House School, Bishop's Lydeard, near Taunton, circa 1954. A boy called Browning. I seemed to remember he was good at soccer. Bit of an athlete. Certainly a monitor if not quite Head of School.

'Sounds like me,' I said.

'No, no,' said Browning, obviously pondering the queer coincidence of there being two writer chappies called Heald, T. 'The Heald I was at school with was very blond and couldn't have been more than four foot eleven.'

I claim about five foot ten standing very straight and my hair has inexplicably gone from fair to mouse.

'If we're talking about *us*,' I said, 'it's forty years on. I remember you as a thirteen-year-old in a blue and gold football shirt.'

He grinned. It was *us* all right. We had a long chat like something from an Alan Bennett or Michael Frayn play and sat next to each other when the Yacht Club people gathered us up for supper at a nearby Burmese restaurant. Browning, son of a West Country vicar, cousin of Daphne du Maurier's husband, Lieutenant-General 'Boy' Browning, hero of Arnhem, had enjoyed an extraordinary and unrepeatable career. After leaving school at St Edward's, Oxford, he joined the Colonial Service and went to Africa, where he was a district officer in what was then Northern Rhodesia. There he saw the Union flag go down for the last time to be replaced by that of Kenneth Kaunda's Zambia. From there he moved to the Pacific, where, as a colonial administrator in the New Hebrides, he was part of the same process. Now in Hong Kong he was, for the third time, an instrument of sovereign change. Indeed he claimed he was the second-last DO in what was once the British Empire. When he came to retire from Sha Tin just before going on leave to England, the only such figure left would be his colleague in Tsim Sha Tsui, the touristy urban area on the southern tip of Kowloon.

I can't say I remembered the boy Browning with any clarity, but I vividly recalled the education we both enjoyed: the team games, the muscular Christianity, the Latin and Greek, the French irregular verbs. Above all we were taught the merits of 'decency and common sense'. We were also led to understand that the privileges we enjoyed carried obligations too. It was very old-fashioned, if in retrospect mostly very admirable (though I, at least, could have done without the corporal punishment). We were educated in a traditional, now deeply unfashionable way and were asked to believe that it was our duty to lead by example. 'Duty' was a vital and integral part of the plot.

That sort of school was designed to turn out men like Browning. I doubt whether such places still exist, at least in quite that form, and I doubt whether such men are still produced. Hong Kong in 1997 was a metaphor for the end of the world they both strove to serve. Whatever the small print, whatever the concomitant details and realities, whatever its meaning for the indigenous people of the Territory, for the leaders of commerce, expatriate and Chinese, 1997 was a symbol of the end of the Browning version of the world.

It was fitting that an old boy of Connaught House School should be going down with the ship. Our headmaster would have approved.

SIX

There is a validity in the first or even the fleeting impression. One afternoon, shortly after I had been interviewed by Andrew Lynch in the *Post*, I sat down in the bar at the FCC and was told by my neighbour that he thought he recognised me. As the photograph of the red-cheeked expatriate perspiring mightily after a half-hour hobble from Bonham Road to the gates of Government House was distinctly unflattering I was distinctly unflattered. My new friend turned out to be Charles Weatherill, otherwise known as Geoffrey Bonsall. He compounded the insult by telling me that I could not hope to capture the essence of Hong Kong in the short time I proposed.

Charles himself had been born in China of missionary parents and was now, in what I guessed to be his sixties, the old China or Hong Kong hand *par excellence*. After a career as publisher at the university press he was now enjoying an Indian summer as a broadcaster with RTHK. He was the world's leading authority on the shorthand notes written by George Chinnery, the contemporary and fellow student of J. M. W. Turner. Chinnery's paintings of Macau and Hong Kong provide the most evocative images of the early Colonial years. Like so many others of his ilk, Charles was fed to the teeth with brash outsiders swanning in and delivering a comprehensive verdict on the Colony after the most fleeting of encounters.

It was Bonsall/Weatherill who asked me: 'Do you think the Governor understands the Chinese mind?'

To which I responded, 'What makes you think the Governor *wants* to understand the Chinese mind?'

This gave us both pause for thought and we arrived at no satisfactory conclusion. His view of the Governor seemed ambivalent, though I suspected he was more hostile than he let on. I explained my relationship with the Pattens, which meant, as usual, that common politeness prevented his being rude about them. He did remark that in the old days the Governor was often referred to as 'His Excellency' or 'HE' for short. He regretted the loss of 'HE' and clearly thought 'Chris' horribly over-familiar. He had met the Governor once when he appeared on the early-morning radio show. Weatherill had made him a cup of coffee, upon which the Governor had complimented him. He would, he said, like to meet him again, properly, for an informal chat. There were things he would like to tell the Governor. Among other retirement jobs he wrote speeches for the legendary Stanley Ho. I said I would trade introductions: Ho for HE.

On the other hand, I explained, I wasn't that close to the Governor and, as he would have observed, he was not particularly susceptible to pressure. In the event, when I did mention the idea to Chris, he managed to pass on to the next topic leaving me unsure whether he had heard or understood what I said. I noticed it more than once. It was quite a clever trick. It avoided any need for unpleasant argument and if one had any nous at all you got the message straight away. Anyway, as far as I know, HE never availed himself of Weatherill's advice.

Perhaps he was right. There is a limit to the amount of advice any one person can assimilate. And, while a man like Charles knew far more about the place than I ever could, there was nevertheless a danger of his being blinkered by lifelong contiguity. Familiarity with Hong Kong had clearly not bred contempt, but it might, in some respects, have dulled his perceptions. His view was that one could not even think of producing a book of any kind, let alone on such a complex subject as mine, without several years of research and contemplation. My argument was that the outsider might perceive oddities and even significances in what, to an 'expert' or 'old hand', might seem everyday. It was possible to *know* everything but *notice* nothing.

A case in point was my esoteric collection of brief stories from the paper. They was small sightings of the hidden mass of Cantonese iceberg beneath the semi-Westernised, usually smiling, surface of the indigenous population. In my early days in Hong Kong I seemed to be forever noticing and recording macabre indications of the world beneath the skin: 'Born-again Christian jailed for frying father' or 'A man, 38, was chopped to death in a Mong Kok Sauna Parlour early yesterday morning.'

After a while, the supply of such stories seemed to diminish. It may be that they really did occur less often, yet I suspect the truth is that I simply became inured to them and that they lost their novelty. Thus, though a Weatherill, with a lifetime's experience of the East, would know so much more, he would lose that capacity for astonishment that the newly arrived visitor possesses. My early innocence was a gift too rapidly squandered. That it was married to ignorance was not altogether a disadvantage. To the old Hong Kong hand the frying of fathers, the selling of under-age girls by fish-ball vendors and the chopping to death of the patrons of Mong Kok sauna parlours were yawn-inducing examples of everyday behaviour. To me they were appalling, though appealing, novelties. Neither perception is right or wrong, but I treasure my early naivety and was sad as slowly and imperceptibly I came to lose it.

94

I also had a problem with the written source. The main point of my book is that it should be the product of first-hand experience. I came, I saw, I reported. I took, often, with a pinch of salt. Yet it seemed to me that, up to a point, the evidence of my eyes and ears was always more or less valid. If I saw or heard or smelt it here in Hong Kong then I should record it. It might not be 'typical' but it was authentic, *real* even. The written source, even second-hand, was important but more difficult to evaluate. There were some books I read which I distrusted very much; others which seemed to hit nails on the head. But I found it difficult to know which to trust, and those whose advice I sought were seldom unanimous.

One book I did enjoy and find thought-provoking was a slim volume called *Borrowed Place, Borrowed Time* by Richard Hughes, which I discovered, looking unwanted and unread, on the shelves of the Hong Kong Club's little library. Hughes wrote it in the 1960s during the time of Mao and the Cultural Revolution, when the present Club building was not even a twinkle in the developer's eye. On 9 May, the day I found his book, the lead newspaper story was that up to 10 per cent of all senior police officers were planning to leave after the transfer of sovereignty in 1997.* I wondered what Hughes would have made of this and whether it was something he had predicted.

On the other hand there was an 'expert', 'old-hand' certainty in Hughes's writing, and with the benefit of hindsight some of it seems misplaced. The whole business of

* This particular report was in the *Hongkong Standard*. It seemed speculative and I was sceptical. Quite apart from the efficiency of the paper's polling, I was dubious on two counts which applied to most predictions about 1997. On the one hand I doubted whether many people told the truth, particularly to newspapers; and on the other I doubted whether they would carry on till 1997 without changing their mind, probably more than once.

democracy, voting, political aspirations and representations already struck me as complicated and shadowy with grey areas. No such weedy havering for Hughes. 'There is no democratic nonsense in Hong Kong,' he wrote. 'There is, to date, no political sense or instinct. There are no serious demands for a vote for a wider franchise or for self-government.'

Hmmmm. I wonder if it was as clear-cut as all that. There was serious rioting in Hong Kong around the time Hughes's book was published. The ostensible reason for some of the trouble was a hike in the first-class fare on the Star Ferry, though this sounds like a doubtful pretext. Thirty years after Hughes, 'democratic nonsense' had become a central issue in Hong Kong and, incidentally, the bane of the last Governor's life. Could the situation have changed so dramatically in that time? Were the seeds of the present discontents already sown? Could Hughes have been mistaken? He himself clearly didn't think so. 'No articulate political sentiment in the Colony,' he opined. This may have had something to do with the character of Hong Kong's inhabitants, but there was, according to Hughes's diagnosis, an overriding external reason. 'Peking's Communists,' he wrote, in those far-off pre-Deng years, 'still expediently tolerate the survival of colonial bureaucracy, but the presumptuous presence of a local, elected, independent Chinese government on Chinese soil would be intolerable.' That seemed to me to be a line that Chris might, with profit, have read and marked. But I suspect that *Borrowed Place, Borrowed Time* is a book more loosely quoted than actually read.

Hughes loved aphorism, which lends itself to certainty. It's easier to turn a memorable phrase. Thus, of expatriates in general and Britons in particular, he insisted that they 'have come to make a living but not a home'. If this was a rule I soon found exceptions to it. Nevertheless the canard was one which many of the local Chinese seemed to endorse and which fuelled their mistrust of the colonial power and its hangers-on. That cruel acronym, FILTH (Failed in London, Try Hongkong), may not have been true but it was widely believed.

I found Hughes consistently more stimulating and provoking than most of the more recent Hong Kong authors, not least because he was so opinionated. Here he is on the four superlatives of China, rendering a traditional native judgement into his own brisk Australian prose style. 'Eat at Kwengchow (Canton): the best food. Dress at Hongchow: the best silk. Marry at Soochow: the best girls. Die at Linchow: the best wood for coffins. So runs the old Chinese code for life and death. It is a definition of Hong Kong which provides the four essentials in combination.'

A little later in the book he amplifies the judgement. 'Hong Kong food is the best Chinese food in Asia (with the exception of Taipeh). Hong Kong shops are the most glamorous and the cheapest. Hong Kong girls are the prettiest. Hong Kong coffins, which the traditionally minded keep under their beds for eventual transportation to a resting place in China, are made of Linchow wood.'

I regretted Hughes's demise. He had his successors, and yet no Hong Kong pundit has quite matched those distinctive utterances. And his conclusion was a yardstick for me whenever I wrestled with the impenetrable question of what was to become of Hong Kong after 1997. 'Whatever happens,' wrote Hughes, 'it is a question which the Chinese will answer in their own time and their own place and their own way.' A chilling verdict, but one to which I often returned as I listened to a later generation with a different perception and a different agenda. The more I thought about it and the more I learnt, the less I felt inclined to trust in the future. I could see that, belatedly or not, the Governor was seeking to establish systems and precedents which would be difficult or impossible to dismantle. These ranged from voting systems and legal procedures of a precise and often intricate nature to something more nebulous and difficult to define but which, in essence, was a climate free from fear. Everything I heard about mainland China, and naturally there was a tendency to paranoia in Hong Kong, led me to conclude that freedom from fear was not a condition to which their leadership aspired. Indeed fear, if I read the messages correctly, was widely regarded as a useful, perhaps inevitable, tool of government.

On the back of a bus that afternoon I noticed a sign which read 'Involvement with triads ends in gaol'. A day or so later the *Post* ran a story about a policeman who had died as a result of his bad debts. The money involved ran into tens of thousands of dollars, and the man was so distressed that he took rat poison and plunged to his death from the ninth floor of a Mong Kok apartment building. In the same edition another policeman fared rather better. Li Ka Shing had hired a former chief of police, Mr Li Kwan-ha, as a 'consultant'. That sounded like a pretty shrewd move all round. Li Ka Shing wielded his chequebook as effectively as Kevin Keegan.* It led to a certain amount of criticism, though not as much, I judged, as would have arisen under similar circumstances in the UK. Still, the appointment made news, and the reaction was not friendly.

None of this signified a huge amount on its own but it was all indicative of a certain climate. This was a society which used the backs of its buses to warn its citizens against becoming involved with organised crime – if that was what the triads really were all about; a world in which a policeman could be so worried about his debts that he

* Keegan, the Newcastle United Football Club manager, hired by the self-made millionaire Sir John Hall to revive the ailing fortunes of a once-great team, was spending millions of pounds of the boss's money in acquiring star players. The idea that money will buy absolutely anything or anyone struck me as very typical of a certain element in Hong Kong.

committed suicide and in which what sounded like a cynical if not downright dishonest private sector job for a recently retired boy in blue was a matter for comment if not uproar.

I felt sure that despite a sometimes murky past[*] the police were pretty straight. Certainly the Governor said so. Not long after I arrived they had to deal with what sounded and looked like unpleasant and dangerous rioting in one of the camps where wretched Vietnamese 'boat people' were detained before being (mostly) forcibly repatriated. The Governor was full of praise for their efforts and paid a special Sunday-morning visit to say a personal thank-you. Unsurprisingly, whenever I visited Government House, I was greeted with exemplary courtesy by the policemen at the gate, but I got the impression that the average copper on the Hong Kong street was a benign presence. I saw them walking around, usually in pairs, smiling, stepping off the pavement to let me pass (my early stick or crutch was obviously a help with this), and generally behaving in the 'Dixon of Dock Green' fashion which is so often extolled in law 'n' order debates in the United Kingdom.

On the other hand that 10 per cent departure intention among senior officers was disturbing. And, unlike British policemen, they all seemed to carry guns. I later discovered that at some time or another they all undergo paramilitary training, and the sense that they are almost as much soldiers as policemen is exacerbated by their uniform, which is khaki with black leather webbing.

Such cosmetic considerations may seem trivial, but images like these are powerful. Part of the still-comforting appeal of

[*] The fortunes of the Force reached their nadir in the 1973 investigation of Chief Superintendent Peter Godber. Godber, who paradoxically had served with distinction during the riots of the 1960s, was found guilty of accepting bribes on a massive scale. As a result an Independent Commission Against Corruption was set up by Governor Maclehose and large numbers of Hong Kong police officers left the Force in a hurry.

the British policeman derives from the lack of firearms and, even more so, the Gilbert and Sullivan uniform, epitomised by those mildly ridiculous helmets. No one wearing one of those could possibly be a licensed thug or bully. By the same token the Army-style outfit of the Hong Kong police always made me slightly apprehensive and feel as if I was, as perhaps I was, in occupied territory.

On the evening of 30 June 1997, apparently, every one of the Force's 27,000 officers will unstitch their shoulder flash, bearing the legend RHKP, and sew on another which will no longer have the initial 'R' for 'Royal'. When I was there some policemen still had a patch of red cloth under the metallic number on their shoulders. This indicated that the wearer was fluent in English. Although the essential character of the Force is supposed to be preserved for at least fifty years I wondered how long the red insignia would stay. I also tried to think how, as a gweilo in the street, I would react to such a trivial detail as the loss of the prefix 'Royal' from the police force upon which I relied. I decided that even though it was a tiny matter I would view the loss with nostalgia and misgiving.

It was 11 May when my new friend Mike Sinfield 'phoned to draw my attention to a story in the newspaper which echoed this impending piece of sartorial republicanisation. My eye had, as usual, been caught by one of those headlines which emphasised the exoticness of the place,* but Sinfield wanted me to have a look at the story headed 'Royals Face the Chop as Clubs Eye 1997'. This was the top front-page story in the *Post*, which as usual my local 7–11 did not have that morning. What they did have was an astonishing array

---

* 'MEDICINE TRADE POSES THREAT TO SEAHORSES'. Apparently Hong Kong was 'absorbing' three million seahorses a year. They fetched HK$55 a kilo and were used to treat asthma, incontinence and goitre.

of condoms, as well as drinks called 'Slurps' and 'Gulps'. The latter both came in three sizes: Junior, Medium and Big.

'Royals Face the Chop' was one of those classically insubstantial newspaper stories which raised at least as many questions as it answered. The basis of it was that the three 'Royal' clubs were debating whether or not they would have to drop the 'Royal' from their title and there were quotations from a recent past president of the Golf Club, Sir Gordon Macwhinnie; the chief executive of the Jockey Club, Major-General Guy Watkins; and the commodore of the Yacht Club, Tony Scott. They all seemed a bit vague. Macwhinnie was quoted as saying that 'we have to recognise that things are going to change'. Watkins apparently said that the timing of any change had yet to be decided, but that he could see the logic of all three clubs changing their names at the same time. Scott said that he was already on record as saying he wanted the 'Royal' dropped and the sooner the better. Inside there were potted histories of the three clubs, parts of which caused some irritation, especially a passing reference to 'the notorious Yacht Club Ball'. Yacht Club members didn't think their ball in the least 'notorious'.

Despite the commodore's remarks the constitution of the Yacht Club made it quite clear that any change in its name had to be referred to a vote of the entire membership. It looked as if the Yacht Club membership was split and undecided. The *Post*'s story suggested that all three clubs would synchronise the name change so that the stigma of disloyalty to the British Crown would attach to all three equally.

The Jockey Club, however, was in a completely different position from the other two. Like the Marylebone Cricket Club it was a private club with a public function. With its monopoly of legal gambling in the Territory, its contribution to a whole swathe of charities and good works was monumental. It was no more a private club within the meaning of the act than the Tote or William Hill in the UK. Under the post-1997 regime, however much the Chinese might go on about 'one country, two systems', there was no way a vastly profitable quasi-public body like the Jockey Club could go on calling itself 'Royal'. The yacht and golf clubs, however, were private recreational organisations with no other function than to make their members happy. One added wrinkle was that, whereas the Yacht Club had enjoyed royal patronage since 1894, the Jockey Club had become royal only in the 1950s. Their royal tradition was correspondingly flimsier.

The story was, unsurprisingly, picked up in the British press. It was a colourful way of symbolising the transfer of sovereignty. I wondered whether the Chinese cared about such nomenclature as much as some of the British. Clubs such as these were, after all, symbolic of colonial rule and, although they now admitted Chinese members without prejudice, that had not always been the case. In 1949 a prominent Chinese businessman offered to pay off the Yacht Club's debts to the Hongkong and Shanghai Bank if, in return, he could become a member. The offer was declined. Three years later it was proposed that members should be allowed to invite guests to the club 'irrespective of their race'. In support of this revolutionary suggestion the pro-poser cited the example of the Hong Kong Club, which had recently changed its attitude and 'found that no harm had come by it'.

It would not be altogether surprising if the Chinese with their famously long memories were to punish the clubs for the past. On the other hand they might derive some amusement from allowing them to remain royal and using the anachronism to humiliate them in some undreamt-of and exotic manner. Or they could be really sophisticated and ignore them altogether.

Just as I found it virtually impossible to talk to anyone

without becoming embroiled in speculation about 1997, so the Governor was ubiquitous. I couldn't escape his presence. This was partly because any author in Hong Kong was presumed to be preoccupied with these two topics and partly because I was known to be something of what caustic locals referred to as a 'Governor luvvie'. One of my problems was trying to work out whether Hong Kongers found 1997 and the Pattens the two most absorbing topics of conversation or whether it was simply something to do with me. Part of me suspected that your average local was actually preoccupied with sex, the weather, the cost of living and the other topics which are the mainstay of casual social intercourse in Britain. This side of me believed that people's apparent obsession with the great inevitable historical change and the personality of the Governor who was most intimately concerned with it was just a reaction to the task I had in hand. Had I simply been an itinerant banker or English kith visiting English kin I might not have felt that the whole of Hong Kong life was dominated by the countdown to 30 June and by the elusive truth about the last British occupant of the big house in the Upper Albert Road. Another part of me believed that whenever two or three were gathered together they did inevitably turn to talk of the inexorably approaching change of government and the last instrument of British colonial rule. I could never know for certain, but I was trapped. No matter how much I might want to absorb the truth about what Hong Kong was thinking I was always going to be confronted with thoughts that my new acquaintances and friends wanted to test against what they assumed to be my interests and even my areas of special knowledge. This meant 1997 and Governor Patten. Try as I might, the two subjects were always with me.

I had always expected that one Hong Kong contact would lead to another. This tends to be so whenever one is a newcomer to a strange society, but even more so in a place

103

like Hong Kong where the ever shifting quality of the expatriate population seemed geared to the assimilation of new faces. There was a conveyor-belt quality to the place, so that it sometimes seemed like a school or university, always with a group of new boys and girls who had to be initiated, shown the ropes and introduced to colleagues, acquaintances and friends. But there was also always a balancing squad of school prefects, wise in the ways of this little world but, just as they were beginning to understand it, poised for departure.

One of my first formal invitations was to dinner at the Cornishes'. A 'phone call from Francis's secretary came first, followed by an embossed stiffy 'pour-mémoire'. It was impressively formal – 'The First British Trade Commissioner and Mrs Cornish' – though unlike a surprising number of Hong Kong functions it called only for lounge suit and not for black tie.

Not for the first or last time I found myself pondering the relationship between Britain's Trade Commissioner and the Governor. Cornish was so many things the Governor was not. It wasn't just public school, Sandhurst and Cavalry. There was also the LVO* garnered after a stint as assistant private secretary to the Prince of Wales. I didn't think the Governor would be tremendously impressed with an LVO. Cornish's diplomatic career was immaculately fast-track, including three years as high commissioner in Brunei and, latterly, public-relations jobs as head of the British Information Services in New York and head of the News Department at the Foreign and Commonwealth Office in London itself. He certainly didn't strike one as fusty; indeed he had a fine line in caustic indiscretion. At the same time he had an old-school side to him, with a patrician hauteur which

* Lieutenant of the Royal Victorian Order. The Royal Victorian Order is reserved for personal services to members of the royal family.

sometimes bordered on disdain. He came from a quite different stable from the Governor and he also had an essentially different brief. Or so it seemed. Where the Governor was allowed or even encouraged to be tough and confrontational, the Trade Commissioner's role was to be emollient and accommodating. It suited their respective training and temperaments, even though there was a waspish side to Cornish and an ingratiating one to the Governor. Whatever the reasons, I sensed tension.

The Cornishes lived in an enormous new apartment on the thirty-sixth floor of the Albany building immediately below the penthouse occupied by Baroness (Lydia) Dunn and her husband, Michael Thomas, a former Hong Kong Attorney General. At this stage I was still awestruck by panoramic views of Hong Kong, especially of the harbour. The Cornish vista that night, from a large, rather windy terrace, was spectacular and, perhaps symbolically, afforded an intrusive bird's-eye view of Government House and its gardens. Looking up, one was confronted by Lady Dunn's plate-glass windows, big as cinema screens.

This was a duty dinner. There were about twenty of us, relatively few of whom seemed to know each other and at least one of whom, other than myself, professed to have no idea of why or even how he had been invited. The ritual of the business cards, still a novelty, was as embarrassing as it always was. By the time I left Hong Kong I had a large collection of these trophies. Unfortunately, however, I lacked the discipline or common sense to annotate them properly, so that most of them became completely mysterious by the following morning. It was just like this with the Cornishes' dinner. Over Ah Non's sculpted breakfast mango and melon the morning after, I shuffled a set of cards around the tablecloth as if playing Pelmanism, trying to fit the strange names and titles to the faces I had encountered the previous

105

night and, for the most part, failing dismally to make the right connection.

At table I sat between the boss of the local Marks and Spencer organisation (business apparently booming), who was, to my surprise, a chemical-engineering graduate from Aberdeen, and the wife of Philip Chen, the managing director of Dragonair, the junior sibling of Cathay Pacific Airways. Mrs Chen had done an MBA in Boston. When I asked her about Dragonair, she said jokingly that the airline flew to all those places to which no one wished to go. She mentioned Cambodia by way of example.

I also spoke to a German in textiles who was predictably disparaging about British business. I was not surprised by this, though I would have thought he might have expressed himself with marginally more restraint given the occasion and the place.

A more unexpected figure was the civil servant who appeared to be in charge of translating Hong Kong law into Chinese. He unaccountably failed to produce a business card, which made him a man apart. I never saw him again, partly, I suspect, because he was not supposed to talk to visiting writers and would not have done so 'on the record'. The final translation, he told me, would run to around 21,000 pages and, although he thought his team was already halfway through and would meet its deadline, the task was effectively impossible. Under similar circumstances – he mentioned Canada – completely new law had always been drafted from scratch. The idea of *translating* a law from one language to another seemed to be unprecedented.

In this case the problems were conceptual as well as purely linguistic. The ideas that underlie Chinese law are simply not the same as those underlying English law. There is no better insight into this than Austin Coates's marvellous little memoir, *Myself a Mandarin*. Coates, long retired and living in Lisbon, was for years a magistrate in the New Territories, and spent a lifetime trying to see fair play while satisfying the judicial requirements of his colonial masters at the same time as those of his indigenous subjects. As far as I could tell, he muddled through successfully, but only because he was essentially a man of integrity as well as pragmatism. You can't assure these by translating words, however inspired your translation.

My fellow guest at the Cornishes' produced just one example of the difficulties involved in his task. In English law, he said, the word 'satisfy' was important. The idea of a judge being 'satisfied' was integral to the way in which English law was practised and understood. There was no such word in Chinese.

Part of the reason for this was, he implied, that the concept was not comprehended. After much mind-cudgelling, the new translation had settled for the word 'happy', which he said was the nearest they could get. Of course it wasn't the same. He shrugged apologetically. So often, the future seemed to depend on grand gestures and orotund pronouncements, but I was more intrigued by the fine print. I never again heard any argument about the difference between 'happiness' and 'satisfaction' and yet it spoke volumes. A 'happy' judge was not the same as a 'satisfied' judge. I found the idea of a culture which couldn't see the difference profoundly disconcerting.

SEVEN

My image of Hong Kong was essentially of a concrete jungle. Some of the jungle was swagger international bank and some was grand hotel, but it was all Manhattan East. Even the squalor was urban. The shanty towns might have been corrugated iron rising on bamboo stalks out of foreign mud but they were vertical perpendicular. No ribbon development here. Not a blade of grass. Plenty of elbow grease but not much elbow room. No space, no space.

Even after a few days I knew that this was not entirely true. My early weekend with the Pattens at Fanling and aboard the *Lady Maureen* had shown me a world of wilderness and ocean which I had barely suspected. Lunch at David Tang's exquisite rural villa with its cropped verdant sward leading off towards an idyllic view of yachts and junks bobbing in aquamarine waters against a backdrop of rocky islets and other millionaire retreats reinforced this vision of another Hong Kong. So did my merchant banker's picnic aboard the junk.

Yet this was rarefied stuff, and treating it as typical of the Territory was like making a generalisation about the Home Counties from a weekend at Windsor Castle or lunch in the Cartier tent at the Guards' Polo Club. It was an easily observable fact that the majority of local people lived in high-rise blocks and even the relatively well-to-do often had quite small apartments. It was a recurring grumble.

Stuart Wolfendale's grouchy column about the tedium of Sunday junking had jangled a chord too. It painted a dismal picture of being trapped among the towers of downtown with nowhere to go and nothing to do except to prop up some dimly lit bar and drink until it was time to start work again on Monday morning. Even old Hong Kong hands told me there was no point in venturing beyond the city limits because the whole of the New Territories was covered in asphalt and new housing developments.

I am as sceptical as the next man about statistics but my few highly privileged rural adventures had already suggested that there was a world without the city walls, and the figures supported my view. They present a picture so far removed from what I believe to be the popular perception that I think they are worth quoting.*

In all, Hong Kong was 1,084 square kilometres but, of this, only 14.9 per cent could be described as 'developed land'. There were 41 square kilometres of 'residential' land, though this did not include the 11 square kilometres devoted to 'public rental housing'. Thirty-seven square kilometres were empty but waiting for some sort of development. If I were playing a game of word association with Hong Kong I would have put 'commercial' at the top of the menu headed 'land usage' and yet 'Commercial' accounts for a mere 2 square kilometres, or 0.2 per cent of the total.

The undeveloped or 'non-built-up' part of Hong Kong accounts for over 85 per cent, of which 413 square

* Like most of my facts and figures these are taken from the annual government publication, the 1995 *Hong Kong Year Book*. The date is slightly misleading because the book deals with events in 1994. These particular figures were accurate as at 31 March 1994, but such is the pace of land reclamation that Hong Kong would have become significantly bigger by the time of writing.

kilometres are covered by a Country Parks Ordinance which protects vegetation and wildlife. In other words there is ten times as much country park as residential land. And that's not all. Almost twice as much space in the Territory is occupied by 'badlands, swamps and mangroves' as by roads and railways. Almost six times as much of Hong Kong is given over to arable farming as to industry. And, my favourite extrapolation of all, the area occupied by commercial property is just one-eighth the size of all the fishponds put together.

It sounded from this as if there was enough open space to provide for more than the occasional governor, millionaire or merchant bank. Every weekend during my first few weeks friends of Liz Dewar would arrive to take the dogs off for serious exercise. They went, I was told, to Sai Kung. At this stage I had no idea what Sai Kung was, beyond the obvious fact that it was, at least relatively speaking, a wide open space where the caged canines could be unleashed and roam more or less at will. Certainly when they returned from these forays they seemed agreeably bushed and almost reluctant to chase the cats and gnaw through my wrist or the flex of the fax machine. It was only subsequently that the HKTA gave me a series of pocket guides, one of which began, 'There are few areas in Hong Kong that can rival the scenic splendour of the eastern New Territories, known as Sai Kung.'

My first experience of the place was with my long-lost prep-school contemporary, Browning. Browning had once had a share in a boat but had, in effect, exchanged this form of weekend escape for a share in a cottage in the Sai Kung country park. A friend of his, a stockbroker called Robin Lindsey-Stewart, was in town on business, and Browning and his Colombian wife Coco were taking him out for a walk and Sunday lunch. Would I like to come along?

We rendezvoused at the Mandarin, where the stockbroker was staying. He and Browning had been district officers together in Northern Rhodesia, so they were old chums. There was talk of hippopotamus dung and strange native dialects and a local chief who had inherited the title of Lord High Admiral of the Upper Zambesi River. This had been bestowed by none other than Queen Victoria herself, and the chief's ancestor had handed down not only the title but a fancy Gilbert and Sullivan admiral's uniform to go with it. According to the two old chums the sight of the Admiral sitting in a magnificent dug-out during the tribal regatta outdid even the classiest of Hong Kong's famous dragon boats. They discussed the old colonial days with pride and nostalgia and waxed irritable about the press they and their kind received these days. It was fashionable to rubbish the British Empire, but these two, who had been its servants, felt unfairly done by. They had, they said, administered their charges efficiently, honestly and with much mutual respect and affection. They certainly had nothing to be ashamed of. It had been, in their estimation, a job well done.

It was only 8 kilometres to the town of Sai Kung, which is the hub of the district. Of the nineteen administrative districts in the Territory this is the largest. It is 126.8 kilometres square and includes about seventy islands, and yet only 150,000 people live there. The roads were crowded at first, but by the time we had passed the town itself the traffic dwindled. The island-dotted seascape was scattered with yachts, junks and pleasure craft; the country near the shore had seen a mild building boom of an affluent-feeling holiday-home nature. The dominant style appeared to be modified Spanish villa, so although the scenery was unSpanish there was a prevailing air of Costa.

Shortly after the town the road turned inland and we passed through the gates into the country park itself. Here there were hardly any cars and few houses. Scrub-covered hills ranged high on both sides and we passed a small herd of apparently untended brown cows grazing by the roadside. It was vaguely reminiscent of a tropical Lake District.

The Brownings' cottage was simple but adequate, a far cry from Fanling Lodge or David Tang's place. It was one of a terrace of old village houses, rented to them by an elderly widow. At the far end there was an operating shrine or temple with smouldering joss-sticks. Along the front there was a terrace with a table where we would later have an alfresco lunch. It had a sort of cowshed feel, but there was hot and cold running water and a shower.

The two district officers and I set off along the well-kept tarmac road for a briskish walk. I was still on a stick and limping quite heavily, but with no real pain. It was steamy hot, though Browning told me this was nothing to what would come in July and August. Presently, after passing some embankments heavily reinforced against the omnipresent threat of landslips, we turned off the road and on to a well-marked footpath which ran steeply up the hillside. The old Africa hands seemed fitter than I and both had two sound legs. They also had the gait of experienced walkers. I panted along behind, pretending that my lack of speed was due to the Achilles tendon rather than to general seediness.

The walk was a revelation. I am no botanist, and the vegetation was not particularly dramatic. 'Scrub' sounds a dismissive word but I can do no better. It was, for the most part, low-slung green stuff. The advantage of this over imposing trees was, of course, that it allowed unimpeded views. And the views were glorious. After half an hour or so we were on the spine of the hill and could gaze all round. In the distance a peninsula sloped down into a still, turquoise sea. Green hills rolled around us. And there was hardly a house in sight. The track continued, clear and well marked, until for the final few hundred yards it changed into a staircase of stone steps back to the road below. In two hours we passed only one other walker, a local Chinese. Browning said this was not unusual. The only time this walk seemed populated was early in the morning. Sometimes when there was mist and the dew hung heavy on the bushes he would encounter little lines of loping Chinese, hurrying, head down, from the sea to the enveloping anonymity of the big smoke. These, almost certainly, would be IIs, or Illegal Immigrants, newly arrived by boat from mainland China, heading off for a new life in capitalist Hong Kong.

I was sodden with sweat by the time we were home. Like other Westerners I never came to terms with the humidity of Hong Kong. The Governor told me that he was quite used to changing shirts several times a day even though, tennis apart, he led a largely air-conditioned life. I can't think how earlier generations of Britons can have managed with only solar topees and aircraft-propeller fans to keep them cool. Hong Kong in summer without 'air-con' must have been unendurable. The cold beer and the shower were essential.

We were a cosmopolitan crew at lunch: Coco from Colombia, of course; we three walkers from England; and another Englishman in the government service, formerly district officer in the old Suzie Wong area of downtown where he was famous for a tree-planting initiative and acquired the nickname 'the sheriff of Wan Chai'. He had an Oxford degree in English and was much given to reciting Shakespeare. There were Chinese, Canadians and French. One expatriate couple were leaving in a week or so and the shadow of their departure lay, for a moment, heavily on the gathering. Most of the others would not long outlast 1997 and there was a sense of abandoning ship, of wondering who would be the next to climb overboard and wave farewell. There was no escaping 1997, even here, eating ceviche (a South American dish of raw fish marinaded in lime and/or lemon juice) and drinking chilled white wine until the sunshine turned to that dramatic unEnglish rain which comes down so hard it seems to bounce back upwards and which on this occasion sent us all scurrying indoors for shelter and coffee.

My notes tell me, unconvincingly, that the cottage was in a place called 'Fok To', adding the admonishment, 'I must get a better map.' Shortly afterwards I did. The Browning cottage, I realised, was just off the road to Wong Shek pier where a small ferry or *kaido* sailed down the sound to remote settlements and islands I hoped to explore before I left. The highest hill seemed to be called Ngam Tau Shan and the villages along the road, in descending order, were called Ko Tong, To Kwa Peng, Pak Tam Au, Pak Tam, Tsak Yue Wa and Pak Tam Chung. Alongside these names were Chinese figures. I assumed that the European rendering was a translation but after a while I was not so sure. Nomenclature baffled me and I came to wonder if the Anglo-Cantonese names used by the British were not only 'wrong' but also some sort of elusive Chinese joke at gweilo expense.

I could never work out why some places were given completely English names while others were phonetic renderings of Chinese ones. Quite often there were two completely different versions. If, for example, you wanted a taxi to take you to Mount Davis Road there was absolutely no point in saying 'Mount Davis Road'.* Instead you asked, more or less, for 'Maw Seen Leng Dough'. For a while I assumed that this was an exact translation. It was only later that I was told that it was Cantonese for 'Reach for the Stars Road'. The confusion was most evident on the underground or MTR.†

* Named after Sir John Davis, Governor from 1844 to 1848. Davis was also responsible for Hollywood Road, Hong Kong, which was so called because his English home was Hollywood Towers.
† Mass Transit Railway. Hong Kong is unusually fond of abbreviations, acronyms and initials. This compounds the bafflement and often seemed to me deliberate. The most bizarre of all is 'Route Twisk', which is the road between Tsuen Wan and Sek Kong in the New Territories.

The Hong Kong Island line has fourteen stations. Eight of them have romanised Chinese names and six have English ones: Sheung Wan, Central, Admiralty, Wan Chai, Causeway Bay, Tin Hau, Fortress Hill, North Point, Quarry Bay, Tai Koo, Sai Wan Ho, Shau Kei Wan, Heng Fa Chuen and Chai Wan.

Sunday out with the Brownings was my introduction to a kind of middle-class expatriate New Territories living with which I could identify. A few days later Basil Pao introduced me to everyday life on an island.

Not that 'everyday' is a word I should really use to describe Basil Pao. I had been given his name by Anthony Sampson, the author, who had worked with him on journalistic assignments. Basil was a photographer, best known for his association with Michael Palin. The two had collaborated on Palin's round-the-world adventures and were shortly to set off on another trip, this time round the Pacific Rim. Sampson described Basil as 'rather exotic', which turned out, I thought, to be pretty accurate.

He lived on Cheung Chau, an island about an hour's ferry ride west of Central. Every morning he came over to Hong Kong Island to leave his daughter at school. Then he would breakfast at the FCC before attending to any business he might have in Central and then heading back to Cheung Chau in time for lunch. His American wife, a successful casting director specialising in Asian actors for Western movies, usually did the afternoon pick up.

Basil's father had been a warder in Stanley Prison but took early retirement and began a second career as an actor – becoming, Basil told me, a popular performer in Chinese TV soaps. Basil himself was educated at Kingswood, the Methodist public school in Bath, and then at art college in Los Angeles. He worked for a while as an art director in New York before moving to Cheung Chau a decade earlier. He

115

lived on a hill just outside the main village, but had a photographic studio above a downtown shop. Slim, tall, with dark hair (which everyone had told me would be very long and possibly pony-tailed, but which had recently been cut short, almost *en brosse*), he had an air of perpetual interest and amusement. He spoke completely fluent colloquial English, dressed in the flappy wide-bottomed trousers I tend to associate with art directors and had what for Hong Kong struck me as an unusually but agreeably languid manner. Our first breakfast meeting, for instance, progressed to beer, Bloody Bullshots (a lethal mixture of vodka, tomato juice and consommé which I had first encountered at White's Club in London), to a beef and pasta lunch in what he described as 'the best noodle shop in town'. I was the only non-Chinese in the place and I would never have dared venture in on my own.

Basil travelled extensively on the mainland, where his appearance and fluency in local languages obviously made him an inconspicuous and trusted figure. Like David Tang he was manifestly Chinese, and yet his Western experiences gave him a cosmopolitan veneer. He appeared completely at ease with himself and yet his identity, especially to one like myself who felt so irredeemably and utterly British, was puzzling. He was not really a Hong Konger. Indeed his quasi-exile on Cheung Chau was almost a deliberate effort to distance himself from mainstream Hong Kong. When I first met him his application for a British passport had not been accepted. He had expected it to be a formality but was surprised to face a thorough interrogation by officials and was even required to produce his GCE exam certificates, something he was, after an interval of more than twenty years, quite unable to do. Various British friends had interceded on his behalf. Indeed, when I mentioned his predicament to the Governor, Chris looked marginally exasperated and said, 'Oh, is that the man everyone keeps writing to me about?'*

Partly because of his personal situation, the question of 1997 and its aftermath loomed large in our conversation. However, quite apart from his own predicament, he had a lively intellectual curiosity about events as well as a shrewd and unusual perception of them. Almost his first question to me after we'd sipped our coffees and exchanged thoughts on Palin and Sampson was, 'What if there's no one for the British to hand it back to?'

In my innocence I was quite taken aback by this. It simply hadn't occurred to me.

He looked at me with something approaching pity. 'After Deng goes they'll be at each other's throats. After all, the boys who did the Long March together still tried to cut each other's throats. If they did it, what do you expect the new boys to do?' He shrugged. 'They were brought up with Stalin.'

Everyone else I had spoken to, from the Governor on, tended to speak of 'China', 'Beijing' (or 'Peking') and 'them', as if there was a unified team or collective which would take over the government of Hong Kong without dispute. But here was Basil Pao putting forward theories about what he described as 'turmoil' with rival warlords and provinces ranged against each other so that when it came to handing back the keys to the colony the British would genuinely not know who the correct authority was. The scenario sounded like something from a 'Carry On' film. I imagined the different Sir Humphreys – or rather the different Percy Cradocks – all giving the Governor completely different but completely authoritative advice about who precisely was in charge. What if half a dozen different representatives of

---

* A few weeks later his application was successful, though, as is the way with such matters, it was unclear how or why the original had been reversed.

117

different factions within the People's Republic were to arrive in the Territory just before midnight on 30 June? They would all claim to be the proper authority and no doubt they would all have a plausible case.

'The Chinese,' said Basil, 'are searching for a reincarnation of the Emperor.'

I digested this for a moment and wondered, as so often, whom he really meant by 'the Chinese' and how it was possible for someone who seemed Chinese himself – third-generation Hong Kong but forebears from somewhere north of Macau – could speak of his fellow countrymen in the third person as if they were nothing to do with himself.

Wasn't he 'Chinese'? I had been hearing about the mystical, animal bond that all ethnic Chinese had with 'Mother China'. Did he not feel this?

He shrugged and smiled again. 'I get no joy from saying "We invented gunpowder". Well, whoopee! So what?'

After a while I came to think of this as a very characteristic Paoism.

Our next meeting was on his home turf, which meant that I got my first serious ferry trip. Ever since my original press trip I had loved the double-decker Star Ferry across the incredible shrinking Victoria Harbour. The twelve ships operating three separate routes between Kowloon and Hong Kong Island carried more than thirty-six million passengers a year. They were one of the few working relics of old Hong Kong. The stubby green and white vessels looked like a child's idea of a ferry. Given the space-age design of the harbour-front buildings one might have expected the Star ferries to have become tarty hydrofoils with fins, but although there are plenty of state-of-the-art vessels plying to Macau or Disco Bay* the lines of the Star Ferry remain

---

* An isolated purpose-built enclave for the aspiring upwardly mobile. On Lantau Island and only accessible by boat, it reminded me of somewhere unfashionable on the outskirts of Bournemouth. I was shown

118

resolutely traditional. The ships still had stern signs requesting passengers not to spit and to beware of pickpockets. The ingenious wooden benches had backs which swivelled from side to side so that you could change the direction in which they faced. Time was, before the tunnel, when they were the only way to cross. They were also, I suspect, the only ferries in the world to have provoked and given their name to their very own riots. Luckily, the woman often credited with having sparked them off was still alive and well and living in Hong Kong. I looked forward to hearing Elsie Tu's account of these bizarre events.

The voyage to Cheung Chau was something else. The island ferries, seventy-four of them in all, operating twenty-four different routes, were similarly antiquated but run by a different company – the Hong Kong and Yaumati Ferry Company, otherwise known as the HYF. The ships operated by this company carried 107,885 passengers a day as well as 2,872 vehicles. With more than 230 islands in the Territory, Hong Kong, was not just a concrete jungle, it was an archipelago, and for many of the inhabitants the ferries were a lifeline. To be sure, you encountered tourists on them, but most of the travellers were working commuters. Part of the pleasure of the ferries was that they provided a rare opportunity to mingle with ordinary Hong Kong people. They were less antiseptic than the MTR trains and less threatening than the buses. On a ferry I nearly always felt confident that I knew where I was going, and on every single occasion this confidence was rewarded.

Basil had told me to get a De Luxe ticket because this would entitle me to a seat in the air-conditioned upper deck,

---

round it by an improbable resident, Barry Girling, a local freelance writer who turned out to have cut his journalistic teeth in Cambridge while I was doing the same in Oxford. Like so many people I met in Hong Kong we had friends in common. He was too smart for Disco Bay and really should have been a neighbour of Basil's.

or alternatively give me the opportunity to sit out on the open deck at the stern. I bought the ticket for $14 but was confused by the boarding arrangements and found myself on a lower-priced lower deck, though I was able to position myself next to the rail and take advantage of the breeze. My ferry was named the *Man Fat*, which Basil told me could loosely be translated as 'May the people prosper!' Several of the ferries were called *Man*; indeed my return journey late that night was on the *Man Hong*. But the *Man Fat* was my favourite.[*]

That magic harbour with its exotic assortment of ferries, junks, sampans, yachts, visiting warships, rusty Conradian freighters, top-heavy container ships and all manner of other vessels is best experienced from its midst.[†] The traffic was so heavy and so multi-directional that it seemed extraordinary that there weren't more collisions. But it was the sheer contrast that was so bizarre. One minute you were watching a junk or sampan with Chinese fishermen in blue pyjama bottoms and straw lampshade hats casting out nets, the next you were being passed by three Royal Marine commandos in a high-speed inflatable. Panama and Liberia seemed the most popular flags of convenience and there were some extremely rusty and dubious-looking ships from both countries. However, easily the rustiest and most alarming-looking were ships flying the flag of the People's Republic of China.

[*] After my return my daughter Lucy decided to form a Ladies' Dragon Boat crew at Nottingham Trent University. At my suggestion they agreed to christen their boat the *Man Fat*.
[†] The Hong Kong Shipowners Association controls a fleet of 1,300 ocean-going vessels. There are 16,000 local craft, including 1,600 lighters and 500 motorised cargo boats. The government alone has a fleet of 341 powered vessels, including police launches, fireboats, airport-rescue craft and pollution-control craft. Hong Kong is the biggest container port in the world. In 1994, 185,000 ocean-going and river-trade vessels arrived in Hong Kong. They handled over 141 million tonnes of cargo and twenty-one million international passengers.

That dazzling high rise of urban Hong Kong fell away rapidly and we were soon in open sea with distant and, for me, as yet unidentifiable islands all round. The *Man Fat* throbbed noisily and smelt of oil. Passengers drank cans of soft drinks and slurped at bowls of noodles. The sea was placid, the sun hot. I dozed.

Basil had described Cheung Chau as 'a cut-price, low-rent Riviera' and I knew what he meant the moment I saw it stretched out in front of me. For a start there were no cars. Basil was waiting on a wide jostling promenade fronted by inviting-looking restaurants with tables and chairs outside.

'Good afternoon, squire,' he said, and we set off on a quick tour of the island.

I am glad to say that Basil's approach to sight-seeing was that of J. G. Links, author of the world's greatest guide book, *Venice for Pleasure*. Links's attitude is that, although the Tintorettos in the Accademia are deeply wonderful, they will still be there the following day or the next time you come to Venice. Meanwhile it is hot and you are thirsty and there is an agreeable café in a shady piazza near by, so it is only sensible to rest your feet and enjoy a cold Campari.

We dawdled along Praya Street, past the cooked-food market with its stalls selling noodles and *won ton* soup and the Regional Council Building which housed the library, post office and a food market with more than 200 stalls. Turning inland we entered a narrow lane with tiny shops on either side. Most of them seemed either to be grocers selling a strange mixture of Chinese staples such as dried squid or shrimp and imperial gastronomic relics like tins of spam or condensed milk, or repair shops of one kind or another. The more I wandered streets such as this the more I became familiar with dark caves inhabited by frowning figures squatting over dismembered bicycles or elderly wireless sets.

We paused at Basil's studio, which was adequate but basic, and left a bottle of white Oxford Landing in the

121

fridge. There was a tantalising selection of Hong Kong books on his shelves, the legacy of a film script he had once composed. It was the story of a ferry from Hong Kong which somehow lost its way on the voyage to Cheung Chau. This was the pretext for a cinematic canter through the Territory's history, but the film never got made.

From the studio we strolled to the Pak Tai Temple, which overlooked the municipal basketball pitch and playground. I wish I was better at temples. The two most memorable features of this one, also known as Yu Hsu Kung, struck me as the gold crown worn by Pak Tai, the sea god to whom the temple is dedicated, and its central role in the Cheung Chau Bun Festival. The significance of the gold crown is that it was presented by a local woman to commemorate the visit of Princess Margaret and Lord Snowdon in 1966. Basil was unable to explain more than these bald facts. The incongruity reminded me of the photograph of Prince Philip which is venerated in Vanuatu. He is still worshipped there, despite the fact that the former colony is now independent, so there is a precedent for thinking that Princess Margaret's crown will survive the transfer of Hong Kong's sovereignty.

I missed the Bun Festival, which struck me as one of the jolliest-sounding of Hong Kong's many festivals, even though I think it was taking place around the time of my arrival. There is a certain haziness about the festival dates because they are, literally, in the lap of the god. The organising committee casts lots in front of Pak Tai, also known as the Spirit of the North, and he decides when the Bun Festival will be. The only guidelines appear to be that it should take place between the last day of the third moon and the tenth day of the fourth moon. It isn't a very old festival but began at the end of the last century after Pak Tai saved the villagers from the plague.

The blame for the plague was laid at the door of the victims of local pirates, and to placate their vengeful spirits the survivors offered them buns. This is apparently the Chinese religious custom. At first they just put small piles of buns on the corners of an offertory table but nowadays they erect three fifty-foot towers of buns outside the temple. These are not to be touched until the gods have eaten as many as they like. Afterwards people used to climb to the top of the towers in order to retrieve the highest bun, which was supposed to bring luck throughout the ensuing year. Nowadays the buns are distributed by the Rural Committee and the significance of the top bun has disappeared. The buns are distinctly Barbara Cartland in appearance, white with luminous pink calligraphy.

The main attraction of the festival is the carnival parade, in which children between the ages of five and seven appear to float at head height. They are held aloft by a complicated system of hidden rods and wires. They wear elaborate make-up and fancy dress as either religious or historical figures or – according to the HKTA guide, which is more informative than Basil – 'as figures in television drama series and novels'.

The temple was built in 1783 during the Qing Dynasty and is located in a good *fung shui* position. *Fung shui* deserves (but will not get) a chapter on its own. The literal meaning of the words is 'wind and water' and it has to do with 'geomancy', a term with which I was not previously familiar. My *Concise Oxford* doesn't have it. *Webster's* has a definition which is much too limited to do justice to the baroque apparatus of superstition or religious belief which it involves. At its crudest it seems to mean that the best site for a building, particularly a temple or a grave, is one which faces water and backs on to a hill or mountain. The Pak Tai Temple on Cheung Chau fulfils these requirements. It also has a snake and a turtle underneath Pak Tai's feet. They symbolise his dominance of the sea and all the creatures therein. In front of the altar are statues of two warrior gods called Thousand Miles Eye and Favourable Wind Ear.

123

During the Bun Festival, Pak Tai is carried outside in a hundred-year-old sedan chair together with a lucky Sung Dynasty sword. In two side-chapels are carvings of the Green Dragon and the White Tiger, both significant *fung shui* figures. Pak Tai's birthday, incidentally, is on the third day of the third moon of the lunar calendar.

'You've probably had enough temples for one day,' said Basil in his most sympathetic J. G. Links mode.

So we ambled off along the seashore to the Cheung Chau wind-surfing club, home of Hong Kong's only world champion in any sport, and had a can of Tetley's beer sitting on a stool at the open-air bar. Presently Basil's goddaughter came in on her way home from school. The bar of the wind-surfing club was obviously one of Basil's regular haunts.

'Drink up, squire,' he said suddenly, 'we've got to get back for the floor show.'

So we walked back along the beach and then through the alleys to collect the Oxford Landing, then down to a Thai restaurant on the waterfront where we bagged an outside table. Presently the 'floor show' began. Around 6 p.m. the pulse of the ferry pier began to quicken. *Man Fats* and *Man Hongs* started to arrive more and more frequently and as they did they disgorged more and more passengers. These were not the casually dressed travellers of the day but men in suits and girls in tight short skirts and side-alley designer jackets with padded shoulders, that ubiquitous sleek black hair and those pencil-thin figures. Basil sprawled back in his chair and smiled the superior smile of a man who enjoys his work and is not chained to a desk and regular hours. Occasionally he would hail a returning commuter. Some came and sat with us before passing on to a restorative shower and change of sweaty clothing at their cut-price home. Two men, English, pink and perspiring, joined us for a jar and ogled the mini-skirts. They were the chief of the island police and his number two. Another photographer arrived. And a French-Canadian who dealt in real estate. The Oxford Landing disappeared. We drank some beer and ate seafood and rice with lemon grass and coconut milk and gradually the ferries became less frequent and the returning office workers' tide dwindled to a trickle.

At last it was time for me to catch a ferry home. Basil felt a cold coming on. His nose was slightly dry and he had a tickle in his throat.

'I'm sorry, Tim,' he said, 'but I must go and drink some bees.'

'Bees, Basil?'

'Of course. Surely you know that dried bees are best for a sore throat. Bees, ginseng and boiling water.'

He looked at me as if I had never heard of aspirin or paracetamol.

On the ferry home I imagined Basil with his head lowered over a steaming dried-bee soup, just as I had in childhood inhaled Friar's Balsam, and I remembered Charles Weatherill at the bar of the FCC.

'Do you think the Governor understands the Chinese mind?'

It was a tiny surprise in a place which was nearly all surprise, but I was still taken aback. Basil had seemed so completely 'one of us', so utterly, if exotically, the Western photographer with his dispassionate views on the 'Chinese', his taste in English beer and Bloody Bullshots. But somewhere among the fast-receding twinkling lights of Cheung Chau Basil was drinking dried bees to treat a cold.

EIGHT

From the three-cat, two-dog, one-amah basement apartment in Bonham Road I moved to a one-dog, two-amah, five-storey house on Mount Davis Road in Pok Fu Lam. This was also due to the Yacht Club network. Indeed the owners of the house were close friends if not quite surrogate parents of Liz Dewar. My new friend Mike Sinfield had been out sailing with Hector and Phyllis Ross in their yacht *Uin-na-Mara*, Gaelic for 'Bird of the Sea', when he had mentioned that I was looking for somewhere to live for a month or so. Hector and Phyllis were heading off to Scotland and Spain for a long holiday to coincide with their son's wedding. For a very modest consideration they would be prepared to let me sleep in their guest bedroom and use Hector's top-floor office. There was even a deck outside it and views across the nearby Chinese cemetery to the sea, with the island of Lamma in the distance.

Once more I was spoiled appallingly. If I wanted clothing washed and ironed I was simply to drop it on the floor and Ah Wah, who was that relative rarity a Chinese amah, or Lou, who was from the Philippines, would do the business. Ah Wah had been with the Rosses for years and had indeed helped bring up the son who was getting married in Scotland. She was so much part of the family that she would be flying to join them for the ceremony. Ah Wah cooked very well, but Lou didn't. Indeed she flew into a panic when, after Ah Wah went to Scotland, I said that I was having people in to supper. She seemed horrified that her lack of culinary expertise might be exposed.

Every so often the amahs would leave a grocery bill on the kitchen table. I have kept one, carefully written out in pencil, as a souvenir – apple 6, orange 8, water melon 12, mango 8, grapefruit 5, banana 4, kiwi 6, lichee 15, cherries 10, choi 6, mushroom 18, tomato 4. Seldom in my life have I eaten so much fresh fruit and veg, and cheaply too.

Hector and Phyllis were 'old Hong Kong', though their daughter was married into an even older Hong Kong family, the Bragas, who had been one of the first half-dozen European families to settle in the 1840s.* Phyllis was actually born in Hong Kong. Her father had arrived from Detroit with the Ford motorcar concession only to find that there were as yet no proper roads in the Colony. Being an enterprising fellow he was undeterred and set about building roads himself.

Hector settled in Hong Kong in the early 1950s after serving with the merchant navy. He was a Clyde man who first went to sea in 1948. In those days Britain still had a huge fleet: Clan Line, Blue Funnel, the Asiatic Steam Navigation Company . . . the nostalgic names tripped off his tongue. He sailed from Calcutta down to Australia and back on various elderly coal-burning steamers, plainly loved the

---

* One of the Bragas was the first person to introduce double entry book-keeping to Japan. When the Japanese invaded, the Bragas were living in Kowloon and produced a thank-you letter, replete with scrolls and hieroglyphs, signed by the man whose company had initiated the double-entry book-keeping. He was now a general. This so impressed the Japanese that the Bragas were not interned, like most gweilos, but allowed to remain at large throughout the occupation. 'Left to starve,' the Rosses' daughter Cathy told me, with feeling. It was hard to say which side of the barbed wire was easier during the war years in Hong Kong.

127

sea, but was disturbed by the alcoholism which seemed to be endemic among the ships' officers. 'It was the done thing,' he said, 'to open a bottle of gin or whisky and throw away the bottle top.' One day he was contemplating a chief officer drinking himself to death and realised that alcoholism was not only an occupational hazard but one he could do without. 'I think I'd rather go ashore,' he said to himself, and left the ship in Hong Kong, where he applied to the Crown Agents and was taken on as a revenue inspector grade 2. This involved chasing illicit distillers all over the New Territories and sounds fun. He also played rugby for Hong Kong. A big tall man, he was one of nature's second-row forwards, and there were team photos in the house to prove it.

He first had a flat in Kowloon overlooking houses with gardens – a far cry from contemporary housing styles. 'I liked the place,' he said. 'It was much healthier than India.'

After a while he took the exam to transfer to the executive grade and spent two years as cipher officer at Government House during Sir Alexander Grantham's time. It was Grantham's American wife who gave her name to the Governor's yacht. Then he worked at the Urban Council's secretariat, in Immigration and at Transport, before taking early retirement in order to spend more time with his family.

Plainly he has always loved the sea and he has been a serious recreational sailor for years. A vice-patron of the Yacht Club,* he took part in the infamous Fastnet Race of 1979 when several competitors were drowned and his own yacht 'pitch-poled'.† He survived this nightmare but it was

---

* The other two were the Governor and Pat Loseby, formerly doyenne of the Dragon class in Hong Kong. The Patron was Her Majesty the Queen.
† This meant that the yacht somersaulted in the heavy seas and capsized stern over bow or, as the Yacht Club bar would almost certainly term it, 'arse over tit'.

not his only brush with death. In 1969 he was arrested while sailing to Macau, the ancient Portuguese colony forty miles to the west of Hong Kong. A sizeable flotilla was making the voyage, but all except for Hector and an American sailor left on Friday. Hector and the American yacht waited until the Saturday morning and five miles off Macau they were waylaid by an official Chinese vessel. It was Chinese New Year and Hector's view is that they were out to have fun. He also reckons that their prime target was the American, who made matters worse for himself by getting into a panic and flushing his passport down the lavatory.

They put a tow-line on to Hector's boat and took him to a port some 8 miles north of Macau. There they subjected him to interrogation. Sometimes they would question him at two in the morning. Sometimes they would let him go to bed at nine only to wake him three-quarters of an hour later, haul him up on deck and shout at him. It was impossible to know how to respond. If you responded in kind and were rude to them they would say you weren't doing your case any good. Matters were not helped by the fact that the interpreters suffered from sea-sickness.

Hector remembered some of the phrases his interrogators repeated as if they were mantras: 'Why are you intruding on Chinese waters? There are no Hong Kong waters ... they are Chinese waters ... you are not showing the right attitude.' Chinese waters or not, 'these people', as he disparagingly calls them, had no respect for the well-established concept of the 'rights of innocent passage'.

He was not unduly worried for himself, but his daughter, then only ten or eleven years old, was on board with him. Also Phyllis was at home in Hong Kong with an infant child, completely ignorant of what had happened to her husband. The other yachts had, obviously, reported Hector's failure to arrive in Macau, but there was no word from the Chinese authorities. Rumours abounded. 'Sightings' were reported. It was said that Hector and his daughter had been taken to Peking under arrest. His yacht had sunk. And so on. Phyllis was beside herself.

And then, as suddenly and inexplicably as they had arrested him, Hector's captors let him go. He had suffered six weeks of boat-arrest and, inevitably, the experience coloured his attitude towards the 'Chinese'. Both he and Phyllis seemed to view the future with unease. As long-standing, long-serving inhabitants they felt proprietorial about Hong Kong. In the context of the times this was an unfashionable, politically incorrect point of view to express in public. The attitude of Western Hong Kongers was that it was they who were the natives and the Chinese who were the aliens. In the case of the Rosses I felt some sympathy. Who understood Hong Kong better? The couple who had made it their home throughout the better part of their life? Or the Illegal Immigrants who had arrived a mere two years before? Because the former had pinko-grey skin and English was their preferred and native tongue they were popularly deemed to be alien, whereas the latter with their demonstrably Chinese appearance and Cantonese mother tongue were considered to be *real* Hong Kong.

'I'm very unpleased about the change,' said Phyllis. 'I don't think they'll look after it.'

The sentiment might not have been universal but it was certainly widespread. I had some sympathy with it. There were a number of gweilos in Hong Kong who had a far greater stake in the place than many thousands of Chinese – emotional as well as material. I felt they were entitled to be concerned about the neo-colonialism of Peking. Phyllis was Hong Kong born and bred, which was more than you could say for Lu Ping.

Life on Mount Davis Road was undeniably comfortable and privileged and the chores I had to perform in order to live there at such minimal cost were few and, on the whole,

130

quite entertaining in a mildly surreal way. I had to photocopy Ah Wah's visa application; move the Mercedes a few feet so that the parking bay could be hosed down; and on one occasion bring the Rosses' hound Chico to heel after he bolted from the house as I let myself into the house after a dinner party. I'm sure the sight and sound of a slightly inebriated gweilo trotting breathlessly up and down the street shouting after the hound's fast-disappearing tail 'Come here, you bloody dog!' must have caused much merriment. I was terrified Chico would end up as someone's gourmet meal. How would I explain that to Hector and Phyllis?*

On a more mundane level it was life *chez* Ross that taught me to love the bus. The diminutive cream and green 54 which ran on a circular route between Pok Fu Lam and Central was almost the only bus with which I really came to terms. Sometimes I took a cab. The big apartment building at the end of the private road to the Ross terrace was full of taxi-users and sometimes I coincided with an alighting passenger. Otherwise taxis were infrequent, for the road was not particularly busy. There was something eerie about hailing one when there was no one about, for Hong Kong taxis were the only ones I have ever encountered which have automatic rear doors. When one stopped for you the passenger door would open silently and without any apparent human aid. I always felt as if I was about to step into an ancient *Avengers* episode.

The 54 bus, however, ran approximately every quarter of

* Chinese attitudes to dogs were quite mystifying. Betty Wei gave me a graphic description of the grief of her own servant when the family's pet dog died. Yet the same person would happily tuck into the same animal suitably cooked. On the other hand what is logical about a society that makes a cult out of the film *Babe* while still numbering frankfurters and spare ribs among its most popular foods? Perhaps we aren't as different as we think.

131

an hour and took about thirty-five minutes to get down-town. In the course of the journey the population of the bus seemed to change completely around three times and I was usually the only person to make the entire journey myself. The only regulars I recognised were the schoolgirls who got on and off a few hundred yards down the road. They seemed resolutely cheerful and chattery but above all immaculate in crisp and freshly laundered uniforms of white. I never ceased to be amazed at the neat cleanliness of Hong Kong schoolchildren, which contrasted so very obviously with the self-conscious grubbiness of the ones I was used to in England.

The 54 seemed to be very much a community bus, with a great deal of conversation. Passengers spoke to one another and to the driver. The driver himself often joined in the chat, which was, of course incomprehensible to me, but it was reassuring, for Hong Kong sometimes seemed an unsmiling place, its people shut off from one another in the crowds. The 54 was cosy by contrast. I also liked the plastic flowers, miniature gods and sometimes even cage-birds which the drivers kept above the dashboard. Above all I knew where it was going. It's true that I never quite worked out the optimum disembarkation point. There was a moment in Central when it suddenly executed a U-turn and began the homeward journey to Pok Fu Lam. Sometimes I got out just before this point, sometimes just after. Feebly, I tended to follow the crowd, hoping, by joining the general stampede, to avoid notice and not to make a fool of myself.

The beginning of the journey was essentially rural with ocean views. Indeed my Hong Kong A–Z* identifies the area immediately after the Chinese Christian cemetery – almost as much of a concrete jungle as downtown – as 'Ocean View'.

* Officially entitled *Hong Hong Guide Book: the most up-to-date bilingual guide for locating buildings, gov't offices, hotels etc.* Published by Universal Publications Ltd. HK$60.

132

Away to the right on the slopes of Mount Davis itself there was an ancient reservoir where people walked their dogs and, out of sight, a disused battery, a youth hostel and a 'Microwave Station'. After 'Ocean View' came 'Honey Villa'. On the waters of Sha Wan or Sandy Bay a fleet of freighters bobbed at anchor, coming ever closer as the bus ran down the hill and Mount Davis Road became Victoria Road. This was on the very border of the sea. The neighbourhood felt opulent and verdant. The houses had security gates.

Presently, however, the bus passed from this plush suburbia into Kennedy Town. Suddenly the pace changed and all became bustle. The first of the Territory's ubiquitous McDonald's appeared. Just before Sai See Street and over to the left there was an abattoir and an incinerator. Immediately afterwards came a sprawling vegetable market. I noticed the Cutie Club, Sam's Fast Fried Chicken, the Joyful Building and the William Property Agency, but many of the signs were, to me, indecipherable. The place felt working class and crowded and impenetrably Chinese, despite such superficial Westernisms as the Cutie Club and McDonald's.

The bus was almost always full by now. Frequently, when would-be passengers stepped into the road with a hailing hand aloft, the driver would roar past. If there were just a few vacancies aboard he would raise the appropriate number of fingers to show the waiting throng how many he would allow to join us. On the right Cadogan Street, on the left Kin Man Street, East and West as always rubbing shoulders in uneasy proximity. After a while Victoria Road ends and Belcher's Street begins. Belcher Bay lies away to the left, and to the right, just after Holland Street, comes Belcher Gardens. Belcher was Captain Sir Edward Belcher of HMS *Sulphur*. It was Belcher who first raised the Union flag at Possession Point on 26 January 1841. The occasion was marked with a loyal toast and three cheers from the ship's company. I can't help feeling that Belcher's will be one of the first names to be removed in 1997.

In Shek Tong Tsui the Captain's Street reaches a T-junction with Queen's Road, one of the principal island thoroughfares. The 54 turns right and then, just after Dragonfair Garden, jinks left and hangs a right into Des Voeux Road, which runs parallel to Queen's and carries the famous island tramway with its thin double-decker tramcars, at a standard fare of less than HK$2 one of the cheapest forms of transport in the world. I tend to agree with Governor Patten's recommendation of the tram as one of the three essential experiences for the short-term visitor to his domain. Des Voeux, pronounced inexplicably 'De Voe', is the eponym of Sir William, the Patten predecessor between 1887 and 1891. His road was officially opened in 1889 by Queen Victoria's son the Duke of Connaught. Unfortunately Des Voeux was absent on one of the long leaves for which he was apparently famous. He was a sickly fellow and left most of the governing to his private secretary F. H. May. The one aspect of governing he really enjoyed was the opportunity to entertain distinguished guests, so he must have been dismayed at missing the Duke's visit, particularly in view of the road opening.

The 54 route followed Des Voeux until shortly after Dr Stanley Ho's Shun Tak Centre, which is not only Ho headquarters but also the gateway to Macau. Thereabouts Des Voeux appears to merge with Connaught. Just after the Sheung Wan MTR station, the beginning of the island line, there is a short road to the right which brings you out on Des Voeux Road Central, which now runs parallel to Connaught Road Central. In 1889 the Hong Kong topography around these two roads would have been quite different. Obviously the Macau ferry terminal and the underground station are very new, but in the last century much of this land would have been harbour. The Duke of Connaught not only named

134

the two new roads after himself and the Governor, he also initiated a new land-reclamation scheme, the first proper one since 1862. As a result of this the waterfront was extended to provide land not only for the new roads but also for the Supreme Court building, which now houses the Legislative Council; for the cricket pitch, now built over; for the Hong Kong Club; and for the celebrated tramlines.

By the time I reached my destination the surroundings had become Westernised almost to the point of parody, Cartier and Dunhill seeming even sleeker than their Paris or London counterparts; the doorman outside the Mandarin more suavely epauletted than his equivalent outside any European Ritz; the office buildings more ostentatiously marbled and elevatored than New York's. Yet only a little further back were those curiously hybrid signs and hoardings that were already beginning to seem so quintessentially Hong Kong: the Sweety House; the Wah Yen Tang cake shop; a general practitioner called Dr Wong Wing Tim; the Sweet Maid Bakery; Wing Hing Shark Fin. Often I sensed an element of English kitsch among the exoticism of the East. Essex and the Orient mingled oddly. Once, shopping with Ah Non for her favourite Thai mangoes, so much greener than their Filipino counterparts, I paused outside a salon full of Chinese women, their black silken tresses obscured under old-fashioned driers. It was called Winnie Hair Design. That seemed to sum it up. Romford meets Sai Ying Pun.

One morning I jerked alert halfway along the 54 route and realised that I had my head buried in the *South China Morning Post* and that it had been there since I boarded the bus in Mount Davis Road. I hadn't stared out at the miraculous harbour and the Cutie Club and the Wah Yen Tang cake shop and those endless wizened old ladies pushing trollies groaning under the weight of countless black dustbin liners filled with God-knows-what. I had lost a little of my wonder and surprise and acquired a little blaséness. I felt

135

guilty and cross with myself, though at the same time it made me confident again of the value of novelty and first impressions. Familiarity with Hong Kong could surely never breed contempt, and yet that particular moment made me wonder.

The essence of any place is elusive but my little bus journey captured, for me, a small part of *real* Hong Kong. It was very different from travelling in the back of the gubernatorial Daimler or even Range Rover, though that too had its *reality*. Both seemed important in constructing a picture of the place, for a true portrait needed to be a mosaic, a jigsaw. I was anxious that it should be what someone said of another, earlier attempt at prose portrait painting. It should be 'loose-fit'. In 'shooting history on the wing', which is what I was doing in Hong Kong, you cannot be definitive or have the final word. A certain sort of soap-box punditry attempts such precision, but it is a neatness, I think, which begs more questions than it can ever hope to answer.

One Sunday morning I stopped off in the daylight dusk of the Captain's Bar at the Mandarin Hotel for a glass of champagne. I can't think why. I was on my own, but it suddenly seemed appropriate. It set me back a cool HK$130. A glass of ordinary white wine at the FCC or the Hong Kong Club would have been HK$20. My newspaper was HK$6. My bus ride HK$3.40.

An American, plump, middle-aged, was sitting at the bar with a bird-thin Chinese girl.

'You tried a Singapore sling?' he asked her.

She dimpled and gave him a Princess Di look through fluttery eyelashes. 'What's that?'

'A drink.'

'What's in it?'

'Everything.'

After finishing my own ridiculous drink I took the Star

Ferry to Kowloon and wandered around the concrete harbour front, with its walkways charmless in much the same impersonal manner as London's South Bank, though with incomparable views across to Hong Kong Island. There was an advertisement for a concert by the Hong Kong Philharmonic under the baton of their lady maestro, Wing-Sie Yip. The soloists were Warren Mok, Eric Moo and Shirley Kwan. I pondered the improbability of three soloists called Warren, Eric and Shirley with the surnames Mok, Moo and Kwan, then remembered the American saying that 'everything' went into a Singapore sling, and wondered if there was some profundity to be manufactured there. Perhaps not, but somehow they contributed to the complexity of the mosaic. Even tiny pieces are crucial to the jigsaw.

I went to church that morning, not so much because I was feeling religious but because I felt in need of the soothing noise the Church of England made and also because I wanted to see what had happened to 'church parade'. Time was when matins at the Cathedral would have been a compulsory full-dress affair with the Governor and the GOC leading the troops in Hymns Ancient and Modern. Being of an ecumenical disposition, Catholic Chris had visited St John's Cathedral and had even preached there on St George's Day. I suspect that like that other improbable pulpit frequenter, Richard Cobb, the Governor was rather tickled by the idea of preaching. For a politician as for a don, the sermon had the unusual benefit of generally being heard without interruption.

I was not present when the Governor preached, though I acquired a copy of his sermon from the Dean's secretary, Mary Whitticase. Her son Matt had been at university with my daughter and had spent part of the previous Christmas with my family. The sermon was typed on small sheets, sixteen of them, with the first sentence of each page printed at the bottom of its predecessor to ensure greater fluency.

When the Governor was Chairman of the Conservative Party he gained some attention by using what seemed to me at the time to be uncharacteristically populist imagery: thus 'porky' (Cockney rhyming slang – 'pork pie' for 'lie') and 'double whammy' (which sent the etymologists of the press scurrying for their *OED*s and *Brewer's* to little conclusive effect). Here in the cathedral he referred to the Vatican's removal of England's patron saint from the Calendar of Saints as 'the ecclesiastical equivalent of a red card'. I could imagine the quizzical smile with which he would have accompanied this footballing analogy, as well as the quick glance over the top of his glasses to see if the congregation appreciated the joke. I wondered how many of the audience tittered.

I enjoyed reading his text, which was typically literate with references to Spenser's *The Faerie Queene* and Carpaccio's paintings in the Dalmatian College in Venice ('St George coping elegantly with a rather fey-looking dragon'). He was sound on patriotism and loyalty – an apposite quote from the Harvard University war memorial. He invoked Scott and Grenville; quoted Browning, Stanley Baldwin and Thomas More – a curious trio but united, I suppose, in their absolute Englishness; and he ended with a statement of ringing religiousness which sounded strange coming from such an essentially (I think) secular figure as the Governor of Hong Kong.

It was his fourteenth point (they were all numbered in his text). 'So,' he concluded, 'in celebrating the values of patriotic citizenship today – responsibility, duty, decency, integrity, honesty, courage – let us not forget, in St Paul's words, that "the word of God is not shut up", is never shut up, and that it is the word of God that must finally determine our behaviour as citizens in the kingdom of this world, in order that we may enjoy with Him life in the next kingdom

138

that He has prepared for us through His own agony, death and resurrection.'

He mentioned Hong Kong only once as far as I could see – at the end of a longish list of places for which he felt 'a loyalty, an affection' – and even then it came after a dash, which suggested that it was something of an afterthought. Essentially it was a thoughtful but very English piece of prose. Given that it was a St George's Day sermon, this was perhaps appropriate, though I was quite surprised that he did not use his pulpit to convey some specifically Hong Kong message. And I was struck too by how comfortable he seemed with the form. Other governors, other politicians, might have faltered in the face of the challenge and have simply served up an all-purpose ecumenical feel-good speech which they could equally well have delivered at the opening of a new factory or someone's National Day. This, however, was an authentic sermon, which might have been delivered by some visiting bishop from Britain.

I found myself wondering, more or less idly, whether Chris would have been a successful cleric. He was probably too worldly to have been a contemporary cardinal but he might have enjoyed crossing encyclicals with Mazarin, Richelieu or even Wolsey.

Morning service almost exactly a month after St George's Day was a drab, rather dispiriting affair. Several lines of huge fans hung from the ceiling and rotated listlessly. They made no apparent difference to the humid heat. The bearded gweilo priest sweated profusely into his cassock. I was the only member of the sparse congregation wearing a jacket, let alone a tie. The pews were comfortable wickerwork. The vergers wore drab grey tunics which made them look like prison warders.

'Lord Save the Queen,' said the priest.

'And teach her councillors wisdom,' the congregation was supposed to reply, but we did little more than mumble.

139

The church was largely bereft of monuments and memorials. Apparently the Japanese had stripped it during their occupation. For a while it had continued as a church, served by Norwegian clergy. But in 1944 the Japanese turned it into a social club. The Roman Catholic Vicar Apostolic arranged for some of the furnishings to be taken away and put in store, but some of these were destroyed in an air raid. When the cathedral was liberated there were 'no stained-glass windows, a ruined organ with a few remaining pipes which looked as though they had been targets on a rifle range, no mural tablets or monuments, no altars, no choir stalls, no Lady Chapel, a desecrated font, a shell-hole through the tower'. *

I noticed a simple plaque in memory of Governor Youde, who died in office, in Peking, on 5 December 1986. It was 'erected by we the Civil Servants of Hong Kong'.

Outside there are three memorials. The cross in memory of the dead of the two World Wars is the second to have been erected, the first having been reduced to a straight granite column by the Japanese. The grave of Private Ronald Maxwell, a 'Volunteer' who was killed aged twenty-two during the battle for Hong Kong, is the only grave within the cathedral precinct. His comrades buried him there because it was the only green space apart from the cricket ground on Chater Road.

Finally there is the memorial to Captain Bate RN. This is a rose-granite tablet on the north transept. Originally it was part of a grander memorial comprising a pillar with a globe on top, but this was knocked down, in true Hong Kong fashion, when Garden Road was widened in 1954. It is 'sacred to the memory of Captain William Thornton Bate

* The words are those of A. S. 'Bunny' Abbott, who worked for the Hong Kong booksellers Kelly and Walsh for thirty years. A devoted friend of the cathedral, he published a private memoir of words and photographs in 1955 in aid of the building of 'The New Hall'.

140

RN who was killed under the walls of Canton at the storming of the city on December 29th 1857 in the 37th year of his life'. The ensuing inscription is a fine example of imperial Victorian respect which, after praising his professional career and duties, concludes: 'The Christian virtues and consistent piety which adorned his private character and the amiable qualities of disposition which endeared him to a large circle of friends combined in rendering his untimely death the occasion of universal mourning among the foreign community in China.'

Alas, poor Bate! He was one of only ten Allied combatants – the storming of Canton was undertaken by an Anglo-French force – to be killed in the engagement. The Governor of the day was Sir John Bowring,[*] who had been demoted from the rank of plenipotentiary by the 8th Lord Elgin, son of the man who made off with the marbles. Elgin, who was later responsible for the equally contentious sacking of the Summer Palace in Peking, had a low opinion of the British in Hong Kong. When calling at the Colony he preferred not to come ashore; he complained that the Hong Kong Chamber of Commerce was run almost as if it was a department of Jardine Matheson; and he stigmatised his compatriots as 'brutes – lying – sanguinary – cheating – oppressive to the weak, crouching before the strong'.

This sounded like one of Peking's diatribes against Governor Patten almost one and a half centuries further on. What intemperate language and actions Hong Kong has produced! I was reminded of the Chinese hauling Hector Ross from his bunk and shouting at him for not having the right attitude. At least he had lived to tell the tale, unlike Captain Bate RN.

[*] Sir John's descendant, Philip, a freelance journalist and former editor of the *Far Eastern Economic Review*, could sometimes be found at the bar of the Foreign Correspondents' Club, of which he had twice been president.

Outside the cathedral the chorus of Filipina maids was eating noodles, bartering clothing and chatting in their inimitable piping Tagalog.

But that's another story.

NINE

Time was when the *Times* correspondent in a foreign land was almost as eminent a Victorian as the British Ambassador himself. Times and *The Times* have both changed, so that neither British ambassadors nor *Times* journalists rate quite so highly. There are fewer of them, and they and their country cut less ice. Hong Kong, even in its imperial twilight, was something of an exception. In real terms both the Governor and the *Times* man were increasingly crepuscular figures with ever more vestigial power and influence. Yet reality, as so often, lagged behind appearance. Just as the Governor *seemed* to wield the power of his omnipotent predecessors, so the *Times* correspondent *seemed*, at least to some, to have all the authority and influence of a William Russell. Other journalists, of whom there were many, resented this, some privately and some more overtly. Dr* Mirsky seemed to be the only journalist in town who really did have the Governor's ear. He certainly bent it on occasion, but the Governor did not seem to mind unduly. Dr Mirsky gave the impression of regarding himself as a player in the great game that was being played out in Hong Kong rather than just a spectator. When, for example, the

---

* Unlike Stanley Ho's, the Mirsky doctorate was earned in a conventional academic manner and was no mere honorary degree.

Governor committed what Dr Mirsky regarded as a *faux pas* or indulged in the unpardonable sin of seeming to be even remotely soft on Peking the *Times* correspondent would present himself at Government House and tell the Governor where he had gone wrong. Despite this, perhaps because of it, the Governor spoke more highly of Mirsky than of any other local journalist (not difficult), and the two dined together informally in each other's homes.

Mirsky was seriously well educated (Harvard and King's, Cambridge), knowledgeable and informed, and he had good connections. In this respect his very public commitment to what was crudely described and perceived as the 'democratic' point of view could have been construed as limiting. As the *Observer*'s correspondent in Peking he had reported on the massacre in Tiananmen Square, as well as making numerous broadcasts for the BBC. For this he won awards in the UK but less than golden opinions from the old men of Peking. As a consequence he was *persona non grata* in China and not exactly popular with the New China News Agency people, a.k.a. Xinhua. Under a pseudonym, Jane Whistler, he also wrote a weekly column for the *Eastern Express* which regularly lambasted the Peking regime.

We had friends and colleagues in common so we spoke several times while I was still in England and he kindly asked me round to lunch at his airy and, especially by local standards, spacious apartment. This was in a building called the Villa Elegance at Number One Robinson Road and was on the sixteenth floor, from which he had a breathtaking view across the towers of Mammon to the harbour and Kowloon beyond. Like Lady Dunn and the Cornishes he also looked almost straight down on Government House, though he said that he could no longer actually see the Governor coming in and out of his front door. In his previous apartment, in the next-door building, he had been able to exercise precisely that detailed surveillance. When I was at

144

Government House I had felt overlooked, but I hadn't then realised quite how true this was.

Dr Mirsky was a stimulating and amusing host, though in my notes of that first encounter I did add that he was 'prickly'. I don't think I was entirely mistaken with this first impression because a few weeks later he became the only person I have ever known who walked out of a meal because of a disagreement with his fellow diners. The argument wasn't about anything of world-shattering importance nor was it of a particularly personal nature. It had to do with the cleanliness of Hong Kong's beaches and the politeness of the Territory's shopkeepers. Dr Mirsky was unconvinced of either, though to this day I'm puzzled why this should have turned into what the Governor would describe as the dinner-party equivalent of taking an early bath.

At our first meeting he was a fund of excellent, gossipy insider stories; searching questions about the Governor's early life; and shrewd observations about Hong Kong. For instance, he told me that in Hong Kong people getting into a lift immediately press the 'close door' button even if there is a long queue of people still trying to get in. The other day he was behind a woman who did just this. Mirsky was a bit slow off the mark and was bumped heavily by the closing doors. Nevertheless he managed to make it into the lift, muttering imprecations and rubbing his bruised jaw. His fellow passenger shook her head. 'I just hate people who press the "close door" button like that,' she said.

Mirsky regarded her incredulously. 'Then why did you do it?' he asked.

She hung her head. 'I am a very bad person,' she replied.

He said this was a *very* Hong Kong story.

After lunch he had to go to a press conference given by the American Chamber of Commerce, whose delegation had just returned from a mission to China. I tagged along. The conference was held at the Conrad Hotel on the other side of

145

the botanical gardens from the Villa Elegance. It was an agreeable quarter of an hour's walk and I couldn't help thinking how enviable the *Times* correspondent's lot was compared with that of his colleagues in Fortress Wapping in London's East End miles away from West End hotels, Parliament and, in short, the action. Their man in Hong Kong not only had an elegant eyrie dominating his domain, he was also within walking distance of everywhere that mattered.

Outside the Conrad there was a magic fountain. Water cascaded in an apparently solid wall apart from one gap in the circular liquid curtain. You could walk through this and then sit down on a bench in the core of the fountain. Doing so was one of Mirsky's favourite minor pleasures and he always made a point of it when visiting the Conrad. His other, similar diversion had been removed by Li Ka Shing's demolition of the Hilton. This was a large globe which balanced, apparently precariously, on a jet of water in the foyer. Mirsky's little joke was to attempt to dislodge the globe. This was, for some obscure reason of aqua-dynamics, impossible; but he enjoyed the anxiety on the faces of the hotel staff whenever he attempted it.

The press conference was run of the mill: six TV cameras, assorted hacks, two mildly shifty men in suits producing such lines as 'some tremendously complex dynamics are in play' and 'surprisingly the Taiwan question did not surface'. The Taiwan question was whether or not the Taiwanese President was going to be allowed into the USA to get an honorary degree from his alma mater, Cornell. The reason 'it did not surface' was that the delegation from the Chamber of Commerce was, as their name suggested, interested in doing business. Awkward questions about honorary degrees for sworn enemies of Peking were absolutely nothing whatever to do with them. In fact they were less than nothing

146

whatever to do with them. They were there to do business, goddammit.

This was a line which was to become familiar. The British were just as guilty. On his several visits to drum up exports in China, Michael Heseltine was just as reluctant to raise anything approaching a moral issue. It is a common enough form of selective political myopia and I had run into it often when I was involved with the PEN Writers in Prison Committee.* Business and Trade were not always the sworn enemies of Ethics and Morality, but businessmen and traders were not governed by the same motives as civil rights activists or liberally disposed politicians. Fact of life; and nowhere more so than in Hong Kong.

I admired the Americans' logo, which was a sailing junk decorated with stars and stripes, but I also found it faintly alarming from a patriotic point of view. I wondered if British business was being as hard nosed. Mirsky was voluble and disputatious, though sitting near the back. He was, by some distance, the most aggressive questioner and the most self-confident. It seemed clear to me, and I would have thought to everyone else, that he alone among those in the audience regarded himself as at least the equal of those on the platform. He was probably correct. But I wasn't sure how well it would play in government press briefings after 30 June 1997.

A few days later Jonathan Dimbleby was due to visit Hong Kong again. He was dining *chez* Mirsky and I was generously invited along as well. I had not previously met Dimbleby and was mildly apprehensive. We were both, up to a point and in a manner of speaking, suitors for the Governor's hand. True, his priority was a BBC TV programme, whereas mine was a book, but, as with his

* PEN is an international writers' organisation for Poets, Playwrights, Essayists, Editors and Novelists. It Writers in Prison Committee was a precursor of Amnesty International.

programme about the Prince of Wales, there was a book riding on the back of his Governor as well.

I thought it polite to take a bottle of wine along, but Mirsky had already said enough to suggest that he was something of an expert, so rather than risking the 'wrong' claret I decided on a bottle of Great Wall. On my earlier visit to the People's Republic I'd been introduced to Chinese wine and it had seemed perfectly drinkable. Much of it seemed to be the product of joint-venture schemes with European or New World companies. Certainly Western-style wines were being produced over the border, and climate and soil conditions were suitable for grape-growing. The Great Wall bottle I purchased at my local 7–11 claimed that it had won a Gold Medal at the 3rd International Conference of Alcoholic Beverages in Madrid in 1984 and also at the 12th International Food Fair in Paris in 1986. I was sceptical about this, suspecting that few serious wines would enter this kind of competition. I doubted whether Château Lafite would be on the starting grid at an International Conference of Alcoholic Beverages, but I didn't know for certain. Like so many recent Chinese developments it was difficult to be sure how far the wine-making was indicative of a great leap forward and how far it was simply cosmetic. Distinguishing between real progress and artificial window-dressing was a fundamental problem for Hong Kongers trying to second-guess the true identity of the 'new' China.

When I arrived again on the sixteenth floor of the Villa Elegance I found the Doctor in a state of considerable excitement. A story of great significance had just broken. He was just finishing a telephone conversation with the apparent villain of the piece, the Australian David Armstrong, editor-in-chief of the *South China Morning Post*. Armstrong had fired the *Post*'s cartoonist, and Mirsky was filing London soonest. Even as he talked he was tapping away at his Apple

Mac, hair standing on end as if electrically shocked. In front of him the plate glass framed the glistening city below.

I'm afraid my irreverent thoughts bounced between a vision of Woody Allen and Dr Strangelove. This, I told myself, was a bad example of 'going native'. The poor fellow had obviously been away too long, had become so immersed in the incestuous little world of Hong Kong that he had come to believe it was the centre of the universe. How could he possibly believe that the sacking of a cartoonist from a colonial paper with a daily circulation of little more than 100,000[*] was going to make headlines in London? The sacked cartoonist was an American called Larry Feign and he produced a strip cartoon called 'The World of Lily Wong'. As far as I was concerned the axing of Larry and Lily was about as significant as the *Daily Express* dropping Rupert Bear.

Not so, explained Dr Mirsky patiently. Feign's strip was highly political and consistently hostile to the Chinese. He had recently been featuring the infamous organ-transplant trade, revealed in a savage BBC exposé by Sue Lloyd-Roberts. In the cartoon that appeared on the day of the firing, the Chinese premier Li Peng was described as a 'fascist, murderous dog'. This was the sort of vivid language his own propagandists usually reserved for Chris Patten. The story-line of the same strip was a man-in-the-street agreeing with the remark (made by an *agent provocateur*) and being arrested in order to provide 'corneas for the client in Kowloon Tong'. Not exactly calculated to bring out a sense of humour in Peking's corridors of power or at Xinhua.

Sacking Feign, argued Mirsky, was a clear act of political censorship. This was a harbinger of what was to come after 1997. Press freedom would vanish. Armstrong, on the

---

[*] The latest available figure from the group's annual report was, at the time of writing, 105,458.

'phone just now, had claimed that the action was dictated entirely by economic considerations. Well, he would say that, wouldn't he?

I remained unconvinced. It still seemed, from a British standpoint, like a storm in a provincial teacup. Surely there were other more serious Hong Kong stories around? Unemployment, for example, had just 'leapt' up to 3 per cent, the highest figure, astonishingly, for nine years. This was being blamed on the government's imported labour policy. There was also the unpleasantness with the Vietnamese boat people. How could you compare the sacking of a cartoonist with riots and baton charges?

I was wrong. The story did indeed play in the UK, fuelled in part by *The Times*'s own coverage. In Hong Kong itself the row, exacerbated by the dismissal of twenty-five *Post* journalists shortly afterwards, rumbled on for most of the year. At first the Territory's chattering classes were firmly on Feign's side. A while later, however, he was invited to speak at the annual Press Club Ball and managed, by negative force of personality, to turn a sympathetic audience into a hostile one within a few minutes. Much later I discussed the matter at some length with the new *Post* editor, Jonathan Fenby. Fenby was too new on the scene to know the story at first hand, but he seemed genuinely to believe the view promulgated by his editor-in-chief.

But, then again, he would, wouldn't he?

That night at the Villa Elegance, however, I obviously misread the significance of the story. I found Hong Kong persistently fascinating but I retained sufficient prejudice (which I thought of as 'objectivity') not to consider it the centre of the universe. And when, during the meal, I heard Jonathan Dimbleby describe the Territory as 'easily the most significant item on the British government's agenda' I thought to myself that these were the words of a man charged with making a mega-documentary on the subject for the BBC. Of course it was a problem for me too. In order to find out one has to immerse oneself in one's subject. In doing so one inevitably runs the risk of losing a sense of proportion. During my time there, however, I increasingly felt that although there might have been a time when Hong Kong was at or near the top of the British agenda that moment was now past and was unlikely to return.

Before embarking on the meal that evening Jonathan Dimbleby said there was just one item of business he wanted to get out of the way. Whenever he read about my intended book, he said, it was alleged that I was going to call it *The Last Governor*. He was afraid I couldn't use this title as it was his and had been since he first thought of it. I didn't reply that it wasn't a particularly original idea; nor did I tell him that the first person who had suggested it to me was my mother's hairdresser in Wiltshire. I did say that, as far as I was concerned, it was only a running title. Since my book was about Hong Kong, including its last Governor, but was not a biography of Chris, it probably wasn't a very apt title for me anyway. In the end, however, as he well knew, the decision would be taken by the marketing department, and in any case there was no copyright in a title.

The following weekend, in its diary column, the *Sunday Morning Post* ran a not very accurate, but trivial and harmless, story about this exchange, thus provoking an unamused 'phone call from Dr Mirsky. Later the item was picked up by his own paper in London and they too ran a little piece in their diary. This irritated Mirsky yet more and even led to Jonathan Dimbleby's agent complaining to my publisher. Like the Larry Feign episode I could not help wondering if, at times, Hong Kong induced a loss not just of perspective, but of humour too. The result, predictably, was that I thought of a better title though pleased to have the words 'Last Governor' in the sub-title, not least as an assertion of independence.

151

Even old Richard Hughes could lapse into portentousness in Hong Kong. This was a place, he wrote, where East met West, 'on common grounds of pretence and expedience, corruption and logic, hypocrisy and morality'.

I'm not entirely sure what he meant by this but when one came down to specifics it seemed to me that what really characterised the meeting of East and West was mutual incomprehension too often clouded by mutual antipathy. On the morning of my meal with the two Jonathans an Arsenal footballer called Ray Parlour was fined HK$2,000 after his team had beaten the local Rangers side by four goals to nil. Parlour had evidently gone off drinking in Wan Chai, consumed twelve pints of beer and then thrown several handfuls of prawn crackers under the bonnet of a cab. He then hit the driver so hard in the face that he needed five stitches. Mr Parlour apologised to the court and said he could not remember anything about it.

At different levels in Hong Kong, from the Governor to the visiting Arsenal footballer, this was, too often, what actually happened when East met West.

Not that it was always that bad. In the case of my long-lost fellow prep-school pupil David Browning I felt that the incomprehension level was high, in much the same way that it had been with his witty predecessor, Austin Coates. The antipathy level, on the other hand, was low. Browning, like Coates, was quite happy to concede mystification but he positively oozed goodwill, and when I saw him *in situ* his local staff in Sha Tin oozed goodwill back even though they seemed to regard him with the same quizzical headshaking that he afforded them.

He took me out to Sha Tin one day, and showed me his office, in a modern block above the railway station on the main line from Kowloon to Canton. There was a Marks and Spencer in the shopping centre. As my fellow guest at the Cornishes had claimed, it was doing good business though it

152

was noticeable that, whereas in England Marks and Sparks nowadays feels like a food shop, here there was hardly anything in the food line. All the emphasis, as it used to be in the UK, was on sensible, fairly priced clothing. Hong Kong's market food is so interesting, variable and cheap that it would, presumably, be folly to compete. The centrepiece of the mall was an ingeniously complicated fountain which gushed in time to music. The town hall was playing host to an orchestra from Leipzig. As it was Thursday the library was closed. Outside the cinema there was a poster of a child with the caption: 'Child over one metre in height should hold ticket – if you're taller than me you need a ticket.'

Twenty years ago there was nothing here but paddy field. It was a place you came to picnic. Now it was like Milton Keynes squared, a moon city of high-rise apartment buildings bisected by the neat, canal-like Shing Mun river – which, it was hoped, would soon be a stretch of water suitable for Olympic-standard rowing.

Touring round this newest of new towns I was reminded that Browning's father had been an Anglican vicar in Somerset. His parishes were North Curry and Sampford Arundel, and in a sense it was difficult to envisage places more different. Yet there was a sense in which I felt that the Reverend Mr Browning showing me round Sampford Arundel would have been not so unlike District Officer Browning conducting me about Sha Tin. Both, in essence, were involved in community care. When the young Browning talked about the chairman of his District Board, a restaurateur who had spent a quarter of a century plying his trade in Dublin, he spoke in much the same way as I would have expected his father to refer to a difficult but likeable chairman of the parish council. When he introduced me to his deputy, an elfin local girl in her late twenties with an English degree from Cambridge University, he did so with

153

the same sort of avuncular pride that the vicar might have taken in a young curate.

In an article in the *Far Eastern Economic Review*, Browning was described as 'an archetypal British colonial administrator with a barrel chest and lantern jaw'. He objected to the 'barrel chest and lantern jaw' description but did not argue with the rest of it. Being such an archetype is not an exact science. Nor, contrary to the cliché, does it involve a draconian exercise of discipline. It's much more a question of holding the ring and creating an atmosphere of civilisation and fair play. 'The status of the DO,' he told me, 'is very high. But in fact he has very little power.'

There was a small but potentially explosive dispute simmering in the District when I visited. It involved a new custom-built health centre which Browning was due to open at the weekend. In the previous doctor's surgery there had been a noticeboard on which anyone who wished could advertise free of charge. Now, however, the doctor had decided that the practice was no longer appropriate and would be discontinued. Word had reached the DO's office that some form of disruption was to be staged at the opening ceremony. This would be embarrassing, but there was no way in which Browning himself could become personally involved in the dispute. Therefore one of his staff was instructed to sort it out. By the time we finished the day's work a compromise had been worked out which allowed a saving of face all round. Browning never told me what form the agreement took. I'm not even sure he knew himself. The point was that, with much nodding and winking, a deal was arranged.

I was reminded of Austin Coates's exasperation on being confronted with a particularly intractable dispute involving concubines and cows. His solution was simple. He got a minion to do as much sorting out as possible.

His man was called Mr Lo. Coates's instructions to him

154

were straightforward: 'Mr Lo, will you please take these people out to your office, disentangle the facts, and when you are able to explain the thing to me clearly, bring them back, and we'll go into it.'

'Thereafter,' wrote Coates, 'this became the procedure. It did not eliminate the absurd misunderstandings of which my own ignorance was a main cause; but it did at least minimise them.'

Nevertheless, Browning said, you can't really run a colony as a democracy. It's a contradiction in terms. Because of this he took the view that the British would be criticised for not having introduced enough local democracy. Running a dictatorship – which, if we're honest, is what a Crown Colony always was – may be enlightened and for the general good, provided the dictatorship was benevolent – as, Browning thought, it nearly always was under the British. On the other hand it was a system tailor-made for exploitation by a tyrant.

There were some 570,000 people in Browning's district, the vast majority of whom – although there were the vestiges of one or two ancient settlements – lived in brand-new blocks. I encountered mixed views about Hong Kong's public housing, but Browning was enthusiastic. 'They're all beautifully kept,' he said. 'There's only very occasional vandalism. They really look after them.' He paused. 'It works. It works.'

The scale of this new housing is unprecedented and unparalleled. Some two million people have been accommodated in just over twenty years. About half the population – more than three million citizens – are in subsidised public housing. There are an estimated 879,000 such flats on 290 estates. Nor is the building rate slowing. The Housing Authority plans another 292,500 flats by the year 2001. The private sector averages about 30,000 new flats every year.

155

Browning's office helps to organise a 'mutual aid committee' in every new block. Each floor elects a representative, which means that there are around thirty delegates on each committee. There is also a management office where complaints can be registered. In theory at least any problem with plumbing, crumbling fabric, drains, neighbour noise and so on will be sorted out rapidly.

Of course there are some horrid, squalid apartment buildings, often surmounted by a temporary, unauthorised shack or two of corrugated iron. I later went to one or two with the Governor, and we were duly appalled. The Kwong Yuan estate that I visited with David Browning, however, seemed intelligently planned and bearable to live in. There were shops, restaurants, sitting-out areas, a corner where the village elders were able to congregate to play mah-jong and Chinese chess. The apartment we visited was small: two bedrooms, a living room, kitchen and bathroom. There was an enormous stereo and TV set; a mother and three young children with pudding-basin haircuts studiously engaged in the afternoon's homework. It was light and there were views. The lift worked and there were regular buses to the downtown area. No, I would not have wished to live in such an environment, much less bring up small children there. But, considering the population explosion, the huge immigration from the mainland, the lack of space and all the other problems, it was miraculous. To be sure the evidence was anecdotal: one literally in a million. But, if Browning was right, it worked.

A few weeks later, after the local dragon-boat regatta, Browning went on leave to his native West Country, never to return to Sha Tin. When he did come back it was to a low-profile office job in Customs and Excise. A year earlier he had told the *Far Eastern Economic Review*, 'We buggers are dying off.' It was true. Even if he was still in Hong Kong beyond 1997 it seemed hardly likely that it would be for

156

long. His successor would be Chinese and, like Browning's young Cambridge graduate number two, possess much superior academic qualifications. Whether they would be as streetwise or savvy, at least in the short term, I rather doubted. I wasn't sure if they would possess the same sense of fair play that Browning learned from the Vicar of Sampford Arundel and from Connaught House School, Bishops Lydeard.

Once a year, and once only, he made a speech in Cantonese – at his own reception in celebration of the Chinese New Year. If he had an expertise it was in dealing with people in general rather than Hong Kong people in particular. All round his office were the souvenirs I came to recognise as ubiquitous thank-yous for anyone who had ever had to dig a hole for a tree, unveil a plaque or cut a ribbon. They were cups, salvers and other trophies, in gold and silver with red ribbons, bearing such inscriptions as 'Guest of Honour Opening Ceremony' or 'Presented to Mr David Thomas Browning, Sha Tin District Officer. In appreciation for officiating the opening of the Exhibition on Office Health.'

They will provide an unusual talking point for visitors to the Browning retirement home in the Quantock or Brendon Hills. I should be interested too to hear what the old District Officer has to say once he has retired from the service and feels, perhaps, less constrained. I'm sure he will look back with nostalgia and pride – though, even when we were in Sha Tin, he shook his head ruefully and conceded, 'I'm basically out of date.'

I wondered also if he would suffer the same fate as Austin Coates, who remarked as he finished his career in Hong Kong, 'All trace of me as a Westerner would not exactly be obliterated; it would be treated as a fact which did not exist.'

Sometimes in Hong Kong I wondered if that was what the Chinese had in store for everything the British had done during their period of occupation. For as Coates concluded: 'For the Westerner – or for the West – to believe it is possible in any way to influence China is chimerical. When a Westerner comes to China, no matter how high his rank or how great his influence, all that he can achieve – all that he will ever achieve – is to add a grain of salt to seawater, since China, like the sea, is adamantine, and of unchanging substance.'

I suspect that may apply to governors as much as it does to district officers.

TEN

I found the idea of confronting commerce and dealing with 'the business community' slightly daunting, though inescapable. Not unlike the Governor. I was frequently told, as a matter of absolute fact, that he 'does not like businessmen'. Certainly I met a number of businessmen who did not like him, though, as I had found from the first, they were nearly always careful to differentiate between the Governor's personal qualities and his political behaviour. 'Nice chap,' they would say, 'but got it all wrong.' I wasn't sure that they did all think him a 'nice chap' but, at least while he was still a power in the land, they thought it politic to pretend.

At the Cornishes' dinner I had got that predictable lecture from the German textile merchant, saying, more or less, that the British were a spent force, incapable of sloughing off their imperialist past. They were indolent, arrogant and further compromised by the Governor's intransigence. This seemed a bit much at a meal hosted by Her Majesty's Senior Trade Commissioner but I was grateful for the German's honesty. Even if I didn't like what he said, I knew there were elements of truth in it. He had argued, among other things, that before long there would be hardly any British left in Hong Kong. And did I know that there were 2,000 Germans in the Territory?

Well, no, I didn't, but I did recall that the features editor

159

of the *Daily Mail* had expressed interest in an article on 'Why are the British messing up in the Far East and letting the Krauts get all the contracts?' There was some evidence for this view. Just when it looked as if General Electric was going to win the contract for the new underground railway in Shanghai, it went to the Germans instead. The alleged reasons were very much those cited by the textile merchant.

The day afterwards I contacted the German diner and he put me in touch with Herr Ekkehard Goetting, Delegate of German Industry and Commerce for Hong Kong, South China and Vietnam. His ultra-smooth office was on the twenty-second floor of the World Wide Building in Des Voeux Road in the heart of Central. Very convenient for the 54 bus, which I guessed Herr Goetting did not use. He had a magnificent harbour view, photographs of schlosses and yachts and two volumes of *Who's Who in Germany*. Also a neat ginger moustache and brilliantly polished shoes. Herr Goetting's organisation was independent of government. 'Not supervised by government,' he said, 'not under *anyone's* hierarchy.'

No, indeed. Herr Goetting struck me as impressively fluent, fierce, competitive, but above all independent. His organisation had just opened an office in Shanghai, and he was anxious to establish strong bilateral relations with the Chinese and take advantage of what he described a touch tentatively as 'the transfer from a state-run economy to elements of the free market'.

He had hoped to gain the co-operation of the Hong Kong government because, he reasoned, a shade disingenuously, he regarded himself and his colleagues as ambassadors for Hong Kong. Support was not forthcoming. 'We are not served well by the Hong Kong government,' he said. 'They take too political an approach. We wanted a Chinese–German Chamber, but they said we were advancing '97. We said, "We're not political. If we do it now we can focus on the Chinese business community." I mentioned it to the former Chief Secretary but he thought we were too much of a nuisance.'

He was posing a difficult problem. His organisation paid out HK$15,000 for a visit to Frankfurt by the Chief Secretary, a rather formidable Anson Chan, appointed by Chris as, in effect, his number two. She was the first Chinese person to hold the post. For this money, Herr Goetting said, he had received nothing. He had still not even met Anson Chan. His organisation had set up between twenty and thirty Hong Kong trade promotions in Germany. This, he said, was hugely beneficial to Hong Kong, and yet the Hong Kong government gave him no support. 'We need ambassadors for Hong Kong ... we're helping this, but we're the only organisation doing it without money or anything from the government. I've lost interest in the Hong Kong government. We've tried everything and we've got nothing in return.' He shrugged. 'Not that we've ever asked for anything.' Clearly he would never demean himself by doing so.

I could understand his irritation. But, equally, the expatriate British who served the Hong Kong government, from the Governor down to the most junior bureaucrat, did have a divided loyalty. So, come to that, did many expatriates working in the private sector. Much later I discussed the question with Peter Sutch, taipan* of the giant Swire Group. He said he had no problem in having been brought up and educated in Great Britain, retiring to Britain, but serving Hong Kong interests unswervingly and, if necessary, in opposition to Britain if so required during his career.

Nevertheless I couldn't help wondering; and the Goetting problem was a very good example of a hopelessly divided

* The *OED* describes a taipan as 'Head of a foreign business in China' and also 'largest venomous snake in Australia'. In this case I mean the former.

loyalty. It was perfectly obvious, was it not, that HK$15,000 from the coffers of the German Chamber of Commerce and Industry to facilitate the Chief Secretary's visit to Frankfurt was good for Hong Kong. So were the twenty or thirty other initiatives made possible by Herr Goetting and his colleagues. Yet at the same time they were equally good for Germany. That was the whole point. Those 2,000 Germans in Hong Kong were not hostile to the Territory. It was not in their (commercial) interests to be so. On the other hand their principal loyalty was to the Fatherland. Where, on the other hand, lay the loyalty of the British? Men like Chris Patten and David Browning served the Queen and therefore, in effect, the British government. They were also required to serve their people and represent Hong Kong. But, on occasion, they might have to make a choice. It was clear that Herr Goetting felt that a choice had arisen in his case and that those concerned had decided for Britain and against Hong Kong.

The reverse of Goetting's antipathy to the Hong Kong government was the warmth and respect with which he spoke of the Chinese in general and their Hong Kong and Macau supremo Lu Ping in particular. Whereas Mr Lu's refusal to meet the Governor was a very public affair designed to seem as humiliating as possible, Mr Goetting apparently enjoyed cordial personal relations with him. 'I'm extremely impressed. He talks to people. He understands everything.'[*] Like many others in or around the business community, Herr Goetting felt that as far as Peking was concerned all his systems were in place. The departure of the

[*] Not everyone believed that Lu Ping had quite the common touch. Nury Vittachi, local writer of humorous books and columns, told me that during one of Mr Lu's visits he went round to the Xinhua house where the supremo was staying. Parked outside was a fleet of remarkably unproletarian automobiles: a yellow Ferrari, a cream Rolls-Royce, an eight-seat stretch Mercedes and eight Nissan Presidents.

British was immaterial. In a sense it had happened already. ''97', he said, 'is a non-date for us.'

When I mentioned this meeting with Goetting, most of my British friends and acquaintances seemed unconcerned. They were surprised that I was in any way surprised myself. It wasn't so much the views themselves as the vehemence with which they were expressed. 'Stupid . . . useless . . . dreadful.' And his English, honed from many years working in North America, was immaculate. He knew what he was saying. Had the British really been so bad? 'The rule of law? Sure . . . The level playing field? Oh yeah. Where were they for the last fifty years?' The Governor himself came in for serious flak. 'Either he's getting the wrong advice or . . .' And now came a conspiracy theory: 'Some people think "they" wanted Chris Patten to run into an open knife.'

It just happened that soon afterwards I was exposed to another example of foreign activity in Britain's last colony. This was an evening of baroque music from the court of Louis XIV at the China Club. David Tang was being invested as a Chevalier des Arts et des Lettres by the ultra-urbane French Consul General. The Governor was present and, as an avowed Francophile, evidently enjoying himself. (Perhaps it was his cosiness with the French which was at the root of German antipathy.) I sat at a table called 'Alice' – nothing as prosaic for Tang as simple numbers or letters – between a svelte Frenchwoman who was the *Elle* magazine Asia supremo and the deceptively dumpy wife of one of the dinner-jacketed Chinese property magnates. She was involved in the government's housing programme. Her daughter was at Wadham College, Oxford, reading Physics. She had been at Roedean previously. Lavender Patten was an Old Roedean girl too. By an odd coincidence Baroness Chalker was at the top table with David Tang and the Governor. She was the Pattens' house guest and not only Chris's successor as Minister for Overseas Development but

163

also a former Roedean head girl. I mentioned this to my neighbour who seemed unsurprised. Clearly life was just one Roedean girl after another.*

As so often I was struck by the way in which people conformed to national type and exhibited the characteristics popularly associated with them. The Americans seemed so jargon-laden and naive, the Germans so ruthless and assured, the French so suave and cultivated, the Chinese so impenetrable. As for the British . . .

The office of Britain's Trade Commission was, perhaps unfortunately in public-relations terms, in the Bank of America Tower. A new, imposing Consulate would, in the brave new post-colonial world, replace Government House as Britain's flagship. Meanwhile by comparison with the Germans' office the British seemed dowdy, with a definite flavour of municipal public library. On the other hand their magazine seemed glossier.

Direct comparisons, however, were not just invidious but misleading. Goetting's concerns were entirely commercial and, as he was eager to point out, he was not employed by government and received his funding from the German business community direct. Cornish, despite his title of Trade Commissioner, was a career diplomat and Consul General presumptive. At the moment he was in the curious position of being, in effect, the British Ambassador to a British colony, but after 1997 he would be in charge of a state-of-the-art building housing fifty UK-based staff and a hundred locals. During the count-down he was popularly

---

* The number of 'Students Leaving Hong Kong for Overseas Studies' declined slowly but regularly in the early 1990s. In 1994 most (4,555) went to the United States of America, followed by Britain (3,222), Australia (3,109) and Canada (2,787). Of these, Australia was the only country whose popularity with Hong Kong students seemed to be increasing. In 1992 she was lying last of these four with only 2,866 as opposed to 4,408 in the United Kingdom. By 1994 she had passed Canada and was within just over a hundred of Britain.

perceived to be a cut-price version of the Governor. Afterwards he would be Hong Kong's top Brit. The Governor's programme was based on the idea of the British departing; the Trade Commissioner's on the notion that the British were staying. The Governor was seen to be at loggerheads with the business community. The Trade Commissioner's job was to cosy up to it. In public, Cornish had, clearly, to support the Governor. In private, however, this might not always be prudent.

When I saw him at his office the Trade Commissioner was musing. He started off by talking about events to 'raise Britain's profile'. Manchester United, the BBC, Princess Anne and a bevy of clothes designers and architects were invoked, as they so often are when questions of British profile-raising are mentioned. Then he asked, semi-rhetorically, peering out over his beaky nose like a latter-day Iron Duke, 'Are we making ourselves so unpopular that they won't buy our stuff?'

We looked at each other, knowing that this was a question which could never be effectively resolved. There was so much bombast and hot air involved.

'People may say,' he continued, 'you lost the contract because of Patten. Well, there's precious little evidence. It's folly to think we don't suffer at all. But I think that equally it's folly to assume that we suffer very much.'

This was a sound diplomatic response. It was predictable that Peking would offer gubernatorial hostility as a reason for British business losing contracts or otherwise having a hard time. It was too obvious a trick to miss, 'trick' being perhaps the wrong word, for it seemed evident that the one thing the Chinese were genuine about was their belief that we were trying to trick them. Precisely how was unclear, and the fact that the feeling was largely mutual made it worse.

'There's no point pretending the lousy atmosphere doesn't matter,' he said. 'It does.'

I thought of the Germans and Herr Goetting. They thought the atmosphere was lousy, but for different reasons. I remembered Goetting's snort of derision at the idea of the British having provided 'fair play' and 'level playing fields'. Then I came across a valedictory essay[*] by the retiring Financial Secretary, Sir Hamish Macleod, who had worked for the Hong Kong government since 1966.

'I have spent much of my career,' he wrote, 'with other colleagues' strong support, in ensuring that here in Hong Kong we operate a strictly level playing field, with open competition and no discrimination in favour of local companies, or indeed in favour of British or Chinese companies.'

I stared at these lines; I considered Francis Cornish's expressions of civilised regret; I thought of Herr Goetting's passionate sense of rejection and foul play. These all were honourable men, were they not? After a while I found I could only take so much of this rather hothouse discussion about the relative values of different cultures and communities. It was time to escape from the tower blocks and computers and see a different side of Hong Kong.

The Tourist Association had arranged a three-day tour, including the New Territories, one of the islands and a taste of the city. I was keen to see what the Association showed tourists, particularly those who had the time or inclination to do more than shop. It is fashionable to be sceptical about tourism, tourist attractions, tourist guides and their ilk, but I was aware, often embarrassingly so, that although in England some 'tourists' never did anything more imaginative than click their cameras at the Buckingham Palace sentries there were a great number who saw parts of Britain that I had never visited. It was all too clear that many visitors never went outside the central district of Hong Kong and

[*] This appeared as 'Hong Kong, a hard-earned success' in the 1995 *Hong Kong Year Book*.

even some veterans seldom strayed from the narrow world encompassed by their office, their club and their apartment.

I mentioned to a long-standing foreign correspondent of the BBC that I was about to see the sights the tourists were shown.

'Oh,' he said, managing to look curious but incredulous at one and the same time. 'What are they?'

I met my guides in the foyer of the Mandarin. They were called Cheryl and Fiona. Fiona was Cantonese and Cheryl came originally from Korea. They were very friendly, smiled broadly and were both almost disturbingly tiny. On the first two days we did quite a lot of walking and now that the heat and humidity were mounting I found that I was sweating disgustingly. Fiona and Cheryl remained fragrant and unperspiring. It was quite unnerving and a major cultural divide. Most gweilos, even ones who had lived in Hong Kong for years, dripped buckets after taking just a few un-air-conditioned steps. Locals in similar circumstances seemed to remain cool as a mountain stream. If they found us uncouth and disgusting I could see why.

Our first call was the Luen Wo Market. The girls had brought along a checklist of fruit, vegetables and other comestibles with translations from Chinese into English. Frequently these were unhelpful because I was as unfamiliar with them in English as I was with them in their original tongue. I could see, for instance, that salted eggs with apparently liquid whites and solid yolks almost certainly derived from chickens, but in no way did they resemble the sort of thing on offer in Sainsbury or Waitrose. Likewise 'durian', a green nobbly object the same sort of size and shape as a rugby football. I had heard already that it was so smelly that in Singapore, typically, it was an offence to be found in possession of one on the underground railway. I looked it up in my Oxford dictionary and found: 'S.E. Asian tree, *Durio zibethinus*, bearing large oval fruit containing

167

pulp notable for its fetid smell and agreeable taste.' I can vouch for the smell but not, I'm afraid, for the taste.

The market is described patronisingly by the *Rough Guide* as 'the tourist attraction touted by the HKTA ... certainly worth a visit, but not nearly as good as the one further up the road in Sheng Shui'. I didn't make the comparison (the road in question is called Jockey Club Road), but the Luen Wo market certainly didn't feel like a tourist attraction in the sense that it was ersatz or artificial. It had the same dark, almost subterranean, Aladdin's Cave atmosphere that I'd met on Cheung Chau with Basil Pao. Apart from things to eat, like thousand-year eggs or mature fomented beancurd, there were Hakka hats with fringes; joss-sticks; red, yellow and gold mirrors to reflect good things; and Double Happiness Safety Matches.

I loved meandering through its honeycomb of booths and stalls, breathing in the unfamiliar smells, looking at alien but apparently edible objects, and watching the Chinese at market. Occasionally one did come across a party of video-toting tourists, but they were few and trod for the most part warily and respectfully, almost as if in church. Meanwhile the shoppers and the stall-holders either ignored them or smiled briefly. This was a working market, or seemed to be. As such it was a daunting place. The basic measurement of weight was the catty. One catty to 600 grams. The measuring was done on scales of the sort that blindfold Justice is holding on top of the Old Bailey. Biblical scales. The bills are calculated by abacus. I would not have felt confident about ordering, say, three and a half catties of Tender Towel Gourd and getting anything remotely resembling what I thought I was going to get. I guessed that most outsiders felt the same. Those who enjoyed local food – and a surprising number of old Hong Kong hands hated it – very often had amahs to do the market shop for them. Many, of course, were put off by the 'nature red in tooth and claw' atmosphere. Live chickens, ducks, rabbits, snakes and frogs were ubiquitous. So were the fish tanks, their occupants pulled out, done to death, scaled, gutted and filleted before your very eyes. Those used to buying their produce off the antiseptic, sanitised, pre-packed shelves of Western-style supermarkets balked at this. I did come across one or two intrepid gweilos who bought their food in local Chinese markets but I certainly saw none that morning in Luen Wo.

After this Cheryl and Fiona took me across the road to a small café with formica-top tables, an indigenous greasy spoon. I eschewed the fish-head congee and the toast with condensed milk and settled, like the girls, for hot, sweet, milky tea, the absolute antithesis of the thin jasmine-scented brew which I had always been led to understand was the mandatory Chinese tea. Cheryl told me that she had studied public relations in Orange County, USA; Fiona that she was shortly being posted to the HKTA office in Pall Mall, London. Suddenly the world seemed very small.

The next stop was Tai Fu Tai at Yuen Long. My geography of the New Territories was still sketchy, but the market was quite close to the Chinese border, almost exactly due north of Hong Kong Island. Indeed Sheng Shui, along the Jockey Club Road, was the last railway station before crossing over to the People's Republic. We followed the road south-west through Mai Po with its wetlands and on down to Yuen Long, which is a new town of 250,000. It is also one end of the Light Rail Transit, a modern tram-type train which runs through the centre of the town to Tuen Mun near by.

Fiona and Cheryl said that Tai Fu Tai is literally translated as 'Important Person's House'. The HKTA's sponsored guide says it means 'The Official's Residence'. Never let it be said that any aspect of Hongkong is straightforward.

The house was built in 1865, the year Lord John Russell succeeded Lord Palmerston as British Prime Minister and also the year in which the Hongkong and Shanghai Bank began trading. It was the sixth year of Sir Hercules Robinson's governorship. When Robinson arrived in 1859 there were, apparently, only four men in the entire Hong Kong administration who had any knowledge of Cantonese, and of these only one, the Court interpreter, could make even a stab at the written language. It seems extraordinary that an intricate, opulent stately home such as Tai Fu Tai, with its walled compound, its orchard of lychees, its peanut-oil tree, its ceramic roof decorations imported from the Shiwan kilns of Canton province, its murals and honours boards and painted windows, its all-round erudition and elegance, could have been constructed next to a British colony whose knowledge of the indigenous population and culture was so minimal.

But, British apologists would claim, therein lay the strength of this sort of colonial rule. Even after they acquired the New Territories in 1897, they did not seek to impose themselves unduly. They did not try to turn the Chinese into imitation Englishmen. Instead, subject to certain basic rules and regulations, they let them get on with it. Thus the clan system persisted and mansions such as this survived.

The house's builder was called Man Chung-luen, chief or at least a prominent member of the Man clan. He could trace his ancestry back twenty-one generations and is said to have been a successful merchant and a considerable philanthropist. Fiona and Cheryl explained to me the significance of the colours: red meant happiness and luck; green was for peace; yellow indicated royalty. They also said that a slippery floor such as this was a very good sign. Tai Fu Tai was deliciously cool on a sultry day and I reflected that Man Chung-luen was clearly someone of taste and discernment. After the Second World War it fell into disuse and was taken over by a destructive pincer movement of squatters and banyan trees. The residence has now been well restored thanks to HK$2.5

million from the Jockey Club. In 1990 the restoration won the Hong Kong Institute of Architects President's prize.

I was interested in our next port of call, the fortified village of Kat Hing Wai, because I had already read about Blake's gates. These, the main entrance to the village, were removed by the British in 1899 during the local militia's armed protests against British occupation of their land. Sir Henry Blake, the Governor, 'a large cordial Irishman', had them taken off to his estates in Ireland, where they remained until they were given back in 1920. I find the looting of the gates a touch surprising because Blake's attitude to suppressing the insurrection was generally humane and enlightened compared with that of his Colonial Secretary, James Lockhart. In a memorable exchange, Governor Blake told his subordinate, 'We have come to introduce British jurisprudence, not to adopt Chinese ways.' To which Lockhart retorted, 'British jurisprudence is excellent in theory, but in practice was quite inapplicable.'

Anyway, there were the gates, and I am bound to say they hardly seemed worth the trouble. I was expecting massive medieval barriers of fiendish ingenuity and impregnability, but these were thin, narrow, pedestrian iron doors wrought in a form of metallic cable-stitch. They looked capable of keeping only the most feeble of hordes at bay.

The village was a miniaturised labyrinth of lanes within the high fortified walls and those weedy gates. It *was* touristy but in a very subdued sense. The shops did tend to sell diminutive Buddhas, carved statuettes and other knick knacks, but it was such low-key tourism that it was almost indistinguishable from real life. In the low doorways old women – never men – in those now familiar lampshade-fringed Hakka hats and baggy pyjamas invited one to take photographs of them. 'Hello! Picture! One dollar!' Some of them seemed impossibly wrinkled and lined with parchment skin stretched thin over sparrow-boned skulls. Importuning

171

passers-by from their doorways, they were like the inhabitants of an old people's red-light district. Cheryl explained that the turtle was the symbol of long life; some of the old women indeed had faces that looked just like a turtle's, though I knew that was not what she meant. Fiona said there were 200 villages like this.

We lunched in Yuen Long on the third floor of the main shopping centre above boutiques with such names as Fantastic Garments Ltd and the Hopeful Textiles Co. The restaurant was enormous, crowded and very noisy: the local equivalent, I suppose, of the restaurant in an English provincial city's main department store. Fiona was amazed when I asked for, and enjoyed, chicken's feet with chili. They were a touch rubbery but full of flavour and well worth the chewing. Fiona said that I was the first foreigner she had ever known who would attempt, let alone relish, such peculiarly Chinese delicacies. In the spirit of gastronomic adventure and discovery it seemed to me only proper, though I never did pin down Steven Wong of the Tourist Association. Steven wrote a weekly food column for a Chinese paper and had agreed to initiate me into some seriously eccentric culinary practices; but sadly this never happened. After the chicken's feet the girls pressed me to try some sweet puddings made from beans, but I liked them less than the chicken's feet. They were like Bird's custard flavoured with candyfloss.

After lunch we inspected a second walled village, this one at Tsuen Wan, another otherwise new town which is the last stop on the MTR. The village, Sam Tung Uk, sat incongruously, in the shadow of the increasingly familiar tower blocks, and was now an imaginative 'folk museum'. The original village was founded in 1786 after a prolonged period of depopulation due to endless raids by pirates. Sam Tung Uk means 'three-beamed dwelling' and refers to the original structure of the village, which was based on three

172

communal halls. The founder was called Chan Yam-Shing, and over the years one Chan begat another until there was quite a large community living around the original halls. Nevertheless there were only a few thousand people in Tsuen Wan until the 1970s, when it was marked down as a suitable site for development. Like their counterparts from the condemned working-class terraces of urban Britain, two or three decades earlier the Chans were moved out and put into modern high-rise buildings such as the one I had visited with David Browning in Sha Tin.

Their village, however, was preserved as a monument to their vanished way of life and thanks largely to the efforts of something called the New Territories Relics Collection Campaign it was extremely authentic, containing real examples of everything from sedan chairs to wedding dresses.

As so often in such places I found the most telling aids were those designed for children. This museum provided a series of cards with a cartoon mandarin figure in the middle asking, in Cantonese and English, 'Nowadays, what would you use to substitute for the traditional household items on the left? Follow the lines to find out the answers. 'Progress' has substituted plastic flip-flops for clogs; electric mosquito repellers for mosquito nets; indoor water closets for spittoons (I somehow doubted that!); soft linen pillows for ceramic ones; plastic electric cooking pots for earthenware ones; electric fans for chimneys; hot and cold running water for 'water vats'; light bulbs for oil lamps. And so on. Was it fair, I wondered, to say that we, the British, had effected such changes? Or would they have taken place anyway? Like so many of the almost post-imperial answers, this one had to be ambivalent. Yes, there was electric light on the other side of the border but I didn't think it was as efficient as Hong Kong's electric light. Yes, they too had indoor toilets but I didn't think they would be quite up to the standards of Armitage Shanks. But then a cranky traditionalist part of me regretted the passing of clogs and spittoons. I was sure (well, maybe not) that the Chans would have been very happy to move from the primitive surroundings of Sam Tung Uk into a state-of-the-art thirty-storey apartment block, but a sentimental part of me wanted them to remain as they had for centuries, hewing wood and drawing water by hand in the traditional way.

A little later we were back in the land of Browning Sin Saan.* When I had stood with him at a vantage point overlooking his city, watching a traffic jam on the main road from Canton and savouring the whiff of one of the regular pig-trains bringing in the daily quota of ingredients for *char siu*† or sweet and sour, he had pointed out the Temple of the Ten Thousand Buddhas. That day we had agreed to skip the temple, preferring to have lunch at the Jockey Club instead, but with Cheryl and Fiona I felt obliged to hobble up the steps, variously estimated at 'more than three hundred' in a book called *Another Hong Kong* to 400 in the *Rough Guide*. I wasn't counting but it was a long climb up the hillside through the ramshackle suburb of Pai Tau. There is a similar problem about the precise number of Buddhas in the temple. Everyone agrees that there are many more than a thousand, each one representing a *bodhi* or follower of Buddha who has entered some sort of Buddhist grace. Once more I wasn't counting. No two Buddhas were the same.

Like many of the holy places of Hong Kong, the temple was not particularly historic. It was founded by a one-time philosophy don from the University of Peking called Yuet Kai. Yuet Kai became an itinerant preacher, fetching up in Sha Tin some time after the end of the Second World War. After establishing a monastery in the Sha Tin foothills he

* 'Sin Saan' is, very roughly, Cantonese for 'Mister'. 'Browning Sin Saan' is the Hong Kong equivalent of the Raj's 'Browning Sahib'.
† *Char siu* and rice was a favourite 'lunch-box' lunch. It was spicy and barbecue-roasted.

died in 1965, whereupon his followers put him in a box and buried him behind the temple. Eight months later they dug him up and found that he had hardly decayed at all. When they photographed the miraculous corpse the prints revealed the image of a tiger around the lower right ribs and a human head on the chest. His delighted disciples painted the miraculous remains in gold leaf, arranged them in the lotus position and put them in a glass case. There he sits to this day, gazing out over Sha Tin.

I didn't take to the Temple of the Ten Thousand Buddhas, despite its golden mummy and the tallest standing Buddha in Hong Kong – I was yet to see the tallest *seated* Buddha, which was something else again. The combination of garish Disney-style elephants and gryphons with tacky incense containers did not appeal. It seemed to mean very little to Fiona and Cheryl either and I understood why David Browning had preferred lunch at the Jockey Club. Perhaps this meant that I was just a little Englander, impervious to the mysteries of the East, and perhaps my scepticism, verging on positive distaste, was evidence of the British failure to truly comprehend the nature of those millions they colonialised. But I wasn't sure that was so. I was finding much to enjoy and admire in the *real* Hong Kong and I felt comparatively open-minded. Yet I couldn't bring myself to love the temples. I sensed about them something profoundly unlike my own notions of what religion was about. Lapsed Church of England and Buddhism make uneasy bedfellows.

The following day the girls and I went to Lamma Island, which like Cheung Chau offered relatively cheap accommodation, a carless society and a laid-back, bohemian lifestyle which seemed to appeal to the more raffish, less well-paid members of the expat community such as freelance journalists. I kept hearing stories of how the quality of life on Lamma had declined. There had apparently been break-ins – unheard of until recently – and I was told that there had been incidents of gweilo beach-bums stealing fish and crustaceans from the tanks outside the island restaurants. And there was a drug problem.

The island is only 3 kilometres from Aberdeen but from Central the ferry took about forty minutes. As with Cheung Chau the transformation from the First World bustle of Central to the Third World languor of Lamma was a severe culture shock. Ambling through the narrow streets of Yung Shue Wan in the north-west of the island we passed several denim- and sandal-clad Westerners of faintly hippyish appearance hurrying towards the ferry terminal, presumably on their way to work in the big smoke. The sun was high and hot and the girls insisted I buy a hat, so we paused in a shop selling baseball hats and wide-brimmed straw stetsons. I bought one of the latter for a fistful of dollars and walked on feeling self-conscious.

The dominant feature of the Lamma landscape is the massive edifice on the coast at Po Lo Tsui which one unkind critic described as 'The Simon Murray Memorial Power Station'. Murray, one of the Governor's closest new Hong Kong friends, used to live on the island, but, as boss of Li Ka Shing's far-flung empire and therefore of his Hong Kong Electric Company, he was responsible for this ugly monster whose two massive stacks are almost inescapable. It's a much resented legacy.

The path to Sok Kwu Wan was concrete, which sounds inelegant but was functional and well maintained. After about twenty minutes we came to a small sandy cove called Hung Shing Ye. The sea was invitingly turquoise, the sand clean, and there was an agreeable small modern hotel called the Concerto, where we sat on the terrace and drank iced tea. It was the sort of small Westernised inn which seemed rare in Hong Kong, and despite the power-station backdrop it was enticing.

From there the track wound uphill to a small pagoda,

where we took a brief respite from the heat. There were some graffiti along the lines of 'Eric loves Sally'; very few people; a scrubby moorland landscape; and, despite reports of three-foot pythons and fluorescent-blue kingfishers, very little in the way of wildlife. Then as the track dropped away the power station vanished to be replaced by another blot – a massive cement works to our left on the far side of what used to be called Picnic Bay. The pity was that the rest of the country was lush and green, and the few houses we passed on the way into the village of Sok Kwu Wan were attractively rustic. The bay itself was full of fish farms – a mesh of floating wooden frames. Apparently the fishermen are not supposed to live over the shop, but it was obvious that many did.

I was awash with perspiration, even though the walk was a scant 5 kilometres, and the row of fish restaurants along the village front was a welcome sight. Fiona and Cheryl remained as unaffected by the humidity as ever. We walked the length of the restaurant arcade and on beyond to the Peach Garden Seafood Restaurant, an approved member of the Tourist Association. This meant that it displayed the HKTA logo and was required to provide 'Reliable and polite service; value for money; accurate representation of products sold; prompt rectification of justified complaints'. The Association made it clear that it took no legal responsibility for its members' shortcomings but pledged itself to 'investigate any alleged failure by its members to maintain the ethical standards expected of them, and, in accordance with its usual practice, assist the complainant to obtain redress of a justified complaint'.

I had no complaint about the Peach Garden, least of all about the steamed whole fish with garlic and ginger. Fiona and Cheryl gave me lessons in chopstickmanship. My technique was very poor, though moderately effective in an uncouth way. The girls quickly realised that my method was essentially flawed and attempted to correct it, but not to much avail. In the days when I played squash a professional once or twice attempted to unstitch my game and teach me to play properly. Alas, in order to get better I would have had, first, to get worse. I felt it was the same with my chopsticks. They did ask, originally, if I would be happier with a fork and spoon, but I explained that like, I think, most English people I would have considered eating Chinese food in Hong Kong with anything other than chopsticks would have been ungracious and almost an insult to my hosts. The girls were appalled that I should have this attitude. They explained that any Chinese would feel much happier that their Western guest should feel comfortable with his eating utensils rather than obliged to do the 'correct' thing. I was interested but not wholly convinced. I was sorry too that they didn't tell me that it was bad form to turn your fish over when you had finished eating the top side. Whenever you did this, apparently, a fishing boat capsized at sea. Much later, dealing with a Macau sole, I committed this unpardonable solecism at, of all places, the Hong Kong Cricket Club. My fellow diners – none Chinese – were horrified.

We took the ferry home immediately after lunch, though I was told a slog up Mount Stenhouse, also known as Shan Tei Tong, was worth while. 'Stenhouse' was Commodore Sir Humphrey Le Fleming Stenhouse, about whom the latest Hong Kong history says nothing whatever. Odd, but perhaps symptomatic, that a man who didn't rate a footnote is nevertheless memorialised by a mountain.

My final day with Cheryl and Fiona was an urban adventure in Yau Ma Tei, including a walk down Bird Street and a visit to the Wong Tai Sin Temple. The area, which meant 'sesame plant growing ground', is between the Mong Kok and Tsim Sha Tsui districts of Kowloon. I was pleased, at the temple, to see more evidence of Governor Maclehose.

178

The classic view of Victoria Harbour and Hong Kong Island seen from Kowloon

Governor Chris Patten on his first day in office, surveying Shatin with District Officer David Browning and Secretary for Home Affairs Michael Suen

Street politics: Governor Patten pressing flesh

The Governor
in High Society
with:

clubland hero
Allan Zeman;

the ubiquitous
David Tang;

the irrepressible
Niva Shaw
at the Foreign
Correspondents'
Club

The Governor at the races:
receiving a miniature Dragon Boat from Martin Barrow, then chairman of the
Hong Kong Tourist Association; and presenting a trophy for a
triumphant horse

The Governor topping out:
the new Hong Kong Convention and Exhibition Centre extension
with Prime Minister John Major; and the new British
Consulate-General with Foreign Secretary Malcolm Rifkind
and First British Trade Commissioner Francis Cornish

The Governor inspecting the site of the new airport

The Governor very definitely absent from this meeting between
Ekkehard Goetting, Delegate of German Industry, and Lu Ping, China's
Director of Hong Kong and Macau Affairs

Two Governors demonstrate a different way of doing things with
Dr Stanley Ho:
Governor Wilson pins on his OBE; Governor Patten greets him at the
launching of the Foundation for Educational Development and Research

Christmas at Government House

Emily Lau
and friends

Christine Loh

The doyenne
and doyen of
the Hong Kong
press corps:
Claire
Hollingworth
and Anthony
Lawrence

Governor Patten takes aim under expert scrutiny from the British Army

General Bryan Dutton, General Officer Commanding British Forces in Hong Kong, greets his opposite number from mainland China

The last Royal Naval presence East of Suez

The new temple was opened by him in 1973 and there is, as usual, a plaque to prove it. The original temple was built in 1921 and dedicated to a Chinese shepherd who, aged fifteen, was miraculously shown how to manufacture a healing drug from cinnabar or red mercuric sulphide. The temple is therefore particularly popular with the sick and infirm, though the god is also supposed to bring good luck to gamblers. Apparently three million people a year visit the temple. I liked it, partly for its bustle, but also because, in among the noise, the importunate hawkers of joss-sticks, beggars, fortune-tellers and worshippers, I sensed far more of a religious purpose than I'd noticed elsewhere.

Paddy Booz, who has written an interesting essay on the place, says that 'above all it is a living place where common people find ways, through ritual and tradition, to keep death and calamity at bay'. I was particularly moved by one woman, quite young and smartly dressed, who prayed prostrate and alone, apparently oblivious to any outside interference. It was the same sort of private solitary worship you sometimes see in dark Roman Catholic churches all over Europe. I was intrigued also by the array of foodstuff, notably whole roast sucking pigs, laid out for the God, though actually eaten, after a suitable interval, by the laity themselves.

There were fortune-tellers operating in English in the arcade of booths, but I didn't succumb. Instead we took the MTR in the direction of Hong Lok Street, otherwise known as Bird Street, pausing for a cup of Five Flower Tea, which included chrysanthemum, frangipane, cotton-tree blossom and some mystery ingredients. Fiona wrote out the Chinese characters in my notebook so that I could order it for myself, though, to be honest, I thought the tea a bit dull and musty. We considered 'turtle pudding', which the girls said was very good for one and utilised only the shells.

Bird Street itself was a dark, congested alley of cage-bird

179

upon cage-bird. The cages ranged from plain to ornate, rather like their occupants. Caging seems to me a terrible thing to do to a bird, though part of me was charmed by the image of elderly local bird-fanciers taking their songbirds down to the park for a morning constitutional while they sat on a bench and chatted to their friends. I can't say either that I was particularly charmed by the cellophane bags full of live grasshoppers which were being offered as an Oriental equivalent of birdseed.

For a while afterwards we window-shopped until finally it was time to part. As a little farewell present the girls bought me a small dragon-and-phoenix cake. They told me that they were traditional wedding sweetmeats made from lotus seeds, flour and peanut oil. In Chinese culture the dragon is a masculine symbol and the phoenix a feminine one. I ate it that afternoon at the Rosses' house in Pok Fu Lam with a cup of tea. It was pleasantly spicy and much lighter than a British wedding cake.

I was sorry to see the last of Cheryl and Fiona with their fluent English and charming anxiety to please. Most of the world's tourist associations provide guides and interpreters for sweaty foreign journalists, and no doubt the HKTA in the new Special Administrative Region of the future will spawn new generations of Cheryls and Fionas. Indeed I had met some on my visit to the People's Republic a year or so earlier. Was it just Western prejudice which made me think that the equally smiling and fluent English-speaking guides up there were just that bit more 'programmed' than Fiona and Cheryl, that their answers came just a bit more pat, that they were less understanding towards the gweilo?

I remembered the chicken feet in Yuen Long and smiled. And why *was* it that they didn't sweat?

ELEVEN

Unlike me, the Pattens failed to attend the Hong Kong Singers' 1995 production of *The Mikado*. As a one-time leading light in the Balliol Players,[*] Chris should have enjoyed it. One of his bodyguards, Howard Leung, was in the audience the night I was there because his wife Kate was one of the three little maids from school. It sounds patronising to say that, for an amateur production, it was extremely accomplished, 'a source of innocent merriment' indeed, though there was the obligatory topical insertion in 'I've got a little list' and the theme of crime, punishment and arbitrary authority meted out by a far-away dictator had a certain 1997 resonance as well.

The Hong Kong Singers were disappointed by the Governor's non-attendance. Previous governors had nearly always turned up on the opening night, and the apparent break with tradition rankled slightly. I enjoyed it as much for its nostalgia as anything. There must have been a time when amateur troupes of British men and women were performing Gilbert and Sullivan all over the pink-coloured globe. This

[*] The Balliol Players were a wandering troupe purporting to perform Aristophanes for the benefit of leading English public schools. When headmasters realised that, in fact, they were actually putting on contemporary revues of a satirical if not quite scurrilous nature they sometimes became upset.

was the sixth time the Hong Kong Singers had put on *The Mikado* since the company was founded in 1931. I had hoped its history was more shrouded in the mists of Victorian obscurity, though its original parent, the Hong Kong Philharmonic Society, also specialised in Gilbert and Sullivan.

The history of the Singers provides some interesting little codas to the grand march of history in Hong Kong. Shortly before the fall of Hong Kong in 1941 they sang Haydn's *Creation* for the troops at Stanley Fort. During the Japanese occupation they were, of course, suspended. Their director John Smith, also organist at the cathedral, was shot dead while interned, also in Stanley.

After the war the Singers' principal revivalist was Sir Lindsay Ride, the Australian Vice-Chancellor of Hong Kong University, the founder of the war-time underground movement in mainland China and a seminal figure in the Hong Kong history of the period – as significant a person, in his sometimes shadowy way, as most governors. After a spell as honorary conductor and then president he became honorary life member.

Even now the Singers provide revealing insights, if not into the life of the Territory as a whole then at least into that of the expatriate community. 'Everyone is so busy,' lamented the director, Ian Robinson. 'Many people need to spend time out of the Territory with their work or are expected to work long and irregular hours and this coupled with unforeseen family difficulties back home which call people back to their native country means it is very difficult if not impossible to get a complete cast together at rehearsals. (I only hope they make the show!) If it was back in the UK it is a situation I probably would not put up with, but in Hong Kong if I asked every person who missed two rehearsals to stand down we would have a cast of three!'

Apart from Howard's wife and Koko, who was played,

182

appropriately enough, by a District Court judge called Bernard Whaley, I had no idea who the performers were. For the most part, however, it seemed that they were quite prominent members of the expatriate community and half the fun was watching 'old so and so', managing director of 'such and such', making a mild fool of himself as a humble spear-carrier in the second row of the chorus. I suppose the Hong Kong Players might survive 1997, but there would be no British Governor to tap his foot to W. S. Gilbert's jaunty tunes and mouth Sir Arthur Sullivan's politically very incorrect words.

> For he might have been a Roosian,
> A French, or Turk, or Proosian,
> Or perhaps Italian!
> But in spite of all temptations
> To belong to other nations,
> He remains an Englishman!

I somehow didn't think it would be advisable to put on *HMS Pinafore* in front of the new Chief Executive of the Special Administrative Region.

When I mentioned *The Mikado* to the Pattens there was a momentary 'Oh, gosh, we were asked to that, perhaps we ought to have gone', but if they went to every event to which they were asked they would never have a moment to themselves, and even as it was they have precious few. There was a popular conceit that some prominent individuals were no longer accepting invitations to Government House and, by the same token, not issuing them to the occupants. If so, I can only think that this diminution of social activity came as a welcome relief.

Having said that, it was quite common for traditionalists to be critical of the Pattens, in particular Chris, for reasons which had nothing to do with politics. The case of the Hong Kong Players was one tiny example. Another was when the

183

wife of a tolerably great and good Hong Konger mentioned that her husband no longer received a Christmas card from the Governor. He had done so under all previous regimes but for some reason his name seemed to have been cut off the list and he was feeling miffed. More than one civil servant said that Chris was bossier, more impatient and less courteous than the career diplomats and colonial administrators who had been brought up not only to wear feathers themselves but to ensure that other people's remained unruffled. I was told that, whereas Governor Wilson *always* told his local officials when he was visiting their territory, under the Patten system the Governor often arrived unannounced. Old-fashioned functionaries considered this bad form, even shading into bad manners. The argument against this was, of course, that the Governor wanted to see things as they really were and not to be constantly exposed to situations which were stage-managed or rehearsed.

Outside Government House few people realised quite the demands on the Governor's time and the constant peril of pitfalls which seemed trivial to most but of huge importance to those intimately concerned. Because I was perceived to be close to the Pattens, people sometimes tried to use me as an intermediary. There was Basil Pao's passport. From time to time PEN asked me to put in a word for some Vietnamese colleague faced with deportation from one of the Hong Kong internment camps. One man even tried to persuade me to obtain for him some sort of gong for services rendered. He had an MBE in mind. Chris and I laughed over this, agreeing that he might have gone for something a little more ambitious. Chris conceded also that he had no great interest in the honours system but probably should since it clearly meant so much to others.

Few people outside his immediate circle appreciated the demands on the Governor's time and the Governor's patience. An officer in the Volunteers said that the Governor

184

had never visited the regiment on its periodic manoeuvres. I asked when would be an appropriate moment and he, in all seriousness, suggested dawn the following Sunday. The laughter round the Governor's dinner table was notably hollow when I reported this.

There were a depressing number of thin-ended wedges. If the Pattens did make a special effort with one organisation there would inevitably be a chorus of jealous disapproval from resentful rivals. When, for instance, Chris said a few words in French at a reception to mark some French national day, the French were delighted. The Italians and Germans and others, however, considered themselves slighted. The Governor had never said a few words in *their* languages at *their* receptions. Much less, as I'd already noticed, Cantonese. Sometimes I felt the Pattens simply couldn't win. In Hong Kong being nice to one person was automatically construed as being nasty to several others.

These arguments could never be wholly resolved, but it was clear that the style of Pattenism was markedly different from that of other governors. The dilemma was similar, though on a different scale, to that facing the monarchy. The Pattens were keen to be less formal and more breezy than their predecessors, but there were those, not necessarily all stuck in the mud, who didn't think governors were supposed to be breezy and informal. And some, not only Chinese, thought it positively rude.

Despite the Governor's absence Judge Whaley, in his tenth year with the Singers, made an impressive and plausible Koko, though much to his chagrin he and Nanki-Poo got in a muddle during one of their dialogues on the first night. (All Nanki-Poo's fault, said the judge.) It was, of course, an apt role for him and when he delivered lines about his 'object all sublime' being to 'let the punishment fit the crime' they were delivered just as if he were in court. Howard, the Governor's bodyguard, in his previous role of uniformed policeman, had often appeared before him officially in real life and said he sometimes had difficulty in distinguishing between Whaley the judge and Whaley the thespian. In a sense this didn't seem to matter. Many judges and barristers are terrible old hams and the two professions have always had much in common.

The question of law and order was being much debated in public and private throughout my stay in the Territory. The Governor, in many of his public utterances, stressed the importance of the 'rule of law' almost as regularly and fervently as he advocated the need for democracy. Popular wisdom, as far as I could determine, seemed to be that, broadly speaking, Hong Kong in recent years had benefited from a police force and judiciary which were efficient and incorruptible. Or at least relatively so. By the standards which prevailed in mainland China they were blameless and razor-sharp. The fears in Hong Kong were that these standards would not survive beyond 1997. The safeguard being discussed in 1995 was the 'Court of Final Appeal', which would take the place of the Privy Council as the last arbiter in the judicial process. Throughout my time in Hong Kong it was not only a subject for dinner-party chatter but a matter for negotiation between the British and the Chinese. Those who distrusted the Chinese wanted the court to include impartial foreign judges and for its authority to be absolute. The Chinese weren't keen on foreign judges and particularly didn't fancy them operating in the sphere of national security. Sceptics in Hong Kong believed that the Chinese simply wanted to be free to put away 'dissidents' for very long terms without having to go through the boring performance of explaining why. Extreme sceptics believed they would do this anyway, no matter how the CFA was constituted.*

* Later in the year, on 13 December 1995, in Peking, the leading

The friend in London who gave me Bernard Whaley's name hadn't mentioned that he was keen on amateur theatricals. I had therefore been a little surprised when he apologised over the 'phone for not returning my earlier call and said that it was because he was so busy rehearsing. Three days a week since January. I was perplexed. An orchestrated show trial in a totalitarian state might need rehearsal but under a British judicial system, surely, the participants ad-libbed.

When Bernard had explained that he was rehearsing for the stage and not for court, we had a slightly nervous laugh about the misunderstanding and arranged to lunch after *The Mikado* had finished its brief run. Off-stage, the judge turned out to be a small, lean man in a dark suit. He had been a barrister in his native Harare, but had practised in Hong Kong for years. He had just moved into a new bachelor pad on the Peak and was suffering withdrawal symptoms from the Singers' production. We met in an Italian restaurant, Rigoletto, in Wan Chai, not far from the law courts, where he was hearing a rather routine robbery case. I said I'd like to see Hong Kong justice in action and he suggested I sit in the public area of his own court after lunch.

We talked about many things apart from the law, but he made two points about the way it operated locally. The positive one was that the Independent Commission against Corruption had done and was doing a tremendously effective and necessary job. The negative one was that as a general rule Hong Kong judges were much less strict and incisive than their counterparts in the United Kingdom.

---

dissident, Wei Jingsheng, was sentenced to fourteen years' imprisonment. No Western journalists were allowed into court and, although the local, official news reports indicated that Mr Wei might be allowed to appeal, the *Daily Telegraph* China correspondent, Graham Hutchings, commented sardonically that no such sentence had ever been reduced, let alone lifted, on appeal.

Counsel were allowed to drone on endlessly to a degree which would never have been tolerated 'back home'.

At the law courts, which were in the archetypal modern Hong Kong high-rise, Judge Whaley left me to find my way to Court 21 where he was sitting. The accused were Messrs Lonny Kwok Ho, Chan Shuk Fan, Lan Sin Fei and Cheng Kwok Chung, all of whom looked about twelve years old. Outside, Wan Chai still had a strong sleaze quotient: Club Superstar, Club Carnival, San Francisco Club, Club Celebrity; a pub called The Old China Hand with photographs of nudes in hats and of aircraft carriers, and a menu with three-egg omelettes and bacon and egg. Somehow this made the courtroom even more of an anachronism. Waiting for the judge's entrance were two female barristers in black gowns and white wigs. One, a mildly blasé gweipo, was powdering her face. The other, Chinese, seemed apprehensive and a touch jittery. The dock was heavily barred. There were interpreters, several policemen, a large royal coat of arms over the judge's bench. Moments later Bernard Whaley entered and we all stood. The transformation was extraordinary. The small, mildly anonymous man eating the set menu in Rigoletto in his dark suit had become the full majesty of the law with a silvery full-bottomed wig, purple robes, a scarlet sash across his chest.

He sat. We sat.

His Honour was right. It was stupefyingly dull. He flicked through the papers in front of him, looked up, glanced round the court with a severe expression, and asked, in the immaculate BBC/Oxbridge tones of the bench, with just a trace of African accent, 'Apart from sections five, ten and thirteen, who provided the rest of the answers?'

'The officer himself wrote it down.'

And so on. Days had already been spent in trying to establish whether or not the witnesses were telling the truth, whether statements had been accurately transcribed, whether they had been obtained under duress. It was immensely painstaking, very dull, but reassuring. A serious effort was being made to establish the facts. This was inevitably a protracted (and expensive) business. Was I being arrogant in thinking that only the British would bother?

The judge wanted to know why one of the defendants had given an answer in his original statement which he was now claiming to be untrue.

The question was translated, slowly, into Cantonese. The defendant replied in Cantonese and this was translated, still slowly, into English.

It was a stunningly straightforward answer which carried conviction.

'I fear he would have beaten me up again.'

There was a prolonged silence. The judge looked concerned.

Eventually we continued. The Chinese barrister did not seem to me to have mastered her brief. This brought out some of the actor in Bernard Whaley. He drummed his fingers lightly on the arm of his chair. He pursed his lips. He turned down the corner of his mouth. Finally he could stand it no longer. Counsel protested to him, 'Your Honour, this is all hearsay.'

The finger-drumming ceased. 'Where are you leading?' he asked the Chinese barrister, with the exaggerated frostiness of a judge in a Boulting Brothers film.

Miss Ho was floundering. The judge's fingers were beating an irritable tattoo, his mouth was a study in vexed impatience.

'Yes, yes, very well . . . very well,' he said, making it quite obvious to everyone in court that all was not in the least bit well and Counsel was making a mess of her case and had better jolly well get on with it if she were not to incur some very severe displeasure indeed.

189

I left soon afterwards, bored yet impressed, and wondering to what extent the proceedings I had just witnessed would continue after 1997. The understanding[*] was that the judicial system would remain just as it was except for the substitution of the CFA for the Privy Council and changes 'consequent' upon it. The process of turning the existing English Hong Kong law into a Chinese Hong Kong law was obviously complex – the pre-1989 *Laws of Hong Kong* ran to thirty-two separate volumes – and, as I had been told at the Cornishes' dinner, was being tackled with rigour. The government's Law Drafting Division, for instance, had a glossary of bilingual legal terms which, in 1995, totalled 12,700 entries and was growing at a rate of about 440 entries a week. Such attention to detail was certainly impressive and it could not be denied that colossal effort was going into the transition from the rule of law under the British to the rule of law under the Chinese.

Despite this I couldn't help feeling that in the future the figure sitting in judgement on the juveniles accused in Court 21 would exhibit more of the characteristics of Koko than of Judge Whaley.

In a way I was ashamed of such scepticism because so much of the rhetoric from so many quarters was designed to persuade me otherwise. Besides, for a number of reasons, some deliberate, some beyond my control, I had not given the mainland Chinese and their apologists what they would consider a fair crack of the whip. Perhaps that is not the ideal phrase.

Accordingly I called on Dr Wu.

The circumstances were mildly mysterious. I had never heard of Dr Wu until I had a telephone call saying that he was happy to see me and giving a time and place which, as it

[*] This is set out in black and white in both the Sino-British Joint Declaration on the Question of Hong Kong and the Basic Law of the Hong Kong Special Administration of the People's Republic of China.

happened, were impossible for me. It transpired subsequently that the interview had been arranged, or so she told me, by Amy Chan, the boss of the Hong Kong Tourist Association. Mrs Chan, who in some ways seemed to epitomise the new localised face of post-imperial Hong Kong, felt, not unreasonably, that I should be exposed to someone who was likely to be instrumental in shaping the image of the Special Administrative Region.* Dr Wu, apparently, was such a one. I mentioned him to Chris's press secretary, the affable Australian Kerry McGlynn.

McGlynn regarded me quizzically and chuckled. 'Ah, Dr Wu!' he said.

But he did not elaborate.

This was not untypical of his sometimes gnomic approach to public relations. The Governor frequently, if obscurely, introduced him as 'the Australian Ambassador'.

Dr Wu's surgery was in a crowded part of Kowloon and was very small. The receptionists, two of them, were in a tiny cubicle off the main reception area with a hatch to connect them with the Doctor's patients. All you could see of them was their heads, and they reminded me of a seaside Punch and Judy show. There were a pile of Chinese papers and magazines, a distilled water container and a number of framed certificates revealing that Raymond Wu Wai Yong was a Fellow of the American College of Chest Physicians and was certified as a medical practitioner by the General Medical Council in the UK.

He seemed cordial but wary. 'First of all, let me emphasise,' he began (he spoke excellent, if slightly stilted English), 'that I do not hold any office in the Chinese People's Congress. I am purely a Hong Kong person. I have no dealings and no business with China. I have no close

---

* After 1997 Hong Kong would cease to be a 'colony' or 'territory' and become, instead, a 'Special Administrative Region' of China.

relatives in China.' The sub-text to these protestations was, of course, that he was his own man, in no sense a Peking stooge, and a true son of Hong Kong. I felt sorry that he had to begin like this, and yet the burden of complaint against people such as him so often took the line that he was in some sort of unholy thrall to mainland China that I had some sympathy. I had to concede that I myself was prejudiced.

Dr Wu came to Hong Kong from Shanghai with his father in 1940 and was so successful in his chosen career that in 1984 he was president of the Hong Kong Medical Association. As such he was one of the Territory's great and good, without being unduly contaminated, despite his professional qualifications, by contact with the West. He was a natural candidate for the Basic Law Drafting Committee to which, along with another twenty-two Hong Kong middle-class professionals, he was duly appointed.

The meetings in China convinced him that the mainland was sincere in its protestations about Hong Kong's future ('Not like 1949 in Shanghai – for reasons I don't want to elaborate'). He remained more dubious about whether the intention will be matched by the execution. 'The architectural plans are laid and finished,' he told me, in what I thought was an apt image for such a swiftly developing landscape, 'but now Hong Kong people need to be construction workers as well.'

When the Preliminary Working Committee was first set up, Dr Wu was the convenor of the political sub-committee. Now there were five 'sub-groups' dealing with politics, economics, legal affairs, social and security matters and culture. Dr Wu was the group leader of the cultural sub-group.

He suddenly looked immensely world-weary. 'When the Basic Law was drafted the understanding was that the Hong Kong and Chinese governments would co-operate to arrange and prepare the transition. For known reasons this mutual co-operation and mutual trust has gone. So China will have to take it over and do it in its own hands.'

This sounded pretty bleak, but the Doctor was not abashed.

'I do not see any difficulty at all. The duties we have are very limited. We only look at matters that are necessary.'

In my notebook I have inserted a bracketed exclamation mark at this point, for the remark seemed so perfectly Orwellian, opaque, impenetrable and chilling. Perhaps it lost something in the translation and Dr Wu did not mean it to fill me with foreboding. It was the riposte of the functionary through the ages and was just as likely to come, I had to admit, from the average British tax inspector as from the average Chinese panjundrum.

'We only look at matters that are necessary.'

Most 'matters' could happily be left to the new SAR government, but a few things had already been dealt with. They were almost all 'trivial matters'. For example the public holidays for 1997 to 1998 would remain as before, in line with the agreed formula of 'one country, two systems'. Dr Wu said that he was concerned to be pragmatic and there would be 'no change for the sake of change'. Pause. 'Apart from abolishing the Queen's Birthday.'

'Abolishing the Queen's Birthday?'

'The Queen's Birthday will become Chinese National Day,' said Dr Wu. 'Liberation Day is substituted with Victory of the Second World War Day.' He paused. 'It is a different name.'

'Yes.' I agreed. It was.

'We will still have Christmas and Easter, even though we will not be a Christian country.'

I wondered about the Cenotaph. Not much chance for that in an unChristian country no longer celebrating Christmas, Easter or the Liberation.

'If the Cenotaph needs to be changed,' said Dr Wu, 'it will be changed. But it does not need to be changed yet.'

'Street names?'

'We don't need to change yet. There is no need for sudden change. It should be gradual.'

He changed subjects quite abruptly. 'We give guidelines on school textbooks. They must be accurate, especially on political and economic subjects. Also history and geography. We are doing this at the request of the publishers. They require a clear guideline.'

I wondered about the honours system. Hong Kong still had its own list. Hong Kongers, even Chinese ones, seemed happy to accept British gongs.

'Each individual may keep as they wish,' said Dr Wu, 'and if the British choose to go on honouring Hong Kong people.' He smiled a little bleakly and said, not altogether convincingly, 'It's a free world.'

'What about organisations?' I asked, thinking of the Yacht Club.

'For any organisation that is private,' he said, 'it is up to the Queen. It is not for the Hong Kong government to prohibit. But with any government-funded or -franchised organisation then the "Royal" has to go. So the Golf Club can keep its name but the Jockey Club cannot.'

I was finding this all a little dispiriting. As so often I asked about 'the last Governor', remembering Kerry McGlynn's enigmatic response to the mention of Dr Wu.

'Before Mr Patten was appointed I went to London to meet him and had a good discussion. He had a noble intention, but his way does not achieve the goal. He probably has his mind fixed. Not only does he ignore our view but also the Foreign Office view. The situation proves he has not succeeded in getting the Hong Kong people what they like to have.'

194

I thought back to Kerry McGlynn and remembered the twitch of his silver goatee beard. 'Ah. Dr Wu!'

But Dr Wu was the future of Hong Kong.

Wasn't he?

TWELVE

When I first arrived in Hong Kong the Governor gave me a book by one of his new friends. It was a real *Boy's Own Paper* effort: the story of a young public schoolboy joining the French Foreign Legion in the early 1960s and surviving with style. It was full of derring-do, amazing feats of bravery and stamina, bloodshed, male bonding, all-night drinking and robust heterosexuality. The young hero had risen to the rank of corporal in war- and revolution-torn Algeria, which was the highest rank to which a foreign national could aspire. He had then retired with honour and gone east to seek his fortune.

A fortune was certainly what Simon Murray appeared to have made. He started with a spell at Jardine Matheson, precisely the sort of old-world *hong** to which an English public schoolboy of restless disposition would apply. Eventually there was a falling-out, provoked basically by Murray's unorthodox and irreverent cast of mind, and after a period on his own he became the first lieutenant of Li Ka Shing. It was Mr Li's company which erected the hideous power station that had blighted my day on Lamma Island with Fiona and Cheryl. Murray once owned a beautiful house

---

* Chinese for 'trading company', but usually applied to the large firms founded by British entrepreneurs of the nineteenth century.

near by and commuted to Central by speedboat.

'I first met him when I was at Jardines,' said Murray. 'I liked him. He had great humility. The two men shared a swashbuckling individualistic approach to business, but the relationship did not last; shortly before my arrival in the Territory the two parted company and Murray took up a new position as the South-East Asia supremo of the Deutsche Bank. It was widely assumed that part of the reason for Murray's falling-out with Li Ka Shing was his outspoken support for the Governor. Mr Li, anxious to please Peking, was at best ambivalent about the Patten regime. Murray, characteristically, liked the idea of a governor who was his own man and who was not afraid of a few verbal slings and arrows.

By early June, when I arrived for a formal interview with him, I was becoming accustomed to Hong Kong power offices and the ritual of the welcome drink – iced water on a salver this time – and of requesting the business or name card which in my case of course I had not got.

I had already met Mr Murray at the China Club on the night of Tang's investiture as Chevalier des Arts et des Lettres. Tang himself introduced us and Murray seemed mildly put out by the fact that I knew he had been at school in Bedford. (This was a small and not very significant fact mentioned as a passing aside in his Foreign Legion memoir.) It was a black-tie affair and we were all smoking massive cigars, courtesy of our ever cordial and generous host. Murray himself was wearing a vaguely Oriental form of evening dress, a sort of black dhoti affair without a collar. He struck me as being one of those Napoleonic figures made extravagantly extrovert and potentially pugnacious by their diminutive stature. He was also doing a lot of kissing.

In his office, over tea, he was naturally brisker and more businesslike, though interrupted from time to time by European telephone calls. It is a fact of international life not

197

often realised by those of us locked into work in a single country that for some people live conversation with counterparts can only take place during a few hours of the working day. When a UK businessman clocks in at 9 a.m. in London it is 5 p.m. in Hong Kong. It's part of the reason so many Hong Kongers work late into the night.

Since moving to the German bank Murray had shifted emphasis in the direction of Singapore. He was still often in Hong Kong but not as often as hitherto. This was just one factor in his make-up which gave him a perspective on events not shared with those whose life and future were more inextricably bound up with the Territory. Like the Governor he did not believe that life began and ended here and he did not have an over-inflated sense of Hong Kong's global importance.

'We're not even in their top twenty problems,' he said, jerking his head metaphorically in the direction of Deng and his henchmen. After all, they had another seventeen million inhabitants coming on the job market every year. How could you provide jobs for 800 million people? How could you make sure they had enough to eat? These were the problems concerning 'up there'. Why should they bother unduly with Hong Kong? They had other fish to fry. On the other hand, he conceded, while Hong Kong might not be in the Chinese top twenty it was incontrovertible that China was very much at the top of Hong Kong's paranoia chart. 'What drives this place,' he said, 'is not greed. It's insecurity. We're all interested in China because we're scared, because it's so goddam big.'

As for the Governor and his proposals, he thought there would be a meeting of minds in due course.

'What Chris is proposing is not a snub to the Chinese, it's a finger-wag to the business community.'

He didn't seem tremendously enamoured of the business community, despite being part of it. I could see why he and

Li Ka Shing might not always have seen eye to eye. Despite his success he remained a paid-up member of the awkward squad.

'Goddammit,' he said, 'I mean, be reasonable. This place is as corrupt as hell. Without the ICAC we'd be back where we were. The corruption thing is potentially a disaster. It's in the Chinese interest to keep Hong Kong on the straight and narrow.'

This was clearly one reason why he was pro-Chris, but I sensed that his support for the Governor was more romantic than pragmatic. He as much as admitted it when he said that he was a hundred per cent behind him because it was so rare for a politician to have qualities such as 'integrity' and 'fortitude' and 'all those words which have almost gone out of the vocabulary'. What a contrast his moral stance was to the secret agenda of 'those fat cats with British passports in their back pocket who go grovelling to Beijing'.

I certainly wouldn't dispute Murray's courage, physical or moral, but I couldn't help reflecting that he too had his British passport and the additional protection of considerable personal wealth. He was characteristically candid about this. 'I'm not so mesmerised by 1997,' he said. 'I've been looking at my fishing rod for some time anyway. I now have a regional role rather than a Hong Kong one. That's not just by chance. And I have a place in England and one in France.'

His Francophilia has endeared him to the Pattens and indeed he was instrumental in helping them find their own new French house. I asked if they were close neighbours in France, and he produced a response which was not only very Simon Murray but also very Hong Kong.

'Well,' he said, after a moment's thought, 'we have a helicopter, so for us it's about twenty minutes. Chris doesn't have a helicopter, so for him it's further.'

Elusive though the place remained, there were a few moments such as that when I felt I had briefly encountered a true and distinctive facet of its character. There was another, shortly afterwards, when I dined at the General's. I had run across Major-General Bryan Dutton in two previous incarnations. The first had been when he was serving with the Devon and Dorset Regiment under the command of John Wilsey,[*] sometime head of my house at Sherborne School. I was researching a book about Old Boy networks. Later Dutton was in charge of Army public relations and our paths crossed again. His presence in the Territory was therefore doubly lucky for me. He came from the family regiment and he was experienced in public relations. His nickname, in obscure rhyming slang, was 'Push Button' Dutton.

He lived, in some style, in Headquarters House on the Peak. Most of his predecessors (who included a Japanese later executed for war crimes) had lived in Flagstaff House, at almost waterfront level. Flagstaff House, its views of the harbour blocked off by modern development just like those of Government House, had now been converted into a tea museum. Headquarters House, by contrast, enjoyed magnificent panoramic views across the harbour to Kowloon. It was on Barker Road, named after Major General Digby Barker, the man who for strategic purposes suggested in 1894 that Hong Kong's borders should be extended to include the outlying islands and the country which became known as the New Territories.

At dinner we ate smoked salmon and prawns, stuffed poussin and a roulade – rather more sophisticated fare than you would have got at the General's table in my parents' day. I sat between Mrs Dutton and a small Chinese wife. Most of the company were British, and of military or Jockey Club tendency, but there were several locals – another

---

[*] Later General Sir John Wilsey. He was one of the first officers to be recruited into the regiment when it was formed following the amalgamation of the Devons and the Dorsets (in which my father and John Archer once served).

change, I supposed, from the 1950s. The dress was lounge suit, but the port circulated.

My sense of pervasive Old Boy network was heightened by the presence of another general, Simon Lytle, the commander of the Army Air Corps, who was on his way to visit some of his helicopter chaps in Brunei. He, like John Wilsey, had been in the same house as me at school and, being a year or so older, had had the power to beat me with a slipper in the dormitory. This he had exercised on his birthday once, I remembered, giving me an extra stroke for cheekily wishing him many happy returns. The day after the dinner he and his wife gave me lunch at the Peak Café and he confided that he and his men had not been too sad when they were moved out of Hong Kong. There was far too little space to play with and the helicoptering had been dull. There was very little for the men to do but play soccer and volleyball and practise their drill.

This reunion was mildly surreal, but at the end of the dinner there had been another moment which seemed even more so and was also more archetypically Hong Kong. As the guests drifted away into the night I asked General Dutton if I might call for a cab to take me home to Pok Fu Lam.

'I live in Pok Fu Lam,' said a pretty Chinese woman, 'I'll give you a lift.'

We went outside, where the only remaining car was a white Rolls-Royce. She ushered me into the passenger seat and took the controls. Like so many locals she was tiny and it seemed to me that her feet could barely touch the pedals. The roads down the Peak were like English country lanes, narrow, hairpinned, the verges thick with threatening undergrowth. And so the two of us swung a touch unsteadily downhill in the Rolls. Her name was Ruby Cheney and she was involved in a lot of this and that including, as far as I could make out, magazines and financial public relations.

Next day I mentioned her to Kerry McGlynn, the Governor's press secretary. Not for the first or last time he raised his eyebrows and his little white beard gave a wiggle of surprise.

'Ruby Cheney!' he exclaimed, in much the same way as he had previously said, 'Ah, Dr Wu!' Once more it wasn't enormously helpful. 'That's Hong Kong!' he added.

How, or in what sense, it was Hong Kong was not quite clear except that the Territory claimed to have more Rolls-Royces *per capita* than any other place in the world – as well, I sensed, as more rich, svelte Chinese entrepreneuses.

Typical or not, it was one of those moments when I had not only to pinch myself but also to tell myself that I was playing out of my league. I was more at home with the hacks at the FCC and old friends like Sheila Macnamara. Despite occasional outings on junks, Sheila was not in the Rolls-Royce-owning class. The *Eastern Express* worked its staff hard and paid them poorly – even by the unimpressive standards of the Hong Kong newspaper industry. Although she was relatively new to Hong Kong she struck me as being as near *real* as I was likely to get. Paradoxically, however, I felt increasingly that the more *unreal* things seemed to me the more *real* they were to everyone else in Hong Kong.

One Sunday I went out for lunch to the house just beyond Sai Kung which Sheila shared with another journalist. I managed the underground and the crowded bus, but the final taxi ride was an expensive mystery. The driver had no English and somehow I had misunderstood Sheila's directions and was under the impression she lived somewhere called Chung Kok. I set off in the cab for what should have been a ten-minute drive and gradually realised, as time and countryside passed, that the driver and I were not at one. In the heart of the country park we found a police car with English-speaking copper and a public 'phone box. Between us all we established that Sheila's village was not Chung Kok but Chung Kok Wan. The Wan was crucial. It was as if I had asked a Gloucestershire cabbie to go to Chipping Camden when I meant Chipping Sodbury.

I found the house in the end and sat with a glass of chilled white wine gazing out at a willow-pattern bay in which, during the last few days, two bathers had been eaten by sharks. Both, curiously, had been hairdressers. The killer shark appeared to operate only for a short period and in a strictly defined area. A bit like grouse shooting.

It was a pleasant, lazy Sunday replete with the same sort of pleasant, lazy chat one might have had in the UK, yet given a peculiar flavour by taking place so far from home. The Governor had produced a thirteen-point employment plan. He had said, 'I want Hong Kong before and after 1997 to be a high-wage, high-growth, high-employment and highly competitive economy.'

On a Sai Kung balcony, looking out to sea, on a wine-fuelled Sunday, this seemed a touch sententious. The vice-chairman of the pro-China Federation of Trade Unions, Tam Yiu Chung, obviously thought so too. 'All loud thunder,' he said, 'little rain.'

The Chinese had a populist imagery the British seldom shared. Confucius, he say . . .

That evening we strolled into Sai Kung town, wandered the waterfront with the ubiquitous restaurant fish tanks, checked an expensive wine shop and a chocolatier, ate a burger in an Australian restaurant and paused awhile to take in a performance by a touring Cantonese opera company. In my notes I described this as 'deeply mad – brilliantly attired actors shouting at each other in high monotones while every thirty seconds or so the percussionist crashed his cymbals. There was an enormous audience in a huge bamboo-scaffolded edifice (a *matshed*) all talking at the tops of their voices and paying only minimal attention to the events on stage.'

203

It was certainly a far cry from the Hong Kong Singers and their *Mikado*. Sheila and I made matters worse for ourselves by agreeing that the performance was straight from *Monty Python* and trying to work out which of the actors was actually John Cleese. Of course this was arrogant and ignorant, and all too typical of foreign devils confronted by the wealth and complexity of Chinese culture. On the other hand the noise had the same effect on me as chalk scratching across a blackboard.

The following week I had another snafu involving Sheila. She was looking for a flat of her own and was inspecting a possible property on Lantau, the largest of the Hong Kong islands – considerably larger, in fact, than Hong Kong Island itself. We took the ferry, then walked along a concrete bicycle track through what appeared to be abandoned paddy fields and gone-to-seed bananas, past some ersatz Spanish colonial villas to a rundown hamlet with a working temple next to which was the house containing the flat. It was unappealing. In the kitchen the stains of smoke and grease made it look as if the previous occupant had run amok with his wok. There was a view of sorts from the roof terrace, but the general feel was squalid. The electrics and plumbing both looked life-threatening. Depressed, we headed back towards the pier. I was becoming quite familiar with the privileged life of the glitterati gweilos, but for an increasing number of Hong Kong expats life was no easier than it was in the UK. In 'real terms', whatever they might be, life for Sheila or Andrew Lynch seemed no easier working for the *South China Morning Post* or the *Eastern Express* than it used to be on the *Daily Telegraph* or the *Observer* back home. FILTH was becoming an anachronistic acronym.

We located a promising-looking restaurant, settled down in front of a large bottle of frosted San Miguel beer and wondered whether we had the energy or enthusiasm to head for the 'world's largest seated outdoor bronze Buddha' half an hour or so down the road. Both of us were feeling J. G. Linksish. The Buddha would be there tomorrow and the day after. The beer would be warm in a few humid moments.

Suddenly there was a shout from down below.

'Mr Heald! Mr Heald!'

I peered over the parapet and saw a beaming Chinese face. It was Howard, the Royal Hong Kong Police Inspector who had been the Governor's bodyguard that first weekend in Fanling and on the *Lady Maureen*. Sheila and I had bumped into him earlier outside *The Mikado*. Suddenly Hong Kong seemed a very small place. Sheila was both amused and irritated. It was serendipitous and coincidental, but there were moments when I too began to think that I couldn't walk down the street without bumping into another solicitous new acquaintance.

Howard was keen that we should join him for lunch. He and Kate were house-sitting for South African neighbours who kept a bar/restaurant a few miles away. We repaired there, ate home-made quiche, drank wine, talked about differences between Hong Kong and England (Howard and Kate had first met in Southport, Lancashire), and forgot all about the Buddha.

We were late leaving and though Howard drove policeman-fast to the quayside, we missed the 4.30 sailing.

This meant that I was going to cut the football match disturbingly fine. The Governor was attending a 'friendly' between the touring Sampdoria from Italy, complete with their Chelsea-bound Dutch World Cup star, Ruud Gullitt, and the local Viceroy Cup champions, Sing Tao. It didn't promise to be a particularly exciting encounter, but it was another opportunity to see the Governor in action. He was a rugby man and, though keenish on spectator sports, not particularly addicted to soccer. I suspected he would have

205

had better things to do on a Saturday evening (a decent claret and a good book at Fanling for instance) and that consequently he would be operating on something approaching automatic pilot. He was, however, too much of an old pro to let it show, except perhaps to those who had known him a long time.

If I had caught the earlier ferry I would have had time to go to the Rosses' house in Pok Fu Lam and change into the dark suit which the occasion demanded. The next boat, an hour later, meant that I might just make it. However, as we approached the Central Terminal, the lowering heavens, which had threatened a deluge all day, finally opened.

Europeans don't experience the sort of rain that is taken for granted in faraway places such as Hong Kong. Serious Hong Kong rain seemed to come from nowhere and hit tarmac so hard that it bounced back vertically like a short ball from a very fast bowler on a blinding pitch. European rain can make you extremely wet but tends to take time. Hong Kong rain could drench you in seconds.

Thus, by the end of the pier, I was a drowning rodent. Besides this, the downpour had the universal effect on the public transport system of rain the world over and there was not a taxi to be had anywhere.

I had two alternatives. One was to go home and forget the whole enterprise. The other was to chance my luck and presume.

I chose the latter, limped, soddenly, to the Mandarin Hotel and dialled Government House.

Eventually the Governor came to the 'phone.

'Hello, Duckie!' he said, encouragingly.

I explained my predicament.

'Oh, come on up!' he said. 'We'll sort something out.'

And so I staggered on up the hill. Presenting myself at the gates the police guards were reluctant to allow me in until a 'phone call to the main house established that I was indeed expected. From exasperated, and entirely understandable, disbelief, the attitude changed immediately to one of solicitous welcome. I could not have been wetter and yet one of the police insisted on raising an entirely superfluous umbrella and escorting me across the lawn to the front door. Halfway up the stairs I bumped into Lavender, who laughed with quite as much incredulity as the Royal Hong Kong Police.

Nevertheless I was speedily shown to the Harbour Suite, where I immersed myself in one of the enormous Government House baths. Soon the Governor arrived with clothing. I chose a natty green blazer with check shirt, matching tie, dark trousers and slip-on brown shoes. Most of these fitted well enough, though they were just a gratifying notch too large, with the exception of the shoes, which were much too big. As I shuffled along in Chris's wake I composed appropriate headlines along the lines of 'Hack not big enough for Governor's boots' or 'Failing to fill the Patten shoes'. At a lunch to celebrate Richard Cobb's seventy-fifth birthday shortly after Chris was made governor, I remarked to a mutual friend how odd it was that, of all of us, Chris should have been the one to attain this exalted position. I was, I'm afraid, rather implying that any of us might have done the job equally well. The friend did not agree, which was very unBalliol of him.

It was a dullish game, as exhibition matches so often are. Sampdoria won 6–3, though the result hardly mattered. The local team was a mixture of Hong Kongers and journeymen British imports; Gullitt sparkled but left at half-time; it rained throughout; the crowd, of 16,876, applauded Chris loudly and warmly when he appeared on the pitch and presented a cup. I sat next to a young American, son of a Patten friend, who was staying at Government House and observing the governorship in connection with his studies at

207

Yale. Chris sat next to a Hong Kong businessman called Timothy Fok.*

Despite his amusement over the business of my clothes – he even managed a laugh when I remarked that this was what governors were for – he seemed tired and out of sorts. The Daimler was repeatedly caught up in throngs of pedestrian spectators outside the national stadium and, though he continued to smile and wave as some of them took flash photographs of him, he wasn't happy. The fingers drummed and he was anxious to get on and get out.

'There are times when you need to shake the dust of this town off your feet,' he said later, over a cold supper.

'People simply don't realise how thin he's spread,' remarked Lavender crossly. As ever she was a wonderfully protective wife, as well, I always felt, as being the person most effective – with the arguable exception of his daughters – at keeping the Governor's feet on the ground.

I was given a lift home that night, mercifully, in one of the smaller cars and found myself, once again, staring without conviction at the back of an official driver's head. I never once drove myself in Hong Kong, though I did take the wheel of a 'moke' in Macau. At least I had the jostling experience of buses and ferries and the MTR to balance this oddly disorienting experience, but although part of me was grateful for never having to deal at first hand with the frantic traffic of the Territory I could see that never being able to take the wheel oneself could be frustrating. Paradoxically it meant that, on the road, one was never entirely in control. The Governor could, naturally, tell his chauffeurs what to do but he was never actually in charge of the wheels, the brake, the accelerator or even the air-conditioning. I wondered if this was a metaphor for the illusory nature of power, and I

---

* Mr Fok was, I'm told, world-famous in Hong Kong. His father, Henry Fok, had made the family fortune. Timothy Fok was best known for being married to a former Miss Hong Kong.

remembered Princess Anne once explaining why she and her father so loved being able to take the helm of a boat. It gave them a sense of hands-on control which was otherwise nearly always denied.

The night before, I was driven home in an ancient jolting Land Rover by a Chinese corporal in the Hong Kong Volunteers, the Territory's Territorial Militia which was disbanded almost two years before the 1997 hand-over. The journey was a nostalgically evocative one, in the small hours of the morning, whining and jolting through the New Territories to Kowloon and Pok Fu Lam beyond – just, I reckoned, as my father must have done, during night exercises with the Dorsets more than forty years before.

The night began at a barracks in Fanling, where 'X-Ray' Company of the Police Tactical Unit was passing out. I had been alerted to this by Kevin Sinclair at the Foreign Correspondents' Club during his lecture about bicycling in the countryside and meeting some *real* people like flower-sellers. Kevin had written an illustrated history of the police, and they too, as far as he was concerned, could be classified as *real*. This time I thought he had a point, so I took up his suggestion of going to a police passing-out parade.

The PTU is, on the one hand, a training scheme through which over 2,000 regular policemen pass every year, and also a crack unit on its own. Although for cosmetic or public-relations reasons the word 'paramilitary' seemed to be used with some circumspection, that is what, to the layman, the PTU felt like. Fanling was their HQ and every year when the company in residence finished its training they held a graduation parade much like that at the Royal Military College, Sandhurst. Kevin Sinclair's view was that I couldn't begin to understand Hong Kong without experiencing the police at first hand, and the passing out of 'X-Ray' Company was a good place to start.

My arrangements had an agreeably cloak-and-dagger

flavour to them. I was to make my way to Fanling station on the Kowloon–Canton railway. Getting out there to the accompaniment of an immaculate BBC-modulated announcement saying, 'The next station is Taipo Market, please alight on the right,' I killed time over an iced milky tea at a small café in the Fanling centre (ordered by sign language with the help of a mini-skirted, mobile-'phoned customer, who was the only person who spoke English) and rendezvoused successfully with two plain-clothes police officers in an unmarked car on the other side of the tracks.

At the barracks gates there was a procession of fond families arriving for the parade, together with a reception committee composed of burly, grizzled gweilo police officers with swagger sticks. I was wearing, half on purpose, the tie of the Buccaneers' Cricket Club, which has, as its motif, crossed scimitars on a green background. Even to the initiated these look very like Gurkha *kukris*. This time I was rewarded, because after a few moments I was accosted by someone called Graeme Large, a former treasurer of Hong Kong University, who asked if I was coming on the manoeuvres.

I tried to look somewhere between innocent and conspiratorial. It transpired that tonight was the beginning of the Volunteers' last-ever weekend battle. They were pitted against the Gurkhas themselves, and Graeme Large was one of the umpires. He had transport arriving to pick him up after buffet dinner in the Fanling Officers' Mess and he would be delighted if I were to join him. Nothing venture, nothing gain, so naturally I said yes.

The PTU passing out was entirely appropriate to a force which had celebrated its 150th anniversary the previous year and whose Commandant General was a member of the British royal family, Her Royal Highness Princess Alexandra. Even the typing of the 'Order of Parade' had an old-

210

fashioned manual sense of orderly-room clerk which felt entirely colonial.

The explanatory wording opposite the actual timetable conveys the flavour:

'X-Ray' Company was the third Company to form at the Police Tactical Unit in 1995. Personnel of the Company were drawn from both Kowloon East and marine Regions. The Officers and NCOs of the Company attended a Cadre Course between 20–2–95 and 18–3–95. The full Company formed on 19–3–95 and has undergone 12 weeks of training. A broad field of subjects including Internal Security Drills and Tactics; Specialised Firearms Training; Crowd Control; First Aid; Helicopter Training; Physical Fitness; Fieldcraft; and other related skills for duty on the SINO-HONG KONG Border have been covered.

The Company now goes to Field Patrol Detachment based at Burma Lines, Queen's Hill, for a sixteen-week attachment along the Border. Then on 1–10–95 it will move to Kowloon East Region for a 20-week attachment and will be based at Airport Police Station. From there it will engage in a wide variety of Police duties as directed by the Regional Commander.

The Company will disband in February 1996 to be replaced by 'Charlie' Company, which has yet to be formed and trained.

The parade itself was taken by Jim Hurst, the Deputy Regional Commander of Kowloon East, who was shortly retiring after a lifetime's service. A bugler played the Last Post; the pipes of the pipe band* skirled; a solitary piper played a floodlit rooftop lament; the company marched past, advanced in review order, presented arms in an immaculate general salute, and displayed its armoured vehicles. I don't

---

* The police pipers wear the Macintosh tartan in memory of Commissioner Duncan Macintosh, who rebuilt the force immediately after the Second World War.

know what effect they would have on your average rioter, but they certainly terrified me.

Afterwards we all adjourned to the mess for a few beers, speeches and a buffet. There were three speakers, all of whom sat on a high bar-level armchair, and gave chappish addresses extolling such old-fashioned virtues as discipline, integrity and immaculate turn-out. The first two were the Inspecting Officer, Jim Hurst, and the Commandant, Gus Cunningham. The third was 'X-Ray' Company's Commander, Superintendent Wong Hung Tak, whose speech was every bit as full of tradition and team spirit as those of his predecessors.

His second-in-command was Chinese as well, and of the eight inspectors at the head of their platoons only two, Inspectors Gore and Tullis, were, presumably, British.

I was quite surprised to find that there were two gweilos in the squad. Whether or not I was prepared to find the Britishness of the parade and its aftermath quite so undiluted I am honestly not sure. Already most of the top brass were no longer British and, as the turn-out that evening indicated, there were fewer and fewer expatriates among the younger officers. I was unsure about the precise intentions and expectations of those who remained. It depended on so many variables. I spoke to several officers that night and to others on separate occasions. Some were bullish and some were sceptical. Their attitudes depended on age, on temperament, on the nature of their employment and much else besides. The official line was, naturally, that 1997 was a 'through train', that, although the 'Royal' would be dropped from the title and Princess Alexandra pensioned off, the essential nature of the force would remain the same, its integrity intact.

I was certainly impressed by Superintendent of Police Wong Hung Tak. He and his men seemed reassuring earnests of the future. Of course, after 1997, the police would be serving the leaders of the People's Republic rather than His Excellency the Governor and Her Majesty the Queen. Yet the sense that night at Fanling was that the police's true commitment was to the community and that this obligation would remain. This is the essence of policing a free society, and the Hong Kong Police should, in an ideal world, be a Great British legacy. It's all there, at least by implication, in the Basic Law, and, on the evidence of that strange anachronistic evening at the PTU in Fanling, one felt the future was in safe hands. Nevertheless I longed to know what thoughts were *really* passing through the minds of the young men of 'X-Ray' Company on that sultry June evening just over two years before the Union flag came down for the very last time.

THIRTEEN

I have before me as I write a clipping which purports to come from the *South China Morning Post*. The by-line is 'Darryl Badmash' and it is headed 'Bludhist Threat Looms'. The essence of the story is that 'The Mad Maharajah of Bludhipore' has embarked with an invasion force and is shortly expected on the shores of Hong Kong. The final barbed paragraph quotes a government spokesman as saying, 'This could, indeed, be a job for the Volunteers – um, er, that is if we haven't already disbanded them.'

Anyone who has ever participated in a military exercise of however rudimentary a nature will immediately recognise the sort of pastiche scenario which has made Army officers chortle for generations. This particular example was handed to me by Graeme Large as we waited in the guardroom for our transport. The true version was that this was Exercise Dragon Apocalypse, a weekend-long battle against the Royal Gurkha Rifles designed 'to bring to a fitting end 141 years of Volunteers' exercises in Hong Kong. The exercise will be concentrated in the hills which overlook the Sek Kong and Lom Tsuen Valleys, particularly Kai Kung Leng, Tai To Yan, Pak Tai To Yan, Birds Hill, Cloudy Hill, Grassy Hill, Tai Mo Shan and the hills along the Tin Fu Tsai track.' Once again I was struck by that curious intermingling of Chinese transliteration and straightforward English names. I wondered too how many of the English names had been conferred by Volunteer officers marking out landmarks on battlefields real or imaginary. There were later references to Routes Rose and Lily; Kite and Hawk; Tiger and Lion. And finally the news that on Sunday, at the conclusion of hostilities, 'a regimental photo will be taken on the final objective, before the Regiment and the Enemy regroup at Gallipoli lines for "Brunch" '.

Sad. The Governor was, in name at least, the Volunteers' Commander, but he did not put in an appearance at Exercise Dragon Apocalypse. Later, he and Lavender hosted a ball at Government House, a symbolic last waltz for the regiment, or, more appropriately, a final military two-step. But I got the impression that the Volunteers would rather have seen the Governor out at night in battledress and charcoal make-up, moving among their camp fires like Henry V on the eve of Agincourt. Whoever wrote the spoof scenario clearly didn't think much of the government decision to disband either the regiment or, which followed, the government itself. 'Asked to comment on the Maharajah's threats a Hong Kong Government spokesman said, "Don't Worry. Be Happy." ' Which is much the same as accusing government of doing a Nero and playing the fiddle as the city burns. That wasn't so far removed from what some members of Hong Kong's doomed territorial army seemed to be thinking.

When our transport finally arrived it contained a visibly agitated adjutant called Simon Lindsay-Lord. Things were running late; chaps couldn't be contacted on the walkie-talkie; some Gurkhas had penetrated the Volunteer lines and, metaphorically speaking, thrown some grenades into our side's billets. And so on. After a rickety ride through narrow country lanes we arrived at what appeared to be a disused camp with Nissen huts within and barbed wire without. Major Lindsay-Lord had trouble getting someone

215

to come and open the gate. There was some rather cross-purpose talk involving passwords and then we were into the camp, where we found a platoon or so of fully kitted soldiery of both sexes sitting by a truck and drinking tea. One was a British regular on secondment. The others were all part-timers.

I stayed several hours moving between the ordinary unit and another Dad's Army group of older soldiers. An Indian sergeant-major called Nat Ulla had some stories of Major 'Charlie' Churn junior. The radio operator was fast asleep. Someone said, 'It's a great opportunity to get away from the desk work.' Another said, 'This is our very last bang.'

And so it was. I felt sad for them in a mild nostalgic way. The atmosphere was much the same as I remembered in my school's Combined Cadet Force forty years earlier. The Volunteers clearly had skills and some up-to-date equipment. That summer one of their girl soldiers landed a big prize at the British Army shooting championships at Bisley. But, in all conscience, it was obvious that they had to go. It was one thing for an essentially autonomous police force, arguably the best of its kind in Asia and essentially already successfully 'localised', to be granted at least a stay of execution. It was quite another for this battalion of ill-assorted irregulars, with their essentially British colonial traditions, to co-exist with the People's Liberation Army, let alone become a part of it. Better for the Hong Kong Regiment to perish honourably than to be transmuted into a parody of its former self.

There were plans for the officers' mess and Old Comrades to continue, though I wondered how easily these institutions, however innocuous they might be, would sit with the political correctness of the new Special Administrative Region. In any event I was sorry to miss the Sunday brunch at the conclusion of Dragon Apocalypse, but pleased to have captured something of the flavour of this left-over part-time

216

battalion. And my drive back to town in the Land Rover with my very own corporal chauffeur was pure vicarious nostalgia. For miles of narrow British-constructed lanes, under the brightest stars and white-painted trees edging our progress, it was as if the new Hong Kong had never come into being. Then suddenly we were on a multi-lane highway, racing giant trucks from Big Brother in the north, then becoming engulfed in the concrete chasms of the city before plunging into the harbour tunnel and emerging on to an island whose resemblance to the island of my mother and father was so pitifully slight.

As it happens the reason why the Governor and Mrs Patten were not at the final regimental brunch was that they were by the harbour, dragon-boat racing. It was, in fairness, a much higher-profile event, a sign of the future rather than a wave at the past. It was also a photo-opportunity. As the guests of honour arrived, a British photographer climbed precariously on some scaffolding and muttered biliously, 'I'm afraid the only thing the UK wants is a head and shoulders of Patten.'

Probably true, alas. It was often said that the advent as governor of a top-whack British politician as opposed to a career civil servant enhanced the international image of Hong Kong. However, there were moments – and this was one – when one wondered whether international interest in the Governor really had anything to do with international interest in Hong Kong. It might well be that a smiling Patten mug-shot would adorn the next day's British papers. Some mention might even be made of the dragon boating. Yet the reason for wanting a photograph of Chris was not because the British public was perceived as being interested in Hong Kong. It was because there was interest in Chris – in his 'secret agenda', in what he was going to do next, in whether he was going to become the best Conservative 'Lost Leader' since Rab Butler.

217

The photographer was probably right. Dragon boats wouldn't play in Wapping, whereas Patten just might. On the other hand it seems to be a running certainty that there will be dragon-boat racing in Hong Kong long after the last Governor has departed.

Kent Hayden Sadler of the Tourist Association was a keen advocate of dragon-boat racing. One night he took me to dinner at an ancient Hong Kong institution called Jimmy's Kitchen – English clubland food in suitably leathery surroundings – to meet Ronnie Wong, a Hong Kong Chinese businessman based in England, who was chairman of the International Dragon Boat Association. As Amy Chan, Kent's boss and also chairman of the Organising Committee of the Hong Kong Dragon Boat Festival International Races,* wrote in her introduction to the programme, 'Dragon-boat racing has, despite its uniquely Asian heritage, become a truly international sport.'

So, indeed, it seemed. I travelled to the event on my favourite 54 bus, which, I realised, seated much the same number as the average dragon boat – about sixteen.† On the journey I noticed the sign of Dr Wong Wing Tim, Top Hit Plaza, the Fancy Hair Club and the Sweety House. It was a foul day, though the New Zealand team who finished second in the mixed event said that the sweeping rain had the effect of flattening the usually choppy harbour, making it easier for those paddlers used to placid waters.

There were forty-three teams from thirteen different countries, so although there were 129 local teams the atmosphere was indeed cosmopolitan. In the men's final the

---

* Apart from these highly commercialised 'international' races, there were also a host of local events for indigenous teams.
† The optimum number for a dragon-boat crew is actually twenty-two, including one on drums and another on tiller. Occidentals, being heavier, often have fewer in their crews. Over twenty of the oarsmen traditionally associated with an Olympic rowing eight would sink a dragon boat.

Indonesians won with Shun De of China second and the Toronto Chinese Business Association third. The women's event was won by False Creek from Canada, followed by Shun De of China again and another Chinese team, Ya Ya, coming third. The mixed champions were Vancouver, with the New Zealanders and Germans, from Dresden, in second and third. In other words, the People's Republic of China were looking ominously good and the home side was nowhere.

As a spectacle it reminded me of my few first-hand experiences of Grand Prix motor racing. The initial impact was stunning, but after the first couple of races it became, for this spectator at least, a bit of a bore. The traditional boats are made of teak, though predictably many of those on the Hong Kong harbour that day were of fibreglass. Although there are discrepancies in size, all those competing in the Hong Kong championships were 11.6 metres long, a metre wide and 43 centimetres deep. The elaborately carved dragon's head and tail are traditionally made of camphor wood and add another metre or two to the overall length. The crew paddle rather than row and may either sit or kneel. The drummer sits in the bows like a Western-style cox, facing the crew, while the helmsman is in the stern.

So far so good. A dragon boat in full cry is an awesome sight, as is an Oxford or Cambridge eight on the Thames, but as with Oxford and Cambridge the race too often seems to be over in the first few seconds and the contest becomes a procession. Of course there were some close finishes and sometimes the lead changed hands. After a couple of races, however, I found myself succumbing to ennui and muttering to myself that one dragon-boat race is just like another. I'm obviously in a minority, but I couldn't help feeling that taking part was more fun than observing.

The Hong Kong Dragon Boat Festival International Races has been an annual event since 1976 and the Territory has been the driving force in making dragon boating truly international. Nevertheless, the real origins of the tradition belong to imperial China. In the fourth century BC in the Kingdom of Chu, a much loved populist minister named Qu Yuan was ousted from office by corrupt rivals (*plus ça change* . . .). Devastated by his exile, Qu Yuan roamed the countryside writing poems in celebration of his patriotism and devotion to his fellow citizens. Finally this melancholy man committed suicide by drowning in the Mi Lo river.

The story is that the local fishermen paddled out in their boats to save him and, having failed, threw silk-wrapped rice dumplings into the water to prevent his body being eaten by fish. Nowadays this unhappy event is commemorated annually on the fifth day of the fifth lunar month in the form of dragon-boat racing and the eating of rice dumplings – wrapped in bamboo leaves rather than silk. This is also considered good for rain-making. The ritual begins with a benediction and 'eye-dotting' of boats at the nearest Tin Hau temple. At the end of the regatta each dragon boat is paddled out to sea on a course at right angles to the temple and then back to the temple. The drummer drums throughout this performance, which is repeated three times. Then the boats are put into storage until the following year and everyone lives happily ever after, enjoying abundant rain, fine harvests and no visitations from unfriendly spirits.

All very Chinese. And as far from the razzmatazz of the International stuff as proper village cricket from the international night-time pyjama game.

The Governor did the honours at the International with his usual, slightly wry grin, rocking gently on the podium-pontoon. I, wreathed against the elements in some particularly shapeless waterproof trousers and jacket, was generally looking hack-scruffy and therefore stayed well in the background. On the whole this meant that I was ignored by those above the salt, though Kent Hayden Sadler did remark

220

that I was more than usually shabby. Eventually, however, the Governor caught my eye and wandered over for a sardonic chat – we both, I think, knew that we were not entirely at home. The effect was extraordinary. Suddenly all sorts of hitherto disdainful dignitaries, including Mrs Chan herself, became affable and almost ingratiating. How seductive and insidious are the powers of office, even at one remove!

It was a shame that the home team did not perform better in the races, but it seemed to me that the day contained an even gloomier message for Hong Kong. Here was an international event hosted by Hong Kong. Hong Kong had arranged massive sponsorship from the likes of Epson, Citibank, Cathay Pacific and Hutchison Telephone. Hong Kong had pioneered this unlikely sport and proselytised on its behalf for almost twenty years. Hong Kong had put dragon boats on the map.

And yet, for what? There was absolutely nothing about your average dragon boat which made it look like a Hong Kong product. There was nothing about international dragon boating which made it look Hong Kongish. Everything about the sport shrieked 'China'. Already Chinese crews were defeating their Hong Kong opponents on the water. Off the water Hong Kong had shown the way and the marketing was brilliant. Yet what credit accrued to Hong Kong? The *on dit* was that when, sooner rather than later, Peking staged the Olympic Games, dragon-boat racing would become an official Olympic sport. Not only would the Chinese – steroids or no steroids carry off a chestful of medals, they would also take all the credit for introducing something which, after all, was born in China 400 years before the birth of Christ.

So dragon-boat racing seemed, in a sense, a paradigm for the whole Hong Kong–China relationship. The phenomenon was quintessentially Hong Kong – a unique combination, if

221

you like, of Hayden Sadler and Wong, Oriental tradition with Occidental marketing. It might all have begun with a dissident Chinese poet, but it took imperialist gweilo ingenuity to turn it into a genuine world-wide sport. Post-1997, however, it would, I guessed, have become a wholly Chinese invention, absorbed and transformed into the motherland, like so much that seemed, even in the twilight of British rule, so distinctively Hong Kong.

This was a media event – not exactly a publicity stunt but equally not the sort of event at which a serious investigative reporter would be seen dead. I found it instructive even though (or perhaps because) it was so demonstrably (though not exclusively) market-driven. In trying to understand Hong Kong I tried not only to be open-minded but also to be open to information of all kinds, no matter how it was presented or whence it came. My scepticism varied according to source, but on the whole I went where the wind blew. It was more fun that way and more *real*. After all, the Governor himself said, as Patron of Dragon Boats, that he wished participants 'great success and great fun'. Even Benjamin Jowett, the apparently austere Victorian Master of Balliol, believed there was no point in 'knowledge' if it was acquired without 'fun'.

Shortly after my dragon boating the wind blew me into the police station on one of Hong Kong's lesser islands. I hate to do this. There is nothing more frustrating than the author's note which explains coyly that a particularly juicy plum has been plucked as the result of 'Private information'. On occasion, however, a source has to be protected. This particular expatriate policeman did not, specifically, ask for anonymity but I feel he should have it, not least because when I mentioned his name to the head of public relations for the Royal Hong Kong Police he went quite white and said that even if I had the stupidity to talk to this policeman I shouldn't believe a word he said. I could see why. He was the

222

perfect antidote to the spit and polish of the Fanling passing-out.

He was about to go on holiday when I called and he was wearing a blue shirt and red Bermuda shorts and drinking lager from the can. On the wall of his office there was a sign saying, 'If you don't smoke I won't fart'; and on the door another saying, 'There they go! I must hasten after them, for I am their leader.'

There was a dog in his office, a nondescript mutt, introduced as follows: 'This is Frank. He's a failed police dog. Friendly, isn't he? Bit smelly, but dogs tend to be round here.'

The policeman was a cross between Alf Garnett and Ealing comedy, his attitude to the natives under his surveillance benign but politically incorrect. There had been some domestic violence – 'They'd been hitting each other about . . . if she wants to make an allegation that's her problem.' The woman was a Filipina, the man Scandinavian. The policeman gave me the official population of the island, but added, 'We think it's more. But, if the government admit that, they have to build a bigger hospital.'

Was this realism or cynicism? I inclined to the former view.

There were eighty police on the island, many of them part-time 'auxis'.* 'They all live on the island and they're our eyes and ears. They work really well. Unique in that respect. Elsewhere they're a pain in the arse.'

He was a real old-fashioned copper, though not, as I had supposed, a British policeman transposed from the UK. After giving up his job as a telephone cable-tester he hit Hong Kong *en route* for Australia in the early 1970s as an indigent backpacker. He then became a barman and an aerosol fly-killer salesman before applying for the police because a

* Police slang for 'auxiliary policeman'.

223

friend suggested it might be fun. He was accepted after what he described as 'an extended interview'. Twenty years later he was on the verge of retirement. He had had a good time and running his island was, plainly, an enjoyable and relaxing occupation in the run-up to his golden handshake. At present he was on a salary of just under £50,000 sterling a year and his contract expired shortly before the Chinese take-over. He was dubious about the future, feeling that all agreements were 'very airy-fairy, very wishy-washy . . . the main thing is that no one ever says it's going to be "good for Hong Kong" '. Nevertheless he liked the place, so he thought he'd take his money out to somewhere where it was safe, then sit back and see what happened. This attitude was, in my experience, not uncommon.

His portrait of island crime made the place sound like an Oriental Clochemerle. 'There's a self-appointed village elder. He got done for corruption but got off. They're mainly fishing people. We get a bit of trouble with drinking. Couple of drunks slapped a girl after a wedding. Two hundred witnesses and not one of them saw a thing. Some of the locals think we're too lenient on smuggling, but I haven't really got a handle on it.'

His most serious problem was illegal immigration. He and his men arrested four or five IIs a week. Time was when the locals were sympathetic to them, but not any more. 'Not with unemployment at 3 per cent. Big deal! It's all bollocks really.' A more publicised headache was the island of Ling Ding, part of the People's Republic of China. The place was apparently crawling with attractive, modestly priced call-girls from the north. One or two smart entrepreneurs were organising special tours in speedboats. The islands were only fifteen minutes away.

My copper's attitude was predictably laid back.

'What's the problem?' he wanted to know. 'I don't give a

screw. In any case we haven't come up with an ordnance to stop it.'

Knowing when to turn a blind eye was plainly his first law of policemanship. You could hardly expect that to be the official line propagated by the Royal Hong Kong force, but I nevertheless suspected that it was nearer the truth. Indeed it seemed to me that this was probably a good rule for most coexistence between members of the occupying power and the indigenous population. The two found each other so incomprehensible that it was arguably better not to even attempt comprehension. Who, in the end, were the more effective at dealing with the Chinese – men like Lord Wilson or Sir Percy Cradock who devoted their lives to unravelling the mysteries of the Oriental mind or those like Governor Patten or Mrs Thatcher who never really tried? In the end it didn't seem to make a lot of difference. The laissez-faire island copper was just as effective/ineffective as his gung-ho Cantonese-speaking counterpart.

Even if Ling Ding did boast a number of unorthodox hairdressing salons I wasn't entirely convinced by its red-light reputation. A little later on the waterfront I bumped into a portly paterfamilias who said that he went there every Sunday for lunch with his wife and small children. The food was terrific and half the price of anywhere in Hong Kong. He made it sound like Montmartre or pre-war Soho, and once again I found myself questioning if not precisely disputing the received wisdom. There were, apparently, no brothels on the island. According to local legend there had been an attempt to establish one, but the fishermen's wives staged a sit-in and the place folded before it even began.

After a couple of beers the policeman showed me his armoury – locked – of firearms and tear gas, and the cells complete with notices of the internees' rights to legal representation and a list of 'duty solicitors'. There was even a prisoner for me to inspect – a wild-eyed, dishevelled man in ragged clothing who was in for drugs and was still, apparently, suffering from the effects.

'Go on, Frank,' said the copper to his dog, 'eat him!' The dog looked mournful, the prisoner dazed and uncomprehending. The copper sighed. 'They're all called "customers" these days and we have to "respect their rights". Personally I'd like to take him out and beat him up.'

He looked ruminative. 'For years they all complained about the Brits,' he said (meaning, among other things, that 'they' all complained about him), 'but now they want them to stay.' (He meant that 'they' wanted him to stay.)

I kept hearing a certain sort of British expatriate say that, just as I kept hearing them say the following, not always as succinctly as my island copper, but meaning much the same: 'The point about Hong Kong is that it's always been the sort of place where you make as much money as possible and get the fuck out.'

While perhaps not a universal truth, there did seem to be something in this. More than anywhere else I had ever been, Hong Kong appeared to be the land of the migrant worker. Some got richer than others; values were relative; but whether you were a British taipan or a Filipina maid you tended to follow your mercenary calling. One became richer than the other, but both made a lot more money than they would have done if they had stayed at home.

'Mr Tim Heald,' said Ah Wah one day, 'I go market.'

I asked her what she was going to buy. Someone was coming to supper.

'Up to you,' she said.

I was coming to the conclusion that I wouldn't have been very good with 'staff'. I thought of Chris and Lavender suddenly thrown in at the deep end over at Government House. At least they had the Duke and Duchess of Kent's former housekeeper to show them the ropes. I supposed that the Foreign and Commonwealth Office trained you for that

226

sort of thing. I wasn't sure that Balliol did. We had college servants known as 'scouts', but that was hardly the same.

'No, Ah Wah,' I said firmly. 'It's up to you.'

She grinned. 'Prawn chow mein,' she said. 'Prawn with noodles.'

The prawns were delicious, but I felt I had not handled the situation with the aplomb of an old Hong Kong hand. In Hector's office on the top floor I discovered a book called *The Maid's Manual*. It was a book designed for novice amah employers such as myself. There was a section on 'The Maid's Visitors' which carried the simple message that the maid should, on the whole, not have visitors and definitely no male visitors. I thumbed through it with gathering depression. Vacuuming should be done two or three times a week. Vegetables 'should be cleaned as soon as they come into the house'. I wouldn't have dared to try laying down such rules even if I really was my amah's boss and not just a caretaker. The idea that there were 130,000 foreign women whose lives were being ordered by this Emily Post of migrant-worker etiquette was disquieting. The notion that there were employers who would otherwise flout these rules was worse still. The Rosses seemed exemplary employers. Likewise Liz Dewar. But there were reasons for thinking them unusual.

The Anglican cathedral was a sanctuary for the Filipina maids, and the afternoon service in Tagalog conducted by a Filipino priest was now the best attended of all. The Bishop (Chinese) wasn't giving interviews, but the Dean (English) was. Christopher Phillips had been dean since 1988 but would not be staying on after 1997. He faced an uncertain future because he had been ordained in the Territory and his priesthood was not, apparently, valid in the UK. The future of the diocese was a bit cloudy too. The idea was that Hong Kong and Macau would together form a province with three bishops, the senior of whom would be the Archbishop of

Hong Kong. Alas, the synod were unable to elect the requisite two new bishops. A hung synod. As far as 1997 was concerned the Dean accepted that 'the assurances are all there under the Basic Law'. Nevertheless he looked dubious. And, if the local Anglicans can't get their act together under the British, what chance of doing so under the Chinese? The Church had 'localised' as well as anyone. There had been a Chinese bishop since 1981 and the diocese was at pains to distance itself from the Colonial Administration. Even though some governors – Governor Wilson was a notable example – had been regular worshippers, it was important that in Hong Kong there should be no suggestion, as used to be the case in Britain, that the Church was simply the Conservative Party at prayer. Unfortunately there seemed every likelihood that the Chinese would fall into that trap. They were unlikely to look kindly on the Anglican Church in Hong Kong. They would consider it part of the Establishment.

The Dean was bothered about the Filipina maids. Indeed I formed the impression that the maids constituted the single most important group in the Church's ministry. They didn't flock to the cathedral on Sundays simply because it was conveniently placed in the centre of town. It was a place of comfort and refuge: a sanctuary. He suggested I talk to Cynthia Tellez, who ran the Mission for Filipino Migrant Workers from an office within the cathedral precinct.

Although the Philippines were 85 per cent Roman Catholic, the Hong Kong Filipinas came from Anglican communities. There had been a schism at the turn of the century and two separate Churches emerged – the Philippine Independent Church, which was basically English, and the Episcopal Church, which was American-influenced. Members of both converged on St John's and both were also ministered to by Ms Tellez and her fellow workers. She had a staff of five, but

228

would have preferred at least nine if there had been the money to pay for them.

A trained social worker from the Philippines, with adult children, she had lived in Hong Kong for about fifteen years. In the mid-1970s under Marcos, she explained, the Philippine government had instituted a Labour Export Programme to boost a flagging economy. Hong Kong had long relied upon domestic servants, but an increase in the demand for semi-skilled labour in factories devoted to the manufacture of garments, toys and everything to do with micro-chips led to local amahs leaving home. In a factory they could, basically, earn more money for fewer hours. It was a classic case of supply and demand. Hong Kong needed cheap domestics; Filipinas could undercut Hong Kong wages and yet still earn 100 per cent more than they would have done at home – even assuming they could get work.

By the time I was in Hong Kong the situation was becoming ever more fraught and unhappy – not least because the numbers of immigrant domestics were growing to ever more unmanageable proportions. 'Hong Kong', said Ms Tellez, 'is not a very friendly place.' Many of these expatriate women were young mothers faced with the unspeakable situation of having to abandon their families in order to be able to give them the necessary financial support. However friendly Hong Kong might be, this would have provoked difficulties. Every day the mission counselled between thirty or forty maids, referring the more disturbed to qualified psychiatrists.

The government, she said, had not been sympathetic, and was convinced that many Filipinas were flouting immigration and employment laws. Consequently, in the late 1980s, it introduced a 'two-week' rule which said that if a Filipina's work was terminated then she must return home within two weeks. The effect of this was, naturally, to terrify many Filipinas, who would risk anything in terms of general hardship, bad pay, substandard accommodation, even sexual harassment or rape, rather than get the sack and face forcible repatriation. A significant proportion of their employers took advantage of these fears and exploited them. An employer might, for instance, demand that their maid work evenings in their grocery business or bar. If the maid complained that this was illegal, her employer would tell her that if she didn't like it then her contract would be terminated and, therefore, she would have to be back in the Philippines within a fortnight.

Ms Tellez's view was that her countrywomen were being wrongly regarded as the villains of the piece and that getting tough with them was unjust and counterproductive.

' "Cracking down" ,' she said, 'is putting the blame on the victims.'

An editorial in the Mission's quarterly *Migrant Focus* summed it up as follows:

> By stipulating that a domestic worker must leave within two weeks of the termination of a contract, the two-week rule creates situations in which domestic workers feel they have little choice but to endure physical and mental abuses if they want to continue to provide support to their families, pay for their children's or their siblings' education, or repay the massive debts they have incurred in the process of immigrating. The other alternative is for a domestic worker to report the abuses to the Labour and Immigration Departments. This means she or he will be subjected to an ordeal of Labour Department hearings, labour tribunals, and possibly also the district courts in order to enforce a labour tribunal award. This process can drag on for more than a year, during which time a domestic worker is not allowed to work and is very unlikely to receive permission to start another contract.

I found these arguments compelling and articulate. 'Overall,' said Cynthia Tellez, 'it's getting worse because of the increasing numbers; but it's getting better because we're becoming used to dealing with organisations such as government.'

Hers seemed a good illustration of the necessity, yet tardiness, of the liberalisation and democratisation which the Patten Governorship was seeking to introduce. In a Western democracy the problem would be acknowledged, the arguments rehearsed and a solution of sorts arrived at, even if the whole process dragged on far longer than any of the protagonists might have wished. It seemed unlikely, however, that there would be a resolution by the summer of 1997, and if the problem were still around after the end of British rule I guessed that it would be solved in a quite different, and probably much less sympathetic, manner.

As well as running the Mission for Filipino Migrant Workers, Cynthia Tellez was also the treasurer of a women's refuge which provided shelter for maids in particularly distressed circumstances. The shelter was founded by Lis Hamark, a Swedish missionary. When she first arrived in Hong Kong, in 1988, she came across that Sunday gathering of women from the Philippines. Her reaction was not unlike my own: 'When one sees their playful manners, their laughing faces and joyful activities, nobody can imagine what kind of difficulties they have, or what kind of sacrifices they have made.'

Imagine Piccadilly Circus, Times Square or the Place de la Concorde brought to a halt every Sunday by an army of laughing, chattering, bartering, picnicking women doing nothing more menacing than enjoying each other's company. It struck me as one of the oddest sights and sounds of odd Hong Kong. It was disturbing to realise, as Lis Hamark had, that the appearance of simple enjoyment masked real sadness; even more so to reflect on their future. Throughout my time in Hong Kong, my cooking was done and my shirts washed and ironed by women such as this. However briefly, I was part of the system which was at one and the same time

231

their exploitation and their salvation. As Mrs Hamark put it, 'To be able to have a family of their own, they have to leave it – in their wish to give their children good upbringing and education, they have to abandon them.'

FOURTEEN

My reading on Hong Kong was eclectic and sceptical, like my general approach to the Territory. This seemed appropriate, not least because writing about Hong Kong was eclectic and often misleading, opinionated or occasionally just plain wrong. One day in the Hong Kong Club library I came across *Rambles in Hong Kong* by G. S. P. Heywood. It was published in 1951 and began, 'The Colony, about 400 square miles in area, is less than half the size of Westmorland but can rival any English county in variety of scenery.'

Much of Hong Kong reminded Heywood of the Hebrides. A few weeks earlier I would have said he was out of his mind. After proper exposure to the world beyond the modern conurbations I began to see what he meant.

On another occasion I was sitting in the big drawing room at Government House and found a new history of the building with some choice snippets: several governors had wanted to move Government House to a site at Magazine Gap, halfway up the Peak; Governor Grantham was particularly keen and wanted Government House turned into a hotel; it originally cost £14,500 whereas Lord Wellesley's palace in Calcutta cost £167,000, but then he needed stabling for 146 elephants; it took 2,000 convicts to build the Upper Albert Road outside; in 1850 Lord Grey declared that he was 'satisfied that the time has come when the

233

erection of a proposed Government House may with propriety be commenced'; it was finally built by Hong Kong's second surveyor general, Charles St George Cleverly.

This was interesting enough reading as I sipped coffee and listened to the shimmer of staff and the tip-tap of Whisky and Soda's claws on the parquet. I was waiting for Lavender and Louise in order to accompany them on one of Mrs Governor's solo trips to a favourite charity, the Heep Hong Society for Handicapped Children. This had been founded in 1963 by a group of women who were concerned about the lack of post-operative care for children recovering from polio operations. Then, as polio became less common and as the society gained in strength, so it broadened its work to include young children with a wide variety of handicaps. It was the only agency in the Territory taking 'multi-handicap-ped' children. When I tagged along to one of their centres with the patron, their staff of 300 were dealing with some 2,000 children and their families all over Hong Kong. Literally translated, 'Heep Hong' apparently means 'to help to health', but with that agreeable ambiguity which so often seemed characteristic of Chinese languages, the characters also suggested 'being united, co-operating to achieve health'.

The Governor himself could be extremely informal, not to say caustic, on some of his more shirtsleeved non-ceremonial and non-political forays into the life of the Territory, but there was usually more of an entourage. Even if the press were not in evidence you felt they might arrive at any moment. And, even in the slums, tenements and backstreets he was invariably recognised and noticed if not actually mobbed. With Lavender on her own the situation felt conspicuously more relaxed and, well, feminine. This may seem obvious but, especially in a place with so many formidable high-profile women, worth stating. Lavender was more than a match for any of them intellectually and also had her steely side when required, but, at least on this

234

particular morning, the whole feel of the occasion was more velvet-gloved than when the Governor was also on stage.

Of course the children helped. Small mop-headed Chinese children often seem more endearing than their Western counterparts and their handicaps gave them extra pathos. Lavender, fond mother of three daughters herself, was not only professional but genuinely warm, tactile and experienced enough to kneel down so as to be on the same level as the children. She also obviously knew and got on well with Nancy Tsang, the impressive and articulate director, and even more so with the board director, Betty Wei, a graduate of Bryn Mawr with an MA in international relations, a doctorate in modern history and two books on Shanghai to her name. Betty was also the co-author of a racy little guide to the Territory which had already become a useful crib on such matters as etiquette on minibuses.

Despite subventions from the government's Social Welfare Department, an annual grant from the Community Chest and the Lotteries Fund, Heep Hong had to rely heavily on private sponsors. These included the Keswick Foundation, Louis Vuitton, the Board of Management of the Chinese Permanent Cemeteries, Christian Dior and the Wah May Garment Factory. But the Patron conceded that funds were limited. That meant that the organisation was never able to pay its therapists a competitive salary and couldn't offer serious career prospects. As a consequence too many staff stayed only for a few short months before heading off for something which offered them a better future. This was obviously disruptive, particularly when dealing with very young and often insecure children.

Such matters were touched on during the visit, but generally speaking the tone was light.

'We very much hope', said Nancy Tsang, describing a new Heep Hong publication, 'that our patron can write a foreword for us . . . we already have a draft.'

235

'Oh,' Lavender laughed. 'How convenient!'

I think that Heep Hong, and several other organisations particularly dear to the Pattens, was in its understated, low-key fashion an interesting indicator of what they would like to leave as a legacy in post-imperial Hong Kong. As Conservatives, they believed that charities such as this should be sustained by a well-disposed private sector just as much as by a benevolent state. Even more fundamentally they, and others like them, were keen that the British should leave behind an example of compassion to what often seemed a ruthless and callous society. It so happened that a little later six people were executed in mainland China for what amounted to offences involving Value Added Taxes. It didn't necessarily follow that such a society could not care about handicapped children, might even prefer to let them die from neglect. Nevertheless the view was widely held, if not publicly expressed, by Hong Kong liberals. The paradox was that the Chinese were supposed to dote on small children, but not, north of the border, in the manner of Heep Hong.

A few days later I went to a small meeting on press freedom convened by Fred Armentrout, the American president of Hong Kong's English Speaking PEN Centre. The idea was to create a movement to preserve the (sometimes precarious) freedom of expression enjoyed under British rule. The basic understanding behind the breakfast-time meeting, which so closely echoed similar affairs I had attended at the Writers in Prison Committee meetings in well-intentioned, often derided, politico-literary London, was that in the People's Republic there *was* no freedom of speech and that it therefore followed that after 1997 there would be none in Hong Kong either – no matter what it said in the Basic Law. Possibly even worse, there were plenty of community leaders in Hong Kong who frankly did not give a damn about such namby-pamby ephemera. In fact I heard about more and more Hong Kong tycoons who regarded the very idea as a noxious gweilo insolence.

Part of my problem, and perhaps part of every foreigner's problem, was that I was having such difficulty working out what was characteristically Chinese and what was characteristically *mainland* Chinese. I had no idea how much the attitudes of either had really changed in the last few decades. What was orthodox and what was deviationist?

One evening more than thirty years after the event, Anthony Lawrence showed me a BBC film he had made with the director Richard Cawston, best known perhaps as the man who made the first and breakthrough *cinéma-vérité* documentary about the royal family at the end of the 1960s. Anthony's 1963 *Born Chinese* had the predictable crackling grey visual quality of its vintage, but the laconic truisms were as sharp as they must have seemed when he had first uttered them. If his subjects were indeed 'born Chinese', Lawrence seemed a 'born' foreign correspondent. Although I had first met him at lunch in the soothingly British environment of Government House, he seemed to have severed roots with 'home' even though he had not exactly gone native. Like so many of the best foreign correspondents, he seemed dispassionately 'outside' everything and everyone, always looking on with keen interest and insights but no longer quite sure where he belonged.

I liked his diffidence too. At the beginning of his film he confessed that, though they say it takes six years to know a Chinese, 'I've only been here four.' He seemed to have made a decent fist of getting to know a family. Watching it himself, peering crouched at the screen with its images of three decades earlier, he remarked that one thing which had not changed was the incessant din of the pneumatic drills. He had lived more than thirty years with the drill as an ever-present anvil chorus. I was reminded of Lavender's complaint as we walked the dogs around the Peak on my earlier visit.

In his eighties, he still had a good BBC voice of the old school – dry, wry and correct without being either starchy or plummy. Part of his commentary was a deliberate send-up of stereotyped attitudes. 'Us' on the Chinese: 'Most of them don't speak English or have contact with the British . . . they all have long black hair and eat with chopsticks . . . the thing about Chinese cooking is that you cut it up very small and you cook it very quickly . . . I think they still dislike the British . . . they think we're hairy, smelly, drunken barbarians.'

I asked him, after the programme had finished, what had happened to the couple in his film. He really did seem to have got to know them even after only four years.

'Oh,' he said, 'they got divorced. We've lost touch.' He looked sad.

Almost a decade later he made another film with Cawston to mark the fiftieth anniversary of the BBC. I enjoyed his definition of colonialism: 'One lot of people running another lot without asking their permission.' If Queen Victoria had asked permission in the first place, what would have been the answer? Had there been a referendum within the Territory to decide the post-1997 situation, what would the people have decreed? If you accepted the Anthony Lawrence definition, the new regime was going to be as colonialist as the old: 'One lot of people running another lot without asking their permission.' For London read Peking.

On the official birthday of Her Majesty the Queen the band of the Royal Hong Kong Police beat retreat on the lawn at Government House. They wore tam-o'-shanters, trews or kilts, and played Elgar and 'Abide with me'. Lydia Dunn, the baroness, was there. She had just held a press conference to announce that she and her husband would

238

shortly be leaving Hong Kong for the UK. Nothing to do with misgivings about the future of the Territory. She would speak for Hong Kong in the House of Lords, have a board-level job with Swire's and live in style in London and the Cotswolds. I was not at the conference, but Sheila Macnamara reported that our friend Dr Mirsky of *The Times* asked the Baroness who would take her place as the most important woman in Hong Kong. She dimpled prettily and replied that it was 'Jonathan' who had first called her that. Sheila, born to a hard, old-fashioned Scottish school of journalism which believes in distance if not antipathy between politicians and the press, was unamused.

I was scanning the lawns for a familiar face when a dapper Indian figure tugged at my elbow.

'I saw you talking to the Governor,' he said. 'How are the shirts?'

It was Manoo, alias 'Sam the Tailor'. The Governor was wearing one of his suits, but changed shortly afterwards into a white tuxedo, also one of Sam's, before leaving with Lavender and Alice for the first night of *Phantom of the Opera*. You had to be quite a quick-change artist to govern a British colony.

That Sunday I met Martin Barrow, chairman of the Tourist Association, a biggish cheese at Jardine's, and a close friend of yet another Balliol contemporary. Indeed the two of them had arrived in Hong Kong together in the 1960s. He drove me to lunch at his grand house in the country, Number Two Shek O. Among those present was a fellow LegCo member, a neurosurgeon who talked with authority about the dawning of political consciousness among local university students in the 1960s. I shared a taxi back to town with another guest, Candy, wife of Mike Ellis, ADC to the Governor. Yet again the world seemed small.

The following day I spoke to Patrick Fegen, manager of my branch of the Hongkong Bank, and the world seemed smaller still. He was the Pattens' bank manager too and had been in the same house as me at school, where, even though he was only a Colt when I was in the house first team, he was a daunting figure on the rugby field. I had forgotten he worked for the bank until I happened to sit next to a colleague of his at dinner in the police officers' mess at Fanling. I also had a word with Nick Rhodes, the public-relations man at Swire's. He told me he had been watching the Governor practising his golf swing on the range at Fanling, thought he looked well enough co-ordinated but probably still had some ground to make up before he could give Lavender a serious game. Rhodes, an Oxford golf blue, offered him a tip or two. He was yet another Balliol man, though younger. He had read zoology in the late 1970s.

Was it my imagination, this sense that the British community in Hong Kong was a mesh of Old Boy networks? Had I really been at school or university with everybody? Was this what used to make the British Empire tick? Was it a meritocracy? Or was it a question of whom you knew rather than what, of where you had been educated rather than what you learned there? Was there something a little moth-eaten about colonists? Modern Britain often seemed inherently, insufferably and paradoxically both smug and second-rate. If this were true, was it not even more so of its last serious colony? I was reminded of some lines I found in a novel by Austin Coates, whose eye was often so fastidiously jaundiced.

Coates referred to 'the suffocating social atmosphere of the government enclave'. He continued loftily: 'At Government House, the influence of the people from the enclave quickly became overpowering round the table, introducing among the royal portraits and crown-studded plates the horrible incongruity of the semi-detached villa.'

But that was a long time ago.

General Dutton had not quite been at the same school but

there *was* the Dorset regimental connection. He even had an ancient regimental pith helmet in his office by way of proof. In that grand house of his on the Peak there was a board, rather like a school honours' board, which recorded the names of all his predecessors. Among them were John Archer and Roy Redgrave. Also on the list were four Japanese vice-admirals, the last of whom was apparently executed as a war criminal.

I wondered whether those Chinese generals who were shortly to succeed him would retain the boards.

They were certainly going to take over the house, for he had recently shown some senior PLA officers around so that they could take stock. They were particularly intrigued by the cartoons and photographs in the downstairs lavatory. The General explained that it was traditional for the British middle and upper classes to plaster the walls of their lavatories with a sort of gentlemanly equivalent of the graffiti which the lower orders scrawled on the walls of public loos.

His Chinese 'oppos' were clearly perplexed by this. There was much head-shaking and muttering. The following evening the General entertained his visitors to what they called a 'banquet' but which he described as 'dinner in the mess'. He naturally put on a bit of a show; dusted off the garrison silver; put the chefs on best behaviour; and finally arranged for a team photograph to be taken of smiling British officers sitting alongside their Chinese counterparts.

Afterwards the senior Chinese chap beamed at General Dutton and said that, now that he understood ancient British customs, he knew exactly where to put this historic photograph.

'Oh,' said the host, arching an eyebrow. 'And where exactly is that?'

'In the downstairs toilet,' replied the Chinese General, quick as a flash.

After dinner, port was circulated. Naturally. Quite apart from the fact that this, too, was an Ancient British Custom, it was a well-known fact that your typical Chinese had a notoriously sweet tooth and, properly encouraged, a marked liking for strong drink.

In time-honoured fashion the port went round the table, passing, as tradition dictates, from right to left. The first time was good; the second better; and, by the time of the third circulation, the atmosphere had become highly convivial.

One of the Chinese generals, slightly the worse for wear, decided that he would like nothing better than a fourth glass and accordingly reached out to take the decanter, which was by now several places to his left.

Without hesitation General Dutton reached out and grabbed the Chinese by the wrist.

For a moment it seemed that there was to be a serious incident, but not so.

'I have just saved you from a fate worse than death,' General Dutton told his guest. 'Had you actually laid hands on the port, without waiting for it to come full circle, you would have brought incredible bad luck upon yourself. To help yourself to port in such a fashion is the very worst English *fung shui*.'

The British General's instinct was entirely correct. Such superstitious conventions as this were readily understood. After this incident the Chinese delegation often made reference to English *fung shui*, and the fact that gweilos were also bound by their own idiosyncratic code of necromancy clearly enhanced their standing.

The General told me these jolly stories over lunch on the understanding that they would not appear in the next morning's popular press. Newspaper speculation about the size and role of the People's Liberation Army in the new Hong Kong was frequent and, in the General's view, ill-informed. It was also embarrassing and possibly even

242

dangerous. With memories of the Tiananmen Square massacre fresh in people's minds it was hardly surprising that the thought of a large garrison of the same troops who had perpetrated that particular outrage was not exactly reassuring. The Black Watch might have caused trouble in the bars of Wan Chai, but that was hardly the same.

Part of the General's problem was, of course, that visits such as the one he described were fraught with potential disagreements and misunderstandings and therefore had to be conducted far away from journalistic gaze. As a former director of Army Public Relations, General Dutton had a sympathetic, if brisk, understanding of the need to get on with your average journalist. This was not shared by the Chinese generals who came visiting. They were so secretive that the British were not told which ones were the bosses and which ones the stooges. They all came in identical mufti with no badges of rank.

'What I'm trying to do,' said the General, with a weary smile, 'is to establish a "liaison". Friendly armies throughout the world do this. They visit each other's messes, they take part in each other's war games and play rugby and ping-pong with each other.'

The British Army was a past-master at such liaisons. The People's Liberation Army had attempted such a thing once in its entire history and that with the North Koreans.

I felt rather sorry for the General. Whereas British GOCs in the past had commanded as many as 30,000 men, the General had a force of about 3,000. Press speculation about the ultimate size of the post-1997 presence was variable, though the General insisted that he hadn't left the Chinese accommodation for more than 9,000 and that they would all be confined to barracks and certainly not allowed out on to the streets to terrorise the citizenry. This presupposed on the one hand that the Chinese squaddie would be given the same relatively spacious room allocated to the British soldier and on the other that the PLA would keep its pre-transition word. I didn't see much reason for believing that either would be the case. Essentially the General's job, like the Governor's, was to continue the run-down until the moment at which he handed over to the Chinese. By then he would have conducted an orderly but irrevocable withdrawal until, by the night of 30 June 1997, he would not even be on dry land but would be commanding the rump of the garrison from a naval flagship somewhere in the middle of Victoria Harbour. However flamboyant the final parade, this was not the sort of operation for which Sandhurst and Camberley had prepared him.

'We're the only British institution which is being replaced by a Chinese one,' he said with an air of defiance. There was something in that – unless one included government itself. Certainly he was living in interesting times. He was taking lessons in Mandarin. He enjoyed most of the trappings of an imperial commander, even though the appearance of power outstripped its reality. It was not an uninteresting job, but I couldn't help feeling that he would have been happier elsewhere. Whereas his contemporaries were dealing with real-life soldiering in Bosnia and Northern Ireland, he was having to be nice to a Chinese Army which was, in effect, about to walk over him without a shot being fired in anger. Even his official 'yacht', the *Jackson*,[*] which looked like something Hebridean that Compton Mackenzie should have described, was up for sale. Worse still, it didn't even fetch its reserve at auction.

The climax of the General's stint in Hong Kong would be the valedictory parade and even that might, if certain people had their way, be little more than a moonlit flit, a slink-away with the tail between the legs before the firework display of

[*] Named not after a soldier, as far as I can ascertain, but after a banker – Sir Thomas Jackson, sometime taipan of the Hongkong and Shanghai Bank. Par for the course.

244

the following morning ('If they think that's going to happen,' said the General, 'then they don't know their General'). I suggested, only half mischievously, that the farewell parade might be a good opportunity for promoting tourism. After all, Kent Hayden Sadler, the HKTA's marketing director, was a former Gurkha and could be relied upon not to vulgarise the affair. Perhaps the General and he should get together?

I had overstepped the mark.

'We certainly don't want *them* involved,' said the General with asperity.

Perhaps because I was an Army brat I found myself saddened by the dilution of the military presence. The Gurkhas seemed to be skulking in the northern hills and there was only a dash of khaki around the Prince of Wales Barracks. I hankered after the thud of boot and drum. I would have liked to see the colours on parade.

Instead it was the Royal Navy which seemed to me to keep the flag flying, and was doing so with a defiance which may have been absurd but nevertheless had a brio I admired. On royal birthdays, for example, one of the ships of the Hong Kong Squadron came scudding into the harbour and then, as the clock struck noon, banged out a noisy, smoky twenty-one-gun salute, only marginally reduced in strength since early days when the report had blown a number of embarrassing holes in the plate glass of progress which stared down on the little ship as she performed a passable imitation of HMS *Amethyst* running the hostile gauntlet of Chinese shellfire on the Yangtse almost fifty years before.

I watched HMS *Plover* perform the ceremony on 4 August, the ninety-fifth birthday of Her Majesty Queen Elizabeth the Queen Mother. The ship made a splendid spectacle in mid-harbour, though I doubt whether more than one in a thousand noticed, let alone had a clue why she was steaming along, blasting off at all and sundry. The timing

245

was ironic, for that same morning it was announced that part of the Tamar basin, where the Navy moored before HMS *Tamar* was removed to Stonecutters' Island, had been sold to CITIC* for HK$3.35 billion. This was 24 per cent more than the predicted $2.7 billion and represented a price of $5,694 per square foot.

HMS *Plover* was one of a squadron of three ships, the only Royal Naval vessels permanently stationed outside British home waters, the last vestiges of that once formidable imperial presence 'east of Suez'. The Navy had been in Hong Kong waters since Captain Eliot arrived in 1841. I felt a certain affinity with the idea of the Royal Navy out here, if only because of my uncles Basil and Tom, both RN.

The traditional task of the East Indian Fleet was to eradicate piracy and safeguard British trade, much the same job as the one being undertaken by *Plover* and her colleagues *Peacock* and *Starling* in the squadron's twilight years. The fleet was a serious affair until the years after Suez, when cuts in defence spending began in earnest. The present custom-built ships took over from converted minesweepers in 1984.

They were a robust, chunky trio, the final Peacock-class patrol craft. Originally there were five, custom-built by Hall Russell of Aberdeen. Two, however, were deemed superfluous to requirements, and were sold to, of all people, the Irish Navy. It is wonderfully Irish to think of their home waters being protected by fully air-conditioned craft, designed to combat *tai fei* speedboats with cargoes of illegal karaoke machines.

One night I went out for a turn on HMS *Peacock*, the seventh to bear that name since a Captain Peacock captured an eighteen-gun frigate in 1651 and named it after himself.

* China International Trust & Investment Corporation. Ostensibly a commercial company but actually the mainland Chinese government in corporate guise. In much the same way the Chinese played politics in the Territory by masquerading as the New China News Agency.

The journey across the harbour to the ship's anchorage at Joss House Bay was an adventure itself aboard a Royal Marine-manned 'bouncy boat', more correctly called an FPC or Fast Pursuit Craft – the Navy likes acronyms. The FPC was a fibreglass boat with a couple of 200 hp outboards which could take it up to over 50 knots. Whereas the less expert police boats would try to ram *tai fei* smugglers from behind, the Royal Marine technique was to draw alongside, leap on board armed literally to the teeth, cut their power lines and interrogate smugglers, impound cargoes and do whatever else seems appropriate. Sean Steeds, *Peacock*'s commander, said that so far the ship's tally of apprehended *tai feis* was ten. His men were known to the Chinese as 'Hell Cats'. Commander Steeds, shortly off to command the helicopters at Culdrose Royal Naval Air Station in Cornwall, said with a certain pride, 'They think we're mad.' Bouncing across the choppy water, knees braced, hands clenching a transom to the front, bottom rammed into a bicycle seat behind, it was still all I could do to cling on. The Marines seemed to manage to stay upright with no visible means of support and to leap from one boat to another with apparent nonchalance. Not that they were reckless. 'It's not worth risking an arm and a leg for a stolen car or a karaoke machine,' said Steeds.

Each of the three ships was 63 metres long, 10 metres wide and had a gross tonnage of 763 tonnes. The ship's company was about forty, which meant they felt crowded, if not quite cramped. This was enhanced by the height of the officers. The captain came in at six foot four (he must have felt even more cramped in a helicopter); the first lieutenant also six foot four; and the sub-lieutenant under training six foot seven.* The officers messed together in a tiny chintzy

---

* His father was the Bishop of Maidstone and he had a degree in music from the University of Durham. His preferred instruments were the trombone and the organ. I like to think these antecedents and attributes were typical of Royal Naval officers past and present.

wardroom and that evening for dinner we had chicken *cordon bleu*, green peas and potatoes followed by apple crumble with custard.* The temperature outside was 32 degrees. My hosts dressed in a mess kit of evening trousers, starched white shirt and cummerbund embroidered with the scarlet and gold dragon insignia of the squadron.

I couldn't help wondering what a common or garden village karaoke smuggler would make of being arrested by HMS *Peacock*. First, the FPC would speed alongside at more than 50 knots; then Marines in combat gear with knives and sub-machine guns would leap aboard, and he would be taken to the mother ship for a confrontation with very tall gweilo officers in dress cummerbunds eating crumble and custard. He could be forgiven for thinking he was in outer space. Sean Steeds confirmed this. 'When we catch them,' he said, 'they're not very happy chappies.'

'Five per cent of our time is spent escorting Chinese gunboats off the premises,' said Steeds. 'We "assist them with their navigation out of Hong Kong waters".' This meant preserving the integrity of a British sovereign territory. 'There's no Royal National Lifeboat Institution here,' he said, 'so we do search and rescue for up to 800 miles from Hong Kong. That's another five per cent. Then ninety per cent of the time is spent "assisting the police" in their anti-smuggling operations.'

The concept of 'assisting the police' was more important than it might sound. The General had already pointed out that the forces were the only British institution being replaced by a Chinese one. In other words, in 1997, the British Navy would go and in would come the Chinese

* The chefs are Chinese and not, at first, used to English cooking. Sometimes the result is 'Chinglish' and eccentric. The original instruction form was misleadingly laid out so that officers found themselves being served with roast beef and custard. As far as the cooks were concerned, this was just a peculiar naval version of sweet and sour.

Navy. The police, however, would remain *in situ*, unchanged before and after the event. If it could be established that they, and not the Navy, took the lead in matters maritime, then the chances of the status quo being maintained after 1997 were greatly enhanced. If the Royal Navy could be shown – whatever the reality – to have taken a nominal back seat to its colleagues in the maritime police, it would be that much more difficult for the Chinese Navy to pull rank after the change-over. That, at least, was the theory.

The atmosphere that night was gratifyingly like a black and white film starring Jack Hawkins with young Richard Attenboroughs and Bryan Forbeses in support. We weighed anchor at six. Fifteen or so convened on the bridge to synchronise watches and learn that there was a 10-knot wind, good visibility and no cloud cover. They were tasked for smuggling and then territorial integrity, maintenance of. At 8.15 the two FPCs were silently winched over the side and sped off like whippets after a hare. On the darkened bridge we watched on the screen as infra-red cameras relayed their position. Very soon they boarded a junk and we heard excited voices on the radio. The junk was unlit and carrying a suspicious cargo.

'Definitely beer, sir!'

'Arrest them and impound the cargo.'

Alas, however, papers were in order and the beer legal.

Enormous binoculars swept the horizon . . . 'Starboard Fifteen' . . . 'Eight cables on the starboard quarter'. The main gun, a 76 mm OTO MELARA, was capable of firing eighty-five rounds a minute at a range of 6 miles and was thought quite capable of frightening off any Chinese naval craft likely to be in the vicinity. The four general-purpose machine guns and the two rocket launchers were deemed enough to cope with any smugglers.

For an hour or so the two FPC swooped about the Hong Kong waters, boarding vessels, inspecting papers, putting the fear of God, and of the Queen, into the natives. I was almost persuaded that in this corner of a far-off sea the Royal Navy did still rule the waves, even if it was only for a few more years. Racing back to the Prince of Wales Barracks in our high-speed inflatables, we zoomed cheekily past a visiting American warship in the harbour, almost flying by in an aquaplaning rude gesture at the stationary might of the United States. Rule Britannia!

Unfortunately, stepping ashore, I stumbled and caught my shin on the harbour steps. As I collected a change of clothes from the nearby Furama Kempinski Hotel, my trousers felt damp and, glancing down, I saw that blood was positively pumping out and was staining my trouser leg crimson. The smartly uniformed concierge in that marbled hall noticed my alarm and saw the blood. His expression evinced not the slightest concern but only outrage and disgust. It was obvious that all he was worried about was getting blood on his spotless floor. For a moment I thought this was a very Hong Kong reaction, but then, grimacing myself, I reflected that it was probably Grand Hotels the whole world over and limped towards the taxi rank, feeling relieved that the officers of HMS *Peacock*, magnificent in their dressy evening kit, were unable to witness this bathetic anti-climax to an evening of Eastern gunboat diplomacy in a Palmerstonian tradition we will not see again.

FIFTEEN

Peter Woo, the suave, plausible multi-millionaire boss of the Wharf Group, told me that he thought of the Governor as the coach of an inexperienced football team. He saw Patten as a gnarled old democrat, veteran of many a cut-and-thrust debate in the Mother of Parliaments, himself an acquiescent victim of the democratic process, architect of one of the most unexpected election victories in parliamentary history, the Terry Venables of free speech and one-man-one-vote. Hong Kong politicians, bright, articulate, well educated though they might be, had lived all their lives in an authoritarian, paternalistic society where the role of the populace was to be seen, not heard. They were the political equivalent of the United Arab Emirates in football. However naturally talented they might be, they needed lessons.

Unfortunately, the arrival of the first 'democratic' Governor – if that was not a contradiction in terms – came only a few years before Hong Kong was to be handed over to a country which made British colonialism look like a laissez-faire Utopia. Many people acknowledged this. Those that didn't tended to react with a petulance that suggested, to me at least, that they didn't disagree with the diagnosis as much as they pretended. As Anthony Lawrence, shrewd as ever, said on the radio one day, 'Anyone who thinks that the Chinese are going to allow Hong Kong to run itself as it

251

wants is living in Cloud Cuckoo Land.' Yet the Basic Law, with its central premise of 'one country, two systems', suggested just that. No wonder, therefore, that in the run-up to 1997 Hong Kong politicians of all persuasions – including the Governor – sometimes exhibited signs of strain. It isn't easy living in Cloud Cuckoo Land.

Probably the best-known politician in the Territory was Martin Lee, the lawyer who led the Democratic Party. Had Hong Kong truly been a democracy, there was a case for saying that Lee would have been its elected leader. As it was, in the sort of half-baked LegCo which was as near as Hong Kong got to an elected parliament, Lee was the closest approximation to the people's representative. I first heard him speak at a lunch in the Foreign Correspondents' Club, where he struck me as a fine example of the best sort of British legacy. Intelligent, humorous, passionate, yet para-doxically *dis*passionate, he seemed the very model of the Lincoln's Inn barrister. He had studied law there in the 1960s, living in reduced circumstances in King's Cross, where he apparently subsisted on a diet of Walls luncheon meat, and fried rice with a dash of brandy. By the time he took to politics in the 1980s he was reputed to be the highest-paid Queen's Counsel in town. His father had been a Kuomintang general.* His son was at school at Winchester.

As much of a *bête noire* to the Communist Chinese as the Governor himself, he was even more of a darling to Western liberal opinion, particularly in the USA. He seemed to be able to command columns at will in the *New York Times* and *Wall Street Journal*, and if a television news programme wanted a 'moderate' (in other words, 'anti-Beijing') voice, then Lee's was top of the shopping list.

Understandably the Governor found this tiresome, not

---

* Kuomintang was the Chinese Nationalist Party, ousted by Chairman Mao's Communists in 1949, but still in power in Taiwan.

least because there was a point up to which he himself played the moral, Christian, Roman Catholic card. It increasingly looked as if Lee had trumped this. Even if he was not actually canonised in certain quarters, he was widely regarded as a politician who somehow contrived to be above politics. Often that summer I heard the Governor complaining that he was fed up with having to treat Martin Lee as if he were some sort of saint. Once when I remarked, naively I suppose, that Lee felt 'betrayed', Chris became quite shirty. 'Where', he wanted to know, were 'they' – meaning Lee and his friends – 'when *we* needed *them*?' It was all very well for them to complain that he was selling Hong Kong short on the Court of Final Appeal, but why had they not said anything when Peking was abusing him in the past?

The Court of Final Appeal was the key political issue during much of my time in Hong Kong, though I felt it was not so much an issue in itself as just another expression of the only political issue which mattered, namely what was going to happen in Hong Kong after 1997. Sometimes this manifested itself in questions about passports; sometimes in questions about the number of Chinese troops to be garrisoned in the Territory; sometimes in questions about the naming of streets and clubs; sometimes in questions about the economy; sometimes in questions about the rule of law. Always there were questions, some apparently trivial, others clearly profound. In the end, they all boiled down to the same question. Everyone asked it. No one seemed able to produce a satisfactory answer.

Without getting too bogged down in the intricacies of the Court of Final Appeal, the issue was what precisely should replace the British Privy Council as the last legal resort of the Hong Kong citizen. In the most extreme example someone condemned to death in Hong Kong under colonial rule had the right to appeal to the Privy Council in London to have the sentence overturned. This meant that independent law

253

lords in Britain had the ultimate and absolute right to determine the course of justice in the Colony.

Clearly this state of affairs could not continue under Chinese rule, but it was agreed that there should be some sort of equivalent. Chapter Four, Section Four of the Basic Law set out all sorts of safeguards which read reassuringly well. It was clear that there was to be a 'Court of Final Appeal' but not at all clear who would sit on it. Article 82 said that the court 'may as required invite judges from other common law jurisdictions to sit on the Court of Final Appeal'. However, I was unable to find any indication of what 'as required' could possibly mean. The wording suggested that the court itself would decide what was required, but I could see nothing to indicate whether the original court would include foreign judges or not. All that was clear was that the court's Chief Justice would be a 'permanent resident of the Region with no right of abode in any foreign country'. Nor was it clear whether there would be any restrictions over the court's jurisdiction.

These and other matters were the subject of negotiation between Britain and China during that summer. The British position seemed to be weakened by their desire to have the new court 'up and running' by the time of the hand-over, whereas the Chinese seemed not to be bothered one way or the other. Britain evidently wanted as many non-Chinese judges in the court as possible. China obviously didn't. China was keen to exempt certain 'acts against the State'. Ostensibly this meant such matters as treason or espionage, though the Martin Lee camp argued that it was a catch-all phrase capable of any interpretation. It would be used, one way or another, to suppress 'dissidents'.

In the event, an agreement was reached. The Governor, clearly not entirely happy with it, took the view, in public, that the compromise was a triumph for pragmatism and *realpolitik.* Martin Lee and his supporters thought it was a sell-out.

Before I talked to Lee himself I spent some time with Minky Worden. Surprisingly, this name seldom if ever featured in reports of Lee's activities. A young American activist, she became aware of Lee while she was working at the Justice Department in Washington and was so entranced that she decided she was going to work for him come hell or high water. She accordingly resigned her job, flew to Hong Kong and, within a few weeks, was installed as Lee's political assistant. I think that gives a misleading impression of her influence. It was clear to me not only that she was the sole way to getting an interview with him but also that she was used to orchestrating what he said and what any interlocutor such as myself should think and write. Before my meeting with the great man, Minky bombarded me with – very useful – faxes as well as giving me a long lecture about the iniquities of the British in general and the Governor in particular. During the interview itself she was present throughout and frequently interjected directions such as 'Martin, tell him about . . .' or 'Martin, you've forgotten about . . .' On the whole, it seemed to me, Martin did as he was told.

Minky was livid about the agreement on the CFA. 'The rule of law was all that was left,' she said. 'Now anything that the Bank of China says or does will be treated as "an Act of State".'

Of the Chinese and Hong Kong she said, 'It's like a gorilla with a Stradivarius.'*

---

* Metaphors and similes such as this were commonplace. A favourite was 'It's like giving a Rolls-Royce to someone who's only ever ridden a bicycle.' Bryan Dutton, the General, produced one of the best when he said the Chinese reminded him of a bashful male wallflower at his first dance. They liked the idea of dancing with a pretty girl, but had no idea of how to set about it.

And of Chris Patten, she said, 'The Governor can't save Hong Kong but he doesn't have to leave them without the means to do it for themselves.'

None of these lines would have been surprising if they had been uttered by Martin Lee himself. I did wonder, despite Minky Worden's manifest inexperience, who in this instance was the organ-grinder and who was the monkey.

I finally met Lee the morning after a vote of no confidence in the Governor was lost by 35 to 17 in LegCo. The odd thing was that those expressing no confidence were those who had previously been thought of as Patten allies – the liberal progressives – whereas those defending him were old-guard pragmatists with whom he was supposed to be out of favour. Lee's office was on the seventh floor of the Admiralty Centre behind a door which was almost a parody of the entrance to any chambers in the Inns of Court. The name of Mr Martin C. M. Lee QC came first, followed by Messrs Wong, Li, Yu and Lung and finally Sir John Swaine QC, LegCo's President. Inside, the office continued the theme, being all leather and law reports, though I was pleased to see a copy of Douglas Hurd's book, *The Arrow War*, about another Chinese conflict in the middle of the nineteenth century.

I found Lee immensely courteous but faintly chilly. Like many politicians speaking on the record, he said little that he hadn't already said in public, though his disillusion with Chris seemed real and raw. He had watched TV when the election result from Bath came through and seen the genuine shock and distress register on both Pattens' faces. It made him, he said, think that he would be dealing with a real human being. 'This guy,' he said, 'has to be an honest man.' Then, when he went to meet him for the first time, he took along a small gift. He had read that Chris had a bit of a weight problem and was trying to diet, so thought that he would present him with a healthy-living book entitled *Fit for*

Life. Inside he wrote, 'For a big man who aspires to be smaller.'

After telling me this, Lee shook his head and smiled ruefully. 'At the time,' he said, 'I did not realise the truth of what I wrote.'

He added bitterly, 'Whatever good he did he has made irrelevant by the deal he did on the Court of Final Appeal. Last night in LegCo the rumour was that he is going back to England and will not come back. He has no friends.'

The CFA was dear to Lee's heart because, as a lawyer, he believed that 'the rule of law is everything. That's why I entered politics.'

There were those who said that he was still, essentially, a lawyer, and had not yet learnt how to be a politician. True or not, he had, despite the coolness, an almost messianic quality about him. 'My biggest worry,' he said, apropos 1997, 'is not for me but for my party and my people, because unless the Chinese government can be brought round to trusting the Chinese people there is no future. How can I help? We have to have dialogue with the Chinese. If the Chinese refuse to have a dialogue there is no hope, but maybe I can find a way by which I could be sitting down with them and having a dialogue.'

I was surprised by this, for I had always thought that Martin Lee was as adamant about not being able to have a dialogue with Peking as Peking was about the impossibility of having a dialogue with him. 'That's what I did before Tiananmen,' he said. 'You have to have a middle man and I am optimistic, maybe naively . . . We keep on winning elections and they know it.'

This was true, but I found the references to 'my' party and 'my' people just a touch unnerving and proprietorial. I wondered whether, given certain circumstances, this Mr Lee had it in him to be as autocratic, despite his credentials, as that other Western-educated Mr Lee, the father of modern

257

Singapore, Hong Kong's most obvious rival in the Oriental city-state stakes. There were similarities – moral and intellectual certainty being the most obvious.

A little later he told me a story, an old Chinese tale whose real meaning eluded me. I think it is a widely held Western belief that many Chinese like to talk in riddles and conundrums such as this, often preceded by the words, 'Confucius he say'.* Such Western prejudices are often wrong, but this one seemed to me to have a basis in truth. The Chinese have a parable for every eventuality.

'I have a dog,' said Mr Lee. 'When my dog sees a stranger it barks at him. I decide to emigrate but I cannot take my dog. My friend will take the dog but he does not like the dog to bark at strangers. So I beat my dog every time it barks so that it learns not to do so. If my friend did it, it would be much worse for the dog.'

End of story.

I was mildly perplexed by it at the time and I remain mildly perplexed by it to this day. I take it that 'I' represents the British; the dog is Hong Kong; and the friend is China. I could be wrong. In any event I thought it characteristically oracular. It was difficult, if not impossible, to know quite how to respond. It might have meant nothing whatever, but it sounded disturbingly mysterious and profound – just as, I judged, it was intended to.

After I left Hong Kong and after Lee's lot did well in autumn elections, a long magazine article appeared in the Territory with a picture of a loin-clothed Lee studded with arrows *à la* St Sebastian and captioned 'Martyr Lee'. It was very much the image he projected and the notion had a glum

---

* My favourite misconception is that the favourite of all Chinese curses is 'May you live in interesting times.' All Westerners, including the Governor, believed this to be true, but my Chinese contacts assured me that this is a fallacy. On the other hand they may well have been pulling my leg.

plausibility. If I were a betting man, I would wager that in the year 2000 Martin Lee will be heading up a successful law practice in Toronto and gilding the lily with voice-in-the-wilderness performances on the North American lecture circuit. But I suppose he is just as likely to be languishing in Stanley prison. Or worse. Certainly his intention when I saw him was to remain in Hong Kong to the, probably bitter, end.

I had not intended to spend too much time on Hong Kong politics in the day-to-day, week-is-a-long-time sense, but there was no escaping the fact that it was a highly politicised place, even though most of the highest-profile politicians were, by conventional Western standards, virtual eunuchs with little more real political clout than the average English rural district councillor. It was significant that the Legislative Council Building was a conspicuously dowdy affair, designed by the same architects who were responsible for the Victoria and Albert Museum and the grim slab-like façade of Buckingham Palace. Like other 'public' buildings in Hong Kong, it was dwarfed by its 'private' rivals.

It was here that I saw Elsie Tu, described by Frank Welsh in his Hong Kong history as 'a shining light of liberal opinion in Hong Kong for thirty years'. Like Lee, she was one of Hong Kong's relatively few high-profile politicians, though dramatically unlike him in almost every conceivable respect except for an awkward integrity and an apparent certainty of belief. She and Lee shared something else – a virulent dislike of the Governor. She herself first came to Hong Kong as a missionary in 1951. She had always lived close to the people and remembered a time when Hong Kong was a very different, down-at-heel community. Earlier in the year she had lost the Urban Council seat she held for thirty years. In the elections for LegCo in the autumn after I left, she lost her place in that body too.

In Mrs Tu's case, there was no question of feeling

259

betrayed, as Martin Lee did. My own sense was that, like many old Hong Kong hands, she would have felt resentful of anyone who came to the Territory with the Patten provenance. This was not surprising. How could she who had lived and breathed Hong Kong for more than forty years think a forceful Westminster-bred, political figure like Chris Patten anything other than a Johnny-come-lately?

She and the Governor got off on completely the wrong foot. In an interview with Fionnuala McHugh, a local journalist who occasionally contributed to the *Telegraph Magazine* in London, Mrs Tu told how the Governor 'called me to his house and he sat me in a chair and he talked to me as if he was cross-examining me. He treated me like a child.'

Mrs Tu was eighty years old at the time and was eighty-two by the time I met her, and impressive. Nevertheless, there was a sort of saintly simplicity in her view of life which an urbane pragmatist like the Governor could well have found ... well, yes ... child-like.

However, that first encounter with the Governor did not end there. According to McHugh's article, as she was leaving, Whisky or Soda entered left, barking. Chris made to pick the dog up and Elsie, who is keen on dogs, went to stroke it. When she did this, Chris, apparently, gave her a filthy look as if, Mrs Tu said, 'My dirty hand shouldn't touch it.'

When I remarked on this story, she was embarrassed and said that it had been very wrong of McHugh to repeat it. (Thinking as a journalist, I thought McHugh would have been very wrong *not* to repeat it.) She did not, however, deny it. My own interpretation was that, knowing his dogs' reputation for taking chunks out of the Government House gardeners' ankles, the Governor was nervous that Whisky or Soda would have a nip at Elsie. When I mentioned it to the Pattens they seemed mystified and also slightly upset.

Elsie protested that she was not, as her critics suggested,

pro-Peking but just pro-Hong Kong. Whether or not this was so, she and the Governor were unlikely to see eye to eye politically. On the other hand, both he and Lavender had genuine personal respect for the redoubtable Mrs Tu's life and achievements. No slight had been intended.

Too bad. 'He'd be much better as an actor,' she told me, at the end of an entertaining couple of hours. 'He'd make a good comedian. He doesn't have the principles to be a statesman.'

I wasn't sure whether she really meant that, whether it was just a commonplace politician's gibe or something more heartfelt. One way or another, I felt the insult wasn't quite worthy of her.

Her father had had no more than a primary education, had come back from the Great War and imbued his family with three subjects – politics, religion and sport. She joined the Plymouth Brethren, perhaps to escape from an unhappy home, left, returned at the persuasion of her first husband, Bill Elliott, went to Shanghai as a missionary, saw people dying on the street with cold, then came to Hong Kong expecting 'something like Britain' but finding instead a colony where 'racial discrimination was terrible'. She recalled something called the 'Peak attitude' which meant that, for instance, amahs were left in sole charge of British children but were not allowed into the clubs where they went for parties, games and other social activities. The British didn't talk about the 'Chinese', she said. They referred to them, contemptuously, as 'them' and 'they'.

She had felt everyone was racist and/or corrupt until the arrival of Maclehose (I was impressed, yet again, at the affection inspired by Jock the Sock). 'Maclehose,' she said, 'was the first one with clean hands. He was actually prepared to listen about corruption. The police were the worst, but it was in everybody and everything. Grantham went home with a boat-load of stuff.' (Just as Maclehose's

261

popularity seemed remarkably endearing, so memories of Sir Alexander and Lady Maureen seemed disturbingly unkind, even though it was almost forty years since they retired.)

Mrs Tu was outraged by the endemic graft in society, but almost as incensed by the concomitant *petit bourgeois* snobbery, so acutely pinpointed in Austin Coates's remarks about the semi-detached enclave around the Governor's dinner table. I had a definite sense that some of her passion stemmed from being patronised by a certain sort of minor public school Brit and his wife. They would see Elsie not just as someone keen to rock the comfortable colonial boat but also as an impecunious missionary married – shock, horror – to a Chinese (her second husband, Andrew Tu, was headmaster of the school she herself had established).

Her finest hour was during the Star Ferry riots in the 1960s. 'They tried to get me into prison,' she said. 'They' were the later-disgraced Superintendent Godber and his corrupt associates. Not just them either. She was arraigned before an official commission of enquiry and given a fearful wigging by no less a person than the Chief Justice. However, at the next Urban Council elections, she was returned with more votes than ever.

At this distance in time it's difficult to be sure exactly what caused the riots, though the one thing that does seem clear is that it had little to do with the ostensible reason, which was a modest increase in the first-class ferry fare. Mrs Tu, then still Mrs Elliott, may not have actually incited the rioters, but she certainly went down to the police station after the first arrest and told the accused that he had the right to plead not guilty.

As she told the story, full of stone-throwing, *agents provocateurs*, gangs of boys, fiendish policemen out to get her at all costs, a lightning trip to lobby public opinion in Britain ('interpreted as running away') and even a suicide threat, her eyes lit up and her voice took on such an urgency that it was almost as if she were back in the fray, a doughty crusader in her prime once more.

She was still indomitable, but she was elderly and she no longer commanded votes. Sadly, she was also perceived in some quarters, particularly those inhabited by Martin Lee and what she referred to as his 'so-called democratic party', as being pro-Chinese.

'In 1984 after the Joint Declaration,' she said, 'I was on top of the world. I was always against colonialism. I was always a supporter of Gandhi and of his methods. I was happy. Everyone seemed happy. Then 4 June 1989 [Tiananmen Square] knocked me right off my feet. My husband, who was very patriotic, broke down in tears. I joined the mourners, but I joined them to weep for the dead, not to shout and bawl.'

Naturally I taxed her with the canard about being pro-Peking. 'I'm pro-Hong Kong. This is where I live and this is where my duty lies. People who spread the story about my being pro-Chinese are doing it for political ends. Tell me one thing I've done for Beijing. We're on very friendly terms, but they know I won't stand any nonsense.'

I liked her very much, not least because she so clearly remained difficult and nonconformist. It might be that she was politically more pro-Chinese than many genuinely democratic people would like, but, even if her head wasn't always screwed on as tightly as a more political politician's, I didn't have much doubt about her heart.

'I suppose,' she said, 'I could fit into any country.' This was manifestly untrue in the sense that she would always be too much of a rebellious individualist to fit comfortably anywhere at all. 'I suppose I'm cosmopolitan. I don't believe in this nonsense about patriotism. I'm patriotic up to a point, but not radically patriotic. I certainly don't believe "my country right or wrong".'

'Nor China right or wrong.'

I overstayed my time with her, causing her to lose at least a further hour out of her still-crowded day. It seemed a pity that she and the Governor couldn't get on.

'Oh,' she said, in a final dismissal, 'he doesn't want to hear anybody who doesn't agree with him. He listens to his own secretaries and what do they know about Hong Kong? He is being led by the nose and I can't forgive that. Now I feel sorry for him. He's lost the support of both sides.'

Ironically I felt a little like that about Elsie Tu. There was no doubt that in her day she was the lone conscience of Hong Kong. She had obviously been an influence for good. Equally obviously, it was now time for a gracious retirement. But, most obviously of all, that was simply not her style.

She would probably never forgive me for saying that her mantle had fallen on anyone, let alone that she had handed on her baton of liberal dissent. Nevertheless there was one member of LegCo who in terms of unorthodox, unafraid unpredictability echoed the prime of Elsie Tu. Emily Lau was American-educated and a former journalist. Messianic though she sometimes seemed, she was no missionary, nor, with her young, windblown good looks, did she really fit into the beige, plum and mahogany of her office in Room 216 at the LegCo Building – but then nor did Elsie Tu, looking like a favourite, if slightly daunting granny, with her white hair, blue cardigan and white blouse.

Emily Lau had been talking to some visiting journalists and seemed bored. I had the impression of someone on a very automatic pilot, particularly when her response to my first question was a barely suppressed yawn and the words, 'I wasn't born yesterday.' By the time I left her office I was becoming quite irritated by being told that Emily Lau wasn't born yesterday. I had assumed that before going to see her, but the lady protested so much that after a while I began to wonder.

The first time she said it was when I asked her if she, like

264

Martin Lee, felt a sense of personal betrayal over Chris and the Court of Final Appeal. 'I wasn't born yesterday' meant that she had seen Chris coming a mile off and, although she hadn't liked Governor Wilson and although she realised that the appointment of Governor Patten represented a change, it was not a fundamental change. How could it be? He was still a British governor. He had to carry out British policy. 'The British were being portrayed as selling Hong Kong down the river,' she said. 'They wanted to change that image without actually changing the reality.'

Not that she was particularly inimical. 'When he asked to see me I went,' she said. 'I bothered to go and see him. The things he said were off the record, which I respect. Whenever I go it's always a very jolly chat, but I don't believe there has been a very fundamental change. How could there be?'

The Lau view of Britain's contribution is orthodox and even-handed. Like others, she talked about the British contribution to 'prosperity and stability' and judged that the Territory's commercial success was due largely to Chinese industry operating within a British framework. As for democracy, well, yes, failure to introduce it two or three decades earlier was part of a 'sorry saga' but she didn't think you could blame it entirely on the British.

All in all, she had mixed feelings. Phrases that recurred were 'sense of impotence', 'no effective feeling of nationality', 'in the fifties and sixties, especially, no sense of belonging', 'abandonment by Britain', 'never been anything other than pessimistic'. For someone who had the reputation of being ultra-feisty she seemed dispirited, if even-handed. Perhaps it was just realism and a greater sense of distance than some domestic Hong Kong politicians were capable of. After all, she had studied journalism at the University of Southern California and international relations at the London School of Economics, quite apart from her stint at the

265

Far Eastern Economic Review under the worldly-wise, even world-weary, editorship of Derek Davies.

No wonder she kept telling me she wasn't born yesterday.

'Of course I feel depressed,' she said, when I remarked on her mood. 'I'm not close to anyone, I'm a real independent and so I only have one vote. I don't feel I want to join a bigger group. I'd like Hong Kong to have a free and democratic future but I can't change the world. The only guarantee for a free and democratic Hong Kong is a free and democratic China, and that could take decades. In the meantime what Hong Kong would like is a separate existence. If China would only leave us alone . . . but all they want is to exercise control.'

And the Governor?

'He could get us some more passports,' she said. 'That's the best he can do.'

Emily Lau's name was often bracketed with that of Christine Loh. Lau and Loh had a sort of music-hall euphony. Both were young, personable, courageous and articulate. Both were members of LegCo. Both commanded column inches. Christine Loh had been at school in Bedford and university at Hull. She had been back in Hong Kong since 1979. I found her, in her office in a block a stone's throw from the LegCo Building, ante-room full of a scrum of supplicant constituents, in a more positive mood than Emily Lau. She reasoned that people in Hong Kong had been trying to come to terms with transition for over a decade and their senses had been dulled. You couldn't feel unadulterated pessimism for a decade and more: 'If you'd been depressed for that long you'd have gone mad.'

She was wearing pearls, a long khaki tunic and black trousers. The effect was cool and just the sensible side of chic, which was overall very much the impression she conveyed. Most other Hong Kong politicians had moments when they seemed really quite silly, but Christine Loh managed to seem reasonable throughout. Even when contemplating her own future she was quietly realistic. She would much prefer to stay in Hong Kong, but if it became impossible to be an elected politician or to earn the money to live then she would have to review the alternatives. And the alternatives would naturally mean abroad. How could it be otherwise?

If she remained as a local politician, there were a number of obvious respects in which life would change. Some were so obvious that they were hardly ever stated.

'In the past,' she said, 'if you wanted to lobby you had to go to London. In the future you'll have to hot-foot it up to Peking.'

This is indubitable. The question, however, was whether people like Lee, Lau and Loh would be given the opportunity to lobby in Peking or whether the only people allowed to trip down the corridors of power would be placemen, apparatchiks, fellow travellers or the corrupt people that Elsie Tu assured me were suddenly beginning to emerge from the woodwork as the day of transformation approached.

Certainly I found it difficult to see how any normal person could find Christine Loh life-threatening. She sounded like the quintessential centre-left moderate.

On Governor Patten for instance: 'Well, his promises are only as good as his officials and their policies, aren't they?'

Fair enough. She told me that, in summary, there were three important areas: democracy, by which she meant the extension of the franchise which had been so important[*] to this Governor; a free society, by which she meant guarantees on freedom of speech, particularly within the press; and the environment.

On these three she seemed to be giving him a sort of

---

[*] Perhaps *too* important. Christine Loh was one of those who had, to his irritation, taken Chris Patten to task for being a 'one-issue governor'.

qualified approval in the beta range. She had liked the appointment because the new Governor was a man of obvious stature: 'He looked good, he sounded good. Of all the governors I've seen he was the most willing to walk in the streets. In some ways it was like going back to Maclehose [that man again!]. He answered questions in LegCo for an hour, which no previous Governor has ever done. That's all very refreshing and if we don't ask the right questions then "boo" to us!'

'On the other hand' – and Christine Loh struck me as very much the politician who always had an 'on the other hand' up her sleeve – 'he has an impossible task . . . Basically we have to give it back.'

I thought the use of 'we' was instructive. Like many of her generation in Hong Kong, she was intrigued and perplexed by the notion of identity. 'It's very difficult for people like me to feel that we're part of the People's Republic of China,' she said. 'I think in Chinese. Our fathers came from somewhere in China. But *we were born here.*'

Quite what that makes her seemed uncertain. She speculated briefly on the nature of 'Chineseness' and then said that in her view there were three distinct Chinese societies – Hong Kong, Taiwan and the PRC (People's Republic of China) – all fuelled by different values and beliefs. She thought that there was something in Hong Kong which was eminently worth fighting for, but it was quite difficult to define.

'I'm in a significant minority when I argue that Hong Kong represents an idea,' she said. 'Most powerful people just say, "Don't mess with China." I think that in this situation you have got to have some core beliefs.'

These she manifestly possessed, but in the end so much returned to her analysis of the impossibility of being governor in these last few years.

'Basically we have to give it back.'

That said it all and, no matter what was done before the

end of June 1997, nothing could alter the fact that once the Union Jack came down the Chinese writ would run. It struck me, however, after my conversations with Hong Kong's allegedly dangerous dissident politicians, that they themselves should form a valuable part of the gift. On balance they seemed a very attractive proposition compared with the average Westminster MP. China should be very pleased to have them, but I somehow doubted that they would see it like that. I had a nasty feeling that the example already set by Baroness Dunn might become the norm and that the effective voice of Hong Kong political dissent would ultimately be a voice in exile. That would be a real admission of failure by the most populous nation on earth.

SIXTEEN

Hong Kong was like a banquet. Or maybe a *dim sum* lunch. There was an old gweilo adage about Chinese meals filling you up but leaving you hungry for more only a short time later, and this was true of Hong Kong. There were times when I felt I couldn't cope with the pace and the strangeness, the permanent transition, the contrasts between street-level poverty and multi-storey magnificence, the comfortable familiarity and the alien terror. But even when I felt I couldn't manage another mouthful of Hong Kong I always knew that I would have changed my mind within an hour or so and would be holding out my bowl like Oliver Twist.

Like *dim sum*, she also came at you in an endless procession of tiny vignettes. An English sign in the Teaware Museum, converted from military usage thanks to the largesse of K. S. Lo, inventor of Vitasoy drinks: 'For your own safety please do not climb up, lean on or play along the staircases.' A taxi driver opening the door of his cab to aim a phlegmy gobbet of spittle into the gutter outside, of all places, the Dunhill boutique in Central. The blank faces of the hostesses at Club Bboss,[*] the biggest 'hostess' club in

___

[*] The Club Bboss was originally called Club Volvo. The Swedish car manufacturers, with lamentable sense-of-humour failure, objected and the name had to be changed. I never discovered why it became 'Bboss', and Tito Catalan was unable to enlighten me.

Asia, sitting out their carefully timed conversations with equally blank-faced Japanese businessmen in suits as I sipped Scotch with the manager, a Filipino called Tito Catalan. Those extraordinary newspaper headlines which told one so much more than the stories underneath them. 'Girl, 12, has biggest breasts in the world.'

Sweet and sour, bland and tart, familiar as Lancashire faggots or so peculiar that you dared not even imagine what unusable part of a snake or dog could have been cased in this delicate pancake or dumpling – the *dim sum* of Hong Kong came thick and fast.

Often, also like a Chinese meal, the most exotic mouthfuls came as a shock in a sea of stodgy rice or bland noodles. So that suddenly, in the middle of an orotund recitation of a company hand-out, someone would lean forward and say something quite shocking, such as 'Quite frankly, old boy, I'm not hanging around till the Chinese get rid of all the Filipina maids and the only available servants won't be capable of boiling an egg in any known language.' Underneath the pleasantry there was hatred in Hong Kong.

And, pushing the gastronomic analogy yet further, one was always up against the problem of assessing an alien cuisine. What exactly was the mystery ingredient in this meatball? Were these chicken's feet typical of the region? Was there anything significant about this incredibly expensive abalone I was being offered by the Governor's egregious acquaintance Cassam Gouljarry, the Mauritius-born Consul General for the obscure African Republic of Gabon? Did Cassam count? Did his generous hospitality indicate anything more than an outgoing personality? Would his drinks business, Caves de France Limited, thrive under the new Chief Executive as it throve under the last Governor?

If I were to attempt a picture of my own home country, how much time, I wondered, would I spend on the grand public observation and how much on the tiny details which

271

are an essential part of the whole? Is a place a seamless entity or a patchwork quilt, a melting pot or a mosaic? Do you learn more from a government white paper or from the graffiti on a station wall? In the upstairs office of the Hector Ross house in Pok Fu Lam there was a framed newspaper cutting about his father-in-law which, for me, perfectly illuminated one facet of the progress of Hong Kong. The event occurred in the lifetime of the Rosses and yet was so archaic that it seemed almost prehistoric.

'Mr Wallace Harper,' it read, 'Ford Dealer at Hong Kong, is a licensed pilot and has his own aeroplane, an American "Arrow Sport". Some time ago a Fordson Tractor part was badly needed at Macau, so Mr Harper flew from Hong Kong to Macau in 30 minutes and the part was installed an hour and five minutes after he left Hong Kong. This is believed to be the first trip of this nature in this part of the world.' I was fascinated by a long technical dissertation from Philip Chen of Dragonair on how his airline was at the aeronautical apex of the Orient, and yet that faded cutting on Hector's office wall conveyed a flavour that no company report could ever emulate.

Sometimes a very grand and important pronouncement such as 'Martyrs are revered in China because there are so few of them' (Discuss) interested me less than something which was apparently far less profound. For instance, I spent one morning on a wondrous if sometimes stomach-turning market tour with the Governor's chief chef. I enjoyed cruising these places – as did the Governor himself. Markets are always revealing, Hong Kong's particularly so, and Patrick was an unusual guide. He had spent twenty-four years with the Royal Navy cooking on the aircraft carriers HMS *Albion* and HMS *Bulwark*. We roamed pleasurably among the salted duck eggs, the Chinese plums and cabbage and the fish slaughterers. How disturbing was the indifference of the old woman brushing the scales off a live garoupa or snapper as it squirmed, biting on the fingers of her rubber glove, like a piglet on a sow's teat, until she slapped it down on the chopping block and beheaded it with a crisp blow of her machete. Parts of the area were more like an abattoir than a market. Live chickens jostled each other in crowded cages and occasionally one was hauled out to be decapitated much like the fish and with the same coolness.

'Governor like chicken?' I asked idly.

Patrick grinned.

'I buy live chicken for me,' he said, 'frozen chicken for Governor.'

It was a trivial enough remark, I suppose, and a mere gossipy titbit of information, and yet I found myself mulling it over, expanding it into evidence of a bunker mentality, of the clash between a live- and a frozen-chicken culture, of the impossibility of West ever truly understanding East. And even now that I contemplate the remark for the umpteenth time I am not sure that it isn't more significant than, for instance, anything that Martin Lee had to say about the Court of Final Appeal. Live chicken for the chef; frozen chicken for the Guv.

Another remark that stayed in my consciousness long after it was made was one from Jimmy Lai. It was Minky Worden who said to me that Lai was the future of Hong Kong and he certainly seemed to me one of the more attractive of the Hong Kong tycoons. He first came came to the Colony as a boy of twelve. He was a street hustler in Canton in the 1950s. 'Life was tough there,' he told me, 'there was no hope.' From time to time he would hustle visitors from Hong Kong. They were good targets, being both susceptible to his routine and also obviously prosperous. He knew that Hong Kong was where he wanted to go, for it represented the possibility of freedom and prosperity. Then one day he fell in with a man from Hong Kong who, halfway through their

273

exchange, produced a paper-wrapped object which he broke in half, sharing it between the two of them.

'Eat it,' he ordered.

Lai sank his teeth into it, tasted chocolate for the first time and vowed that he would wait no longer but would head for the West without further delay. He got to Macau without too much problem and then smuggled himself to Hong Kong on board a ship and made his way to the garment area of Kowloon. Within a decade or so his entrepreneurial skills had made him a millionaire. He hated Chinese Communism, he hated politicians and, in the 1990s, he translated some of his textile fortunes into publishing. *Next* and *Apple* were his flagships, loathed by the conservative Hong Kong press establishment and the Chinese government for their outspoken advocacy of individual rights and capitalism. Despite his riches, Lai seemed genuinely egalitarian and libertarian. When I saw him his open-plan offices were still in the rundown garment area and they had none of the thick carpet and panel of the more traditional fat-cat taipans. His own work space was no more lavish than anyone else's. Lai himself spoke fluent but curious English, putting a 't' on the end of many of his words, as in 'traditionT' and 'informationT'. He was entirely self-taught and told me that he was looking forward to *re-reading* Karl Popper. He wore trademark denim rather than mohair and he kept a cage-bird in his office. I had seen old men walking in the streets with such birds and I had seen them alongside bus- and cab-drivers, but his was the first I had seen in a tycoon's office.

I asked about the bird, feeling that, like so many facets of Chinese culture, there was here a key to something significant.

He smiled.

'He is a fighting bird,' he said, 'but he sings.'

Lai had many more obviously important things to say about the Governor, the British, the future, the significance of information technology and much else besides, but it was that remark and the image of the caged fighting songbird in his office which stayed with me. It could have been a metaphor for the Governor himself, caged in his obsolescent palace – 'A fighting bird, but he sings'.

By yet another of the fortuitous coincidences that peppered my time in the Territory, I found myself the very next day in the biggest bird-cage in all Hong Kong, the aviary opened by Lady Youde in memory of her husband Sir Edward in 1992. Governor Youde died in office in 1986 while on a visit to Peking – an event which was in some quarters darkly suggested to be more than a coincidence. As so often, death in office seemed to have enhanced his reputation, at least in the short and medium term.* The Youde aviary was in the heart of Central, on the hillside below the eyries of 'Mandarin' Mirsky of *The Times*, Baroness Dunn and the First British Trade Commissioner. Although it had once been part of the Victoria Barracks it was as if a giant butterfly net had been thrown across a rainforest.

There were supposed to be 600 different sorts of bird under the netting and, of all the memorials to the British past in general and to the British governors in particular, these were the most magic. Their vivid plumage in the hot damp of the luxuriant foliage was a brilliant respite from the clank and clangour of the moneymaking all around. The names too made as evocative a prose poem as those of the Agincourt dead, memorialised by Hollinshed and lyricised by Shakespeare in *Henry V*.

---

* Frank Welsh describes him as 'dedicated and much admired'. An old China hand, he had been responsible for negotiating with the PLA over the HMS *Amethyst* affair in 1949 and was Ambassador to Peking between 1974 and 1978. After his death, seasoned observers were amazed at the long lines of ordinary Chinese people who queued to sign the book of condolence at Government House.

Here were the Chestnut-backed Scimitar Babbler, the Golden-fronted Leafbird, the Gold-whiskered Barbet, Rothschild's Minah, the Striated Yuhina, the Great Racquet-tailed Drongo, the Fawn-breasted Bowerbird, the Siberian Ground Thrush, the Slaty-legged Crake, the White-rumped Shama, the Black-headed Bulbul and the Ruddy Cuckoo Dove. All that was missing were birds named after the governors themselves. How civilised if, to the 600 existing inhabitants, could be added Youde's Yellowhammer, Wilson's Warbler, Maclehose's Moorhen and even Patten's Puffin. That really would be 'history on the wing'.

But perhaps those are not the memorials men crave. On one of the Governor's visits we homed in on slum dwellings in one of the most densely populated parts of the city, which by definition meant one of the most densely populated places in the world. Quite often the Governor was taken to the most deprived places in his domain almost as if it was therapy or an opportunity for penance. 'Where are the tarts?' he asked good-naturedly, as he peered out at prostitution-free streets. 'Normally I'm shown tarts.'

The Governor could be endearingly self-deprecating. At another moment, gazing on a particularly nightmarish urban landscape with half-completed public works at every prospect, he muttered, 'Something must be done!', and then, catching the echo of the Prince of Wales's sad lament in the South Wales coalfields in the 1930s, smiled his trademark smile and said, almost in admission of defeat, 'Said the Governor.' His sternest critic could not accuse him of not being self-aware.

I had been advised that this particular visit was shirtsleeve order. No formality. More chance of blending in. We travelled in an official minibus. 'Never been in a bus before, have you, John?' he quipped to John Tsang, one of his private secretaries. Tsang grinned but squirmed a little. The Governor's quips could seem the tiniest bit barbed on occasion. I had taken the shirtsleeve order as an instruction to dress down and come in beach or barbecue gear. The private office had interpreted it more literally and had simply taken off the jackets of their suits. There was no way in which they were going to blend in with anyone in Sham Shui Po, least of all the man in the street.

The programme was dispiriting.

3.20 p.m. Drive past work sites of sewage and drainage projects at Yen Chow Street.

3.35 p.m. Arrive Chew On Building. Proceed to the rooftop to see the condition of the building.

Visit an apartment.

4.10 p.m. Depart for Apliu Street.

Drive past Nam Cheong Area to see the problem of illegal workers.

The condition of the Chew On Building was nightmarish – overcrowded, gloomy, exposed wiring everywhere, noise deafening, hygiene non-existent. On the roof were corrugated iron shacks known, euphemistically, as 'illegal rooftop structures'. They were almost more squalid than the apartments except that, being on the roof, they had more sense of air and space. They must have been appallingly susceptible to the frequent extremes of the Hong Kong climate. They reminded me of the hut in which the Japanese guards confined Alec Guinness in the film *Bridge on the River Kwai*.

On the way to the helipad near Kai Tak, the Governor shook his head at his embussed secretariat.

'There's still too much of that temporary housing,' he said, noticing another feature of the local landscape – enclaves of primitive huts for the homeless. 'We've got to get rid of it before I go.'

His enemies might not agree, but he was still enough of an idealist and altruist to want to be remembered as the man who abolished the 'illegal rooftop structure' and 'temporary

277

housing' rather than the Governor who had a bird named after him. Or even an aviary.

'I want to see how people live so that we can understand better how we can help people to live in better places,' he told the young, beige-trouser-suited District Officer in Sham Shui Po. She had the usual bird-like good looks and raven hair. Her name was Linda Lai.

'Let me ask you this,' said the Governor, taking his leave. 'After the Governor's been they'll say, "OK, it's a bit smelly ... it's a bit messy ... but that's Hong Kong. Isn't the Governor just trying to import his Western values to the place?" '

'No,' said the District Officer. 'It can be improved and so it should be improved.'

'OK,' said the Governor briskly. 'We'll follow up.'

More than anyone else in the Territory the Governor ricocheted between the extremes of wealth and poverty. Despite his recently acquired lifestyle and salary the Governor was not rich by the standards of Hong Kong's rich any more than he was, of course, poor by the standards of Hong Kong's poor. Yet he constantly rubbed shoulders with both.

Among the rich, Stanley Ho was one of the very richest. While not as shy as the shadowy Li Ka Shing, he was, when it came to giving interviews, more of a shrinking violet than some of the younger entrepreneurs. He would talk to me only on condition that I submitted written questions in advance and when we met he avoided eye contact almost the entire time, reading from a typewritten draft with only occasional asides. The single most significant departure from his text came at the end of our session when I asked him if, in the event of the post-1997 situation not turning out as planned, he would contemplate emigration.

It was then that he raised his eyes and even, momentarily, twinkled. Like other Chinese people confronted with an awkward question, he did not quite answer but instead, sort of, told me a story. He had been asked this question, he told me, on a previous occasion.

'Dr Ho,' he had been asked, 'why do you not emigrate?'

'And I said, "Where would I go? Perhaps I should go to Canada, but I would not go to Canada because I should freeze to death. Well then, perhaps I should go to America, but I would not go to America because even though I have a lot of money I should not like to have my fortune reduced by half with taxation. Or perhaps I could go to the United Kingdom, but I would not wish to go there because I am too old to learn to go on strike. And finally I could go to Australia, but I do not want to be eaten by flies. So you see I have no alternative." '

I wasn't entirely sure what to make of this, but I felt it was probably typical of the gnomic way in which some Chinese people dealt with the question direct. And, if so, I could understand why, from time to time, the Governor might become frustrated.

And, having said that Dr Ho was a shrinking violet, I should record the heading of his curriculum vitae. It says, after his name, 'OBE., Gr.Cross O.L.D.H., Chev.Leg.-'d'Hon., SPMP., DSocSC., CSTJ.' I wasn't sure what most of this meant but it presumably meant a lot to Dr Ho. The rest of the CV emphasised his fifty years doing business in Hong Kong and Macau (he was, in effect, 'Mr Macau' and likely to remain so after the departure of the last Portuguese Governor, just as he was likely to remain one of the half-dozen richest men in Hong Kong). He had been chairman of the Real Estate Developers' Association of Hong Kong since 1984. His group owned the largest jetfoil fleet in the world and ran approximately 70 per cent of the traffic between Hong Kong and Macau.

Then there were hotels, the three floating restaurants in Aberdeen, tour agencies, endless foreign interests. These were followed by a long list of his charitable interests and voluntary positions. I was intrigued to learn that the Doctor was vice-president of the Hong Kong Girl Guides. He was a year older than my mother, which meant that when she was in Hong Kong in 1952 they would both have just turned thirty. Dr Ho was a famously keen ballroom dancer. I wondered whether they had waltzed together at *thés dansants* at the Pen.

It was perhaps unfortunate that the day before I had been sailing in those waters between Britain's and Portugal's last major colonies that are almost Dr Ho's private sea. There I had heard a Mandarin-speaking gweilo offer the ultimate insult to a Chinese sea-captain: 'You malformed egg.' Nothing the courteous Doctor said could reasonably have provoked such a response, yet the bland urbanity of his answers did slightly stretch my tolerance and I would have been tempted, had I possessed the Cantonese, to try it out.

By now I had become quite fazed by such notions as 'face' and *fung shui*. Helen Hung, Dr Ho's public-relations assistant, had a glass of water. I had a cup of sweet-smelling Chinese tea stylishly served in an elegant cup. Dr Ho had a large mug. So obsessed had I become with the nuances of tea ceremonies and questions of culture that I found myself trying to read all manner of, possibly absurd, significances into this. I almost felt as if I was coming under a spell, deliberately cast.

Because of Dr Ho's interests in Macau, the thrust of my questions was Macanese. I had spent some time in that curious Portuguese enclave, so much more of a time-warp than Hong Kong. Governor Patten had waxed lyrical about the Portuguese Governor's political assistant, who had just taken delivery of a Morgan sports car which he was about to drive from the manufacturers in Malvern to the South of France. I had also been advised to contact a larger-than-life priest called Father Lancelot and indeed nearly had a

280

contretemps with him at the Military Club. My friends and I ordered 'partridge pie' only to be told that Father Lancelot and his fellow ecclesiastics at the top table had eaten the last of it. Macau, a strange mixture of well-preserved Portuguese architecture and cuisine, White Russian prostitutes, gambling and slightly shady-sounding business ventures, was an instructive ramshackle counterpart to the gloss of Hong Kong. If, on the basis of prejudice, you were to create the archetypal British and Portuguese colonies, you would, I think, include at least 50 per cent of the core qualities of Hong Kong and Macau. That, on the basis of a brief stay based on the elegant Mandarin Oriental-owned* Bela Vista Hotel,† was my impression – a first one and by no means conclusive.

Dr Ho's vision, in his glossy annual report, is that Macau, 'at one time reckoned to be the single wealthiest entrepot in the world, is today enjoying its own renaissance as a major gateway to China's Pearl River Delta, linked by superhighways and sea lanes to the area's major cities'. Dr Ho believed, and he was not alone, that within twenty years the Pearl River Delta would have five cities of more than a million inhabitants.

As always, I viewed company reports with suspicion, convinced that their lines were meant to be read between but not knowing quite how to do it. It did seem quite significant, however, that Dr Ho himself owned 161,396,412 shares in the company, which was just over 161 times as many as anyone else; also that in the previous financial year the Group had turned over HK$1,872,803,000 and made a

---

* 'Mandarin' is the common usage, but the correct full name for the hotel and its parent company is actually 'Mandarin Oriental'.
† The Bela Vista used to be agreeably seedy and was the venue for a Bela Vista Ball, a glamorous party for Hong Kong glitterati which has been perpetuated with annual bashes in such places as Cuba, St Petersburg and Victoria Falls.

profit of HK$681,185,000. These figures seemed so enormous as to mean nothing to me. On a more footnote level I saw that among the 'significant events' of the year were the appointments to the main board of the chairman's daughters. Ms Daisy Ho, thirty, was responsible for 'Group real estate and restaurant activities'. Her sister, Ms Pansy Ho, thirty-two, was responsible for 'Group corporate affairs and development, and restaurant activities'. I did not envy those further down the chain of command in 'restaurant activities'.

I could not find any mention in the report of Dr Ho's fondness for ice-cream. One of Shun Tak's subsidiaries was a company called 'Glaces de France'. When in Macau, Dr Ho was allegedly given to sending out for a tub of the stuff at all hours of the day or night. If so, it seemed an endearing enough vice. He was also heavily into golf, and his Macau Golf and Country Club had, by the end of the financial year, sold over a thousand memberships and generated an income of just over HK$25 million.

So this was the shy, elderly gentleman in the surprisingly crumpled suit reading to me over a mug of tea in a huge trophy-festooned office high above his ferry terminal. What he read was not without interest, though it was not as intriguing as actually meeting one of the living embodiments of the commercial success which has, in part, made Hong Kong the object of such astonishment. As so often, my basic reaction was, in John Betjeman's words, that he seemed 'such an ordinary little man'. Yet, manifestly, that was the one thing he was not.

The difference between Hong Kong and Macau, he said, was that Macau was given to the Portuguese whereas Hong Kong was taken – he did not actually say 'stolen' but this was what I inferred. Therefore, Macau had always been a part of China administered by the Portuguese, whereas Hong Kong was a fully fledged British colony. Partly as a consequence, the only serious Portuguese interest in Macau was a note-issuing bank, the Banco Nacional Ultramarino.

In Macau there would be no attempt to adapt the existing Portuguese legal system after the change-over there in 1999. According to Dr Ho, Portuguese law was too complicated and, in any case, there were only two Chinese lawyers in the whole place. Unlike Hong Kong, Macau had a basically unsatisfactory harbour which silted up so badly that Dr Ho's own company had to dredge it all year round 'to make sea transport at all possible'.

He himself was involved in the drafting of new 'Basic Laws' in both colonies. He claimed that these were '95/96 per cent' identical. In the future Macau would have no death penalty and unlike Hong Kong would have no PLA troops stationed there. The hundred thousand Macanese with Chinese surnames would have Portuguese passports which would be 'merely a travelling document' and would not allow them any consular or ambassadorial protection. I had heard about this already. It did not sound like the sort of passport I would wish to have.

Macau, he pointed out, had a population of only 500,000 and its people were 'less educated, less affluent and easier to control than those of Hong Kong'. There were no proper political parties. There *were* trade unions, but Dr Ho obviously didn't rate them. He smiled inscrutably at the mere thought. 'The Chinese keep a watchful eye on them.' I said this sounded suspiciously big-brotherly. 'No,' he said, ad-libbing briefly, 'Macau people are very relaxed. They are not very enthusiastic about politics.'

For thirty-three years Dr Ho had held the gambling franchise in Macau. The vast profits from this were used in part to finance 'Macau's large infrastructural projects'. One of his Macau companies had a 38 per cent stake in the new international airport. That meant HK$8 billion. There was also a stake in the deep-sea terminal and the new harbour bridges. He said that no other private company in the world had such a large stake in a country's infrastructure.

I asked about uncertainty about the future and he shrugged. He had been here before. He had once made a heavy investment in horse-racing when the Shah was in power in Iran. He lost all his money when the Ayatollah took over. But he lived to tell the tale. Maybe he himself was a gambler like his fellow countrymen, on whose passion for games of chance he based so much of his fortune.

If life for Dr Ho was a game of chance, there could be no denying that the odds were heavily stacked in his favour.

SEVENTEEN

One Saturday afternoon in late July, Louise Cox was married in the Union Church with a reception afterwards at Government House. The invitation was a striking example of what Sino-British relations should have been: a joint declaration which showed the way for the Joint Declaration. The invitation was four pages of gold English and Chinese script on a scarlet background. 'Mr and Mrs Peter St John Cox and Mr and Mrs Chum-pui Law', it said, 'request the pleasure of your company at the marriage of their daughter Louise and their son Steve.' Steve was a policeman and the two had met when he was assigned to special duties as one of the Governor's bodyguards.

I arrived at the church shortly after the bride, who was radiant in white. Moments later, the ubiquitous David Tang arrived, cutting it even finer. We sat near the back of the concrete-feeling church and Tang followed the readings in his Bible. The second, 1 Corinthians 13:1–13, was read by Elspeth Collins-Taylor, the housekeeper, wearing a magnificently wide-brimmed hat. The Hong Kong Children's Choir sang 'Amazing Grace' and the Reverend Gene Preston delivered a homily. I could have said that he preached a sermon but that would not have been entirely accurate. The hymns were a tambourine-ish number which began 'Give me joy in my heart, keep me praising' and the more traditional 'Now thank we all our God'.

This mixture of ancient and modern seemed appropriate to the occasion and also to the place. The Union Church on Kennedy Road was first organised as 'an independent, non-denominational Protestant congregation' for the Colony's English-speakers in 1843. The old church was destroyed in the Second World War and the modern description of the new church's function was that it was 'international, ecumenical and welcomes all to its Sunday Worship'.

After the service, the congregation strolled through an octopus of urban highway to Government House. First there was champagne in the garden and a gubernatorial kiss for the bride which made the front page of the following day's *Post*. Then we repaired to the ballroom for a banquet (my Westernised notion of a 'reception' was far too prosaic). We were offered braised baby lobster with pepper balsamico vinaigrette; double-boiled pigeon with fish maw and Chinese mushrooms; passion-fruit sherbet; fillet of beef with red-wine truffle sauce, mixed Chinese vegetables and château pota-toes; white chocolate parfait with strawberry coulis; mocha and Chinese *petits fours*.

Most of us, the Governor included, sat in the body of the hall, but the wedding party occupied a high table facing the guests. As so often in such circumstances, they looked self-conscious, thus displayed, and I felt their mild embarrass-ment was perhaps compounded by an entirely correct seating plan alternating gweilo and Chinese. I wasn't sure the simultaneously translated speeches helped and, watching the bemused, or possibly just inscrutable, expressions on some faces, I scribbled, 'Scottish proverbs don't work in Canton-ese!', which was unkind but not, I still think, far from the truth.

There was rather a lot of scribbling at the Governor's table that night. He was several places away from me, so oral

286

communication was difficult. Instead he wrote a note on the back of his menu and handed it to a rather baffled David Tang, who passed it on. It was about daughters and weddings and he was reflecting on his Kate, Laura and Alice and my Emma and Lucy. Many Patten-observers remarked to me that he was an unusually fond father, though the fondness was often disguised – ineffectually – by the sort of Balliol/House of Commons badinage which was his preferred conversational style.

In a sense, therefore, the note he passed across was predictable: 'Do you have your speech prepared for your first outing? What will be the political correctness test? Will the FCO[*] have to clear the draft?' Louise's father was speaking, touchingly, about the 'joy' afforded to him by his daughters. Characteristically, Chris wanted to know, 'How much joy will you be able to ascribe to your daughters?' and 'Will they knee you in the groin if the word "joy" crosses your lips?'

I suspected the answer to the last question, in both our cases, was affirmative. I also wondered if members of the Peking hierarchy passed such notes to each other during wedding banquets.

A moment later the Governor had penned another missive. The first thought was on the matter of speeches and daughters, conceding that he had 'never been as nervous as when speaking at Kate's 21st' and that, on such occasions, it was unwise to go much over three minutes. He concluded by asking what on earth made me think I would be asked to a daughter's wedding. 'We'll be quite lucky', he thought, 'if we're told.'

Tongue in cheek as usual. Not everyone – Chinese or Westerner – found this easy to come to terms with. I remembered Baroness Dunn telling me what a breath of fresh air he had seemed when he first arrived. And I

[*] Foreign and Commonwealth Office.

remembered writing in my notebook as I sat in the newly decorated waiting room at Government House, 'How extraordinarily unlike Chris all the earlier Governors look' – coming after all those feathers, epaulettes and whiskers, all those hairy men in uniforms, suddenly, unexpectedly, Hong Kong had a smooth man in shirtsleeves. *I* was reassured that he was passing frivolous notes across the table. Others might be perplexed or even cross, but that, in an ideal world, should have been their problem, not his.

He was different and so also, in these final days of British rule, was British style, British certainty, British self-confidence. Perhaps only the British eye for money and the main chance remained the same. It was often remarked that it was typical of Hong Kong that the main statue in the main square should not be that of a great patriot or a great soldier or a great explorer or even a great king or queen but that of a great money-bags: Sir Thomas Jackson Bart, 1841–1915. He stood there, though I doubted whether he would be standing there much longer, because of 'his eminent services to the Hong Kong and Shanghai Banking Corporation whose destiny he guided as Chief Manager from 1876 to 1902'. How many city states beatify the bank manager? Did the Chinese think of us as a nation of bank managers? Was the last Governor not enough of a bank manager himself?

In Macau one black, thunderous, rain-drenched afternoon, I sat over a glass of port with Fernando, who ran an eponymous restaurant on the island of Coloane. Fernando struck one immediately as a soldier of fortune, quixotic, very Portuguese, utterly unbankmanagerial. He viewed the return to Chinese rule with a characteristic shrug. 'The people who make money will go and the sooner they go the better. Then it will be possible to work properly . . . I came here seventeen years ago with no money. If I leave with no money it is not a problem. I've seen worse.'

Sometimes I felt the Patten style might have been better

288

suited to Macau, with its Roman Catholicism, its intriguing cuisine, its abiding feel of ancient Europe and of a byzantine cast of mind so unlike the bluff simplicity of most British colonialism. In some ways it seemed, compared with Hong Kong, so lawless and corrupt. Yet there I had seen a sign which outdid any fierce cock-hatted Hong Kong edict: 'Whoever destroys or in any other way damages a statue or other object destined to the public utility or decoration, and placed by the public authority or with its authorization, will be punished with imprisonment of two months to two years and correspondent fine.' It seemed unlikely that this ruling was ever enforced.

In Hong Kong, however, I saw no such sign, no indicator that the first man to raise a hand against the statue of Sir Thomas Jackson would be imprisoned by the public authority. But then it would probably be the public authority itself which eventually did for Sir Thomas.

Not all these thoughts passed through my mind during the nuptials of Louise Jane St John Cox and Steve Shek-kong Law, but it was a thought-provoking occasion in all manner of ways. After dinner there was dancing, ballroom dancing being a passion among many rich and well-connected Hong Kong Chinese. I remembered that Stanley Ho's love of French ice-cream was said to be matched only by his addiction to the *paso doble* and the Viennese waltz. Very light on his feet, Dr Ho.

Steve's policeman colleague Howard was at the wedding and we had walked from the church to Government House together. Police training, school at Scarisbrooke Hall between Ormskirk and Southport, his English wife . . . the combination made Howard, who was ethnically completely Chinese, also seem completely English. He was exceptionally friendly, articulate and loyal. One day I went over to his home on Lantau Island. (On my previous visit, of course, he had been house-sitting.) He was keen to show me round.

289

Lantau is the largest of the islands in the Hong Kong archipelago, yet has no serious conurbations. This may change when the new airport is complete, but when I was there it seemed wild and remote, like the New Territories I had explored with David Browning. With its soaring mountains and deserted shorelines it felt, as the old guidebook suggested, like the Hebrides, only hot.

Howard's place was cool and spacious and cost a fraction of a comparable home on Hong Kong Island or in smart Kowloon. Among the family photographs was one of his father looking nautical as a pupil at the Hong Kong Sea School and another of both parents on the beach at Stanley when it was almost as quiet and unspoiled as those on Lantau.

As before, driving on the island with Howard was an experience because he had once been the island's traffic supremo and knew every inch of the road as well as every traffic policeman. The roads were surprisingly good, especially the extravagantly illuminated highway on the approach to the greatest of all Lantau attractions, 'the world's largest outdoor seated bronze Buddha'. This was the Buddha that Sheila Macnamara and I had eschewed on my previous visit. Howard was no more enthusiastic about it than anyone else I spoke to. It was a new Buddha, created, allegedly, because various people felt the need to 'shine the shoes of the Chinese'. The ceremony of dedication had been something of an embarrassment with the Governor and Lavender attending and seeming ill at ease. There was an attendant monastery which had a distinctly commercial feel to it. There is something particularly unsettling about Mother Church dabbling in the tourist industry, whether it's Westminster Abbey, Chartreuse or this Chinese shrine where it was rumoured monks had been spotted wearing Rolex watches studded with diamonds. I didn't see any myself but there was a sense of ripped-off bus trip I found unappealing and we didn't stay long. The Buddha was big all right. Howard said it had been engineered by Chinese Aerospace, which made a certain bizarre sense. But there were too many crowded charabancs from the New Lantau Bus Company.

Not many buses in Tai O, however. Tai O was one of the world centres of shrimp-paste manufacture. All along the waterfront, rows and rows of straw trays were filled with pungent, pale-pink paste. They looked like Oriental pizza dishes or surreal waterlily pads. I wondered what happened when it rained. The ferry that crossed the creek which bisected Tai O was a Cherwell punt attached to a rope, hand-pulled by shrivelled old woman in a lampshade hat. We walked on through narrow lanes selling dried egg yolk and fish maw, then on to the point where, under a Union flag, we came to the white colonial police station presided over by a brisk Chinese inspector who produced ice-cold beer from his fridge. He and Howard showed me the plaque commemorating the fatal shooting, in 1918, of Police Sergeant Thomas Glendenning. He was gunned down by an Indian constable who had been arrested on a charge of theft.

Tai O was a cartographical aberration, for the maps showed that it was actually in Chinese waters. No one seemed to know quite how this had happened, but because of it the police station had been built right on the water's edge in order to show the flag in the most demonstrative way. For the same reason, a few yards along the coastal path there was a Royal Naval surveillance station. This was now abandoned, but Howard and the Inspector told me jolly stories of joint police and naval parties made more convivial by the supplies of duty-free alcohol helicoptered in to aid the sailors on their remote detachment. The Chief of Police's office was on the corner of the building and enjoyed sea views from all windows. For an exiled representative of the Raj it would have made a marvellous retreat – just the place for someone of Orwellian disposition and talent to fill idle moments by penning some home thoughts from abroad. Orwell served with the police in Burma, but it could just as well, couldn't it, have been Hong Kong? He wrote *1984* on the Hebridean island of Jura. What if he had been police-man/writer-in-residence here instead?

After lunch in an unassuming tiled café downtown where Howard silkily remarked – as I grappled with *pak choi* with shrimp sauce – that I seemed to have slippery chopsticks, we drove up a narrow Z-bend lane to the ancient Tung Chung Fort, now converted into a village school. Away in the distance lay the site of the new airport, that recurring bone of contention between the governments of Britain, China and Hong Kong. From our vantage point Howard and I could see a great wasteland peopled with scurrying insect-like machines, dust rising in their wake. It had a Moon City feel: progress in a primitive land. It would have been a satisfying post-colonial gesture if, just after the flag came down, the last Governor could have flown out from Britain's final gift to this once-barren rock. Far too satisfying to be allowed by Peking, who, in their own time and their own way, would inevitably subvert progress so that the new airport would, instead, be made to look like a triumph for Chinese invention and industry. Standing in that quiet rural spot with the Governor's bodyguard, I felt as if I was watching the beginnings of a fantasy by John Wyndham or H. G. Wells. All around us was almost as it had been for hundreds, even thousands, of years. But over there, as the mechanical ants scurried hither and yon, a Kraken was waking.

I suspected too that, given time, the Hong Kong flagship airline, like the new airport, would become a hijacked symbol of modern Chinese ingenuity. If, in the future, the airline prospered it would be a Chinese triumph; if it failed it would be the failure of a colonial legacy. I didn't fly Cathay Pacific until my final return, but one could not be unaware of

292

the name when one was actually in the Territory. It was to Hong Kong what British Airways is to the UK, though its image overseas belies that comparison. Whereas British Airways seems to base its international appeal on its Britishness, Cathay appeared, to me at least, to be making as little as possible of its Hongkongishness. Until I saw, at first hand, that it was the national carrier I had vaguely assumed that it was some sort of pan-Chinese pan-Pacific enterprise. I would not have thought it was a Communist airline, knowing that, on the whole, the aeroplanes of such regimes have bamboo or balsa-wood seating, no alcohol and staff who got their basic training in the Gulag. But I might just as well have placed Cathay's corporate HQ in Taiwan or the Philippines. Their latest slogan was 'Heart of Asia'. Anyone living in Hong Kong knew, of course, that this could only mean his home – Hong Kong, an Asian Rome, was the hub of the continent, if not the globe. To a European this was not so obvious.

Cathay's boss during my time in the Territory was Rod Eddington, a forty-something Australian with a doctorate in nuclear physics and a cricket blue from Oxford. *His* boss, Peter Sutch, the head of Swire's,* was also an Oxford graduate, though he was an English public schoolboy, educated at Downside.† Both struck me as notably hard-headed pragmatists. Both seemed profoundly Oxonian, even though they had travelled along different roads, but at the same time they had devoted their working lives to this part of the world. Both aspired, with some justice, to an

---

* Swire's, traditionally the great rival of Jardine Matheson, was one of the original Hong Kong *hongs*. Still immensely rich and powerful though they were, their hegemony had already been largely usurped by newer indigenous rivals headed by the likes of Li Ka Shing and Stanley Ho.
† His brother Dom Anthony, a fashionable Benedictine monk credited with royal princessly friendships, had recently been appointed headmaster of their alma mater.

understanding of the Oriental psyche which was obviously beyond me or even the Governor.

Eddington, who had an Asian wife and had worked in Korea and Japan as well as Hong Kong, made the point that, whereas an Anglo-Saxon will 'get comfortable' with someone very fast, it will take a Chinese person much longer. An Englishman meeting another Englishman for the first time will know within five minutes whether the two of them are going to get on together or whether they have nothing whatever in common.

This was particularly so in the case of the last Governor, he reasoned, 'because he's a strong man and not a chameleon so he doesn't become part of the environment he's plonked down in'. Eddington respected the Governor's 'strong sense of right or wrong', but because this stemmed largely from being a 'bright liberal Anglo-Saxon' it was difficult for the Chinese to comprehend. 'He believes in fundamental things,' he said, 'such as liberal democracy and by pursuing these ideals he has produced conflict. Hong Kong's future masters don't understand where he's coming from.' He paused, not so much, I felt, because he was uncertain what he was about to say next as because he regretted having to say it. 'Perhaps', he said, 'he doesn't understand where *they're* coming from.'

Like many businessmen, though he seemed to have an extra-commercial dimension lacking in many of them, he contrasted governmental dealings with the Chinese unfavourably with those of his own company. 'The Swire Group', he said, 'have been sending their best and brightest to China for at least ten years.'

In contrast there was 'no dialogue' between senior civil servants in Hong Kong and China, which, in his estimation, meant that there was a triangle with only two sides. There was dialogue between China and London; dialogue between Hong Kong and London; but no dialogue between China and Hong Kong. And that was inexcusable. On the other hand it was much too simplistic to blame it on the Governor, even though that was a popular pastime. 'There are plenty of people who, at the beginning, said "he's absolutely right" and then two years later "he should have known better".'

His view was that the people of Hong Kong would overcome this crisis just as they had overcome every other crisis. As for Cathay Pacific, the airline had changed from seeming to regard itself, essentially, as a British carrier in the Far East. Now it looked on itself as 'Hong Kong's premier airline'. That transition was critical and even if there were challenges to be faced they were the same challenges as those faced by most of Hong Kong – not the altogether more difficult ones confronting Hong Kong companies who were still perceived to be British.

The point was echoed, unsurprisingly, by Peter Sutch. 'Swire's were seen as being very British, which is why we took the company public in 1986. We wanted to be identified with Hong Kong.' For generations the company's recruits tended to be bright young Brits like him. They still take on such graduates, but the numbers have dropped sharply. In most years there would be three or four non-Hong Kong entrants to the organisation against about twenty-five locals.

Professing himself a personal admirer of the Governor, he seemed to share Rod Eddington's misgivings about the Patten political performance. How tired I was becoming of these personal caveats from the Governor's critics. I almost wished someone would concede a dislike for the person as well as the policies. However, Peter Sutch did seem able to enthuse about some of the achievements. 'I think', he said, 'that he has woken people up in the business community. After all, we *do* have pots of money and in many ways it is a very harsh community. I think Chris has persuaded people that it is possible to be a capitalist and to have a conscience.'

He mentioned AIDS and drug addiction and other areas of social concern. He thought there had been a change of mood. 'I hope that he's made a lasting difference,' he said.

In the end, though, Sutch will be going 'home' to retire. He said, forcefully, that his commitment to the Territory was absolute. When he felt it right he would stand up for HK against UK. And he could wax quite romantic about the place. On Sundays, sometimes, he would wake at five and drive round reminding himself of things he hadn't seen for an age. It was a vignette I found appealing. It was odd that this endearing image should be balanced by another automotive picture. On the whole he seemed to take a cautiously optimistic view of the post-1997 world, but he conceded that the 'Mercedes syndrome' might be more in evidence.

'The Mercedes syndrome?'

He smiled. 'A few more chaps behind shaded windows in large limos.'

Hmmm. There is nothing in the Joint Declaration or the Basic Law to cover tinted car windows and the cheap crocheted antimacassars which so often, out East, go with them.

Pity.

Of course when it came to large limos few came larger than the Governor's. His, however, despite the informality of these final months, had a sedate pomp which seemed ever more anachronistic. Despite oases of quiet, antiquity, elegance and sophistication, I was coming to believe that the essential Hong Kong was noisy, brash and vulgar.

Alan Ziman might have conceded 'noisy' and 'brash', but never, I think, 'vulgar'. His was a literal story of rags to riches, for a quarter of a century earlier he had been a struggling businessman in Montreal, importing cheap garments from Hong Kong. Now he was the rich entrepreneur who, almost single-handed, was responsible for the creation of Lan Kwai Fong, the Soho of Hong Kong. This was an area of Central just behind the FCC. It was quite unlike the old sleaze and Suzie Wongdom of my imagination, though I had glimpsed the remains of that neon girlie-bar world in Wan Chai and round the tourist hotels off Nathan Road on the other side of the harbour. That old world served the Hong Kong where the Fleet put in. It was part of the Rest and Recreation for the fighting men of Vietnam. Lan Kwai Fong, however, catered for the Hong Kong of the mobile 'phone, the Armani suit and the minuscule black skirt. It was a land of frozen daiquiris or Clare Valley Chardonnay in Happy Hours, chrome bar tops and rock music to shout over. There were restaurants which shaved parmesan over warm salads of chicken liver and rocket leaves.

The Belavistas, the small group of Hong Kong glitterati who invented the Bela Vista Ball, were epitomised for me by two exuberant independent PR women – Lynn Grebstadt and Mary Justice Thomasson. They struck me as the cheerleaders of Lan Kwai Fong. It was somehow symptomatic that neither Lynn nor 'MJ' much cared for Chinese food. But they knew everyone; they liked to party; and their photographs were often in the *Hong Kong Tatler* or on the social page of the *Post*.

'Fifteen years ago,' said Ziman, over a drink in his trademark bar, California, 'this was not the Hong Kong of today. The big event was "the Hotel". Everything happened at the Peninsula or the Mandarin. But there was nowhere for the sort of young people working for me to go. I figured that every city can use a Soho, so I came up with California.'

Other successful Hong Kong entrepreneurs have taken different routes and operated in different areas, but in some ways it seemed to me that Ziman was typical. He was a living demonstration that over the previous decade or so it was possible – especially if you were involved in property – to move from relative prosperity to serious wealth. I wasn't sure precisely how he had done it, but I suspected that he,

297

like others, had not got where he was by applying precisely what is taught at Harvard Business School. Above all, he seemed an enthusiastic risk-taker with an eye for the main chance and a grasp of the blindingly obvious which often eludes people of more conventional temperament and intelligence.

Back in Montreal at the beginning of the 1970s he had been paying well over 50 per cent income tax. In the Far East, where he was doing so much business, tax scarcely existed. It didn't take a genius to realise that if he shifted his base to Hong Kong he could earn less money but still have more in his pocket at the end of the year.

This he did. And before long he found that he was doing a lot of business in the Hunan province of China, which he described as 'truly Communist but exciting'. The experience helped him, he thought, to 'understand the Chinese mind' (though by now I had been in Hong Kong long enough to be becoming both tired and wary of this claim). He believed first of all that it was impossible to change the 'culture', which was too unassailably old, and therefore you had to learn to work with it rather than against it – something of a sideswipe here at the last governorship, which to him seemed to be working consistently against the grain. Within the culture, he continued, 'face' is the most important thing.

'The sooner the Westerner realises this, the more successful he is.'

I could see this, but I still found myself irritated. It seemed such a one-sided view. More than once I heard the Governor complain, only half jokingly, 'But what about the Governor's face?'

Perhaps, by always allowing the Chinese to maintain 'face', businessmen like Ziman could make more money, but why did the Chinese, to whom their own 'face' was so important, apparently refuse to concede that a gweilo might have 'face' as well? It seemed to me dangerously close to arguing that you must always let the Chinese have the better of any argument because if the Chinese loses an argument he loses 'face'. It was one thing to recognise the place of 'face' in Chinese culture but quite another to accept it unquestioningly. Why should we take them at 'face' value? On the other hand it was abundantly clear that doing so had paid handsome dividends for Alan Ziman.

Besides, when, as happened, the local (Chinese) residents of Lan Kwai Fong objected to what he was doing, he didn't really allow them much 'face'. He took them to court and won.

'When I came up with California I bought the old Keng Fung Supermarket. The owner wanted out. After that, whenever a shop or a warehouse in the area became vacant I bought it.'

Real estate is also expensive in Tokyo, which he knew well, and one result is that some buildings there have restaurants and bars on all their floors. He applied the same technique in Lan Kwai Fong so that, for example, the whole of the Yat Fung building, of which California occupies the ground floor, is rented out to other eating and drinking places.

'Suddenly the whole place started to have atmosphere. You've got to understand that there are a lot of young Western kids here and they get homesick. This has become the first place to come and have a hamburger. It's a little village now and I own the major part of it. I did quite well.'

This is true. And he had every intention of staying on. 'This is my place,' he said, 'I belong here. I know there'll be changes after 1997, but there's no way they'll screw it up. There are enough smart people in China and Hong Kong who want to make it work to make it work.'

We didn't discuss democracy or the Court of Final Appeal. For once the topics simply didn't arise.

'The secret of Hong Kong,' he told me, 'is the low tax base and laissez-faire.'

It will be interesting to see whether China agrees. It was a widely held point of view, although in a way it told one more about those who expressed it than the place about which they were expressing it. As the historian Elizabeth Sinn put it, 'I try to be objective but you can't help being your own person.'

Dr Sinn was often mentioned to me by thoughtful gweilos. She was an academic at the Hong Kong University specialising in the unfashionable subject of Hong Kong history under colonial rule studied from a Chinese point of view. English historians, like the seminal Endacott[*] (whose original draft had once, I was told, been rejected by the poet Edmund Blunden when he was on the staff of the university) and his latest disciple Frank Welsh, wrote inevitably from an English point of view. Chinese historians, with comparatively few exceptions, dealt with the vast themes of Chinese history rather than the footnote sideshow of the Chinese in Hong Kong. Apart from its relative insignificance, the story of the Hong Kong Chinese between the early nineteenth and late twentieth centuries was not exactly 'face'-enhancing.

'Each historian is constrained by her own circumstances,' Dr Sinn told me, a touch severely. She knew I was a friend of the Governor, and although she was welcoming and polite there was just a hint of frost. She was very much the professional historian and I think she suspected a lack of intellectual rigour in my approach. At one point in our conversation she said that it was impossible to write proper history until about fifty years after the event. 'Events like 4 June' – she was referring to Tiananmen Square – 'we discuss and think about but without the detachment you need as a

---

[*] G. B. Endacott, *A History of Hong Kong*, Oxford University Press, 1958.

historian.' No historian could exercise the necessarily impartial judgements about things which happened in their own lifetime. She almost said that no historian could *ever* be sufficiently impartial, period. 'Endacott', she said, 'is Eurocentric. Historians such as he only look from the top down. I try to compensate and turn the case upside down. I want to do that because I am Chinese. I can talk to people. I can read Chinese texts . . .'

She paused. I felt inadequate on a number of crucial counts. When I asked her if one recent authority, extravagantly praised by Dr Mirsky of *The Times*, was a book upon which to rely, she said succinctly: 'Not scholarly.' That verdict made me feel very unscholarly indeed.

One of Dr Sinn's most important books was a history of the Tung Wah Hospital. In earlier times the directors of the hospital performed the dual function of interpreting Chinese laws and customs for the benefit of a largely ignorant British government and also of acting as spokesmen for the Chinese community. They ran the hospital, too, but this was almost a secondary consideration.

I had a fascinating tutorial from Dr Sinn, though later I learnt from a friend of hers that she might have been more forthcoming had I not been so apparently tarred with the imperialist and journalistic brushes. 'Colonial and imperial writers will say that the Empire was the best thing that ever happened,' she said, 'but actually if you look at the ways in which laws were enacted it's not such a pretty picture.'

'It was not', she conceded, 'a black and white picture', but on the whole she seemed to be saying that the colonial administration left a lot to be desired. In the 1950s and 1960s there was 'rudeness, mistreatment, social injustice, an unfair distribution of wealth'. There was no labour protection in the 1960s; no compulsory education until 1973, and even now it was free only till the age of fifteen. And when I talked so blithely about Hong Kong Chinese, who did I

301

mean? New Territories families who had lived there for 700 years or more? Or people like her whose parents came from Shanghai? What is one to make of a scholarly intellect such as hers, feeling on the one hand perfectly at home with Chinese opera, music and literature and yet brought up to sing 'God Save the Queen' and play hockey and netball?

'Hong Kong was part of China and is becoming part of China again,' she said. 'There is no controversy about that. But we need to balance the rhetoric of Empire against the reality of Empire.'

I thought of Alan Ziman sitting in his very contemporary bar in Lan Kwai Fong, letting me into the secret of Hong Kong being low-tax and laissez-faire. I'm afraid I chickened out of telling Dr Sinn what he had said. The two people and their points of view were so far removed that there seemed little point in trying to construct a bridge. It was not that one was right and the other wrong, but that they were not talking the same language.

Having been brought up in the twilight of the golden age of newspapers, I still attached a lingering importance to journalism. I believed that, at its best, it could legitimately claim to be 'history on the wing' and that, *pace* Dr Sinn, this was a legitimate subject. After all, when, in fifty years' time, 'scholarly' historians began at last to deal with the events of today, what better source could they have than contemporary newspapers? The principal players in this drama would be long since dead; their diaries and memoirs hopelessly *partis pris* or bowdlerised. But the newspapers, with their privileged ring seat and their instant recording of events, would be colourful and authoritative. They would be the record on which subsequent analysis would be based. That was what newspapers were all about.

My previous encounters with Jonathan Fenby had suggested that all was not entirely well at the *South China Morning Post*. No sooner had he arrived than his star cartoonist was fired from under him, closely followed by 10 per cent of the staff journalists. There then ensued an amalgamation of the daily and Sunday papers, both to be edited by Fenby. He was also, it seemed, in the awkward situation of being answerable to both his proprietor and his predecessor. Rumours, some of which turned out to be true, abounded. Very early in his editorship Fenby was seen walking from the newspaper building to the management office with the editor-in-chief, Armstrong. Everyone immediately 'knew' that both men had been fired and that Tony O'Reilly* had bought the paper. An announcement was scheduled for 6 p.m.

In the event, of course, none of these things took place.

There was anxiety in the Territory about press freedom, and I had attended two meetings on the subject. The sense of both was that, while there was no direct press censorship as such, most publications and radio and TV stations were already practising some form of self-censorship. The fear was that, if such restraint did not produce the requisite results, the new post-1997 regime would step in to do the job itself. The Governor, publicly and privately, expressed a genuine and heartfelt belief in press freedom. But I got the impression that we all knew that he was whistling in the wind. After the hand-over his writ would no longer run and there was also an uneasy feeling that the more loudly he protested the more the Chinese would clamp down when their moment arrived.

As far as the *Post* was concerned I didn't feel that it was being censored either from within or from without. I didn't have the sense that its finger was on the pulse or that it was really required reading, but that was different. In any case

---

* Dr Tony O'Reilly, former rugby international, proprietor of the *Irish Independent* chain of papers and an increasing number of newspapers worldwide, was a voracious empire-builder whose name was inevitably linked with any publication considered vulnerable.

those criticisms were true of almost every newspaper in the modern capitalist world. Greed and technology had more or less finished off serious print journalism.

Fenby was happy for me to sit in on a day at the office, though when we met for lunch he was nursing a heavy cold and contented himself with an iced tea and a veggiburger. Both his leader writers had been off the day before and he felt uncomfortable writing editorials unassisted. Although he had now moved from his hotel to an apartment in Old Peak Road, I didn't feel he had yet really come to terms with the place. He said Chinese people he met were surprised when he referred to such things as 'discussions', 'meetings' and 'consultations'. They evidently expected an editor to hire, fire and throw his weight about. Not Fenby style.

He also confirmed that editing was a very electronic affair these days. The *Post* had arrangements with many other newspapers and all of them made their copy available on screen. Whereas a newspaper editor in the days when Fenby and I began our careers in Fleet Street would have briefed and directed his own foreign correspondents, he now seemed to have a much more reactive role. For example, the big story of the moment was the arrest in China of Harry Wu, a prominent dissident who, despite being of Chinese origin, now had American citizenship. Washington's reaction was obviously a major news item. The *Post* had a Washington correspondent of its own but he was on holiday. No matter. Fenby could call up at least two other papers' stories on his computer screen, decide which one he preferred, and pull it out for the following day's *Post*.

This form of editing was not peculiar to Hong Kong, but it was not what I was used to. Nor, I felt, perhaps priggishly, was it what one should expect from a serious newspaper. At that time, the news editor Simon Macklin told me, there were nineteen general news, eight political and five court reporters. As Jonathan Fenby had told me earlier, there was a conscious shift away from being a sort of London *Times* in exile. 'In the old days,' said Macklin, 'when the House of Commons had its annual debate on Hong Kong we'd report it almost verbatim. Now it doesn't make page one. In the old days whenever any old MP arrived from London we'd go down and interview him. Now we wouldn't bother.'

This seemed reasonable enough. The fact that the *Post*'s coverage of Britain no longer featured the views of any boring knight of the shires or trade union nominee jetting in on a parliamentary freebie was a realistic reflection of the changing political scene as well as a sensible idea of what constituted 'news'. On the other hand, there was a depressing tendency to suggest that the only news coming out of Britain concerned the peccadilloes of the royal family. In fairness I had to admit that this was not a view confined exclusively to the pages of the *South China Morning Post*.

'There's nothing happening in the world very much,' said the editor morosely. So it seemed at conference, as the staff ran through their agenda. One story about a triad godfather in Chinatown elicited the editorial response, 'That one's been on the list for as long as I've been here.' There was a story about the official abandoning of the one-cent note – now worth next to nothing – and it was suggested that a reporter try to conduct a transaction using one. This idea was abandoned in favour of a 'whimsical leader'. Fenby must have been as aware as anyone that he didn't have an equivalent to *The Times*'s Philip Howard on his staff. 'We'll see how whimsical it turns out to be,' he said. 'We'll have Wu on the front ... and a picture of the mass Korean wedding ... sport have offered us the Tour de France ... I'm keen to do this pop group Blur, though the trouble is no one will recognise them.'

There are few places more dispiriting than a newspaper office on a slow news day. To while away the time I was given a crash course on the new technology. As technology it looked brilliant. There was hardly any paper in the building. Everything was sent by computer to the new print plant at Taipo in the New Territories.

'Basically,' the production chief told me, 'you can produce everything anywhere.' The *Straits Times*, the famous old Singapore newspaper, was apparently now being sub-edited in Australia. I could see that this was technologically amazing, but I couldn't help wondering how much feel a sub-editor in Sydney would have for a story in Singapore. It reminded me of the last days of *Punch*, when the staff spent more time performing conjuring tricks on their computers than thinking of something funny to write. One older *Post* sub-editor, an Australian – practically all the subs seemed to be Westerners – told me that the next wave of machines would enable editors to watch TV and a video and sub copy, all at the same time. Big deal, I thought, wondering why anyone should wish to do such a thing. And, of course, although boffins, hackers and other techno-groupies say otherwise, the new systems are fallible and when they fail they fail with a spectacular finality. The previous night the main leader had frozen on screen. The technicians spent twenty minutes trying to move it and then admitted defeat. The only way to unblock the system was by losing the whole leader.

Such is progress.

More impressive was a major row between the *Post* and the French Consulate. Fenby had taken a tough line on French nuclear testing in the Pacific. The Consul General, with whom Fenby, a serious Francophile, had been on cordial terms, became incandescent and faxed Fenby to accuse him of stirring up hatred against his country. Then, after an unfortunate frog-bashing article on Bastille Day ('Nothing to do with me,' said Fenby), the Consul General made a public speech attacking the *Post* for racism.

Fenby was not altogether happy about it all. 'Now I can't

306

even go to the French cinema club to see my favourite films,' he complained.

And despite new technology there were still rules to be observed and problems to be resolved – at least by someone brought up in the old ways like Fenby. 'Oh God,' he said as he tapped away at his keyboard in his poky office on the twenty-eighth floor, 'split infinitive.' And then, as we watched jet after jet roar into Kai Tak on the other side of the harbour, he struggled over a headline. He wanted something witty and elaborate, but after typing the words 'Boat People' found that he had run out of space. Perhaps editing was still the same as ever, despite the obfuscation of the new screenpower.

'Can you say', he asked in quiet desperation, 'that more people watch the Tour de France than any other sporting event in the world?'

Neither of us could answer this knotty question and we fudged the issue. Then, earlier than usual, still suffering from his cold, Fenby toured the premises, chatting away in an informal, shirtsleeved manner to the night staff, before fading away to his apartment halfway up the Peak. I wondered if he would still be editing the paper after the Governor had gone. 'I hope so,' he said. 'The lease on the apartment expires in mid-July 1997.'

Always one returned to that date, even though there were those who scoffed and said it was just a date and had no real significance and life in Hong Kong would just roll on like some seamless carpet. The *Post*, however diminished, was a symbol of the status quo; its continued presence a reassuring sign that all was fundamentally well. Even after a short stay there were for me many such aspects, both people and places. Most significantly, of course, I knew that if, after 30 June 1997, I were to return and find, as inevitably I would, that Chris, Lavender, Alice, Whisky, Soda, Louise and Elspeth were no longer in Government House and had been

307

replaced by strange Chinese substitutes, I would feel threatened and unhappy. And the same went for a whole host of other familiars. How would it feel, I wondered, to be Peter Sutch, rising early on Sunday morning to drive round his favourite memories, and find them all gone or changed for ever? Rhetorical question.

One such institution was Sam the Tailor. So much so that the old Hong Kong hands warned me off on the grounds that he was over-exposed and too expert at self-promotion. Probably true. But I liked Sam. He was an institution. And he was 'By appointment to the Governor'.

'Everybody is nice in the world, sir . . . all is written . . . it is karma . . . for you I make a dark-blue suit because you have bright shirts . . . a quick measure with a very light touch . . . the secret is in the cut . . . if the cut does not fit the altering does not work . . . you have to see the customer's body . . . Bingley is where the material comes from . . . it takes time . . . first a captain comes . . . then a major . . . then a colonel . . . you have to be patient . . . Coutts Bank are my bankers . . . The Governor has visited my workshop because he wanted to be sure . . . I have made him thirty suits since 1988 when he was MP . . . I have made Mrs Lavender's suit.' He produced a Reuter's report clipped from an obscure American paper: 'Tailor to the rich and famous,' it said. 'Clients include Prince Charles, Richard Nixon, David Bowie.'

'You can't write about Sam,' said the old Hong Kong hands, with smart streetwise scepticism, 'everyone writes about Sam.' The man at the Hongkong Bank regarded me with mild disdain. 'We get rather fed up', he said loftily, 'with journalists who get parachuted in and interview the same six people, then go home and write as if they knew all about the place.'

Well, yes, I concede, Sam is probably one of the same six people. But he was a fixture in the Hong Kong I got to know, whether in his shop or lurking, smiling, in the shadows of the Queen's Birthday party at Government House. Surely Sam will be there after 1997? Sam himself won't say.

'It is written,' is all he will vouchsafe. The new regime will want Sam's suits and shirts. Won't they?

'What about Sam?' I asked one of his loyal customers. 'Will he be all right?'

'You don't have to worry about Sam,' came the reply. 'He's got a million-pound mansion in St John's Wood.'

Hong Kong wouldn't be the same without him.

But then Hong Kong won't be anyway.

EIGHTEEN

August is the cruellest month in Hong Kong. The heat is at its most heavily sodden and it is typhoon time. Those who can afford to tend to make themselves scarce, and this includes the Pattens. The new house in France beckoned with siren promises of sun, silence, anonymity and *vin de pays*. After a while even the most robust constitution is debilitated by votes of no confidence. In April I thought the Governor seemed ebullient and gung ho. Almost four months later he struck me as pensive and a little jaded. He was nowhere near the beleaguered, marginal figure his critics described, but he still appeared out of sorts and in need of a break.

I had seen more of him over the last few weeks than in the previous few years and it was fascinating to follow him round the slummish tower blocks and the drug clinics, to hear him fielding questions in LegCo, watch him tripping the light fantastic at David Tang's China Club party and breast-stroking himself slowly round the *Lady Maureen* in Double Haven. But so far I had not sat down and conducted a face-to-face on-the-record interview and although, for the most part, I was not writing that sort of book, let alone his biography, I still felt I should capture some more formal structured Governor's thoughts to set alongside his sardonic off-hand quips, his public pronouncements and my own observations. I wasn't intending a self-consciously gritty TV-style interrogation full of lines like 'With respect, Governor, you haven't answered my question' or 'Did you or did you not intend to fly out from the new airport in 1997?' I wanted something more ruminative.

So one day after Lavender and Alice had departed for France and just before he followed them I presented myself at Government House for the last time, armed with a tiny Microcassette-corder newly purchased from an electronics boutique in Prince's Building. The rain was bucketing down and the Governor regarded it morosely. 'No tennis today,' he said. I asked how long he was away for and he said he had to be back in Hong Kong for the fiftieth anniversary of the Liberation from the Japanese. He accepted the duty with good grace, though I sensed a slight embarrassment. The occasion could hardly do other than exacerbate anti-Japanese sentiments. The reality of the 1990s was that he, Britain and Hong Kong had to rub along with the present generation of Japanese, and especially the Consul General, whom he regarded as 'rather a nice chap'. It wouldn't be all that easy to strike the correct, delicate balance.

When he was first offered the job in 1992 he had spent the whole of his working life in domestic British politics. For more than a quarter of a century he had been a Conservative politician and for half that time he had been an elected Member of Parliament. He had been to Hong Kong only once in his life and his working experience of foreign affairs was confined to three years as Minister of Overseas Development. Unless you count his time as a junior minister in Belfast he had no experience of colonial administration. Nor was he expected to be any old colonial governor. His task of preparing a British possession for its return to another sovereign power was unprecedented. I wondered if in the beginning he really knew what he was letting himself in for.

'I'm not sure', he said, 'that I knew what I expected. I

311

always thought it would be difficult, tiresome and long drawn out to deal with Chinese officials, to negotiate with the Chinese. I think that the state of the leadership in Peking, and the stage of evolution it's in, has made it even more complicated and even more of a problem than it would have been otherwise. There are some of my Foreign Office officials who have been involved in virtually every negotiation with China over the last fifteen or twenty years and there are some of them who say that they don't think it would have been possible to negotiate the Joint Declaration in the present state of politics in Peking. So that's been more complicated than I thought it would.

'The politics here in Hong Kong has been both more moderate than I expected – given the huge issues that are at stake and are debated, the political dialogue is very reasonable and pretty calm – and at the same time it's cruder than I expected in the sense that the analysis is so angular. On the whole, people only have two keys on the word processor. It's either "c" for confrontation or "k" for kowtow.

'I underestimated the amount of media interest there'd be, both in the international media and in the local media. And not just interest in me as governor but in the governor's family. In fact Alice has managed to cope remarkably well and been pretty normal. I think Laura found it more difficult.'

In fact the media fuss generated by Laura's short skirt, when they first arrived, turned out to be an Andy Warhol fifteen minutes of celebrity.

'I also think', he continued, 'that the Mayor of Hong Kong side has been more fun than I'd expected. Running a city of this size without any of the financial constraints which one is used to in European politics makes a bit of a difference.

'So I guess my stumbling answer is that there are several ways in which it was different . . . some things you can't entirely anticipate. I both have and haven't felt lonely from time to time. I have very good officials. I have extremely good personal staff and have done right since the beginning, but there are times when you feel very much at the end of the branch. In a Cabinet job at home even when you're under a lot of pressure there's a sort of collegiality about taking the brickbats, whereas that isn't true of this job. People have been very kind. I'm on the 'phone a lot to friends, but I don't think one can quite predict in advance just how far away London is in sentiment.'

I was reminded yet again of the 'home thoughts from abroad' above Governor Maclehose's name in the Post Office. All Governors represent Her Majesty in theory and Her Majesty's Government in practice. That means constant contact with London. I had been quite surprised at how easily I seemed to have, temporarily at least, sloughed off London. But unlike Chris I had no official umbilical cord connecting me to 'home'. It was probably not a good idea for the Governor to go native in any case. Locals and others who sneered at the 'bunker mentality' of Government House rather missed that point. If it sometimes seemed more like an outpost of Whitehall than part of Hong Kong itself, that was not necessarily a bad thing.

It seemed to me that the honeymoon with the press was long gone and I wondered if the constant drip of press hostility had had the debilitating effect on him that it would have had on me. After having to defend the poll tax and the Conservative Party, however, the Governor had developed a thicker skin than mine. He shrugged. 'I don't think it's as bad as the Prime Minister's had in the UK. I mean the endless, remorseless criticisms from the press. Here most of its copeable with because it's so daft . . .'

It was tedium which wore him down as much as criticism. 'The days I find most exhausting,' he said, 'are the ones where I have a visiting foreign minister, a journalist I've got

313

to speak to, a bank chairman and a delegation from the American Bar Association. On some days I feel I've been speaking and *have* actually been speaking for five or six hours just going over the same old stuff over and over again. I watch my private secretaries sometimes when they're noting these meetings and they have a sort of code: the X story, the Y story, A anecdote, B anecdote . . .'

He shook his head and half laughed with the only slightly amused exasperation I'd often noticed.

I wasn't altogether surprised that boredom depressed him more than animosity. All the same I wondered if the level of hostility he'd been subjected to from mainland China was something he expected. He thought for a moment and shook his head again. 'No,' he said, looking as if he was thinking about it for the first time. 'No,' he repeated, and then brightened enough to chuckle.

'It's quite funny, the poor President of Taiwan* is now being subjected to it. There's a cartoon strip in the *Hong Kong Economic Journal* called Fat Pang's Theatre. It's very funny. They've had me cheerfully on the 'phone to the President of Taiwan during the last few days.

'The Chinese invective seems to have been so much water off a duck's back. It was so sort of Cultural Revolution childish: "whore" . . . "prostitute" . . . I think there's still a leftist element there, particularly in their propaganda organs and bureaucracy.'

Nevertheless the Chinese outrage has seemed genuine and not all the criticism has come from such predictable *parti pris* sources as Sir Percy Cradock. There must have been moments when he wondered if he might have behaved differently?

'Well,' he said, 'the smart criticism used to be "Of course

*The Taiwanese President had just returned from his visit to his old university in the USA. This had excited much the same sort of Chinese invective as that to which the Governor had for so long been subjected.

314

we sympathise with what he's trying to do but if only he'd gone about it differently." Well, that's not actually the point at all. We spent a year trying to negotiate a deal with them on the electoral arrangements and the truth of the matter is that they were incapable of compromising. Their notion of what was tolerable was so many miles distant from ours. No, I don't think to be honest I'd have changed fundamentally and I certainly wouldn't have changed what caused the row, which is that we had a bottom line. Somebody who was here in the Cradock days was saying to me recently that during his period every argument was resolved by a telegram from Cradock – or inspired by Cradock – saying, "No, but this is a *principled position* for the Chinese and we'll have to back off.' No *principled position* for Hong Kong or Britain. And that's *really* what the row was all about.

'It's also worth pointing out that if we hadn't been prepared to stand up for clean elections, if we hadn't been determined not to connive at arrangements for throwing Martin Lee and others out of the Legislative Council, the row we're having at the moment over the Court of Final Appeal would have been as nothing compared with the international obloquy and the local row we'd have had. It would have been extremely destabilising. Also, if I'd done what some people now say they think I should have done – not to set out some general proposals to discuss with the Chinese in public but to go off and try to negotiate a deal with them in private and come back with it – we'd probably have found ourselves in exactly the same situation as we found ourselves in with the CFA, which was exactly the product of that sort of diplomacy. We negotiated a quote secret deal unquote with the Chinese and then couldn't sell it to the Legislative Council, so four years on we're desperately trying to get something set up before we go.'

At times he must have had doubts? He smiled and half agreed. 'There were days in the autumn of 1992 in particular when the Hang Seng index was down four hundred points when one had to hold on pretty tight.'

Some months earlier David Tang had told me that his friends in Peking had trouble coming to terms with the notion that this Governor was not simply an emissary from Britain but a substantial political figure charged with making policy as well as executing it. I wondered to what extent Chris really did have genuine autonomy or whether he had to do as he was told by London. 'I've pretty well had a free hand right the way through,' he said, 'I mean I have to get the cover of the Foreign Secretary and the Cabinet and the Prime Minister and there have been moments, particularly in 1992 and 1993, when we've had to get the stamp of Cabinet committee for the policy being pursued. That's constitutionally proper, but with the exception, a bit, of the Court of Final Appeal there haven't been endless attempts to second-guess us. And on the CFA, once Cabinet ministers had agreed that if we didn't get a deal we'd have to go ahead and legislate on our own, they left the playing of the hand to me. It means that we can make decisions very quickly, we can adjust and manoeuvre much more rapidly, and sometimes I think the Chinese are rather surprised by this.

'The Chinese used to say that what they wanted in this last period was a senior political figure as governor who was close to the Foreign Secretary and the Prime Minister and who could make decisions on the spot, and they got one.' He said this with a short laugh, making it quite plain that Peking didn't like it but that in his opinion it served them right. 'I think the Chinese know perfectly well where policy's made,' he continued. 'One of the early things we did was to install secure lines between us and Peking and between us and London, and I'm not so naive as to think that the Chinese don't know when we're going "secure" – not to put too fine a point on it. And throughout the negotiations in 1993 they knew perfectly well that the Ambassador was reporting back

316

to me after every round of negotiation, which he did superbly incidentally – he's a very good man, Robin Maclaren.

'So there are always the same clutch of stories about Hong Kong politics: there are the "secret deal" stories, the "Governor's about to go home" stories, there's "the Governor doesn't really care about us, he's only doing this for his greater glory in Britain so he can go back as foreign secretary", there is "the Governor's not making the policy any more", there's "the Governor's a lame duck", there's the Governor's "secret agenda", there's the Governor's "isolation" . . . you can go on for ever. And they've been running since whenever it was, July 1992, when I first came.'

I recalled my first visit when we had passed like ships in the night and he had been attacked on the front page for going back to England so often. He sighed. 'The story about me being away too much was entirely a *South China Morning Post* story which got picked up by other people. Two weeks ago they ran an editorial saying that I wasn't going back to London *enough* and how this was an indication that London didn't care about us any more and how irrelevant we all were. When the "Offshore Governor" stories were running we actually sat down and very patiently counted up the number of days I'd been away, compared it with the number of days my predecessor had been away. We showed that I'd been away less than my predecessor. It made no difference whatsoever.'

It seemed to me that whereas British journalists, especially the editors of national newspapers, had enormously inflated opinions of themselves and were courted ludicrously by politicians, their Hong Kong counterparts had a wholly different status. At home Chris would have been much more circumspect in his dealings with the press and would have regarded the best journalists as, if not intellectual equals, at least intellectually worthy opponents. That did not appear to be the case in Hong Kong. What's more, the apparently condescending attitude of the Governor was echoed by many other figures in Hong Kong's public life. Hong Kong's British journalists, unlike their counterparts in business, commerce or the law, gave me the impression that they felt a bit second-rate and provincial. I also got the impression that this was the Governor's view as well. Of one persistently hostile hack he remarked that he had a 'chip on his shoulder the size of Epping Forest'. When I floated my own impressions past him he said simply, 'There's a huge amount of chippiness about', before switching to a more constructive vein.

'I tell you one thing that Lee Kuan Yew advised me. He said, "You've got five years. You've got to go there. You've got to set out your agenda. And just deliver it." And by and large that's what I've done, right across the board. We set out a programme of welfare development . . . of education . . . environment . . . in 1992 and we have a report each year of how far we've got and we've pretty well accomplished it. There were three areas I was concerned with: a social agenda . . .' Here he digressed for a moment. 'That's been another of the annoying criticisms – the "one-issue" Governor. You go to a hospital, you come out, you make a statement about hospitals, and they all stand there with their pencils waiting and then it's, "What about the airport, Mr Patten?", "What about politics?" '

He shook his head again, exasperated by such facile perversity.

'Anyway, there are some elements in the social agenda that I feel particularly keenly about. For example, getting a better deal for the disabled, trying to develop a more coherent and successful programme for dealing with drug abuse. The disabled I feel particularly strongly about because it seemed to me that unless we got fairly civilised arrangements in place before '97 they were less likely to be put in

318

place afterwards. Secondly, there were all the window-pane issues as it were – putting in panes of glass in order to protect Hong Kong as much as possible, getting rid of that colonial legislation which has denied a bill of rights, ombudsman, access to information, data protection – all that sort of thing. And thirdly to try to deal, sooner rather than later, with the awkward issues which had been left around. And the most difficult of these were the electoral arrangements.

'Nothing would have pleased me more in retrospect than if these had been agreed before I came. But I also felt very strongly that we had to show that the Joint Declaration wasn't just verbiage, that it wasn't just a fig leaf for us to wear while we fled Hong Kong. And I felt we had to be seen to be standing up for Hong Kong's autonomy. So that was the package I arrived with.

'What's one trying to do here? I suppose one's trying, in a political sense, to keep several plates in the air. Local opinion, Westminster opinion, international opinion, China. If you can keep three in the air that's pretty good going. It's quite difficult to keep the first three in the air and avoid the fourth hitting the ground fairly regularly.'

Having been educated as a historian he took, I think, a longer view than many politicians. Naturally he was concerned with his own personal performance as a colonial administrator, but I expected him also to have some thoughts about the British performance as a whole. How did he think history would judge the British in Hong Kong from beginning to end? 'I think it's a pretty good record,' he said. 'If you think, three-quarters of the people here are refugees or the families of refugees. I was explaining this to an Australian the other day – the Speaker of the Victorian Parliament and I turned to Bobby* and I said, "Bobby, I

---

*Bobby Cheng, assistant private secretary to the Governor.

don't know where you come from?" Well, it turned out his parents had fled Canton in the fifties.

'What did Hong Kong have to offer? Trading post. Good harbour. No natural resources. And almost as soon as the refugees arrrived the trade embargo with China during the Korean War meant that Hong Kong had to start manufacturing or it was finished. And there has been a huge commitment and entrepreneurial vim from the Chinese, particularly the Cantonese and the Shanghaiese who had worked in Shanghai in the textile industry. But what lit the spark has been our political culture: clean, pretty decent public administration, good police, rule of law . . . to put it mildly, no "hidden agenda". British firms have done well out of Hong Kong, but it's difficult to think that "treasure" has been shipped from Hong Kong to the United Kingdom.

'So we provided a home and a refuge for these people which, with our help, they turned into this astonishing place. As I say to every visitor, the only statistic you need to know about Hong Kong is that the six million people who live here produce a gross domestic product which is equivalent to twenty-six per cent of the whole of China.* And today we have health indicators which are better than most OECD countries. A quarter of our eighteen-year-olds go on to tertiary education. Between sixty and seventy per cent of those kids come from public housing. It's an astonishing social revolution. So I think it's one of the greatest success stories of British colonial administration.

'The one area in which it has lagged has been in the development of representative government and democratic institutions. My predecessors in the forties and fifties wanted

*The latest estimate (1995) is that the population of mainland China is 1,200,000,000, so Hong Kong, with a population only one two-hundredth of China's, generates more than a quarter of its annual wealth. The average Hong Konger is therefore more than fifty times as economically effective as his (or her) mainland counterpart.

to develop institutions similar to those that were being developed elsewhere in the Empire. They were dissuaded from doing so by the extreme Chinese hostility to the proposition on the grounds that if people in Hong Kong started voting they might believe that they were actually in charge of their own destiny. There were also those who said – and perhaps they were right – that elections would produce a polarisation between Kuomintang Taiwan supporters* and United Front voters.'

I remarked that there were those, from the late Richard Hughes to many of the people I'd met, especially business-men for whom not rocking the political boat was para-mount, who took the view that Hong Kong people were simply not interested in politics.

He disagreed. 'The truth is that people in Hong Kong are no more and no less interested in politics than anybody else. They're better educated, better travelled, better off, more middle class. They have the same sort of political agenda as anybody else.'

On one occasion he had told me that one British colleague of his absolutely hated Hong Kong. At the same time Chris denied that he felt in the least like this. Nevertheless I sensed an ambivalence in him which was not to do with the rocky professional road he was having to tread.

He thought for a moment. 'There are aspects of it that I find surprising. I think I understand the pretty ruthless, self-protective individualism of some of the leaders of the business community. They are, after all, refugees. They don't see any great distinction, moral or otherwise, between on the one hand opposing any attempt to build into Hong Kong defence mechanisms for the future and on the other making their own arrangements. It is not an unusual experience to

*Many Hong Kongers were sympathetic to the anti-Communist regime in Taiwan.

321

find oneself one day being attacked by individuals who will the next day be asking for British passports. You were asking what initially surprised me and I think I was surprised by that sort of yawning gulf between what people think is acceptable public behaviour and what they do in private. So I guess I understand more about, not just Hong Kong, but human behaviour as a whole. If I'd been a refugee maybe I'd behave like that. What it's meant is that there isn't the sort of corporate identification with the values of the community that I would have ideally expected and certainly that I would have wanted to see. I think the other thing I understand more clearly are the consequences of colonial administration with touches of racism here and there – in both directions.'

A few days earlier there had been a dinner for the whole of LegCo at Government House. Chris and Lavender sat at a table with four LegCo members and their spouses. Afterwards Chris asked Lavender, with amusement, whether she realised that they were the only parents at the table who were having their child locally educated. He looked thoughtful about this and I remembered Charles Weatherill asking me, early in our acquaintance, whether I thought the Governor understood the 'Chinese mind'. I passed the question on and, as I had anticipated, he gave me a derisory look which suggested that in his view the Chinese mind was much the same as anybody else's. 'What are the manifestations of Confucianism in Hong Kong?' he asked rhetorically. 'I mean, give me a break.'

Part of my fascination with his predicament was the effect it was having on him personally. Was he in danger of becoming spoilt? 'The difference between being a Cabinet minister and having a job like this is that all the edges of life are smoothed over,' he replied. 'I don't find myself sitting in quite the same traffic jam as everybody else. We're very well looked after, extremely comfortably looked after. I don't think it's going to be difficult to turn one's back on it. I'm

322

looking forward to spending the next four weeks digging the garden, making ratatouille, driving a car for the first time, shopping, going to market. I mean we've tried to humanise this place, but it's still an astonishing museum to live in.'

But was he in danger of becoming insulated? Or even corrupted? He took some time to reply to this, apparently chewing it over as if he hadn't considered it before. 'I don't think it's "insulating",' he said, 'partly because of Alice and having kids around the house, partly because we've got a lot of friends in Hong Kong and we go to shops and to restaurants and get out a lot. Corrupting? Um, I don't think I've become more grand.' He paused and looked mischievous. One of his predecessor's wives, he told me, said of her husband that he could never say 'I *think*'. The reason for this, she said unashamedly, was because he was the leader of the community and therefore always had to say, 'I *know*'. You wouldn't catch Lavender making a remark like that. 'The best people to ask are my private office.' He said he always makes a point of working in the same office as his staff every afternoon. He clearly regarded the gesture as important for team spirit. Ultimately, though, he was tentative about whether or not he'd been corrupted.

'I won't know until I've finished,' he said ruminatively. 'It'll have been five years. That's quite a big chunk of one's active life . . . I really don't know what I'm going to do next . . .' For a moment I almost got the impression he was regretting his governorship, as if Hong Kong had stolen those five years and prevented him doing something he would have preferred.

I asked if he regretted accepting the post.

'I remember,' he answered, 'shortly after the last election when I'd lost my seat, driving down to stay with the Cranbornes* in Dorset – one of my favourite places – and

---

*Viscount Cranborne, heir to the Marquess of Salisbury, was elected

323

listening to *Any Questions* in the car. Roy Jenkins was being dismissively patronising about me. He was saying, "He's such a bad chooser of jobs ... Environment Secretary, Chairman of the Party, now he's off to Hong Kong ... I was offered Hong Kong in the lavatory at 10 Downing Street by Jim Callaghan and I turned it down." '

Chris frowned disbelievingly. 'I don't know how people can conduct a public career in that way. I've always done what I've been asked to do. I hope that doesn't sound po-faced but I've never planned my career.

'Oh, one exception was that after I lost my seat I felt very strongly that none of the options – a by-election, the House of Lords, staying in government – was acceptable. I certainly didn't want to be hanging around in the margins of politics with a lot of people feeling sorry for me. What I really wanted was another public service job if possible away from Westminster. I couldn't possibly compare my four or five years here with what I might have been doing if things had turned out differently and say that life has been brutally unfair to me. But if you ask if I'd have preferred to win my seat and stay in the Cabinet then yes, of course. That's what my life had always led towards. The one job I shall always regret not having is foreign secretary. But I would like to think that I have another public service job still to do.'

I said that the governorship of Hong Kong was not a bad qualification on one's CV and he snorted. 'It gives you a better quality of bullshit,' he said.

A sceptical part of me believed that although Chris had caused a tremendous brouhaha vis-à-vis the Chinese it wouldn't in the end make any real difference. In ten or twenty years' time, the historian looking back would decide that no matter who was the last Governor the outcome was

---

MP for South Dorset in 1979, the same year Chris Patten first entered Parliament.

always going to be the same. You would hardly expect Chris to concur. 'I hope I will have made it easier for Hong Kong to stand up for itself,' he answered, when I asked rudely if he thought he would have made the slightest difference. 'And I hope that I will have contributed towards the momentum behind what American political scientists call "the institutions of civil society" which will help them to travel successfully through 1997. If I haven't managed to do those things then your question will be decidedly relevant.

'All of us have hanging over us that remark of Enoch Powell's that all political careers end in failure. All that you can really do is to be able to live with yourself and to be able to feel that you actually tried to behave honestly and honourably – that you tried to live up to what you believed in. But I don't look back. I don't keep cuttings. I ruthlessly clear out letters. Life's too short.'

That seemed a good moment to stop. I switched off the tape recorder and we returned to a more private conversational mode. It was the last time I spoke to him before I left, though I was to see him on one more occasion when he did indeed return to lead Hong Kong's Remembrance of fifty years before. Meanwhile I hoped he had a well-earned break. I imagined him sauntering about an open-air French market and prodding vegetables, like Ah Non, my old Thai amah. I pictured him with a glass of good red wine in his hand as he stirred the garlic and the tomato and the aubergine in the pungent olive oil. It would make a change from bean sprouts and soya and sesame, and I felt he deserved it.

NINETEEN

Hong Kong without the Governor felt a little like London without the Queen. The Pattens' French retreat was not Balmoral, but it fulfilled a similar function. One was aware, dimly, that it could be reached by telephone, that the occupant would be kept abreast of events at home, but one knew that for a few weeks life for the Pattens would assume a completely different character and that, for a while, those of us left behind would, effectively, cease to exist. Of course, the Governor was no longer quite the crucial figure that he had been in his Victorian heyday. He, like his boss Queen Elizabeth, no longer occupied the same position as his nineteenth-century predecessors. Yet still the absence of His Excellency and Her Majesty appeared to signify. Without them the place seemed to grind to a halt. Although I knew that the rest of Hong Kong had not actually decamped to the French countryside, it felt as if they had.* Hong Kong seemed half empty. The most important members of the Patten entourage still in town were Whisky and Soda.

Government, during the holidays, moved out of Government House and into the apparently capable hands of the Chief Secretary, Anson Chan. The streets and the waters

---

*Not quite as far-fetched as it might sound. The Governor's friend Simon Murray was, of course, within helicopter distance and his press secretary, Kerry McGlynn, had also taken a holiday home near by.

seemed as crowded as ever. 'Zoo night' at the FCC was still a crush. Yet one felt that just as in London at this time of year the caravan of movers and shakers, great and good, moved off to the Dordogne or Cowes, the golf course or the grouse moor, so in Hong Kong it was not really done to be seen around. On the whole, the sort of people I needed to talk to were somewhere else.

There were sound climatic reasons for this, reasons of which I had a terrified inkling from reading a wonderfully melodramatic Hong Kong novel called *Typhoon*. ('Through the long, hot summer of passion and terror, Typhoon Rose moved relentlessly across the South China Sea towards Hong Kong and its awesome, shattering climax . . .'). Typhoon, which is simply Cantonese for 'big wind', is an infinitely more chilling word than storm, gale or even hurricane, matched only, perhaps, by tornado. Typhoons are killers.

Soon after the Governor flew to France ('fled' to France was what his enemies said), I had my first experience of the language of sub-tropical weather. I was in Macau when they 'hoisted Number One'. The archaic phrase has a literal origin because in the days before radio and TV the storm signals were physically hoisted on a mast in a prominent position where all could see them. In Macau the cones were hauled up on a hill in the centre of the city; in Hong Kong the same ritual was enacted at the Royal Observatory – another institution whose regal prefix had but a short time to live. In addition the warnings were put out at regular intervals on radio and TV as well as appearing in the press and on public buildings. The first I knew of the 'Number One' signal was when I saw it prominently displayed in the lobby of Stanley Ho's enormous and rather depressing Macanese casino, the Lisboa.

For the benefit of innocent tourists, hotels placed laminated explanations of the signals in guest bedrooms throughout the typhoon season. The warnings were graded on a

327

scale of one to ten, though five of the originals had been abolished. It was a little like Pimm's, a speciality of Rupert Chenevix-Trench's* Bentley's† restaurant in Prince's Building. There used to be six different kinds but latterly only gin (One) and vodka (Six) survived.

Just so with typhoons: Two, Four, Five, Six and Seven had all been abolished. Of the remainder, Number One was a very early warning and meant simply that a tropical cyclone was within 400 nautical miles‡ of the Territory and might or might not actually hit town. Old Hong Kong hands paid very little attention to a Number One.

Number Three was a little more serious and indicated that some sort of storm would be arriving before long with winds of 22–23 knots gusting up to over 60.§ When Number Three was hoisted, wise virgins made sure they were within easy reach of home or shelter. It was also sensible to make sure that exposed windows and potential flying objects were secured. The Observatory advised, 'Even at this stage heavy rain accompanied by violent squalls may occur.' The signal was timed to give ships in Victoria Harbour twelve hours' warning of strong winds, though it was less for more exposed waters.

Number Eight was the lowest scale of the real McCoy: gales of 34–63 knots, gusting to over 100. People were advised to stay indoors and watch out for overhead cables and rogue advertising hoardings. Schools, law courts and ferries were all liable to shut at short notice and the heavy rain was likely to cause 'flooding, rockfalls and mudslips'.

*Some sort of cousin of the famously hard-beating former headmaster of Eton – a kinship he found both advantageous and irritating.
†An obvious clone of its London namesake, specialising in fish and school puddings, though in fact no relation.
‡The Royal Observatory used nautical miles in all its weather forecasts, though sometimes the word 'nautical' was omitted for the sake of brevity. A nautical mile is 1,852 metres.
§A knot is one nautical mile per hour.

Eight was bad but still, basically, the sort of storm which would be familiar to most Britons.

Nine and Ten were in a different league. The former meant a sustained wind speed of between 48 and 63 knots and the latter was hurricane-strength with sustained winds of 64 knots or more and the possibility of gusts of over 120. Once Eight, Nine or Ten were hoisted a weather bulletin was broadcast regularly at two minutes to and half-past every hour.

My own Number One turned into a Three on Friday, by which time I had returned to Hong Kong. Later that night Three became Eight and remained so until Saturday evening. She was dignified by the name 'Severe Tropical Storm Helen' and I'm afraid that in my notebook I recorded the assessment 'A tad wimpy'. That was a ridiculous verdict, for the storm was severe enough to be alarming even when indoors. I was supposed to be doing a broadcast with RTHK on the other side of the harbour and chickened out – not so much because of what I could see and hear of the storm itself as because of what I had heard about flying scaffolding falling on people's heads, pot-plants descending from great heights, chunks of rocks hurtling into the middle of the highway, and so on. It was, however, an observable fact that throughout the Number Eight taxis did keep plying for hire, though buses ceased, and pedestrians still scurried along the pavements. In the event, Helen seemed to cause little harm.

As everyone warned me, however, it was the aftermath which proved lethal. By then I had read *Typhoon*. It was not so much the initial impact as the destabilising effect of wind and water on that inherently improbable lunar city precariously perched on those precipitous hillsides. In the novel the two main characters 'saw the great mass of jungle and mud and concrete come sliding down the mountain, and behind it the great mass of mountainside lumbering down itself towards them, tearing itself up and getting bigger and bigger, like a wave'. That was fiction, but it was based on fact. Hong Kong typhoons trigger avalanches – urban avalanches composed not of snow but of mud and rock and concrete. Unlike their Alpine counterparts, the Hong Kong variety descend in densely populated areas with predictably horrible results.

Helen's legacy was four dead, including one particularly poignant tragedy where a young couple were killed as they lay in each other's arms, much like the lovers in Pompeii consumed by the lava of Mount Vesuvius two millennia before. On a more mundane level, roads were blocked all over the island. A Sunday cocktail party halfway to the Peak was almost ruined by a landslip which either sent the guests on a half-hour detour or made them walk the last half-mile. A week earlier I had been sailing with Robert Delfs to the Po Toi Islands on his yacht *Zinfandel*. We had started the day with bagels, smoked salmon and serious coffee in his elegant apartment at Repulse Bay with a matchless marine view of junks and craggy islands. Helen had caused a serious slip either side of Delfs's apartment block, cutting him off from civilisation and hot water. In order to get a shower he had been forced to trek by foot and sampan to the Middle Island branch of the Royal Hong Kong Yacht Club, the best part of a mile away. This, clearly, was the most trivial inconvenience when compared to the literally life-threatening events elsewhere. Yet it brought home once again the precarious, transitory nature of Hong Kong life.

Here today, gone tomorrow.

When the rain cleared and the sun came out I had my black shoes cleaned by a hunchbacked boot-black between the Star Ferry and the Mandarin Hotel. It was the first time I had undergone such an experience since Lisbon a decade earlier. The two cities shared, I felt, more than just shoe-shine boys. They both had an element of hierarchical raffishness. Despite its chrome and concrete modernity,

330

Hong Kong was still the sort of place where one would expect to get a haircut, a manicure and/or a shoe-shine in the street.

My Hong Kong shoe-shiner was a model of his kind with row upon row of Cherry Blossoms and Kiwis, dusters and brushes, tins of water (or spittle?) and one of San Miguel lager from which he sipped as he spat and polished. I was mesmerised by the way he flicked water over my toecaps but most of all by the pack of playing cards which he dealt round my ankle, inserting the cards between shoe and sock, thus protecting the wool from the polish. At the end of ten minutes sitting on his stool, my shoes shone as they hadn't done since I was gently disgorged from the ministrations of the Government House staff all those weeks before.

I meant to return for a retread but never did. However, I walked past him from time to time and every time I did he smiled and waved as if I were a long-lost friend. I found this oddly affecting.

My shoes now shone, but a little further up my leg was in trouble once again. The ruptured Achilles tendon gave no more than a twinge of discomfort now and again and it was weeks since I had needed the stick. The scar, though alarmingly long, seemed a neat tribute to the craftsmanship of Queen Mary's, Roehampton. However, the cut that I had sustained disembarking from the 'bouncy boat' after my evening aboard HMS *Peacock* was another matter. At the time it had caused no pain, despite the buckets of blood. The cut looked as neat as the surgeon's incision on the other side of the leg. However, it did not seem to be healing and moreover it was beginning to look an unpleasant colour akin to the grey-green greasy waters of Kipling's Limpopo. I was afraid hostile microbes from Victoria Harbour might have invaded the wound and wished the Governor had been more successful in cleaning up the pollution outside his back door.

He kept saying he'd get something done, but the water still looked pretty filthy to me.

Enquiries around the FCC, which had by now become a sort of home from home, seemed to point to a doctor called Peter Miles. It was automatically assumed that I would 'go private'. Dr Miles, a club member (interpretation of the words 'Foreign Correspondent' seemed to be surprisingly elastic),* had served with the Australian forces in Vietnam and enjoyed the reputation of being able to cure the most exotic and intractable venereal diseases. Not knowing this at the time, my opening statement – 'I have a problem' – was perhaps ill-advised. It presumably explained the amused arching of the eyebrows which greeted it.

Having inspected my shin, taken a swab and said that he didn't think the bone was affected (this had never occurred to me and really did make me think about harbour pollution), he gave me some antiseptic plasters, some mysterious magic ointment and some antibiotics which wouldn't interfere with alcohol consumption. This last practice was another reason for his popularity at the FCC. I knew that he was a keen sportsman and it transpired that in his youth he had played cricket for New South Wales. We exchanged Keith Miller stories and then moved on to golf. He had come late to the game, was mustard-keen, played off four and was a member of the Royal Hong Kong Golf Club. I commiserated about the club's apparently uncertain future, but he seemed quite sanguine. As a good Australian he was unconcerned about losing the 'Royal' prefix; he said that word had been sent from Peking that the heads of mainland Chinese companies would be expected to apply for membership of the club in the normal way, having to be proposed

*I am being unfair. The club had several categories of membership, by far the largest being 'Associates'. The 'Associates' paid a larger joining fee than 'Correspondents' and 'Journalists'.

and seconded and subjected to the usual rules about waiting lists. There would be no queue-jumping.

Dr Miles said that he had detected a number of small but encouraging signs such as this. He considered the Chinese to be more sophisticated than a lot of gweilos gave them credit for. I thought him realistic and shrewd, filed his thoughts for future discussion with sceptical contacts and paid the receptionist by American Express.

Early one Saturday morning I did a long live radio interview with Chris Hilton at RTHK on Broadcast Drive in Kowloon, reflecting that the instant coffee, the mild shirt-sleeved confusion and the sense of interminable labyrinthine corridor was a disturbingly accurate parody of Broadcasting House in London. Then, by public transport, mainly small island-hopping *kaido*,[*] I journeyed to Tap Mun, one of the remotest parts of Hong Kong. There were shacks with verandahs on stilts built out over the water, and sieves of sprat-like fish, oysters and shrimps drying in the sun. A narrow path led up the hillside, to a graveyard with Christian and traditional Chinese plots intermingled. Some were freshly dug and littered with the remains of fire and charred paper banners. Twice on the track I had to stoop to avoid perfect gleaming spiders' webs, the predatory weavers squatting at the centre waiting for lunch.

In the extravagantly decorated village temple the smoking joss-sticks were stuck into cans of Ovaltine. The incongruity of the grandeur of the carvings, the effigies, the friezes and banners with these discarded bedtime-drink containers was so unEnglish. I imagined incense and Ovaltine in the wedding-cake baroque of Wardour Chapel near my mother's house in Wiltshire and wondered what the fierce Jesuit priest

---

[*]The latest official statistic was that there were eighty-eight of these vessels in operation. There appeared to be no figures for the number of passengers carried.

would have said about it. Was this to be a legacy of British rule?

Lunch at the only restaurant on Tap Mun cost HK$215 for two: fried squid with chili, garoupa with *pak choi* and braised lettuce, two large bottles of Tsing Tsao and mineral water. The proprietor, Mr Loi, was not at home but apparently ran a restaurant in Blackpool and spoke fluent English in an accent as broad as George Formby. The fame of his cooking had evidently spread to Government House, for, near a photograph of the Governor (and other governors), was a framed letter, dated 15 June 1993:

Dear Mr Loi, I greatly enjoyed my visit to your restaurant on Saturday evening. Not only was it a relaxing way to while away an evening but, more importantly, the food was excellent. In particular the steamed fish was excellent.
Best wishes, Chris Patten, Governor.

There were times when I began to think of Chris as a sort of gubernatorial Egon Ronay, but I was glad he had made it to this remote spot and wondered if he had come in the *Lady Maureen*.

After lunch we walked along a narrow concrete track past a police post flying the Union flag and a football pitch to a clifftop look-out with views across the strait to China. The usual rust-bucket freighters chugged through choppy waters and a large sampan was fishing just below us. The obese children of a Chinese family fought noisily and a very old, very small woman with a crinkled face and long, long walking stick stared silently out to sea. Later the little *kaido* pottered from village to village and down the Hebridean fiord where I had sailed that first weekend with the Pattens. This time no police came out to salute as we passed their anti-smuggling boom, though they did come aboard at one stop in order to adjudicate in a dispute between a party of backpacking teenagers and the ticket collector. There was a lot of noisy talk and finger-jabbing, but all was ultimately resolved and we sailed home under gathering clouds before catching a train from the station near the Chinese University.

I loved quiet escapist days like this. Apart from anything else they made me realise how and why the sanctuary of their retreat at Fanling was so essential to the Pattens. It was also instructive to learn that there could be peace and tranquillity in Hong Kong, not just the downtown bustle which was all that so many visitors saw and which was the prevailing image of the Territory abroad. Sometimes, too, I felt I was in danger of being swamped in a sea of glitz, of company junks and David Tang cigars, liveried servants and smiling amahs. Life seen from the back of a Daimler had its own *reality*, but I needed correctives like the incense burning in the cans of Ovaltine.

I wanted too to strike a balance between the expected and the surprising. There were aspects of Hong Kong which fell into both categories. Sometimes I was stunned by the unexpected, on other occasions incredulous at the clichés. When I tried telling other people about Hong Kong they tended not to believe me for two reasons: either what I said was so contrary to their prejudiced assumption that it could not be true; or it was so precisely like what they had seen on the telly that it was manifestly untrue too.

Take speech for instance. There is a sort of pidgin English with which every hack author used to endow his Chinese characters. Political correctness has probably rendered it obsolete, but we are all familiar with the sort of FuManchu-speak spoken by wily Orientals in pulp fiction. If I were to reproduce dialogue like that in a novel I would be mocked and derided by every so-called expert who ever took a degree in Oriental languages.

And yet here are two verbatim examples.

The first was in the Luk Yu Tea House where I shared a *dim sum* lunch with two friends who spoke a little

Cantonese. The Luk Yu Tea House, by the way, is recommended by the Tourist Association and by practically every travel writer who has ever spent more than a stop-over in Hong Kong. In a way that's a pity but it doesn't make it any – or much – the less *real*. It was certainly more luxurious than Mr Loi's joint in Tap Mun and the cooking more sophisticated, but when I lunched there it appeared to be full of a wide variety of Chinese customers, mainly male, doing business and enjoying fine Cantonese cuisine. They looked totally *real* to me.

Tourists, admittedly, tend to be seated downstairs where the service seemed tourist-trap grumpy. Barry Girling, who booked the table, knew this, and insisted we went upstairs. Here too the service was unsmiling at first, until my friends began ordering in Cantonese.

Immediately the waiter's face creased into a grin and he said, simply, 'You number one.'

On another occasion I was in a boutique in Prince's Building with a friend who was an old and valued customer. At one point in our conversation my friend asked after the shop's aged, and absent, proprietor.

The assistant said that he was in good health and fine spirits and then added with a smile, 'When you speak Mr Wong he happy.'

Both these examples of local English are entirely genuine. I noted them carefully at the time. Had I, however, reproduced them without explanation, many experts would have said they were too good to be true. I would have been accused of mocking local Chinese attempts to speak English in exactly the way they would expect of some facile gweilo ignoramus.

The Pattens were still in France when I went on a tour of the 1941 battlefields. In terms of tourism this was a non-starter. Nowhere did it feature in any of the brochures produced by the Tourist Association. Elsewhere in the world, battlefields have become part of the tourist industry. In Europe, the Somme; in North America, Gettysburg. They have their packages, their visitor centres and their brochures. In Hong Kong, however, the old sites are mainly unmarked, sometimes located in restricted areas and seldom visited. The whole 1941 affair was settled in just over a fortnight and was, despite many acts of individual gallantry, a less than glorious episode. For all sorts of reasons many people seemed to think it best forgotten.

The British Army thought otherwise and from time to time 75 Army Education Centre at Osborn Barracks conducted a day-long tour of the scenes of conflict. It was unadvertised and usually confined to military personnel and their families. Since the fiftieth anniversary of the Liberation was being celebrated at the end of the month, I thought that despite the oppressive stickiness of the weather I should go along with Captain Harold Simpson one day to learn how the Japanese came to occupy Hong Kong. It all seemed a long time ago now, but when my parents were in the Territory it was, for many of their local friends, an all too vivid memory. One of them was James Norman, governor of Stanley Prison, who spent much of the war incarcerated in his own gaol.

We began in the countryside near Sha Tin on a section of what was now the Maclehose Trail – South China's answer to the Pennine Way – which Captain Simpson had traversed non-stop during the annual competitive trek. He not only accomplished the journey in double-quick time, he also carried the bulk of his team's food and drink on his back. In other words, he was super-fit, though by the time we had finished he too was steaming with sweat, shirt clinging to his back, as expatriates' clothing in August so often seemed to do.

Here, in 1941, was the Allies' Maginot Line. It stretched 11 miles from the Texaco Peninsula in the west to Ma Lau Tong in the east and was called the Gin Drinkers' Line. The

337

redoubtable fortifications were generally reckoned to be redundant because it was thought unlikely that the Japanese would invade in any case. Besides, at this point in the war, the British had less than scant respect for the fighting qualities of the Japanese. It was widely believed not only that they were physically puny and mentally cowardly but also that they were unable to see in the dark and therefore incapable of night fighting. Moreover if, by some fearful mishap, they were able to penetrate as far as the coast they would never be able to take Hong Kong Island itself, for they were notoriously prone to seasickness and would never be able to complete the crossing of Victoria Harbour.

Arrogance was compounded by ignorance and inexperience. The Governor, Sir Mark Young, had never previously been east of Ceylon and was only appointed in September that year. General Maltby, the military commander, arrived a couple of months earlier. Of six battalions – and the received opinion seems to be that there should have been at least three times that number – the 1st Battalions of the Royal Rifles of Canada and of the Winnipeg Grenadiers got to Hong Kong only in November. Their sole training had been *en route* in Bermuda and much of their equipment was still at sea.

Conspicuously not at sea, however, was the Royal Navy. There had been a cruiser squadron and a submarine flotilla, but they were withdrawn early that year, leaving behind 1,600 sailors including 300 Chinese and Indians. Their commander, Captain Collinson, had a destroyer, four gunboats, eight motor torpedo boats, seven auxiliary patrol craft and an auxiliary minesweeper. Even less impressive was the strength of the Royal Air Force. The RAF had seven officers, 108 airmen and five aircraft. These were two Walrus amphibians and three Vickers Wildebeeste torpedo bombers. The planes were all more than ten years old and none was able to exceed 100 m.p.h. In the event, this hardly mattered

338

as none of them even got into the air. They were all destroyed on the runway by enemy bombing.

British policy over Hong Kong at the time was confusing. Early in 1941 Churchill himself told 'Pug' Ismay, his Far Eastern C.-in-C., that there was no hope whatever of defending the colony if the Japanese entered the war and he wished there were even fewer troops in the garrison. And yet he allowed the Canadians to send reinforcements. There would have been still more had Hong Kong not fallen. Throughout the brief battle the Prime Minister was, in public and private, at his most bombastic, refusing to countenance surrender even when he knew perfectly well that the situation was quite hopeless and prolonged resistance would only result in more British deaths. It was far from being his finest hour.

The core of the first line of defence was the Shing Mun Redoubt. It was still there only a few yards off the Maclehose Trail in the middle of a country park, though if Captain Simpson, nimble as a mountain goat, hadn't been there I would never have known this. The trenches and pillboxes were hidden by undergrowth and completely unsigned.

They were melancholy ruins. The most poignant remains were the names, still carved on the walls of the fortifications: Regent Street, Shaftesbury Avenue, Charing Cross, the Strand Palace Hotel. It was a long way from Blighty.

The Mainland Brigade consisted of three regular battalions and some Volunteers – forerunners of the soon-to-be-disbanded unit whom I had encountered on their last night op a few weeks earlier. The regulars were the 2nd Royal Scots, the 2nd/14th Punjabis and the 5th/7th Rajputs.

At the time of the battle, the hillside below the Redoubt was little more than scrub, though when I saw it the trees had grown so that it had become forest. The ground was steep. The attackers should have been easily visible and

339

unable to make swift progress. The position was well chosen and even though there were not nearly enough British troops it should have been possible to pick off the opposition more or less at will.

It was not a bit like that. The Japanese crossed the border at dawn on 8 December and pushed forward at speed, meeting only light resistance from one forward company of Punjabis. They were well prepared with plans and maps and seemed to be totally aware of the British dispositions. Later it transpired that their intelligence-gathering had been highly sophisticated. One key agent turned out to be the barber at the Peninsula Hotel. Many a senior officer had been guilty of careless talk as the spy gave him his short back and sides.

By the end of the first day the Japanese were well past the Governor's country house in Fanling and were only a mile or so north of David Browning's Sha Tin, then little more than a barren swamp. On the 9th they occupied Needle Hill, just short of the Gin Drinkers' Line and that evening they began the assault of the Shing Mun Redoubt. There were at least 12,000 of them. They had a fighter squadron, a regiment of light bombers, and their nine infantry battalions were supported by more than three battalions of mountain artillery as well as two mortar battalions and siege artillery with howitzers.

Predictably enough, it was all over in a matter of hours. Quite apart from the force of numbers and their superior firepower, the Japanese were also assisted by incompetence and bad luck. The Shing Mun pillboxes were sturdy and well constructed but they had wide, open ventilation shafts. Somebody, surely, should have considered stretching chicken wire across these vulnerable holes, but no one did and the Japanese, scampering up the hill in the dark, simply tossed in hand-grenades and waited for the explosion. But one particularly impregnable fortification withstood everything the Japanese could hurl at it until the commanding officer called up the support of heavy guns on Stonecutters' Island. One of the very first shells fell fair and square on the Redoubt, immediately destroying the one bit of defence with which the Japanese had been unable to cope.

The order to evacuate the mainland and pull back to Hong Kong Island was given at noon on the 11th. Somehow they nearly all made it back across the water, but it was an undignified business. I found it chilling to stand in those surroundings and to think of those wretched men so far from home, abandoned to their fate in those nostalgically named bunkers. They must have felt so lonely, staring out into the black of night and realising suddenly that the derided enemy were deadly after all. I was told by several of the old Hong Kong hands that there was an unofficial understanding that because of the events at Shing Mun in 1941 the Royal Scots would never again be sent to Hong Kong. It seemed a harsh verdict but I supposed I could understand.

On the way back to our transport we passed a family picnicking at one of the park tables – also a couple of yellow-fanged monkeys for which the area was famous.

Like the soldiers of more than half a century earlier, we proceeded south, passing under rather than across the harbour before arriving at the former Lyemun[*] Barracks, where Captain Simpson had some difficulty arranging for us to enter. The Barracks, abandoned by the military, seemed to have been converted into some sort of holiday camp. Some of the buildings had real imperial grandeur, the best of them worthy of Kipling – an Oriental Aldershot.

As far as the 1941 battle was concerned, the relevant remains were down on the waterfront. They were in the same style as the functional concrete slabs up on the Gin Drinkers' Line. Some housed relatively heavy guns, while

---

[*]This seems to be the British military spelling. A more common usage is Lei Yue Mun. As both are transliterations of the Chinese it seems, as so often, impossible to say that one is more correct than the other.

others were home for the Middlesex Regiment, whose 1st Battalion had been kitted out as a machine-gun unit. They were as desolate and isolated as their upcountry cousins. While I was standing on top of one I watched a Japanese airliner drone into Kai Tak airport opposite and I thought of an earlier generation of Japanese aircraft strafing the poor old Wildebeeste and Walrus planes of the RAF in much the same spot.

On 13 December 1941 the Japanese demanded surrender and were turned down. They then bombarded the island until, on the night of the 18th, they took to their inflatable landing craft, scythed through the British defences and went charging on up Mount Parker and Mount Butler. It was cold and wet and they were weighed down with heavy packs, but they were extraordinarily fit and determined and they arrived on the hilltops before some of the ill-equipped Canadians had even taken up their positions. One of them, Sergeant Osborn, after whom the barracks were named, won a posthumous VC somewhere round here, smothering a grenade with his body and saving his comrades. The views were spectacular, though it was so oppressively hot that we 'wimped out' (Army argot) and didn't attempt the stiff climb on foot to the highest summit.

By the 20th the invaders had reached Repulse Bay on the south side of the island. For years it was famous as the site of an elegant old country sister to the Peninsula Hotel, though recently this was demolished and developed. There is still a stylish Palm Court-style area and restaurant, but the Somerset Maughamish building has been replaced by a modern tower with a hole in the middle. Legend has it that the aperture was an example of contemporary *fung shui* and was inserted to allow dragons to pass in and out.

Here the British made their final stand, cut off from the Governor and the General, ordered to fight on by the government at home. They held out until Christmas Day, when General Maltby surrendered, his written order reaching the Brigadier in Stanley shortly after midnight. The Japanese were widely held to have behaved with characteristic barbarity and certainly hospital nurses were raped and murdered and patients bayoneted in their beds. Some authorities, not particularly pro-Japanese, have argued that the atrocities were not as bad as alleged, that Japanese officers did their best to prevent them, that offenders were subsequently shot and that in any case sloppy British command meant that some medical facilities were used for military purposes so that, up to a point, they had only themselves to blame. In all, some 4,500 Allied soldiers were killed or taken prisoner, many of them, together with their womenfolk, dying in the wretched Stanley prison camp.

War cemeteries strike me as almost unbearably poignant, and the one at Stanley was no exception. It was beautifully tended, as they always are, and not all the graves were of the Second World War. There was even one man who 'lost his life by an attack of Chinese pirates in the Bay of Chuckchoo on the 1st May 1844'. But the war graves dominated. I noticed one Volunteer twenty-year-old, killed in the battle, lying alongside his grandmother, who had later died in Japanese captivity. Fourteen were killed in an American air raid in 1945. There was a twenty-five-year-old captain who 'won life for his friends, this ground for Scotland and Glory for God'. There was an eighteen-year-old rifleman, Baker, from the Royal Rifles of Canada, killed on Christmas Day. As always, the most difficult of all to bear were the stones inscribed simply, 'A soldier of the 1939–45 War Known unto God'.

I was glad to have spent a day following in those bloody footsteps, saddened by the futility of the sacrifices, curious about the thoughts of those Canadian farm boys and Indian sepoys, Londoners and Scots so far from home, and of those Hong Kong Volunteers who died defending their own home.

One, lying under the neat, green, almost English grass of the cemetery, was a Chinese man who had served under an English alias. I would like to know what muddle of patriotism and prejudice produced that particular subterfuge. By now, however, I had been in Hong Kong long enough not to be surprised.

It was three years and eight months before British rule was restored, and Stanley was one of the first ports of call for the commander of the relieving force. Jonathan Fenby gave me a photostat of his paper's edition for Friday, 31 August 1945. One of the five front-page columns was headed 'Admiral at Stanley. Union Jack Raised in Enthusiastic Scene. Internees' Cheers and Tears'. Fenby was intending to reproduce the page in its entirety as his contribution to the celebrations of the fiftieth anniversary of the liberation. In those days his paper was the *South China Morning Post and the Hongkong Telegraph* – the second name had long since disappeared from the masthead.

The Admiral in question was Rear-Admiral Harcourt, who entered the harbour aboard the carrier HMS *Swiftsure* at about noon on 30 August together with an escort of fighter aircraft. The Japanese had surrendered, but the British were half expecting suicide attacks, which failed to materialise. There was one alarm which led to the memorable message from one ship to another: 'Junk sunk.'

Subsequent history has given Harcourt's liberation the patina of predictability, but in fact it was touch and go. Throughout the war the Americans, in particular Roosevelt who, despite his apparently cordial relations with Churchill was implacably opposed to British imperialism, were of the view that Hong Kong should, after hostilities, revert to Chinese rather than British rule. It was only due to some fancy footwork and some splendid intractability from Mr Gimson, the senior British civil servant in Stanley Prison, that the Colony was prevented from falling into the hands of

General Chiang Kai-shek. Had that happened, would Hong Kong have become another Shanghai or another Formosa? Even if it had not followed one of those two obvious models, it seems highly unlikely that it would have become the Hong Kong over which Governor Patten presided in the 1990s. In any event, the British *did* resume power and the following year the hapless Governor Young returned to reoccupy the office from which he had been so rudely removed in 1941.

The *Post*'s account was characteristically 'Pathé News' and stiff-upper-lipped to a degree unimaginable to a modern British audience. It remains, however, extraordinarily evocative:

> After the singing of the National Anthem, the impressive and touching ceremony of hoisting the Union Jack and the flags of all nationalities represented in the Camp was carried out. The atmosphere was filled with fervent patriotism and many were the tears shed by internees.
>
> A bugler sounded the Last Post and this was followed by the singing of the hymn 'O God our Help in Ages Past'.
>
> Admiral Harcourt called for three cheers for His Majesty the King, which met with tremendous response.
>
> A voice from the crowd called for 'three cheers for the Admiral', this meeting with great enthusiasm.
>
> Admiral Harcourt, in a few well-chosen words, said that on receiving instructions to take the surrender of the Colony, it was his one aim to proceed here as quickly as was humanly possible to relieve Hongkong. He expressed regret that he was unable to remain in the Camp longer, but he had other urgent engagements to fulfil.
>
> It was a genuine delight for the internees, for the first time in over three-and-a-half years of 'routine existence behind barbed wires', to see bright and cheery British faces.

Not that the liberation was an unmitigatedly glorious affair. Another front-page story under the headline, 'Some disturbances', began, 'It is regrettable to have to report that yesterday was not without unpleasant incidents.' These, naturally, had nothing to do with the British, but it did appear that 'some Japanese were assaulted in cowardly fashion by Chinese hoodlums and some Indians on trams'.

What struck me most forcibly in reading those reports was not the archaic journalese, nor the unashamed bias, nor the raw emotion, but the absolute certainty which came from being British. Later Admiral Harcourt maintained that part of the reason for the operation passing off so successfully was that there was no question of consultation with his superiors nor even of his being given specific orders. Instead he was advised that he had 'completely dictatorial powers'.

Quite so. In those days 'lesser breeds'* still jolly well did as they were told. The British ruled by divine right unassailed by doubt or self-recrimination, let alone by such fantastic notions as 'public opinion' or 'democratic votes'. Why risk abandoning 'completely dictatorial powers' when 'one' was obviously right and everyone else was so obviously wrong. It seemed to me that the greatest change in British attitudes towards Hong Kong in the fifty years between liberating it from the Japanese and returning it to the Chinese was the access of doubt and uncertainty. There was none of that sort of nonsense in the first century or so of British rule. Latterly it had become dominant.

Something of that old-fashioned Britishness returned to Hong Kong in a small way in August 1995, though it was not without significance, I thought, that the Governor returned from France only just in time for the final celebrations of the anniversary. It was not merely that he was wary of offending the Japanese, though this was part of Hong Kong's desire not to make *too* much of the anniversary. He was – obviously – more of a politician in his middle years than the historian he had been in his youth. Politicians, as a rule, don't like looking back. The past has too many

*Kipling, 'Recessional'.

reminders of the ephemeral nature of political power, too much evidence of political fallibility. History imposes verdicts on politicians whereas the present is usually ambivalent and the future nearly always capable of the most florid interpretation. Even for an honest, self-critical politician it was easier, in public at least, to strive for an optimistic assessment of the best of all possible worlds to come than to ponder what might have been *if only*. Perhaps this is just an irrational bias in me. I have always felt uncomfortable seeing the elected politicians of the day solemnly laying their wreaths at the Cenotaph on Remembrance Sunday.

Anyway, it was Anson Chan, the Chief Secretary, who got the Rolls-Royce on 22 August. 'Smiling Death' was how one gweilo described her and while this was, of course, a calumny there was something cadaverously threatening about her stretched public grin. She wore a Margaret Thatcher-style navy-blue suit and looked like the future in a more or less ideal world. By an odd coincidence, one of the battleships in Admiral Harcourt's fleet was HMS *Anson*. This was a link with the past, as was her ADC in the full-dress uniform of a Royal Hong Kong Policeman, complete with epaulettes and a helmet with blue feathers. The sweating veterans, including a handful of sterling former Wrens, were in grey flannels, white shirts and dark-blue berets. They marched with swagger led by an Army band. In the circumstances it should probably have been a band from the Royal Marines, but this was 'the Minden Band of the Queen's Division'. They made a robust military noise, but they were a sign of change, the product of cuts in British defence expenditure, euphemistically described as 'Options for Change'. Time was, and I remembered it, when even the Dorsets had a band of their own. As the Minden Band strutted their stuff I regretted, privately and illogically, that it was not the Dorset regimental band beating out 'The

347

Farmer's Boy' and 'The Maid of Glenconnel' as they used to all those years ago.

The Fleet Vetcrans marched past to 'A Life on the Ocean Wave'. Anson Chan saluted. We joined in the Lord's Prayer and the Naval Prayer, which asks God to 'Preserve us from the dangers of the sea, and from the violence of the enemy'. We sang the 'Naval Hymn' – 'Eternal Father strong to save, whose arm doth bind the restless wave'. Little HMS *Plover* crashed down the harbour firing her gun to signal the beginning and end of a two-minute silence. A bugler sounded the Last Post. The name of 'Our most gracious sovereign lady, Queen Elizabeth' was invoked. Several shed a tear. And one spectator was heard to remark, as the veterans marched off to 'Hearts of Oak', chins up, chests out, arms swinging, dressing immaculate: 'I'd like to see the bloody PLA do that.'

The following Sunday the Governor himself was back to take the place of 'Smiling Death'. The previous Fleet Veterans parade was outside City Hall whereas this, for veterans of all three services, was a full-dress Cenotaph affair with the main grandstand under the front of the Hong Kong Club. The Minden Band performed again and we had 'Colonel Bogey', 'Pack Up Your Troubles' and, during the wreath-laying, 'Nimrod' from the *Enigma Variations*. Peter Sutch was among the wreath-layers, slightly peeved because dinner aboard a British nuclear submarine had been cancelled after she slipped her anchor. The VIPs dined at the Prince of Wales Barracks instead, which was enjoyable but not quite the same. Sutch reported that the Governor had gained weight on his French vacation but seemed in good spirits.

I had watched the Fleet Veterans from a privileged stand but this time I deliberately found a quiet, remote corner on top of the car park near the Star Ferry terminal. This afforded a good view but from a distance. To my right,

348

hidden from the parade by another temporary stand, came the cacophony of starling-shrill Filipina maids, sharing their thoughts, their picnics, their discarded clothes. Behind me the pink-tinged imitation paddle steamer everyone called the 'floating brothel' shovelled through the murky harbour deeps. The Bank of China dominated the parade ground and on the far shore the optimistically inclined new Peninsula tower was a study in indifference to change. Hong Kong, the greater part of it, was pursuing business as usual, barely aware that here, alone in an oasis of imperial nostalgia, a few hundred Britons were celebrating a solemn memory.

Governor Patten was in a dark suit, tailored, I guessed, by the egregious Sam; General Dutton was press-button smart in uniform. Half a century earlier it would have been Young and Maltby. I wondered if history's verdict would be kinder to the men of the 1990s than to those of the 1940s. As the band thumped out those Blighty tunes of the Second World War, the Governor remained standing at attention as others laid their wreaths. He looked respectful and authoritative, despite the lack of feathers. I, on top of the car park, felt the tide of history recede. Perhaps it was my memory of university and the boy in blue denim which made me sense that Chris was not at ease.

Presently the veterans marched off, stood at ease, fell out and adjourned for drinks in the mess.

'What do you think?' one of their number was asked.

He looked out of the window across the foam of his pint at the futuristic skyline. 'It was worth it,' he said.

I took a 54 bus to lunch and remembered the letter that I wrote years earlier urging Chris to take the job. 'Last Governor' would surely ensure a place in the footnotes of British history. Perhaps too his role as 'fat prostitute' would earn him a dishonourable mention in the pages of Chinese history too. Was it worth it? Who knew?

In just under two years' time he would be standing erect

and dark-suited at a yet more final farewell. Who could possibly say what form that last salute would take? Who could evaluate the rule that Britain had imposed for a century and a half, still yet the efforts of Chris, the last Hong Kong Governor from the other side of the world? Would he and the Prince of Wales sail away into the sunset aboard the royal yacht destined so soon to join the Territory of Hong Kong as a lost, last jewel in the imperial crown? Or did the Chinese and fate have a trick or two to play? Was this a dress rehearsal? Or a false dusk?

I remembered the words of the open-air service of remembrance.

> For the healing of memories
> For those who suffer as a result of war
> For all who find it hard to forgive
> For communities where past wrongs and violence persist
> For all in pain or distress and those who care for them
>
> Lord in your mercy *Hear our prayer*
>
> For friendship and trust amongst all
> For an appreciation of our independence
> For the ongoing building of a new world
> And for a world that is in harmony with itself
> Lord in your mercy *Hear our prayer*.

Would that He did. And yet, irreverent though the thought may seem, I had a horrid feeling that when the final trump was sounded by the Black Watch bugler at midnight on 30 June 1997 the only echo bouncing back was going to be hollow laughter and the clash of Chinese cymbals, as triumphant and impenetrable as those I had heard, disbelieving, at the travelling opera in Sai Kung.

It was time for me to shake the dust of Hong Kong from my feet. I had lived with a sense of the place for more than forty years and had the opportunity, now, of measuring my dreams and not-quite-fairy-tales against a few months of actuality. Hong Kong knew my father; my father knew Hong Kong. But that Hong Kong had perished long ago. The place I felt I had, sort of, got to know was very different. The insignificant, archetypal British Colony had become a manic hybrid – independent already in all but name, yet still a vestigial corner of a foreign field that was forever British.

I came half hoping for something recognisably part of a past which I had never experienced, and which had disappeared. There were a few surviving pockets but, on the whole, reluctantly, I acknowledged that Governor Patten, wedged firmly in the present and the future, was clearer about the *reality* of Hong Kong than I, crippled with my naval uncles, my military father and my second-hand memories. I came, I saw . . . was conquered. Hong Kong was seductive, elusive, easy to explore, impossible to understand. It was a privilege to see this barren rock turned into a chrome and tinsel wonderland; at one and the same time, perhaps, the final significant pink dot in the British atlas, and also the harbinger of a new Chinese hegemony.

If there was an example of 'history on the wing', this, I felt, was it. It was a privilege to be a part of it, albeit vicariously. I understood and yet did not understand, for Hong Kong was always a paradox. When I finally took off from Kai Tak on Heathrow-bound Cathay Pacific 251 late at night on 30 August I realised that I was flying on a leading Chinese airline from an important Chinese airport. Yet when the captain came on the tannoy he said his name was Nigel Best.

Chinese airline, British pilot.

The paradoxes continued till the last.

SELECT BIBLIOGRAPHY

Frank Welsh's 'compendious'* *A History of Hong Kong* (HarperCollins, 1993) lists just over thirteen pages of 'secondary sources' including such unlikely esoterica as a volume called *British Interests and Activities in Texas 1838–46*. I don't think mine is the sort of book which should have a three-hundred-title bibliography, but it might be useful to identify one or two which I found particularly interesting or useful.

The Frank Welsh book is indeed compendious, though there are still those who told me that G. B. Endacott's *A History of Hong Kong* (Oxford University Press, 1958) should be regarded as the standard work. At least one Chinese academic told me they are both too Eurocentric and British in their perspectives. I have some sympathy with this view, but as my interest in Hong Kong is essentially and inevitably British, this didn't bother me too much. Welsh's book is very much a colonial history and not a Chinese history, but as such it's a useful reference book and provides an invaluable historical context.

For more contemporary facts and figures I relied heavily on *Hong Kong 1995* (Hong Kong Government Publications, 1995), colloquially known as 'the Hong Kong Year Book'. I

*Jonathan Mirsky's description, writing in *The Times*.

was frequently warned that this was not as reliable as it looked, but as it came from the horse's mouth it seemed a reasonable source.

In a more personal vein I enjoyed Richard Hughes's *Hong Kong: Borrowed Place, Borrowed Time* (André Deutsch, 1968). Hughes's breezy certainties are endearing – if sometimes mistaken – and he was so much the pre-eminent old Hong Kong hand of his journalistic generation that I found him compelling in a way that some other opinionated books were not. Anthony Lawrence's *The Fragrant Chinese* (Chinese University Press, 1993) was a much more diffident work but just as attractive. And although Lawrence is much too modest a man to take Hughes's place, it is a fact that, when I was in Hong Kong, he was very much the doyen of foreign correspondents just as Hughes himself had been.

Austin Coates's *Myself a Mandarin* (Oxford University Press, 1968) never set out to be anything more than a personal memoir of an unusually sophisticated colonial civil servant, but it has more perceptive insights and observations than many longer and more solemn books.

My favourite Hong Kong novel is John le Carré's *The Honourable Schoolboy* (Hodder and Stoughton, 1977). Although often overtaken by events which have proved stranger even than le Carré's fiction, it paints a brilliant picture of the place and contains, among other things, a terrific pen-portrait of Richard Hughes.

Index

(CP = Chris Patten; HK = Hong Kong; NT = New Territories)

358

Hall, Sir John 98n
Hall Russell 246
Halliday, Jon 20
Hamark, Lis 231–2
Hamilton, Denis 68
Hang Seng Index 87, 316
Happy Valley 4
harbour tunnel 14–15, 78, 217
Harcourt, Rear-Admiral 344, 345, 346, 347
Harley, Belinda 35
Harper, Wallace 272
Hawthorne, Nigel 33
Headquarters House, the Peak 200
Heald, Alexander (author's son) 5
Heald, Emma (author's daughter) 287
Heald, James (author's brother) 1, 3, 41
Heald, Lucy (author's daughter) 120n, 287
Heald, Colonel Bill (author's father) 1, 2, 3, 351
Heald, Mrs (author's mother) 77, 280
Heath, Sir Edward 22–3, 78–9
Heep Hong Society for Handicapped Children 234–6
Heseltine, Michael 42, 147
Heywood, G. S. P. 233
Hickman, Lesley 65–6, 70
Hill, Christopher 43
Hilton, Chris 333
History of Hong Kong, A (Endacott) 300n
HKTA *see* Hong Kong Tourist Association
Ho, Daisy 282
Ho, Miss (barrister) 189
Ho, Pansy 282
Ho, Dr Stanley 87, 93, 134, 143n, 278–84, 289, 293n, 327
Hollingworth, Clare 68
Honchow 97
Hong Kong
    agreement to return to Chinese rule in 1997 4
    as an archipelago 119

as the biggest container port in the world 120n
colonial administration 301
defined 2n
as driven by 'insecurity' 198
education 320
Europeans in *see* Europeans
factory work 229
GDP compared with mainland China 320
health 320
housing *see* housing; public housing
Japanese occupation *see* Japanese occupation
population 50
portentousness about 148–50
and question of the correct authority in 1997 117–18
question of elections 321
refugees in 319–20
reliance on domestic servants 229
riots (1960s) 79, 99n
as a Special Administrative Region of China (SAR) 191, 193, 216
speech in 335–6
as a village of networks and universal acquaintance 13–14, 240
war years in 127n
Ziman on the secret of 299, 302
Hong Kong and Yaumati Ferry Company (HYF) 119
Hong Kong Chamber of Commerce 141
Hong Kong Children's Choir 285
'Hong Kong Chinese' 301–2
Hong Kong Club 54, 56–7, 61–2, 64, 95, 102, 135, 136, 233, 348
Hong Kong Country Club 19, 86
Hong Kong Cricket Club 178
Hong Kong Davis Cup team 15
Hong Kong dollar 62
Hong Kong Dragon Boat Festival International Races 218–20

361

appoints Anson Chan 161
as the architect of Britain's
    Hong Kong policy 39
autonomy as Governor 39
and the business community
    159, 165, 198, 295
as Chairman of the Conservative
    Party 4, 138, 324
Chinese attitude toward 38, 39,
    314
and the Chinese language 72–3
and Christine Loh 267–8
and the climate 113
and Cornish 40–41, 104, 105,
    165
and dedication of new bronze
    Buddha 290
and democratisation 12, 231
Dr Wu on 194
and dragon boat racing 217,
    220
Eddington on 294
and Elsie Tu 260–61, 264
Emily Lau and 265, 266
employment plan 203
as Environment Secretary 71,
    324
and fiftieth anniversary of the
    Liberation 311, 325, 346
as a Francophile 163, 199
French vacation 325, 326, 327,
    336, 348
'friendly' football match 205–7
heart attack 12–13, 15
and the Hong Kong Volunteers
    215
and the honours system 184
interest in environmental issues
    71
interviewed 310–25
involvement in the community
    76
and the Legislative Council
    demonstration 33, 34
and liberalisation 231
loses his Bath seat (1992) 4–5,
    256, 323, 324
and Martin Lee 252–3, 256–7

as Minister for Overseas
    Development 5, 163, 311
Murray's support for 199
in the Northern Territories
    70–76
opposition of Hong Kong old
    guard 12
and Pao 116–17
Patten style as Governor 185,
    287–9
Peking's attitude toward 11,
    141, 149
portrayed 67n, 69
preaches at St John's Cathedral
    137–9
and press freedom 303
robust attitude to Peking 12
Roman Catholicism 40, 137,
    252–3
and Sam the Tailor 239, 308
and slum dwellings 276–8
Sutch on 295–6
systems and precedents that
    would be difficult to dismantle
    97–8
traditionalists' criticism of
    183–4
and Vietnamese 'boat people'
    rioting 99
visits territories unannounced
    184
Weatherill and 93
and wines 31
Woo on 251
Worden on 256
Patten, Kate 5, 287
Patten, Laura 287, 312
Patten, Lavender 6, 14, 16, 20, 28,
    29, 30, 32, 42, 43, 207, 226,
    239, 307, 322, 323
as a barrister 17
and CP's heart attack 12–13
and CP's losing his Bath seat 4
and dedication of new bronze
    Buddha 290
education 5, 163
and Heep Hong Society for
    Handicapped Children 234–6

Sinn, Dr Elizabeth 300–302
Sino–British Joint Declaration on
    the Question of Hong Kong
    (1984) 12, 190n, 263, 285,
    296, 312, 319
Skidelsky, Lord 20
Smith, James 80
Smith, John 182
Snowdon, Earl of 36, 122
Social Welfare Department 235
Sok Kwu Wan, Lamma Island
    176, 177
Soochow 97
South China Morning Post 13, 34,
    35, 44–5, 52, 81, 88, 92, 98,
    100, 101, 135, 148–51, 204,
    214, 286, 297, 302–7, 317,
    344, 345
South China Sea 8, 88
Special Administrative Region of
    China (SAR) *see under* Hong
    Kong
Spectator 69
Stab in the Back club, London 68
Stalin, Joseph 117
Stanley 290, 343, 344
Stanley Fort 182
Stanley Prison 115, 259, 337, 344
Star Ferry 14, 58, 78, 96, 118–19,
    137, 262, 330, 348
Starling, HMS 246
Steeds, Commander Sean 247, 248
Stenhouse, Commodore Sir
    Humphrey Le Fleming 178
Stonecutters' Island 246, 340
Straits Times 306
Strategic Waste Disposal Plan 71
street names, change of 194
students 164n
Suez crisis 246
Sullivan, Sir Arthur 181, 182, 183
Summer Palace, Peking 141
Sunday Times 68
Sutch, Peter 161, 293–4, 295–6,
    308, 348
Swaine, Sir John, QC 33, 256
Swiftsure, HMS 344
Swire Group 89, 161, 239, 240,

293, 294, 295

Ta Kwu Rural Committee 72
Tai Fu Tai, Yuen Long 169–71
Tai O 291
taipan 161
Taipeh 97
Taipo, NT 306
Taiwan 146, 321
Taiwan, President of 314
Tam Yiu Chung 203
Tamar, HMS 246
Tamar basin 246
Tang, David 23, 48, 116, 285,
    287, 310, 316
    complicated position 39
    on CP 38–9
    education 36–7
    as a friend of the Pattens 18, 36
    invested as a Chevalier des Arts
        et des Lettres 163, 197
    as a millionaire entrepreneur
        and socialite 35
    personality 39–40
    rural villa 35, 108, 112
Tang Chung Ling Ancestral Hall
    73–4
Tang clan 36
Tap Mun 334, 336
taxis 131
Tea Museum 200, 270
teas 179
Telegraph Magazine 260
Tellez, Cynthia 228–31
Temple of the Ten Thousand
    Buddhas 174–5
Tennant, Basil, RN (author's
    uncle) 8, 246
Texaco Peninsula 337
Thatcher, Baroness (Margaret) 12,
    18, 225, 347
Thomas, Michael 105
Thomasson, Mary Justice 297
Thomson, Lord 68
Tiananmen Square massacre,
    Peking (4 June 1989) 144,
    243, 257, 263, 300
Times, The 11, 42, 84, 143, 146,

369